Archibald Clavering Gunter

Bob Covington

A Novel

Archibald Clavering Gunter

Bob Covington
A Novel

ISBN/EAN: 9783337001384

Printed in Europe, USA, Canada, Australia, Japan

Cover: Foto ©Andreas Hilbeck / pixelio.de

More available books at **www.hansebooks.com**

BOB COVINGTON

A NOVEL

BY

ARCHIBALD CLAVERING GUNTER

AUTHOR OF

"MR. BARNES OF NEW YORK"

ETC., ETC.

LONDON

GEORGE ROUTLEDGE AND SONS, LIMITED

BROADWAY, LUDGATE HILL

1897

CONTENTS.

BOOK I.

A LUCKY YOUNG MAN.

BOOK II.

A VERY UNFORTUNATE YOUNG LADY.

BOOK III.

HOW HE LOVED HER.

BOB COVINGTON.

BOOK I.

A LUCKY YOUNG MAN.

CHAPTER I.

THE RACE BETWEEN STATES.

IT is a day of battle in New Orleans—not the battle of men, but the battle of horses—this Saturday, this first day of April in the year of our Lord eighteen hundred and fifty-four, upon which the Great Interstate Post Stake is to be fought out upon the Metairie Course, each commonwealth backing its own horse with State pride and local prejudice, and, above all, the good round dollars of Uncle Sam, twenty thousand of which make the purse, and several millions more, not only in coin, but in corn, cotton, and sugar crops, present and to come, have been wagered on the result.

Kentucky is playing its bay colt Lexington with every dollar it can raise on corn, corn-juice, and fast horses; Alabama is piling its bales of cotton on its flyer, Highlander; Mississippi is going cotton and sugar as well on Lecomte, and Louisiana betting on its pet and pride, the chestnut Arrow, corn, cotton, sugar, rice, and tobacco; every one of the States throwing in lots of "niggers" besides.

And all this in a country where a man's horse was his friend, companion, and sometimes, on his long journeys over the lone prairies and through the pathless wilderness, his safety and salvation—a country in which the greatest criminal was the horse-thief—aye, over road agents, bandits, or even assassins.

So, under the soft sun of a perfect Louisiana spring day, the breeze from the lake being just enough to temper the heat, have gathered together the beauty, fashion, wealth, and sporting blood of all the Gulf States, even to far-away Texas, and the whole valley of the Mississippi, with New Orleans thrown in—New Orleans in its hey-day—New Orleans in its before-the-war splendor when it was the center of all who lived in the land of the cotton and the cane ; when the Crescent City was supposed to beat the world in everything ; when the *salons* of the St. Charles and St. Louis showed more feminine beauty and more Parisian furbelows and Brazilian diamonds to the square inch than any other hotels in America; when New Orleans boats were supposed to run faster and blow up slicker than any others on the Mississippi River; when the planter-aristocracy of that region, piling up their bales of cotton and rolling up their hogsheads of sugar, lived like patriarchal princes, surrounded by hundreds of slaves and dependents; when money flowed like water in the gambling saloons of Canal street and the Rue Royal; when, as Colonel Pike, of Arkansas, remarked, "This is a town that makes you think of hell, but you cotton to it as if it were heaven." In short, the New Orleans of the great slave States, before their power was broken and their chivalry went down under the onset of overwhelming odds and the impact of greater resources.

In the judges' stand are some of the most distinguished men in the South. Ex-President Fillmore, Wade Hampton, Col. Hughes, Bob Evans, and Judge Smith, chosen to represent their several States, entering horses in the contest. On the quarter-stretch and in the betting-ring under the grand stand, are seen all the well-known turfmen of America, wagering their money with the careless ease of ideal sportsmen. But others are betting also. Jammed into a seething mass along the stretch, oystermen from Barataria Lagoons, Italian fruit dealers, Irish butchers, even darky roustabouts from the levee and cotton press, are backing their horses.

On the grand stand, which now looks like a bouquet of beauty—gloves, gowns and other feminine nick-nacks are being risked by lovely and excited girls. The belles of Lexington and Louisville, who have come to bet for Kentucky's glory; the beauties of St. Louis and Memphis, each one of whom has picked out a winner; aristocratic loveliness from South Caro lina and the shores of the Gulf of Mexico, which never sent a finer gathering of beauty than the fair Mobil- ians who are here this day to do honor to Highlander, Alabama's horse, by clapping of dainty hands and wagering, with feminine prodigality, gloves in dozens, hats, bonnets, and robes from Madame Olympe on the pride of their State.

But, of course, in greater quantity, and therefore more dominant, is that peculiar, soft, tropical loveli- ness, that wondrous Creole beauty pertaining to Lou- isiana, in whose race have been blended the blood of the Castilian and the blood of the Gaul, productive in its women of a delicate, sensitive, though sometimes sensuous beauty, giving to them the eyes of Castile, the ankles of Seville and the graceful vivacity of Paris, all moulded together and made softer by blossoming under the sun of the tropics.

The horses are coming upon the track. Lexington, ridden by that slight, pale, consumptive white boy, Henry Meichon, Mississippi's Lecomte, bestridden by Black John, Highlander, by Gilpatrick, and Arrow, upon whose saddle sits Mr. Kenner's boy, familiarly known as "Old Abe," a soubriquet he has borne from pickaninnyhood. All these as they leave the paddock are eyed very critically by the crowd of gentlemen who love sport for sport's sake and know a horse; among them, Bob Covington, a young Kentuckian of bright, fresh, keen face, honest eyes, hearty manner, and off- hand, devil-may-care bonhommie.

"Bet on any other than Lexington ? Not by Daniel Boone ! " he says, " Gentlemen, I will take Lexington at one to two against the field. Three horses against one poor little Blue Grass colt; but I couldn't go back on corn-fed horses and corn-fed girls."

"Done with you for five hundred ! " remarks Henri La Farge, a young Louisianian, who is considered by Creole ladies the very best *parti* in New Orleans.

"Do it over again!" says the Kentuckian. "I have got a stock farm I'll put against your cotton crop." .

"Supposing we do it twice over, in thousands?" suggests young La Farge, who raises lots of cotton and any quantity of sugar, and can afford the luxury.

"That makes twenty-five hundred," replies Covington, "that I wager against your five thousand dollars."

"Certainly. I'll do it over again!"

But a detaining hand is laid upon the Kentuckian's shoulder, and old Colonel Dick Talliaferro, of Louisville, says: "Look here, Bob; don't you think you've done it enough?"

"Can't have enough of a good thing! Don't you see, the track is heavy with mud from yesterday's rain? Was there ever a horse trained in Kentucky that was not a mud-horse?" whispers the young man to the older one. Then he cries to La Farge: "Do it again! Only the winner is to give a champagne supper."

"With pleasure; at the Orleans Club."

"Very well. That is five thousand dollars to your ten thousand dollars."

About this time, probably thinking that he has put up enough of his goods and chattels even for the honor of his State, the young Blue Grass sportsman permits himself to be led away and introduced to Major McBurney, who has just been remarking to Talliaferro: "By Davy Crockett! That's a fine specimen of a man you've brought down with you, as well as a fine specimen of a horse."

"Yes," whispers the veteran Kentuckian. "His grandfather was an Indian fighter along with Daniel Boone, and the race don't deteriorate."

Looking at him, McBurney thinks it does not. For Bob Covington, as he is familiarly called by his friends, is a great big strapping fellow, just over six feet high, and though not carrying much flesh, has enough of solid muscular tissue about him to give him not only strength but a wiry activity peculiar to so many of the natives of that region—traits that have probably come down from those who had to cultivate them to save their scalps from marauding savages but two generations before. As it is, Bob has keen, bluish-gray eyes, a complexion as fresh as that of a girl, a light, hearty, whole-souled laugh, and a soft voice that goes straight to the heart of man, and also—of woman.

"Major McBurney, this is my young friend, Robert Boone Covington. I call him 'Bob,' having dandled him on my knee!" remarks Talliaferro.

"Ah! Come down to see Kentucky horseflesh beaten by Louisiana horseflesh, I hope," laughs McBurney, extending a cordial hand.

"I am not sure that I ought to be so enthusiastic," returns Covington, "about beating Louisiana. You know I have some Creole blood in me ; my mother came from Assumption Parish in this State. She was Miss Isabelle Tournay."

"Ah! Mademoiselle Isabelle, sister of Prosper Tournay! I knew the *savant* poet well," replies the Louisianian. "I have played poker with your romantic uncle at Duval's, and danced with your mother, young gentleman, in the old Orleans ball-room."

"Yes—but please don't talk of my—my mother!" mutters the Kentuckian, and the young man turns away, his eyes growing very sad.

Looking at him Talliaferro remarks to the Louisianian: "Bob's father and mother were carried off by that rush of cholera in 1850. He hasn't forgotten it yet."

But the Metairie race-course this day is not a place for memories of any kind—the present is too dominant. Sauntering across the stretch, Covington suddenly grows a little less interested in the horses than in something else—much more beautiful. A moment after, he steps up to Henri La Farge and says: "Do you see that lady?"

"What is the matter?" remarks his friend. "Lecomte just came past in his preliminary canter, and you didn't notice him!"

"No—I—Do you know who that lady is ?—the young one. The one in the barouche there, sitting beside a lady of more certain years."

"Oh, the one apparently just out of mourning?"

"Well, I don't know what you call her dress, but it's thundering becoming. The one with the white-headed coachman. No, not the four-in-hand—the *pair* I'm speaking about. Do you know who she is ?"

"Ah ! The one who has just thrown back her veil to get a better view of the course. *Parbleu*, she is beautiful !"

"Beautiful! I should think so! Do you know who she is? You're acquainted with everybody in New Orleans—by sight any way. Why don't you speak ?"

"I'm looking!"

"And so am I. Isn't she a leetle the purtiest thing you ever put your eyes on ? That face is as clean cut as a cameo—but what a soul is in it! And you don't know who she is? You New Orleans gentlemen are not very active and ambitious. If this were an old Kentucky race-course there'd be more boys playing about that barouche than flies in summer time. Our Blue Grass girls are a sight to make a man open his eyes; but this one is a—a little different."

"I don't know who the young lady is, but I can find out for you, I think, if she lives in Louisiana. I thought I saw Martineau near her carriage. I will inquire."

His friend leaves Bob looking at the young lady in the carriage. And well may he look, for he is gazing upon an almost perfect specimen of Creole beauty. Though not a brunette, the girl's eyes are a blue that will shine with excitement, but will grow dark if touched by passion. Her lips, exquisitely cut, are red as blushing poppies, yet tender and full of sentiment, suggesting that a very warm heart is beating in the fair body beneath them. Her hair is wavy and brown, growing very much darker in the shadows, but when tinted by the sun—brown. Her nose, clean cut as a cameo, with a trace of retroussé in it, just enough to make it piquant or haughty, as its owner wishes. The forehead not too high, but broad. The brows cleanly penciled, just strong enough to indicate force, but not severe enough to lessen by an iota the feminine grace that adorns and beautifies every expression of the face and every pose or movement of the rounded contours of the figure. As Covington looks at her the young lady is in repose, talking carelessly to her companion or chaperone, and the Kentuckian thinks her slightly haughty. A moment after, she smiles, and it is as the sun breaking forth to give joy unto the earth.

Just at this moment La Farge stands beside him and says: "I have discovered her name. Though they have a house in New Orleans she does not live here. The young lady has come up to the races, I presume. Her plantation is down on the Atchafalaya. She is Miss Louise Tournay, the daughter of old Prosper Tournay, the *savant*, who was suddenly killed by the accidental explosion of his shot gun ibis hunting a year or so back—— But where are you going ?"

"I'm going over to see my cousin," says the Kentuckian suddenly and proudly, "I'm much obliged to you. I will introduce you afterward."

Then he vaults over the palings into the stretch, runs across, despite a shriek of warning from a track-keeper, swings himself over the other fence, pushes his way through the crowd, and a moment after, to the astonishment of a very beautiful young lady, who is gowned very fashionably and exquisitely in white trimmed with lavender, takes off his hat, makes an old-time bow, and says : "Permit a relative to introduce himself, and ask a thousand pardons for doing so. I am Bob Covington, of Lexington, Kentucky, and you are my first cousin, I believe, Miss Tournay; my mother was your father's sister, Isabelle."

After a second's surprise, the young lady replies, looking earnestly at him: "I am delighted to meet you, for you are the only relative I have in the world, as far as I know, except my sister. I have heard my father speak of my aunt. She is dead now. I have often wished to see her, but Louisiana is a long way from Kentucky, and——" here the young lady bites her lip.

"And," remarks Bob, "I believe there was some estrangement. But neither you nor I, Miss Tournay, know anything about it, and as I have not another first cousin in the world, I think we had better shake hands over the old disagreement. It never grew to a family feud, I believe, it is a thing of which we know nothing—and this generation should become better friends than the last." His hand is half held out.

There is something in the frank, open-hearted, care-less, and impulsive, but thoroughly honest method of this young man's speech, address and bearing that Miss Louise, murmuring: "Your face reminds me of my father," extends a daintily gloved, exquisitely small patrician hand. This is literally smothered in the big digits of the Kentuckian, who has great difficulty in constraining himself from giving it a grip that would have caused its beautiful owner a pang or two.

"You will excuse me, I hope, Mrs. Joyce, but this advent of a relative came suddenly. Let me present my cousin, Mr. Robert Covington. You see your name is familiar to me," she adds graciously, while Bob is bowing to a lady of rather prim appearance who is sitting in the barouche beside Miss Tournay.

"I am most happy to meet you," says the chaperone, for that is evidently her office. "Since we came down to the Beau Rivage plantation we have led rather a lonely life."

"Of course—I understand," murmurs the Kentuck-ian, gazing at the girl's half-mourning. "But now I reckon you've just run up from Assumption to bet gloves, bonbons, furbelows, gimcracks, and perhaps a robe or two from Mme. Olympe, on Arrow, your State's horse, and have the beginning of a thundering good time," adds the young gentleman, suggestively.

"No; I believe I have only one little wager—a half dozen pairs of gloves with my family lawyer. I know very few people here. You see, I was educated in the North and have only lately come to Louisiana. Be-sides we live about seventy-five miles from New Or-leans," answers Miss Louise. "But here comes the gentleman of whom I spoke."

A moment after, Arvid Martineau, a typical Creole of French descent, of about sixty years of age, with slightly grizzled moustache, slightly silvered hair, the manners of a Parisian, and the dignity of a man practicing at the New Orleans bar, one of the most dis-tinguished of the day, strolls up. "Monsieur Martin-eau," remarks Miss Louise, "permit me to present my cousin, Mr. Robert Boone Covington, of Lexington, who has come down to see his horse beaten."

"I am very glad that I have come down, whether my horse is beaten or not," returns the Kentuckian, and his voice says he means it. "I am very much pleased to meet you, Monsieur Martineau"——but here a peculiar expression in the face of the lawyer makes this volatile young gentleman pause. The look is not of dislike, but certainly not of cordiality, and perchance almost of consternation.

"You—you are not well?" suddenly asks Miss Tournay, for Martineau's face is deathly pale.

"No! I *was* perfectly well, but the sun—I believe is a little too warm—perhaps the excitement. You know I have backed Arrow rather heavily for a man of professional income," murmurs the attorney.

"I'm afraid you've lost your money," remarks Bob, who can't help thinking: "What the deuce in my appearance had such an effect upon this man? By Daniel Boone! That Creole looked at me very much as if I were an Indian with a scalping knife in my hand." Then he suddenly cogitates: "I've hit it! He doubts the genuineness of my relationship. Thinks I'm flying false colors to get acquainted with this pink of perfection who is under his charge."

Acting on this idea, Bob suggests: "Miss Tournay, permit me to put your carriage in a little better place, near the judges' stand. I know a good deal about horse-racing, and I can locate you so you will get a good view of the final struggle."

"I am very much obliged to you," replies the young lady, and a moment after she finds her barouche, under the experienced guidance of her new-found cousin, placed in the best position to give its fair occupant a first-rate view of the finish of the great four-mile race.

Then, with a sudden thought, "I'll show him I am genuine," Bob says to the French lawyer: "Stroll over with me; I want to introduce you to my Kentucky friends. Be back in a few moments." Raising his hat the two stride off together. For, curiously enough, Arvid Martineau is anxious to know if this gentleman's name is genuine; if so, he is very well aware that the relationship is genuine also.

Of this he gets ample proof in the next two minutes,

being introduced by this rapid young gentleman as "the family lawyer of my cousin, the belle of Louisiana," to Ten Broeck and Kenyon and Huddleston, and half a dozen more prominent Kentucky turfmen, and they all go under the grand stand to the clubroom of the Metairie Jockey Club and take a drink.

"You know there's a change in the betting," remarks Talliaferro, chancing along. "Lexington is coming up in the odds."

"Well, I've put all the money I want on our horse, and now I've something pleasanter to look after. I think I'll walk over and see the race from my cousin's carriage," says Covington. "Won't you come with me, Monsieur Martineau?"

"Yes," replies the family lawyer suddenly, and they are just in time to cross the track before it is cleared for the first heat.

While they are walking the lawyer is speaking. "I am very glad," he remarks, looking the young Kentuckian over, "that you take such an interest in your cousin."

"Who would not?" says Covington enthusiastically. "There's no first cousin in the world, in my opinion, up to her in good looks. Gaze over on the grand stand. There sit the prettiest women in America, every girl of them in her best bib and tucker, but hang me if I think there's one of them that quite comes up to my cousin Louise."

"Yes; she is very beautiful."

"All I wonder," says the young man, "is that there is not a crowd of bucks and bloods round that carriage. There would be in Lexington. The boys here seem to me rather slow on the trail."

"There would be here; but your cousin knows nobody, or very few. Miss Tournay has lived on the plantation ever since her return from school. She has only been in New Orleans two days. This is the first time she has been seen at any public festivity."

"I'm rather delighted to hear that," remarks Mr. Covington. "It saves me trouble."

"How?"

"Well, I've got a clear course for this afternoon.

After that I expect to have to run heats with every dandy in Louisiana. Ah! She sees us! See, my cousin Louise waves her parasol! Look at me! Observe Bob Covington making hay while the sun shines."

A few seconds after they stand beside Miss Tournay's carriage, and the lawyer, gazing on, chews his grizzled moustache grimly, but smiles as he notes that the lady and gentleman seem to become, almost on the instant, very well acquainted.

Miss Tournay is chatting pleasantly and with less constraint than is usual to New Orleans young ladies, especially those of the Creole population, who are brought up very much after the manner of the French. But Louise has been educated at a New York boarding school and has absorbed some of the manners of the Northern metropolis.

A moment after Mr. Covington strolls away, to bring the last news from the horses, which are now getting ready for the start.

Taking advantage of the young Kentuckian's absence, Monsieur Martineau, getting close to the young lady's pretty ear, remarks: "I have just been over with your cousin, Miss Louise, talking to the magnates of his State. Mr. Bob Covington seems to be about as much the pride of Kentucky as that beautiful horse Lexington who is cantering up the track. Your cousin is a very gallant representative of the Blue Grass region."

"I am delighted to hear that; but who would not have known it by his face," returns the young lady. A moment later she makes Mr. Covington very happy, for as he steps up to the barouche again, she addresses him as "Cousin Bob."

"By Heaven! Cousin Louise," exclaims the gallant, taking off his hat, "you've made me happier than if Lexington won the race; and that means the happiest man upon this earth."

"Well, you know 'blood is thicker than water,'" returns the young lady. "Since my father's death I have had no relatives except my little sister, who is away from me in a New York boarding school. Therefore you come in very opportunely; don't you, Cousin Bob?"

She emphasizes the name by a slightly heightened color in her soft cheeks and a look in her eyes that makes the Kentuckian know Louise Tournay means what she says.

"Let's have a *cousinly* wager to celebrate the event," laughs Covington, very proud of his new found relative.

The young lady, gazing at him, hesitates. The color on her exquisite face, already heightened, is now a burning red. Into her mind has flown, "A *cousinly* wager may mean, perchance, a *cousinly* kiss from this young man of rapid action, impulsive bearing, and warm heart."

But Bob, catching the big blush, and Miss Louise's embarrassed manner, begins to grow red himself, and blurts out, "I—I didn't mean that!" Then recovering himself, goes on, with a gallant mien and very earnest eyes: "Though I shall feel the most honored man on earth, when Cousin Lou considers Cousin Bob worthy of such a mark of kinship." To this he adds quite pathetically: "You know, I have never kissed a cousin in my whole life."

"No?" murmurs Miss Louise, caressing the tip of a very dainty *petite bottine* with the end of her white parasol. Then she cries suddenly: "Of course not! I am the only cousin you've ever had," blushes once more and bursts out laughing; and this incident seems to do a great deal toward sweeping away any extreme punctilio between Cousin Lou and her just-discovered Cousin Bob.

"What I meant was, Miss Louise, to give you a cousin's privilege of naming your own horse or horses and your own odds in gloves, nicknacks or feminine furbelows," remarks Mr. Covington, gazing with admiring eyes on the pretty picture made by the young lady, who is now a charming melange of blushes, laughter, and sparkling eyes.

"That means," murmurs Louise, "you want to make a—a cousinly present."

"Not exactly. But I can tell you I'll lose to you with better grace than I would to any other human being. Let's make it gloves," continues the young man eagerly. "You name your two horses and number of dozens. I will take the nags you reject."

"Very well. I select Arrow, our Louisiana horse, and, in compliment to my Kentucky relative, Lexington." Then she laughs. "I think I will only rob you of a dozen pairs of gloves, Cousin Bob."

"How I shall enjoy paying this wager! That's kind of you, that's heartfelt, that's cousinly, betting on our horse, Cousin Lou," cries Covington, elated. "Besides, I can tell you, with this muddy track," he whispers this, "Lexington is sure. You might as well tell me the number of your gloves even now."

"Five and three-quarters. But be sure and get Jouvin's, with long fingers," remarks his cousin.

Looking at her delicately gloved patrician hands, one of which is lying in easy grace over the edge of the carriage and the other dallying with her parasol, Mr. Covington thinks that if anything, five and three-quarters will be too large for her pretty digits.

While this conversation has been going on Monsieur Martineau has been chatting with Mrs. Joyce, casting now and then a glance at the beautiful young lady and her cousinly cavalier. The more cordial the young man gets in his manner to the young lady, the happier the family lawyer's face.

"Don't you think it a rather quick assumption of relationship on the part of Mr. Covington," whispers the chaperone nervously.

"No; there's no doubt of Cousin Bob's standing in his State and with the Kentucky gentlemen who know him. I believe they think of running him for Congress up in the Blue Grass District. There's no doubt of his relationship to Miss Louise. He is a noble, whole-souled fellow and—and I'm very glad of it."

This last is said with a curious twitching of the Creole's grizzled moustache.

But now there is a wild buzz of excitement from the crowd that lines the Metairie race-course and through its grand stand—next breathless silence. The horses are at the post!

Then in all this multitude, who have forgotten even

numan life itself in their thoughts of horseflesh, one man, Arvid Martineau, utters a profound sigh.

"Sighing, my dear fellow?" remarks Henri La Farge, who has strolled up to him. "Do you think you've backed the wrong horse?"

But Bedlam now breaks loose! The drum has tapped, the horses are away, all in a bunch together. At the turn Lexington leads, Arrow second, Lecomte third, and Highlander well up.

"My two horses first! Lexington and Arrow!" cries Miss Louise excitedly, clapping her hands. "The gloves are mine!"

"Yes; I think they are. But four miles isn't won in the first quarter," laughs the Kentuckian. "You've not been accustomed to horse-races, Cousin Louise. We'll have to educate you in the Blue Grass region."

A moment after, the young lady gives a gasp of dismay and mutters: "Lecomte! Those are his colors, aren't they? Lecomte is ahead. Oh, goodness gracious! He has passed Lexington."

But a moment after the chestnut falls back behind the bay. This is the second mile, and they hold this position for the third time round the course. But the mud is beginning to tell upon the lighter-limbed Arrow; his speed has slackened, and Highlander is now in third place, Lexington first, Lecomte second.

"I tell you, it will be a contest between Blue Grass blood," remarks Covington, eagerly. "Lecomte, who was foaled in my own region but trained down here, and Lexington, who has been fed on blue grass all his life. And true Blue Grass *wins!* Old Kentucky forever! Old Kentuck *wins! Lexington!* LEXINGTON!"

This cry is taken up all along the home-stretch! The Louisville girls on the grand stand are waving scarfs and handkerchiefs and clapping their hands, and from up the course there comes the Kentucky yell, for Lexington has won the first heat.

"I have half gained my gloves already," remarks the young lady, "would you like to compromise on half? Say, Cousin Bob, would you like to compromise?"

"You're a thrifty soul," laughs the proud and happy Covington, "with one of your horses, Arrow, distanced,

and out of the race." "But I would not compromise any of my bets. I shall have as much pleasure
in giving you the gloves as I will have in taking twenty
thousand dollars from the gentlemen about here, who
don't seem to appreciate that Kentucky produces the
best horseflesh and the prettiest girls in the world."
Then looking at the fair face that is gazing rather
quizzically into his, he murmurs gallantly, his eyes
growing bright with admiration. "All except one, my
Cousin Lou, the Rosebud of Louisiana !"

CHAPTER II.

THE SECOND HEAT.

THEN comes the excitement between heats, the making of new wagers, and arranging of different odds.
"I think I'll step over and hear about the betting,
just for a minute, Cousin Louise," remarks the Kentuckian. "Besides, I would like to see how our nag
works out after this heat."
In pursuance of this idea, Mr. Covington, elbowing
his way across the track and passing the grand stand,
very shortly finds himself at the saddling paddock,
which is a little to the rear and somewhat to the right
of the grand stand. Clustered about the entrance to
this Walhalla of horseflesh, to which admission can
only be obtained by permission of the Jockey Club,
is a crowd of frantic bettors, stablemen, touts and the
riff-raff of the race-course, who are very anxious to
know what chances the other horses have in the second
heat, for which the odds have already changed, Lexington being now a favorite over the field. As Covington pushes his way through this throng and obtains
entrance to the wished-for land, he is gazed after with
hatred by some and envy by all.
"By the Lord Harry!" mutters a broken-down sporting man. "These bloods always get the inside information! These chaps that put up the many dollars
have a pull over us that put up the few dollars."

"*Sacré Dieu!* That's what has ruined me, Monsieur!" mutters an old weazened-looking man of Creole accent, parchment face, and piercing black eyes. "I have lost on every race this Spring meeting. Now I can only play my little game—which is a fair one, gentlemen—will you not bet upon it? The selecting of the jack when I shuffle them so——" and he begins a game of three-card monte into which he would lure the lookers-on. "Will you not bet? See, it really is simple. I throw them about so! You have the advantage. Your eyes watch my hands; your glance is quicker than my movements, for I am growing old. I will give you the odds, two to one. You name the jack as I shuffle them."

But the other mutters: "I'll be cursed if I'll be skinned on cards as well as on horses! And with niggers round me, too!" Then he cries, "Get out, ye coons! Get out o' here!" For a number of darkey stable-boys and grooms have gathered about, and the irate gamester moves away, driving these sons of Ham from his path and cursing: "By all the Philistines, every nigger in town is out here! There won't be a woolly-head in our hotel to wait on the table this evening!"

In the paddock, Covington finds the elite of the sportsmen of that day, in all the varied joys, hopes, and fears of a great race which is as yet undecided. They are gathered about the horses, discussing the heat and watching their nags sweat out. The Kentucky party, among whom are Talliaferro, Ten Broeck, and Colonel Bruce, are inspecting Lexington, as the bay colt is being walked up and down under blankets by a negro groom. The Mississippi party, who have not yet lost hope, Lecomte having made a very fair showing, are gathered about Colonel Wells and his gallant chestnut. Alabamians are trying to keep up their courage, talking about the "bottom" of Highlander, for he has still another chance. It is the Louisiana party, among them young La Farge, for whom there is no balm in Gilead. Their horse, the distanced Arrow, is being sent to his stables, followed by old Abe, his jockey, who is sobbing bitterly and cursing the mud that has told so heavily against the light-limbed gelding that has carried the bulk of sugar money.

The Kentucky party Bob joins, and they go to discussing their nag with all the enthusiasm of happy boys, Talliaferro crying that their colt is sweating out beautifully and will be as lively for his second heat as a mosquito in spring, and Ten Broeck adding: "I'm glad to hear that, for I've bought him—all of him! This pride of my State is now mine—all mine!" the joy of the owner of great race-horses coming into the sportsman's eyes.

Then one of them suddenly says: "Great Taylor! Look at Col. Wells! He's taking that negro jockey, John, off by himself. They're holding a consultation. Look at that darky's face as his owner speaks to him! The next will be a desperate heat!"

"Well, all the talk in the world won't make that track light," replies Covington. "This india-rubber, gutta-percha mud, twenty pounds of it sticking to every horse's hoofs is what makes it dead sure for us."

After a little he turns to go back to the fair young lady, the glory of whose eyes still lingers in his mind, and tell her he thinks her gloves are very safe.

As he comes out of the paddock, however, he is detained by the old French three-card monte man, who, stepping in front of him bows and says: "Monsieur, you are a member of the Kentucky party?"

"Yes; don't I look like it? Who've the happy faces on the track to-day? Blue Grass boys!"

"Then, Monsieur, can you give an unfortunate a little information?"

"Yes, if it won't take fifteen seconds to do it."

"Please step aside with me, Monsieur. I am in despair. I have lost more than I can afford upon the horse that is going to the stable." And there are tears in the old man's eyes that make the Kentuckian pity him—though the picture before him is not a pleasant one. Old age, decrepit, broken down, though the soft manners of the Creole suggest the man is more educated and refined than his present appearance indicates. His dress of black broadcloth has once been fashionable. It is very neat and clean now, but the elbows of the coat and the knees of the trousers are shabby-genteel to shininess.

"I have but one pleasure in life, monsieur—betting. The only one left me."

"Yes, so I presume. What can I do for you?" remarks Covington, anxious to get through with the interview.

"You can tell me how to place my money."

"Well, I never saw a horse-race that was *dead* sure, but with that mud on the track—go and inspect it, and if it's as heavy as it seems to me, you can back the horse with the big fore-shoulders. You know what nag I mean—the one that won the last heat. By mathematics Lexington has now two chances to one against any other horse; by horseflesh sense, ten to one on this muddy track."

"Thank you, Monsieur; I shall never forget the tip," murmurs the Creole monte man.

"I never give tips," replies the Kentuckian. "I simply give advice founded on common sense and horse knowledge. Only don't curse me if Lexington gets knocked down—that's about the only thing that'll beat him."

With this, he elbows his way through the crowd, on his way to the side of Miss Louise Tournay. But as he passes the grand stand he is detained again; this time in a much more pleasant manner. A very beautiful young lady, magnificently arrayed, with the soft hazel eyes and sunny brown hair so peculiar to Kentucky's daughters, and a rounded form which unites the beauties of Venus and the graces of Hebe, bars his way with detaining parasol, and murmurs plaintively, "Mr. Covington, are you not going to stay and rejoice with us?—over our great horse!"

"I could rejoice," replies the gentleman, gallantly, "with Miss Sally Johnson, without anything else to make me happy."

But Miss Johnson does not get the benefit of *tête-à-tête*, though perchance she would like it; for Bob seems to be as popular with the ladies of his region as with the gentlemen. In a jiffy he is surrounded by

Blue Grass girls, all of them wearing Lexington's colors, and all of them happier than any one should be this side of heaven.

To them he must give the latest news from the paddock; to them he is compelled to make engagements for the grand ball this night at the St. Charles Hotel.

But though bright eyes gaze into his and pretty lips whisper to him and he has enough beauty around him to drive average manhood to distraction, Bob does not forget the charming young lady who sits in the barouche upon the opposite side of the track. Very shortly he is standing beside Cousin Louise and taking off his hat to Mrs. Joyce, to whom he says: "Wouldn't you like me to put a little wager for you on the race? You *should* have a bet! *No* lady should be without one to-day! I can win a year's glove-money for you, as easy as jumping off a log! Say the word and let me put a little bet for you, Madame."

"Bet for *me?*" gasps the astonished chaperone. "My dear sir, I never bet in my life!" Then she adds, in prim severity: "I have not been brought up to *gamble!*"

"No," remarks Miss Louise, playfully, "Mrs. Joyce has conscientious scruples about betting and also in regard to another peculiar institution of our Southern life. She comes from Vermont."

"Oh!—Ah! I understand. She doesn't know that the only happy people down South are those who have got no care and are taken care of," laughs the Kentuckian. "Why Mrs. Joyce, I envy Mr. Cæsar, my body-servant. He hasn't half my work to do; he gets his board and clothes as well as I do, and never wonders where the money'll come from; and that's all any of us get in this world. But the horses are coming up, and judging by the look on darky John's face, he is determined to win, if Lecomte can do it!"

A moment later Covington, who must be talking or doing something, remarks: "I'll tell you a curious story about that negro jockey. It is rumored round the stables that his owner, Col. Jeff. Wells, went down to see John and tell him he'd got to win the race, and asked him what kind of wager he'd like, to make him dead sure to try his very level best. Darn me if the boy—he's a foolish fellow, half-witted, I think, except as regards horses—didn't ask him if he couldn't bet himself agin' the victory."

"Bet *himself?*" shrieks Mrs. Joyce. "What do you mean by that?"

"Well, darky John meant if he won he was to have his free-papers. And I tell you, he made Colonel Wells cry. Wells broke out and said: 'Haven't I been the best master on earth to you, John? Did you ever want anything in the universe? Darn me, haven't I always given you all the money you wanted to spree and get drunk on out of the racing season? Hasn't your mammy got the best cabin on the plantation? Don't you do as you darn please? Don't you boss *me?* Don't you know I'll take care of you as long as you live, and bury you when you're dead?'"

"'That's all right, sir,' replied the boy. 'I'll not leave you for anything, as long as you live. But I was just thinking if you died *fust,* I'd like to pick out the next stable I ride for; though you've got me as long as you want me, living or dead. I'd be your jockey and you'd be my master if I had a hundred thousand dollars and free-papers.'

"'And by Jove!' remarked Wells, who is as noble a fellow as there is anywhere, 'Boy, you can have it!' So that darky is riding to win *himself.* But he's got to lose! The mud is too heavy on that track for John to get a chance to make a darned fool of himself to-day."

This oration is cut short by the excited Louise, who cries, clapping her hands: "Oh, the drum has tapped! They're off the second time! Highlander is ahead—your horse, Cousin Bob!"

"No; Lecomte! Lecomte is first! By the Goddess of Liberty and Uncle Sam!" ejaculates the Kentuckian, "How that darky jockey is riding!"

"Yes! Riding for *freedom!*" snaps out Mrs. Joyce at him.

So they go on, all lapped together, for two miles. People gasping with excitement, boys cheering, girls screaming, as one or the other of the horses takes the lead; men growing pale, and one or two darky stable lads butting their woolly heads together from very nervous excitement.

Now the horses are in the third mile, Lecomte still leading. Highlander is making his rush to pass Lexington, but he can't get there, for the bay now makes his brush also, and the mud soon flies from the Kentucky colt's hoofs in the faces of both the Alabama and Mississippi horses.

"It's Kentuck once more!" cries Covington. "Both Blue Grass bred, but only one Blue Grass trained and Blue Grass all over! Oh, what a State we have! Cousin Lou, come up and see our State!"

But Cousin Lou has a dozen pairs of gloves on the race, and that is what her vivacious, sprightly, feminine spirit is devoted to at this moment. She is crying: "Oh, they're at the third quarter; it's the last mile! Gracious, they're locked together! Which is going to win? Oh, merciful goodness! My horse is being beaten!" and her lovely cheeks grow pale.

The päle, consumptive boy on Lexington is now calling on his horse. The mud is telling against the Southern nag. Those great foreshoulders of the son of Alice Carneal are pulling him through the india-rubber track of the Metairie Jockey Course fatally well!

But darky John is riding to win *himself!* He won't give up, and plies his game mount with whip and spur! So the two come tearing on, Lecomte and Lexington, side by side like quarter-horses. Again the cries of "Mississippi!" and "Kentucky!" fill the air.

A moment after, the cries are all "Kentucky!" and there is a gray-faced darky jockey on a beaten horse four lengths behind Lexington, as he wins the final heat of that great race, which has been turf talk for many a day before and will be so for many a day thereafter.

But Mississippi men won't accept the test. "It was the heavy track! Lecomte was not trained for mud! We live in a decent climate down here!" exclaim some of his backers.

"We'll do it over again!" remarks Lexington's owner blandly.

"Done!" cries Colonel Wells, as genuine a turfman as ever owned a horse. And he backs his nag Lecomte against the Kentucky champion for another race, to be run upon the coming Saturday. With this he steps over to the paddock, where Black John is standing rather ruefully as the chestnut Lecomte is being led away to the stable.

"Please don't think it my fault, Colonel Wells, for I rode for my—my life," says the boy eagerly; then adds: "It war the mud. Yo' know de colt hasn't had a heavy track for his training."

"I imagine you're right, John," says his owner, "though the horse that beat him is a good one, too. But I'm going to give you another chance next Saturday. The track will probably be light and dusty by that time, and perhaps these Kentucky cockadoodles won't have so much to crow over then."

"Bet de same bet, Massa Jeff?" asks Black John breathlessly.

"Certain! You shall have another chance to win yourself, just the same as that colt shall have another to be considered the best horse in America. No, don't thank me—" For the boy, forgetful of the difference in race and station, is clasping his owner's hand and muttering: "God bless you, Colonel! I'll train my-sel' as well as de horse fo' dat race. You can bet yo' money! I'm a-ridin' for my freedom!"

"Why one would think I had been a bad master to you," says the Colonel grimly, "when you know——"

"Yo' have been de best on earth, sir, and I'll ride fo' you till you die. But I've set my heart on owning myself, dat's all—dat's all."

The veteran turfman brushes his hand over his eyes as he turns away. Then he sees something in the face of his jockey that makes him return to the betting ring, though he has lost very heavily on to-day's trans-actions, and begin to make his book on the coming race, backing his own colt very freely and very heavily at the odds that are offered him; for Lexington is, of course, a favorite for the new event.

A few minutes after, it is buzzed about that the Jockey Club has offered a two-thousand-dollar purse, in addition to the side bets, and the two sons of Boston will fight it out over again one week from this day.

This is delightful news for all the storekeepers on Canal street, the proprietors of all the magazines of the French quarter. The boss of every gambling house rejoices and every Boniface is happy, because this means that most of this large concourse that have been drawn to the city by this great race will remain to see another great race and make this first week in April as brilliant as Carnival and Mardi Gras, scattering their money among the New Orleans tradesmen and greasing with American dollars the wheels of local business.

"*La semaine prochaine* will be grand. The hotels will be full. The young ladies who have graced the grand stand to-day will probably favor my bazaar of Parisian novelties," remarks Pierre Larost, of the *Magasin de Sud*, to Kitson Jarvis, his social *confrère* at billiards and dominoes.

It is a curious intimacy; for Monsieur Larost is of Creole blood, small of stature, and has a French face, while Mr. Jarvis is a great, big-limbed, uncouth creature, comes from Cincinnati, and has a peculiarly shrewd Yankee physiognomy. But both these gentlemen are useful to each other, not only socially, but in the way of trade; Mr. Jarvis doing a small, but rather smart, attorney's business, chiefly among sea-captains and shipmen, his office being near the levee, and Monsieur Larost keeping shop upon the *Rue Royal*. Consequently Kitson has been able, from his acquaintance with sea-captains, to secure a good many customers for the Frenchman's wares. Larost, in return, has frequently, through his knowledge of the Creole population of the city, been of service to Mr. Jarvis in some of the petty lawsuits that have come into his hands.

The two together, like everybody else in New Orleans to whom it has been possible, have made a holiday of this day and are now strolling across the race-track preparatory to their return to the city. This evening they will have a game of billiards, after a dinner at Mme. Duparc's café on Bourbon street,

and perhaps wind up at Mr. Tom Placide's Variety
Theatre, or possibly at one of the French playhouses,
as Mr. Jarvis has succeeded in acquiring the dominant
language of the Creole, finding it very useful to him in
his various business affairs.

Forced by the crowd, they are now pretty close to
Bob Covington and one or two of his friends, to whom
the young man, excited by the enthusiasm of victory,
is remarking:

"This has been a great day for old Kentuck! And
I'm the luckiest man on the track."

"Well, come and get into our cabriolet with us," returns Talliaferro. You can expand, enthuse, and blow
your trumpet, my boy, as we drive into town."

"You'll excuse me, Colonel; that's what I came to
see you about," remarks Bob. "I have accepted the
offer of my cousin, Miss Louise Tournay, and her
chaperone, Mrs. Joyce, to drive into town with them."

"You're going to stay over for next Saturday's
event?" asks one of the young men.

"Stay over? I could live and die in Louisiana;
only give me such racing and such girls! Of course I
stay over! By the by, La Farge, I owe a supper at
the Orleans to you and friends. I hope all you gentlemen will consider yourselves invited; supposing we call
it next Wednesday. And now—good-bye, for the
present. No; not even a julep! My cousin must not
be kept waiting even for a parched throat."

With this the Kentuckian moves off. Though he
does not know it, he has a follower. The minute he
has announced himself as the cousin of Miss Louise
Tournay, Mr. Kitson Jarvis, after one start of astonishment, has drunk in every word Cousin Bob has uttered.

With a muttered "Excuse me, Larost; I'll meet you
at the cars in a few shakes of a lamb's tail," the attorney makes his way as best he can through the surg-
ing crowd and succeeds in keeping in sight the tall
form of the Kentuckian, though he does not get
very near him. . However, he can see Mr. Covington
distinctly as he steps up to the barouche in which
Mrs. Joyce is seated by the side of her charming
charge.

Putting his eyes on the group and finally getting nearer to them just as their carriage drives off, this gentleman of the law notes the ardent admiration in the Kentuckian's face as he gazes at the beautiful young lady sitting as his *vis-a-vis*. Then he catches the enthusiastic Bob's words as he says: "Of course *we* race next Saturday, Cousin Louise; we must all drive out together and back Lexington again!"

Then, gazing at the supreme loveliness of the lady, so daintily arrayed and talking so vivaciously to the gentleman, Mr. Kitson Jarvis mutters to himself these astounding words: "By heaven, he's a lucky man!" Next laughs to himself sneeringly: "Won't that chap jump out of his boots when I tell him my little tale?"

Apparently the lawyer has his "little tale" still on his mind when he joins his friend Larost at the cars, for his words are few, and he goes into a brown study, to his companion's astonishment. For Mr. Kitson Jarvis is generally a man of a good deal of small talk, and has a habit of telling facetious stories, perchance not over delicate, but usually having a good deal of brutal point to them.

Entirely unaware of the attorney's interest in him, Mr. Bob Covington contrives to make a very pleasant journey of it, chatting breezily to the ladies as they drive slowly into town, the concourse of carriages upon the shell-road preventing any attempt at speed.

"We'll have a great week of it!" he remarks, airily. "The week *between* the races. Neither you nor I, Cousin Lou, know New Orleans very well; we'll do the town!" unheeding the suggestion of Mrs. Joyce, who remarks that young men and young ladies, especially among the Creole population, are not supposed to go wandering about together.

"That may be all very well!" replies Bob, promptly, when they are *not* relatives! But, you see, Miss Tournay and I are first cousins, Mrs. Joyce. Besides, has not Cousin Louise a chaperone in you?"

"I think that you, Pamela, will cover all the ground," remarks the young lady. "First cousins, only relatives in the world, and your *watchful* eyes!"

She says this archly, patting her companion's hand. "Besides," she continues vivaciously, noting that her conversation makes the young Kentuckian's face happy, and perhaps being willing to please him by this time, "I have not been brought up exactly in the Creole manner. My experience at Miss Martin's boarding school in New York, where you looked rather strictly after me, Pamela, has given me some different views; and, above all, the ties of blood——"

"Yes; but not very close ones," suggests Mrs. Joyce. "Not close enough to —— " The rather prim lady bites her lips at this point, for Cousin Bob's face has grown a little red and Miss Louise has put on a very pretty blush.

"That's true!" cries the Kentuckian. "We're just near enough together to be —— *right!*" Then he goes on in his fly-away manner: "I wouldn't be your brother, Cousin Louise, to be Samson and Goliah of Gath combined."

By this time, the carriage having driven up to the family house of the Tournays on Dauphine Street, Mr. Robert Covington assists the ladies out, perchance holding his cousin's hand a little longer than her chaperone's as he bids them adieu at their door.

Even as he turns away he is made very happy. Miss Louise, taking a step toward him, says: "You have no engagement this evening, I hope, Cousin Bob?"

Then Cousin Bob lies—he knows he has half a dozen; but he answers: "Not a one!"

"Very well; suppose you come and see us *en famille.* Perhaps we may become a little better acquainted."

"That's the talk!" replies the gentleman heartily; "though I feel very cousinly *now.*" And he does, as he takes the dainty hand that is extended toward him again in his and gives it a little family squeeze, and strides off to St. Charles Hotel where he has rooms— the happiest, dashiest and most run-away Kentuckian in all that town, and New Orleans has many of them this day in which the pride of their State has beaten the next best nag in the world.

As he strides down Dauphine Street the sharp eyes of Mr. Kitson are still upon the young man. Having

arrived in town a little ahead of him, and knowing
the *locale* of the Tournay town house, the attorney has
watched Mr. Covington assisting the ladies from the
carriage; he has noticed the Kentuckian's eyes as he
has bid the girl farewell; he has observed her wondrous beauty, and he thinks: "By Jehosh! If she isn't
a sky-rocket!" then cogitates: "That letter from
California is already overdue; it must be here soon!
If it doesn't come, I'll speak to him anyway before this
fortunate young buck gets out of New Orleans. By
Joseph and his brethren! this may be the most tarna-
tion lucky stroke of legal business, Kit, you've struck
in the Crescent City."

CHAPTER III.

BLUE GRASS GIRLS.

PROMPT to his appointment this evening, Mr. Robert
Covington handles the knocker at the spacious portals
of the Tournay residence.

He is apparently expected.

The door is opened almost immediately by a bright-
eyed, bright-skinned mulatto girl, who courtesies to him
saying: "Glad to see yo', Mistah Bob! Does us all
good to have a gent'man of the Tournay blood roun'
dis house once more. I'se Lorena, Miss Louise's
maid."

"Well, Lorena, I'll tell my man, Mr. Cæsar, what
a pretty girl there is about here. Shouldn't wonder if
Mr. Cæsar turns up pretty often with messages from
me, after he has seen you," laughs the Kentuckian in
the easy way common to Southerners of that period,
when family servants were almost as much a part of the
family as the family itself, and the tremendous social
gulf of blood and class, permitted a careless familiarity
between master and slave, who by no accident could
ever change their stations.

"Why, Mr. Cæsar has seen me already, sir. He
brought a bouquet from yo' about half an hour ago,

with a note for Miss Louise," giggles the girl. "Mr.
Cæsar's now in the kitchen, sir. We're treating him
right smart. It's a great thing for the Tournay family
servants to all get together once more, sir. Mr.
Cæsar says he feels just as much to home as if he'd
been born here, sir!"

"Yes; I have no doubt Mr. Cæsar *is* making himself at home. He has a habit of doing it with me!"
laughs Covington, as he is ushered into the courtyard of the house, which is made pretty by growing
bananas and tropical shrubs and has a little fountain in
its centre. On each side of the front entrance, which
is arched and runs through to the *patio*, two flights of
stairs in old-fashioned style in the courtyard lead to
the second floor, upon which the reception rooms are
located. Ascending one of these the young man is
ushered into a pretty parlor full of old-fashioned bric-
a-brac, furniture and pictures, some of its adornments
dating from the time of Louis Quinze.

Here a few minutes after he is welcomed by his cousin
and her chaperone, Miss Louise extending her hand
very cordially and Mrs. Joyce bowing in prim gracious-
ness.

After a few minutes' general conversation Pamela,
remarking: "I have a little embroidery to do this
evening," steps into another salon only separated from
this one by portières, to devote herself to her worsted
frame upon which she is embroidering in colored wools
a flower-piece which, though admired at that day, is
now one of the admitted monstrosities of art.

Seated in this room, Mrs. Joyce is with, and yet apart
from her charge. The chaperone is following the *convenances* of Louisiana life in their form but not in their
spirit, as she is giving Mr. Robert Covington oppor-
tunities of *tête-à-tête* with a young lady that are altogether beyond the precepts of Creole etiquette.

But Pamela Joyce has a Yankee way of looking at
the affair. She reasons: "They are first cousins;
he is the only gentleman relative Louise has in the
world. Probably they have family matters to talk
over, in which my immediate presence would be
a restraint. Any way—what does it matter? These

Creoles treat a girl as if she were not to be trusted, and I know Louise. She never flirted at Miss Martin's boarding school, though half the others did. Her eyes were always straight ahead of her, whenever we marched them down Lafayette Place for our morning walk."

Noting this fact, Mr. Covington for a moment wonders if some hint from his pretty cousin has produced this delicious opportunity of private converse, and is very happy over the idea. But a moment after he forgets everything in the extreme beauty of the young lady who sits before him and fascinates his very soul.

The evening dress Miss Louise wears, after the manner of the period, has added the charms of ivory shoulders and snowy arms to the graces the young lady had displayed on the race-track. It is a pretty gown of white. Made almost after the manner of the First Empire in its simplicity of detail, it clings about her and displays the rounded curves of beauty in every movement, in every pose.

Bob also notes Miss Louise's tresses are banded round her graceful head and tied in a knot *à la Grecque.* Two little Ionian curls float down on one side of her white brow. A single white camellia, set in her soft, dark-brown hair, is the only ornament she wears. So Miss Tournay sits before her new-found cousin, all in pure white, even to petite slippers and weblike hosiery, of which the short gown of that period gives Mr. Covington one or two rap' urous glimpses.

But it is not the young lady's beauty that is productive of all this effect upon the young gentleman. She has a very gracious manner, and her eyes are lighting with varying emotions as these ripple one after the other over her vivacious features. Her smile is merry, her laugh is hearty, and her gestures naively piquant; though as he looks at her Mr. Covington cannot help imagining that at times the young lady may be distant and even haughty—peculiarities of her disposition of which some day he may have further proof. At present, however, Louise is amiability personified, and seems very happy in entertaining her new-found cousin. She sings for him one or two little French *chansons*, accompanying herself very prettily, and asks him if he has heard Jenny Lind, remarking: "I did once. Miss Martin took her whole boarding school to one of Mr. Barnum's concerts at Castle Garden." Then, for variety, she warbles a soft negro plantation melody, imitating the banjo upon the piano, after the manner of Monsieur Gottschalk, who is at this time the rage, remarking about this celebrated exponent of sensuous melody: "You know he is a Creole himself, born here in New Orleans."

A moment after, perhaps to give the young gentleman a chance to talk, Louise asks, suddenly: "Do you dance?"

"Do I dance?" cries Bob, anxious to make a showing for himself. "Do I *dance*, Cousin Lou? Ask the *Louisville girls*."

"The Louisville girls?" remarks the young lady contemplatively; but adds airily: "I am not acquainted with them." There is a trace of pique in her voice, her delicate lips tremble. Then she says, slowly: "Suppose you tell me a little about yourself and the Louisville girls. Eh, Cousin Bob?"

Louise has swung around upon the piano stool. Her piquant nose is gradually going into the air; her eyes have almost a reproach in them.

"Oh, blow the Louisville girls!" cries Covington, uneasily, "Let us talk about ourselves, you and I, Cousin Lou."

And, this seeming to set him right with the young lady, they wander into a very genial and somewhat confidential conversation, each telling the other a good deal about their past experiences and a little about their future hopes; Mr. Covington informing his cousin that he has been educated at Princeton, but had left a post-graduate course at that college, recalled to his Kentucky homestead by the sudden death of his father and mother in the cholera epidemic of 1850.

"For the last year or two," he says, "having got my farm into the best of order, I have been ranging about and seeing a little of the world. I've done Charleston, Washington, New York, and Philadelphia, and have even seen the top of Bunker Hill Monument; but, supposing *you* say something. How did you like your New York school ? Tell me all about yourself since you were knee high, Cousin Louise."

"Oh, that won't take long," answers Miss Tournay. "My mother died just after Nita's birth, when I was seven years old. After that I ran wild on the plantation, the pet of all the darkies, negro mammies and all that. Papa was too engrossed in his science, his books, and his poetry to give such a little girl very much attention. You know, down in Assumption and La Fourche, Papa was called ' *Savant* Tournay' by the country people."

"Yes, but afterward ?" asks the gentleman.

"Afterward ?" murmurs the girl. "Afterward, I went away to school."

Then the young lady goes on to tell her listener that for six or seven years before her father's death she and her younger sister Nita were placed at Miss Martin's academy in New York. While in that institution, to them had come the news of their father's sudden death by accident, about a year and a half ago. That when she had returned to Louisiana she had left her sister Nita still at school, but had induced Mrs. Joyce, one of the assistant teachers at Miss Martin's, to take the trip with her, not caring to make the long journey alone; remarking: "Since then, Pamela, that is, Mrs. Joyce, has been kind enough to live with me at beautiful Beau Rivage."

Then she makes her hearer very happy by adding: "You brag of your Blue Grass region; you should see our beautiful Atchafalaya—and see it you shall and must, some day, Cousin Bob!"

Looking at the young gentleman as he sits before her in the elaborate evening dress of a beau of the period, his trousers very tight, though very much spread out over his patent-leather boots, his waistcoat white as snow, his immaculate ruffled shirt and his swallow-tail coat with high-rolled velvet collar, Miss Louise thinks Mr. Covington, with his broad shoulders, frank manner, and honest, laughing blue eyes, a very gallant and handsome relative.

A moment after, perchance from some feminine coquetry—perhaps just to see how he'll take it—she strikes the Kentuckian a deft little blow below the belt as she murmurs: "But we now think of going to Paris, where my sister Nita can complete her education."

"Going to Paris?" ejaculates Covington, aghast.

"Yes; very soon.   Monsieur Martineau has advised it."   Then she affrights her hearer by remarking demurely: "Do you know I rather imagine he would prefer that I married in Europe? *Un beau parti*—eh, Cousin Bob?"   And she smiles archly at the gentleman.

But Cousin Bob bursts out: "What! A French jack-a-dandy of a husband for you? Mr. Martineau's French blood makes him too kind to Parisians! The Blue Grass bucks are the dandies for an American girl like you! When you have once seen Kentucky in its glory, at a State fair or race meeting, you will never think of Paris or Parisians or French horses again!"

But though Mr. Covington may decry Paris and the Parisians, his trachea seems to have a lump in it for a day or two afterward, whenever he thinks of "*un beau parti.*" Perchance he would even go away dejected, did not the young lady, gazing on his rather woe-begone countenance, now raise him to the seventh heaven of delight, as she says very cordially: "You suggested, Cousin Bob, that we do the town together.   What do you say to a visit to the market to-morrow morning, Sunday?   About nine o'clock, I believe is the fashionable hour, if Mrs. Joyce will kindly assist us to Creole propriety."

"Done!" cries the Kentuckian.   "Here's my hand on it," and Miss Louise's pretty digits get a grateful squeeze, as the two walk in and ask Pamela if she will play chaperone at a jaunt to the market.

To this request the lady gasps: "Sunday!" What are you thinking of, Louise?" and would doubtless make refusal did not at this moment Lorena, with a courtesy, announce Monsieur Arvid Martineau.

"I had called to see you at your hotel, to welcome you to our city, Mr. Covington," remarks the French gentleman, after he has greeted the party, "but learning from your friend, Colonel Talliaferro, that you had come to visit your cousin, I gave myself the same pleasure and followed you here."

"And just in time!" cries Louise. "Just in time to explain to Mrs. Joyce that it is quite the proper thing to visit the market on Sunday morning." Then she adds, with feminine subtlety, "You know, Monsieur Arvid, that Cousin Bob has asked me to go with him, but without Pamela it is a social impossibility." This she embellishes with a very pretty little *moue* that apparently wins the French gentleman.

The trustee of the Tournay estate immediately says: "My dear Mrs. Joyce, you need have no hesitation in playing chaperone. A visit to the old French market is nearly as much *de rigueur* here on Sunday mornings as going to mass."

"That's the kind of talk I like! Martineau, I am forever obliged to you," cries the young Kentuckian, "and will be more obliged to you if you will join the party. Now I think of it, we'll do the market, take breakfast at Victor's Café, Creole fashion. After that we'll run down and view the New Orleans battlefield. My grandfather fought there under Jackson, but he didn't fall there, thank God! Then we'll drive out to the Spanish fort, there we will dine and look at the lake, and in the early evening come home along the shell-road. What do you think of that for a day? It is *my* party, you are *my* guests, and I'll take refusal from no one of you."

"I accept with all my heart," says the French gentleman. "I have several important papers to look at to-morrow, but I throw them aside at your invitation."

Though Pamela would raise her voice deprecating Sunday outings, that worthy lady finds herself overwhelmed, especially by the French *avocat*, who practically says she *must go*. He seems very anxious to put the two young people together as much as possible. In fact, after Mr. Covington and Miss Louise have strolled off into the other parlor and got to their *tête-à-tête* business once more, Martineau very frankly states this to the chaperone.

"You and I," he says, "my dear Mrs. Joyce, will make a quiet day of it together. But we will let these young cousins enjoy each other's society."

"Don't you think it is putting them very much together?" whispers Pamela, pursing her lips.

"I *wish* them together. It is for Louise's interest that she should be on very good terms with her cousin. He is a fine young man, thank God!" This last is said with much more earnestness than the case apparently warrants, and makes Pamela gaze at him surprised as he goes on in explanation: "He is Louise's only male relative. To his protection she must turn some day, perchance, both on her own account and that of her little sister."

"Pooh!" says the schoolmistress grimly. "By that time Louise is sure to be married."

"Sure to be married! What makes you say that?"

"Well, I have been a schoolmistress a good many years, and I know the kind of girls who get married *soon*. Louise is one of them."

"Nevertheless," answers Martineau, "I think it very important that you, Madame, do everything in your power to bring about all possible good will between a young lady, whose interest I have as much at heart as you, and the young gentleman who is at present feasting his eyes upon her beauty, and giving her hand a cousinly and tender squeeze." He shrugs his shoulders in his Gallic way and utters a slight chuckle, as he turns his eyes into the other room, for this is exactly what Mr. Robert Covington is doing to Miss Louise Camours Tournay.

A few minutes afterward the lawyer rises and says:

"Will you not walk along with me towards my residence and my office, where I hope to have the pleasure of seeing you very shortly, Monsieur Covington?" Then looking at the elaborate array of the young man, he adds: "I suppose you will favor the ball at the St. Charles with your presence. Miss Johnson of Louisville, the great belle of your part of the country, with whom I was conversing not over an hour ago, stated that she had promised you the honor of a dance—the first waltz, I believe."

"Oh, of course, Sally Johnson; yes! By Jove, I had forgotten all about her! I must be going! " cries Bob, suddenly.

At this they all burst out into a little laugh, and Martineau says: "*Mon Dieu!* Miss Johnson, the very richest and most beautiful girl in all Kentucky, and he treats her so?" A remark that brings a very happy look into Louise's pretty eyes.

And she is very happy; for a few minutes after the gentlemen have taken their leave she runs up to her chamber and cries to her maid: "Oh, mercy, Lorena! What am I to wear to-morrow? He is coming at nine o'clock! What am I to wear? Make me as bright, dainty, cheerful, and alluring as you can. My Cousin Bob is coming to-morrow morning."

"'Deed I will, Miss! Yo' will beat a bird of paradise! There ain't no young lady in the French quarter that can hold up her nose with yo' if yo' will let me have my will on you. Laws! If Cousin Bob was proud of yo' to-day he'll be prouder than a thousand-bale planter to-morrow morning."

And, this kind of talk seeming to please the young lady, Miss Louise, very shortly after this, placing her fair head upon the snowy pillows of her dainty couch, closing her eyes in drowsy contentment, murmurs softly through her coral lips: "Cousin Bob," and goes into happy dreamland.

As for the gentleman whose name she has mentioned, he walks along, chatting pleasantly with the French attorney, for they have both got on a subject they wish to talk about: *i. e.*, the beautiful girl who has just said good-night to them.

"Isn't my cousin Louise a wonder!" remarks Covington to the attorney. "Did you ever see such luck? Saw the most beautiful woman on the race-course, asked her name, and—by George— found she was *my* cousin."

"Yes; Mademoiselle Louise is very beautiful—and her little sister Nita is also a very pretty child; she is thirteen now. Both are so very attractive, I—I sometimes fear for their future," murmurs Martineau with a slight sigh.

"*Fear* for their future? Why so? The prettier a girl is our way, the better chance she has of picking up a fine young fellow."

"Well, you see," answers the *avocat*, "their father's death left the young ladies in a very unfortunate position. They are almost without friends, and have no near relatives except you."

"Tournays, and without friends—in Louisiana! I can hardly understand that."

"Yes; almost without friends, because they are unknown. Their father, Mr. Covington, was a very peculiar man. Prosper Delaunay Tournay, even in his younger days, though a harum-scarum dandy about town was a poet and a dreamer, but after his sister's— your mother's—marriage and departure for Kentucky, these eccentricities—if I may call them that—were accentuated and became more pronounced as he grew older. He buried himself on his plantation, *Beau Rivage*, except when he was on a smaller place of his, near Guidrys in La Fourche Parish, which was convenient to him, being close to the bayous, marshes and swamps about Barataria Lagoon, where he was engaged in collecting specimens of the birds, reptiles, and animals of Louisiana. For, among other pursuits of Tournay was that of natural history, which brought him his sudden death!"

"How so?"

"He wanted a red ibis, and, too lazy to load his gun, ordered a darky to load it for him. Cuffy put two charges in one barrel, and Prosper Tournay never knew what hurt him. The consequences of his eccentricities were that his children were brought up wild on the plantation, until they were removed to Miss Martin's school in New York, eight years ago. As a result, Tournay's early friends in New Orleans forgot him; therefore the young ladies are practically known to no one here but myself, who have charge of the affairs of the estate, and to you, their new-found relative, whom I am delighted to meet, and, thank God!—find so respected and honored by both the gentlemen and ladies of your native State. Miss Johnson spoke of you in the kindest manner—but we are at Custom House Street. I must say *au revoir*."

"By Jove, I must also bid you good-bye; otherwise Miss Sally Johnson may not speak so kindly of me the next time you see her," laughs Bob. "I expect I'm about due at the hop at the St. Charles."

Shaking the old gentleman cordially by the hand, Mr. Covington steps out rapidly for the great hotel, cogitating: "Martineau must have been making inquiries about me, not only from the gentlemen but from the ladies of my native State. Well, I'm not afraid of investigation. What Bob Covington does is above board. He makes his mistakes openly and does his little wickednesses with frankness and dispatch."

A few minutes after he enters the melange of belles and beaux that are thronging the parlors of the superb hotel, making the scene one of great magnificence and splendor, for the elite of most of the States south of Mason and Dixon's line are there in all their "before-the-war" glory.

Fortunately he is in time to do his dance with Miss Johnson. But, though Miss Sally's hazel eyes are very beautiful, and her charming figure rounded most gracefully, her shoulders and arms white as driven snow, and her costume—imported for the occasion—exquisite in detail and gorgeous in ensemble, the Louisville beauty does not seem to have any great effect upon her partner as he trips his measure with her. And for that matter, neither do the conversation nor the charms of the many delightful young ladies he meets that evening affect the dashing Bob very greatly, though he seems in the best of spirits.

"They are all very well," he thinks, after stepping a polka with Miss Amy Peyton of Virginia, and takin' Miss Laura Singleton, of South Carolina, into supper— "but I know one who suits Bob Covington a *leetle* better!"

After an hour or two of this he strolls away with his friend La Farge to St. Cyr's where he and some other young bucks have made up a game of poker; but Mr. Covington, though generally great at this sport, plays very badly this evening, and loses a little of his turf winnings.

Even this does not destroy the buoyancy of his

spirits, for at the hotel at two o'clock in the morning, just before he turns in, this gallant young sprig says, looking in his mirror: "Oh, you lucky dog! The prettiest, sweetest cousin on earth! The little darling! And the hand of her!—dainty enough to juggle sunbeams! And the foot of her!—small enough and light enough to jump on rosebuds and not smash their dewdrops! And to-morrow a whole day with her! Maybe Bob Covington isn't shouting, but he IS!—loud enough to beat the calliope of a Mississippi steamboat!" Then he looks at himself astonished, and mutters: "Great Taylor! You villain, you've gone back on Blue Grass girls!"

CHAPTER IV.

SUNDAY MORNING AT THE FRENCH MARKET.

BUT this reflection on the charms of the Blue Grass girls does not seem to weigh heavily on this gentleman's conscience. He gets up very brisk, enthusiastic, and "chipper," as his body-servant, Mr. Cæsar, remarks when he calls him at half-past seven in the morning.

"Move along, Cæsar," cries his master briskly, as he sips his coffee. "The sun is out, the breeze is right, and we'll make a great day of it!" This gives a financial opening of which the darky valet promptly takes advantage.

"Yes, sah, yo' may make a great day of it, but I'se kind o' low down in the pocket to make a great day of it," ruefully suggests Mr. Cæsar, who is a mulatto gentleman of very crisp hair, dark eyes, white teeth, and dapper figure, with a melancholy grin.

"Low down in the pocket! Great crocodiles! Didn't I give you money to bet on the horse-race? You ought to be in funds for months!" Then Mr. Covington adds, turning severe eyes on his factotum: "By Daniel Boone! You don't mean to say you bet *against* Lexington, you infernal idiot?"

" No, sah! I ob course backed the Blue Grass colt, and won considerable, sah. But last evening, after returning from Miss Tournay's residence, I was in-,veigled into a little game of poker, sah, with some of the Louisiana gent'men, sah—Mistah Rufus, Gen'ral Hampton's man ; Mistah Washington, Major Bee's factoter, and Mistah Caucus, Colonel Jones's body-servant, sah. And they cleaned me out, sah."

"So that accounts for your not being here when I turned up last night," laughs his master. "You played as bad a game as I did, eh ? Well, here's a V for you. Trot off and give Lorena a jaunt about town. Do the thing up handsomely for the honor of old Kentucky. You're sparking that bright-eyed wench of Miss Tournay's, I imagine. Oh, don't attempt to deny it! I know what your grin means. And, furthermore, don't indulge in any more poker. By the immortal Simon Suggs, do you want to ruin me, you grinning imp of Eblis ?" For Mr. Cæsar has received the five-dollar bill with an unctuous guffaw and a tremendous show of the ivories.

"Yes; give me that slouched hat—not that high tile," cries his master. "This is not Broadway or Bleecker Street I'm going to do to-day!"

Then a handsome barouche, with a pair of fine trotters and stylish coachman being ready for him, Mr. Bob Covington drives over to the Tournay residence, picking up on his way Arvid Martineau.

"I am delighted to see you so well, Monsieur," remarks the French attorney, looking at the handsome young fellow, noting his frank face and countenance slightly flushed by apparent eagerness and expectation. Covington, however, as he returns the other's gaze, cannot help thinking that the lawyer's eyes are, as he expresses it, wistful. In fact, all this day Arvid Martineau whenever he glances at the young man, though it is often with pleasure at his honest utterances and very frequently with admiration at his dashing manner, and sometimes with veritable joy as he sees him do some act of gentlemanly courtesy to his pretty cousin—and Bob Covington does a good many of them between sunrise and sunset—always does it with a latent anxiety in his look, and once or twice almost a tear in his sharp, though kindly eyes.

A few minutes after, the carriage rolls into the courtyard of the Tournay residence, the massive gates being already thrown open for it. Apparently the ladies are expecting them, for Mrs. Joyce immediately trips down the stairway from the second story and remarks as she greets the gentlemen: "Louise will be here in a moment. I believe it's her bonnet strings. I think she wishes to make a very perfect toilet."

"Please don't tell tales about me, Pamela," cries Miss Tournay, making her appearance and tripping hurriedly down, a flush of excitement upon her fair face, for in truth the girl has been driving her maid Lorena to despair this morning, nothing being *just* right. Though it surely is *just* right at present, for no prettier picture ever greeted Mr. Covington's ardent eyes than Miss Louise as she extends her daintily gloved hand to him and murmurs: "I hope I did not keep you. I am as anxious for *le Marché Française* and breakfast as you are."

"Not at all!" answers the Kentuckian; then adds, gallantly: "Though even a moment of your society is important to me!" his earnest glance emphasizing his remark.

"Then," says the young lady, archly, "I must always be very punctual with Cousin Bob." And accepting his hand, he places her in the carriage beside Mrs. Joyce, while Martineau and he take seats *vis à vis* to them. Then the equipage drives off, and passing along Dauphine Street, turns down Dumaine Street straight for what is now commonly known as "the French market."

As they approach, Miss Louise suddenly exclaims: "How bright! How fascinating! How vivacious!"

"By Martin Scott's coon, what a crowd!" ejaculates the Kentuckian.

"Yes; the crowd of a Sunday morning in New Orleans," answers the French *Avocat*, as the carriage draws up and Covington springs out, anxious for a touch of Miss Louise's light hand as he assists her from the carriage.

And he is right, for clustering all about them, coming up St. Philippe Street, moving along Decatur Street thronging from St. Anne Street and also from the early mass of the nearby cathedral, in one heterogeneous concourse, are all the types, classes, and nationalities peculiar to the New Orleans of before-the-war.

Old negresses are carrying on their heads baskets of fruits, *dulces*, and candies. Dissipated looking, foreign catch-penny fellows are tricking boys out of their picayunes at card games. Slaves are bartering poultry and country produce from their own plantation plots. Fishmongers from Cook's Bayou are calling: "Oysters, fresh and salt!" Girls of all sizes and colors, white, black, and chocolate are selling bouquets of flowers. Planters, in the light suits of the tropics; mountain men, in buckskin suits and coonskin caps, who have come down to see the great race from the far off prairies; Texans with their inevitable slouched hats and Cubans from Havana are mixed in with business men from New York, Philadelphia, and even Chicago, which is just now beginning to make itself felt in the Western world. This concourse is beautified by pretty girls from the Gulf towns, Kentucky, and St. Louis, who have all come to see the great race and remaining for the other great race, are now enjoying the sights of the metropolis of the Southwest.

But, if the costumes are diversified, the voices, *patois*, and languages are even more so, varying from the sharp, shrill twang of the Green Mountain boy who has brought some fast trotters to sell to New Orleans sportsmen, to the soft rhythm of the Creole, the babbling *patois* of French and Spanish negroes, the peculiar lingo of the Acadians, who are peddling Perique tobacco, together with some excited semi-Indian jabber from a few remnants of the Choctaws and Chickasaws that have not entirely been effaced from the soil of Louisiana, and who drive a thriving business in beaded work and Indian knick-nacks. These, mixed with the sweet voices of pretty girls from everywhere, make, as Mr. Bob Covington expresses it, "a roar of sound that beats the Italian opera and the Tower of Babel banged together!"

Edging their way carefully and followed by Mrs. Joyce and Monsieur Martineau, the two cousins soon find themselves passing under strings of pineapples and bunches of bananas which perfume the air. But the odors of the fruits are as nothing to the fragrance of the flowers. Cape jasmines, early magnolias, sprigs of orange trees laden with both blossoms and fruit, and limes from Mexico scent the air from neighboring flower booths adorned by potted plants, palms, and flowering shrubs.

"How beautiful! How delightful! I think I'll come here shopping every morning. Can't I do the housekeeping, Mrs. Joyce?" laughs the young lady, turning her head toward the ex-schoolmistress, who is immediately behind her.

"Yes; I rather like it myself. Let us come down every morning, Louise;" returns the chaperone—who has a Yankee love for bargains—"Coffee at three cents a cup" having just struck her eye.

"Gracious! You can buy everything here," exclaims Miss Louise, who is now astonished at the sight of a bazaar of fancy goods, clothing, and underwear.

So they pass on in the *Halle des Boucheres*, looking at tempting steaks off Texas cattle that are already becoming celebrated; past fishmongers' stalls with red-snapper, sea trout, barracouta, and pompano, diversified by shrimps, rosy from the boiling pot, oysters of enormous size, snails ready for cooking, frogs' legs, and crabs of wondrous smallness.

So many eatables produce an effect. The Kentuckian says: "I believe I suggested that we breakfast Creole fashion. Suppose we go to Victor's."

"Anywhere for a starving girl," exclaims Miss Louise.

Therefore they stroll out of the market; the babel of many *patois*, many languages, and many tones seems more pronounced. Above them stridently comes from negresses with little cakes fried in grease: "*Bels calas! Tout chauds!*" Others are screaming: "*Belle fromage à la crème!*" while boys are yelling "*Cinq a deux sous!*"

"Mercy! I'm nearly deaf!" murmurs Miss Tournay

as the Kentuckian puts the ladies into the carriage.

He is about to order the driver to go to Monsieur Victor's restaurant on Bourbon Street, when Martineau remarks: "I know New Orleans better than you. If you will permit me to advise, a little quiet breakfast at Madame Labat's."

This will probably afford him a better opportunity of *tête-à-tête* with the beautiful young lady who is looking into his face, and the Kentuckian jumps at the suggestion. Then the coachman makes one or two sharp turns, and draws up in front of an old-fashioned Creole house, and very shortly afterward the party find themselves on the second floor of the establishment, in a room with sanded floor, plain wooden furniture, napkins and lingerie white as snow, and a fat creole woman effusively and gesticularly suggesting to them a little breakfast of the dainties of New Orleans cuisine.

She is jabbering French to Martineau, who acts as interpreter to the Kentuckian, who finally says: "Tell her to have her way; though I believe she intends to provision us for a campaign."

Madame Labat having left them, there comes to their ears an excited jabbering with the French cook in the next room, as the party sit and look out on the veranda, which is filled with potted plants and flowering shrubs.

"If she would only begin at something!" murmurs Miss Louise, plaintively; and a moment after, their hostess does.

Their palates are enlivened with red shrimps as appetizers. Then come oysters, fat and luscious, followed by crabs *à la Creole*, gumbo soup, pompano, *a fillet au Chateaubrien*, an omelet *aux fines herbes* all these being "lubricated" as Bob remarks with the celebrated C. C. Claret. This meal is finished by the freshest of strawberries in their leaves and on their stems after the French fashion, and coffee—the coffee of New Orleans—the coffee of the Creoles.

This pleasant affair takes an hour or two. The conversation has been as bright and pleasant as the meal itself—all seem in exuberant spirits except Martineau. A little episode now comes to place the girl and her cavalier rather closer together, though it hardly appears to please the *avocat*.

It happens, almost as they finish their breakfast, Monsieur Martineau has murmured contemplatively: "I hope you enjoyed yourself at the ball last evening, Mr. Covington. Were you in time for your dance with Miss Johnson?"

"Yes, fortunately," replies the young man, then laughs with Western modesty, "We Kentuckians generally are, when young ladies are in the case."

"I suppose the ball was a very gorgeous affair," remarks Miss Louise suddenly, then adds: "Suppose you give me a little description of the fête?"

This Bob does, winding up with: "It was the biggest show of diamonds, feminine dresses, kickashaws and highfalutins I ever looked on. All the pretty girls of the town were there—except one." His eyes suggest to whom he refers.

For a moment Mademoiselle Louise bites her pretty lip; then, suddenly, what is in her mind trembles on her tongue and comes forth.

"Don't you think, Monsieur Martineau," asks the girl, eagerly, "that it's about time for *me* to go to balls? I have been out of school for over a year."

"Ah, yes; but in—in half mourning," murmurs the French lawyer, apparently in uncalled for consternation.

"Half mourning? Is *this* half mourning?" says Miss Tournay, archly, looking at the exquisite toilet in which she is arrayed. Though not of brilliant color, it is light, pretty, and gay, being a simple white muslin, trimmed with very pale pink ribbons, and dotted here and there with sprigs of little rosebuds. Beautifully made, fitting her graceful figure *au marvel*, from beneath it peep two little French bottines. Above it, on her fair head, is a piquant Paris bonnet of light straw, adorned with a few of the same flowers that spray her dress. Altogether, it is a simple yet very charming costume for youth and beauty, and certainly not suggestive of grief.

Then she adds: "Papa has been dead eighteen months. Of course I wish to do all that is right in respect to his memory. But everything seems so joyous now, why should I not go to balls, as other girls?" She looks at Martineau with an alluring but pleading *moue*.

"And you shall!" interjects Bob, suddenly. "There's a ball to be given on Thursday evening by the Pelican Club, the swellest affair in New Orleans. I know most of the members. I'll get you an invitation!"

"Thursday night! Oh, heavens, what shall I wear?" This is a cry of almost consternation from Mademoiselle Louise. Then she rattles on, joyously: "But I know both Mesdames Olympe and Sophie have received new stocks of robes from Paris on account of these races. Oh, they can't have sold them *all!* Monsieur Martineau, to-morrow morning I shall buy the finest ball dress Madame Olympe has!"

Then, looking at the attorney's face, which has grown very gloomy, as he is whispering: "Not yet! Not yet!" she falters: "Oh, don't say no! You can't say *no!* It will be my first ball!—And I dance very well. Mrs. Joyce will tell you at Miss Martin's the professor of dancing said I could polka and waltz as well as any young lady in the establishment, and I'd— I'd like to have a chance to show my Cousin Bob how well I do dance!"

"By the Lord Harry, you shall! You shall dance with Cousin Bob until you're black in the face!" cries the Kentuckian; and, looking at the lawyer savagely, who is apparently about to dissent again, he mutters: "Why the deuce shouldn't she go? It's the most exclusive ball in New Orleans society."

To this the old lawyer does not reply, but murmurs: "We will see. We will see," in a dazed and curiously abstracted manner.

"Yes, we *will* see!" cries Louise, clapping her hands. "We will see what fine dresses we can get to-morrow. We'll see what a hole we will make in the Tournay bank account! We'll see, we'll see! Cousin Bob, my first ball!" And she goes into such an ecstasy of expectant delight that a tear comes into the eye of the French attorney, though his face has grown very white. Then she laughs: "You look horrified, Monsieur Martineau—horrified at the size of the bills I am going to send in to you! And you're—you're in a brown study—a brown study at the frightfully expensive young lady I shall be when I am in society! The Tournay diamonds shall be there! I know there are a few locked up in the strong box. Pamela, you'll be my chaperone, won't you? Oh, a polka, a waltz!"

And the girl, rising from her seat, in the excitement of the moment, trips a few measures with exquisite grace and poetic abandon, until Mrs. Joyce shrieks: "Louise, have you forgotten it is Sunday?"

"Yes; but I must rejoice! I have entered on my life! When are you going to take us out, Cousin Bob? You said you would drive down to the battlefield, then to the lake—I'm told Monsieur Miguel's cuisine is excellent. Dinner! Next a drive along the shell road! Oh, Cousin Bob—Cousin Bob! All the way I shall be thinking about that ball at the Pelican Club! You'll —you'll get me lots of nice partners, won't you?—and you'll introduce to me that handsome French gentleman, Monsieur La Farge, and that great turfman, Colonel Talliaferro of your State, and all the young beaux? Young Soulé and Auguste Maurey—Monsieur Martineau pointed out some of them at the race-course. And oh, Cousin Bob, I'm going to the ball!"

This mention of partners in all the young bloods of New Orleans makes Cousin Bob scowl once or twice, but he says: "Yes; I'll introduce every one of them. They'll be round you thick as bees round flowers." Then breaks out: "Great Heavens! don't you suppose I'm proud of my new cousin? There won't be a girl in the ball-room can hold a candle to you! You'll be as great a belle as that little French girl was at the French Hollow shake-down when Tom Burt told her daddy his daughter was a *screamer*, and nearly got killed for the insult."

He would go on effusively in this strain, did not Mrs. Joyce say: "Good gracious! Stop talking that way. You will make her too vain."

"He can't do that," says Louise, airily. "I'm as vain as a peacock already. I admit it—I admit it.

When such a cousin is doing so much for me, who would not be vain?"

A few minutes after, they pass out to the carriage again, to drive to Jackson's battle-ground, Miss Louise all this day harping upon the ball and growing happier and happier about it. And Cousin Bob looking at her grows happier also.

CHAPTER V.

THE SPECTER OF THE PELICAN BALL.

"I suppose I ought to be able to tell all about the battle of New Orleans," remarks Mr. Covington as they drive away. "My grandfather fought in the third company of the First Regiment of Kentucky riflemen, but that's all I know of the affair."

"Then permit me to assist you. I shall enact the rôle of oldest inhabitant and play cicerone," suggests Martineau, attempting a playfulness he does not feel.

"Very well; we will appeal to you as a Creole guide-book," laughs Mrs. Joyce, whom the breakfast has placed in the best of humor.

"Then, first and foremost, there are two heroes of this battle of New Orleans, on the American side: General Jackson and Jean Lafitte, the pirate."

"Oh, yes, I have heard of him," remarks Louise. "He had a rendezvous on Barataria Bay, not so very far from Guidrys, near our little plantation on Bayou La Fourche. He was a pirate, burned and scuttled ships, made men walk the plank, and buried treasure—for darkies to dig for and never find. Every negro on our plantation, I imagine, has had a hunt for it some time or other when he was not too busy looking for 'possums and 'coons."

"That is the popular idea of Jean Lafitte," rejoins Monsieur Martineau. "But some Louisianians think a little differently about him. At all events, he had as much to do in saving this State to the American flag as any one who lived in Louisiana, and possibly as much as General Jackson.

"Originally he was a blacksmith; his forge was once at that corner;" and the lawyer points up towards Bourbon Street as they are crossing St. Philippe. "Afterward Jean Lafitte threw down the sledge-hammer, sailed the seas, and wielded the sword, very successfully for himself. He was the head of all the smugglers of this region. Their headquarters were at Barataria Bay, as you say, Miss Louise. He was also a privateersman, first with a letter of marque from the French crown against the Spanish nation, afterward from the Republic of Columbia or Carthagena, which had just taken up arms for liberty against the parent State. The captured Spanish merchantmen brought into Barataria Bay were numerous. Their cargoes, immensely rich, were doubled in value by being smuggled free of United States duties, into New Orleans, to be sold on Levee Street, to the despair of the shopkeepers of his day, who could not compete with goods that originally cost nothing, and in addition paid no duty.

These tradesmen naturally made out Monsieur Lafitte and his brethren as no better than they should be, branding them as pirates, cutthroats, blackguards and buccaneers. And perhaps they did do a little of that, for privateering in those times was nearly the same as piracy, legalized. At all events the United States government thought so—though whether it was to protect their revenue or Jack 'Tar I cannot say. They sent an expedition against him under Commodore Patterson, with orders to burn, shoot, and destroy on sight. Monsieur Lafitte wisely fled from the terrors of Uncle Sam's navy.

"About this time, naturally supposing he was filled with rage against all Americans, Pakenham, in command of the English expedition against the United States, communicated with Lafitte as to the prospects of an attack upon New Orleans. Being a Frenchman, Jean naturally hated the English even more than he did the Americans who were making war upon him. By his skillful negotiations and intrigue the British advance on New Orleans was delayed until General Jackson arrived with four thousand Tennessee and Kentucky militia."

"Here my grandfather enters the combat," interjects Covington, laughingly. "First Sergeant, Third
Company, First Regiment, Kentucky Militia."

"Well, Jackson's four thousand Kentucky militia,
your grandfather included, I presume," continues
Martineau, "were in a very bad way. They did not
have flints for their muskets or rifles; there was no
fit powder and ball for their cannon. These were
all furnished by Lafitte from his private plunder.
Then, after the British landed, no one could keep a
better watch on their movements, because no one was
so well acquainted with the shoals, creeks, and bayous
extending from Rigolets and Lake Borgne to the Barataria Lagoons. The consequence was that the British
advance was delayed until Jackson got his breastworks
erected, his cotton bales up, and his guns in position
down at Chalmette, where, having done their scouting
work, Lafitte and his band joined him to the number
of five hundred, manned his battery of heavy guns,
with the use of which the Kentucky and Tennessee
riflemen were unacquainted, and fought in a way that
was most disastrous to British arms. The flower of
England's warriors dashed themselves against rifle
balls fired by marksmen who could hit squirrels in the
eye and cut off the heads of partridges and turkeys.

"Valor is naught against cold lead, and twenty-five
hundred of the veterans of the Peninsula War under
Wellington went down before backwoods bullets.
Pakenham paid for his rashness with his life, and the
New Orleans question was settled."

"My grandfather always said it was a slaughter, not
a battle," remarks Covington. "He said he hated to
kill brave fellows whose foolhardy general never gave
'em a chance."

"But curiously enough, Lafitte's assistance to the
American cause came very near being entirely neutral-
ized by the double-dealing of one of his agents," adds
Martineau. "This far-seeing scoundrel, putting his
eye on the future, saw that in all probability if the
great pirate assisted the American arms, he and his
followers would be pardoned by the government of the
United States; that being permitted to settle down un-

molested with their accumulated gains would certainly disintegrate the band from which he was making a good deal of money by acting as their agent. Accordingly the despatches of General Jackson to Jean Lafitte came very near not being delivered. This was never discovered until a year afterward; if it had been found out at the time, Jackson would have hung the agent of Monsieur Jean, if Lafitte had not slaughtered the traitor himself. It would have probably furnished a new yarn for the novelists: 'Lafitte's last butchery!' 'The execution of Faval Bigore Poussin,' 'The Notary that walked the plank!'"

"Oh, I knew him!" cries Louise, opening her eyes. "When I was a little girl Monsieur Poussin patted me on the head. He had small dark eyes, and was dried up and yellow and looked a hundred years old——But is not that the United States barracks?" and she points to some low brick buildings.

A few minutes after the carriage drives onto the plain of Chalmette, to which spot a good many tourists are coming this day, the city being full of sight-seers.

"Goodness! We're already on the battlefield!" remarks Miss Louise, as if she had suddenly awakened from a day-dream. Then she says, pointing to a structure of white marble: "I wonder what Jackson used that for? Did he have guns up there?"

"Gracious, Louise! That's the monument being erected to commemorate the battle," ejaculates Mrs. Joyce in school-mistress horror. "Don't you remember your United States history?"

"No, I don't!" says the young lady; then murmurs archly: "You know I was always at the foot of the class in history. I could not remember it then; do you think I can remember it now, when I've so many more pleasant things on my mind?"

"Well, that ball is running in my mind also," says Covington, as the party alight; for this young gentleman has already seen himself in imagination floating about to the music of Monsieur Julian, with the pretty young lady who is walking beside him, and thinks of the admiration and envy on the faces of La Farge, Soulé, and the other bucks of the Pelican Club.

Just here both of them are recalled to the field of carnage by Mrs. Joyce suddenly coming to them and saying: "I have engaged a guide who declares he fought in the battle, to give us the various points of interest for one dollar."

Gazing at Pamela's discovery, the Kentuckian sees the three-card-monte man who had got a tip from him at the race on Saturday. This old shriveled-up individual is bowing politely and saying: "Yes, Monsieur; I had the honor of fighting under General Jackson."

"Well, you look old enough to have fought under General Washington," returns the young blood, easily, then queries: "How did you come out on the horse-race?"

"Ah, Monsieur, I am forever obliged. The race-week, which would have been a despair to me—under your advice—became a delight."

"Always back old Kentuck!" cries Bob heartily; then adds: "Perhaps you can tell me where my grandfather fought. First Sergeant, Third Company, First Regiment, Kentucky Militia."

"*Certainement!*" replies the guide. "We fought next to him. Here is the cotton battery, with the heavy guns, where I stood, together with Dominique You and the sea-dog Bluche. There are the three trees down the river, half a mile, where Pakenham's headquarters were. Here General Jackson stood," and he goes into an elaborate description of the battle.

To this Covington listens unheedingly. He is looking at the beautiful young lady by his side. Probably Miss Louise pays little attention also, as she suddenly says: "I wonder whether blue gauze or white tulle and pink flowers will become me most. What are your favorite colors, Cousin Bob?"

"Wood-violet eyes and dark brown hair," murmurs the gentleman, abstractedly.

At which a sudden blush flies over the young lady's face. She cries: "Don't be foolish!" then laughs a little embarrassed laugh and wanders away, but does not get very far, as somehow Mr. Bob Covington is never very far behind Miss Louise Tournay during this day.

Mrs. Joyce does not pay very much attention to this. She is determined to get her dollar's worth of information from her salaried guide, and is now asking more questions than he seems to care to answer. Finally she says: "You say you fought with the big guns on this battery?"

"*Oui, Madame.*

"Was not this Lafitte's battery?"

Some called it so," answers the man, politely, though he now edges away from Pamela and breaks in upon the happy *tête-à-tête* of the Kentuckian and Miss Louise. "If Monsieur would tell me a little about the chances of Lexington for the next race," murmurs the guide, bowing. "The track will probably be dusty."

"It will be dusty for both nags!" returns Covington, savagely.

"Ah, yes! But in the absence of mud ?—— If Monsieur should hear of anything, would he kindly give me the benefit of his advice ? Here is my address." And the Creole produces from a greasy, worn, and dilapidated pocketbook a more greasy, worn, and dilapidated card.

This he hands to the Kentuckian, who shoves it into his pocket, saying: "All right! If I get anything definite I'll let you know," then turns away, anxious to resume his *tête-à-tête*.

A moment after, the party go to their equipage, for they have now to drive to Spanish Fort in time for dinner. So, calling to Martineau, who has wandered off by himself, apparently in a brown study, Covington puts the ladies into the carriage again and they get under way once more.

Two hours later they are on the borders of Lake Pontchartrain, upon whose banks in the distance the green of the cypress and the oak can be seen, meeting the soft waters. In one or two places there are traces of beach, in another a white light-house, and in the distance a long pier. They drive beside its limpid waters, and very shortly find themselves at those old moss-grown fortifications called Spanish Fort, whose guns even now are rusty and dismounted, and beside whose crumbling earthworks, grown up with flowering thickets of peach, flows the Bayou St. John, upon whose sluggish waters float a few schooners and sailing boats.

Here, in addition to a long wharf, are some rose gardens, a shooting alley or two, and various other places of entertainment, among them the celebrated restaurant at which they are going to eat one of its famous fish dinners.

The place is crowded by a merry throng of ladies and gentlemen, it being quite the thing to dine by the lake side. The breeze from the water has given the party an appetite, and they seat themselves at one of the tables in a hungry expectation that is not disappointed. They all would enjoy the meal very greatly, did not with their coffee come to them an episode that puts Miss Louise in the seventh heaven of delight, but seems in some way to bring consternation to the French *avocat*.

Among the gay crowd at the restaurant—for the buzz is kept up very merrily, the laughter of fair women and gallant gentlemen is in the air, and the popping of champagne corks punctuates the buzz—Louise's bright eyes catch the graceful form of Miss Sally Johnson. This young lady, with some Western gentlemen, two or three St. Louis girls, and a dashing widow for chaperone, is at one of the neighboring tables, the ladies of the party making a great show of beauty.

This Louisville belle has been pointed out to her on the drive by Monsieur Martineau, and remembering Mr. Covington's engagement with this young lady the evening before, Miss Louise looks at Miss Sally with an interest that at the moment she does not understand, but which produces some later effects.

Conspicuous also is Henri La Farge, the aristocratic Creole and probably the greatest beau in New Orleans. This gentleman and Covington are quite well known to each other, having met the year before in New York, and at Saratoga, where they drank the Congress-waters and ran through the usual round of watering-place gayety. Though they have never been intimates, they have always been very good friends.

The Creole is now seated at a near-by table. Catching view of him, Bob hastily whispers: "If you'll excuse me for a moment, I'll speak to La Farge."

On his journey, chancing to pass quite near Miss Sally Johnson, Miss Louise thinks—for her bright eyes are on him—he whispers into the pretty ear of the Louisville beauty. Then some new passion the girl has never felt before, comes into her to make her eyes sparkle and her delicate foot tap the sanded floor petulantly, angrily.

She dislikes Miss Sally, though she has no reason to, for the pretty Kentuckian is simply saying: "Mr. Covington, who is that beautiful creature?—A cousin? Ah! you were always lucky!—But I see you're anxious to speak to your friend, Monsieur La Farge."

A moment later he is very kindly greeted by the young Creole exquisite; then after a few minutes' conversation, both gentlemen stroll over to Covington's table.

"Permit me to introduce Monsieur Henri La Farge," remarks Bob, presenting his friend to the two ladies. "Monsieur Martineau and you are acquaintances, I believe."

"Old ones!" returns the Creole, greeting the *avocat* very cordially, but keeping his eyes upon Miss Louise.

To her he says: "I am delighted to welcome Mademoiselle Tournay to New Orleans. Your family have been away from the city too long. The Crescent City without a Tournay, twenty years ago, would have been considered not quite New Orleans. But I am happy to learn that you have concluded to put aside mourning and enter society," and manifests a desire to sit by the side of the young lady, whose beautiful eyes and piquant expression seem very attractive to him; but Martineau uneasily rises from his chair.

"I see your party are preparing for the drive back," continues the Creole exquisite. "Mademoiselle, may I hope for the pleasure of a dance next Thursday evening?"

"Certainly," answers Miss Louise, with more than debutante's *naïveté.* "I only know *two* young gentlemen in the town, you and Cousin Bob."

"Then Mr. Covington and I are both very fortunate," murmurs the gallant. And he moves away, to be almost immediately petitioned with much anxiety and eagerness by Miss Johnson and her party for just another invitation for the approaching ball for Miss Carondelet of St. Louis; these Pelican fêtes being the most gorgeous and select in all the West, and *entrée* to their portals being as difficult to obtain, and as much longed for by the fair sex as the opening of the gates of Paradise to outside Peris.

A moment after, Louise, whose eyes have become very bright at the thought of social success and social gayety, passes out of the restaurant, leaning upon Covington's arm and murmuring: "Am I not a fortunate girl? Monsieur La Farge is one of the Pelican Invitation Committee, is he not? You are making this a new world for me, Cousin Bob."

Among the crowd lounging outside and looking at the equipages driving up and the ladies and gentlemen taking departure is Mr. Kitson Jarvis. This worthy's face brightens and his eyes become very keen as they catch sight of the beautiful girl the Kentuckian is placing in his carriage. His ferret glance rests on the graceful outlines of Miss Louise, from dainty head to exquisite foot and ankle, and, noting the gallant bearing and ardent eyes of her escort, Kit rubs his hands together and mutters: "Gee-whiz! Perhaps next week I'll have something to tell you, my gorgeous buck, that'll make you look two ways for Sunday, you lucky dog!"

But Miss Tournay and Mr. Covington are becoming so engrossed with one another that they are oblivious of outside comment or remark.

So the party drive in, as the evening is descending, along the shell-road that borders the banks of the canal, which lies on one side of them and is made bright by pleasure boats, a few schooners that are making their way to the city in spite of Sunday, and some little steamboats that ply up and down its waters. On their other hand is a sea of green, live oaks, swamp-cypress, and palmettos mixed. . The road is full of laughing parties in dashing equipages, mingled with vehicles of all kinds, from the hired cabriolet to the fast American trotting buggy. As they near town, pickaninny boys and pickaninny girls offer them bouquets from the roadside, and the guffaws of many darkies come from little cabins, some of them bowered in shrubs and palms. Every one, black and white, is enjoying himself this soft, spring night.

So, coming into the city, they leave the more modern houses and passing Canal Street, the great thoroughfare, which, with its *banquettes* even now crowded with gayly dressed ladies, is the dividing line between the American and Creole quarters, drive up Dauphine Street. At the Tournay residence, the gentlemen would take their leave, did not Miss Louise remark: "It is very early. Send your carriage away! Come in—I want to talk to you."

"About what?" asks Covington, eagerly accepting the invitation, and followed, almost perforce, by Martineau.

"About my dresses for the ball, of course!" And the girl goes into an excited dissertation upon the various styles, modes, and fashions of that epoch, winding up her remarks by crying: "Monsieur Martineau, you must open your strong box and let me have the Tournay diamonds!"

To this her trustee makes no immediate reply; but, apparently wishing to throw the subject off his mind, enters into conversation with Mrs. Joyce, leaving the young lady and gentleman to their discussion of the frivolities of this world, and so brings upon himself another spasm of dismay. Mrs. Joyce, in that pursuit of information peculiar to schoolmistresses, must now know everything about the battle of New Orleans, dates, figures, and the losses of both sides, and goes to questioning the *avocat* eagerly.

Finally, Pamela asks one or two questions about Lafitte and his men, and what position that buccaneer took in the battle, and who fought under him, and getting answer to them, she electrifies the party by a series of faint screams, and, faltering, gasps: "My! That wretch is a pirate! Oh, mercy! Oh, my!"

"What wretch?" cries Covington, disturbed in conversation with Mademoiselle Louise.

"Oh, that creature who guided us over the battle-field! Oh, heavens! that I should have spoken to a *real* pirate!"

"What makes you think that?" queries Martineau, struggling with a laugh.

"Why, you just said all who fought in that battery of heavy artillery were Lafitte's men, and that awful old man told me, though with reluctance, that he commanded one of the guns."

"Well," laughs the Kentuckian, "he didn't make you walk the plank, any way;" then adds jocularly: "Would you like the address of your buccaneer?" Fishing in his pocket, he produces the card given him by the Creole guide, and gazing at it bursts into a guffaw; for this is what he beholds:

M. FAVAL BIGORE POUSSIN.

NOTAIRE FRANÇAIS
17 Fulton Street.
N. B. Reliable information and valuable tips given on horse-races, and tickets supplied for Vasquez' cock-fights, Monday and Thursday evenings.

Then he passes this to Miss Louise, who laughs till the tears are in her eyes. Finally it is given to Mrs. Joyce, who cannot help smiling, and by her it is handed to Arvid Martineau, who gazes at it through his eye-glasses with quivering lips and paling face.

But the rest of the party do not notice this, for Miss Louise is crying: "It's the notary—the old notary at Guidrys! I thought I had seen those cat-eyes before! Monsieur Martineau, it's the man who was a traitor to General Jackson! You remember?"

"Ah, yes, yes! The infernal scoundrel!" mutters the Creole attorney, trying to hide concern by simulating contempt.

"The miserable tout wants my information to sell tips on. But Monsieur Poussin won't speculate on my knowledge," exclaims the Kentuckian, and jeeringly tosses the card out of one of the open windows, where it floats into the darkness of the courtyard.

A moment after, the *avocat*, rising, remarks brokenly: "I—I must take my leave. I must bid you good evening."

"Going—so soon?" murmurs the young lady; then suddenly ejaculates: "You are not well!" for the attorney's face is drawn, his eyes contracted, his lips pale.

"Yes; I—I am not accustomed to such prolonged exertions in the heat of the day—our long drive. The fresh air outside will do me good," falters the old gentleman, and takes his leave, declining assistance, though Covington offers to walk home with him.

But, getting down the stairs into the courtyard, the old *avocat* suddenly goes to searching vigorously but quietly in the darkness among the flower-beds just outside the open window of the parlor, and finally discovers the dirty card Bob had carelessly thrown away.

This he carefully puts in his pocketbook, and suddenly shudders; for through the open window comes the hum of happy voices, and Covington is saying: "I arranged that Pelican affair with La Farge; your invitation will be sent to-morrow."

Then he hears Louise's voice, in innocent joy, exclaim: "Thank you, dear Cousin Bob! You are making my life very happy!"

From this scene the old French *avocat* flies. But, getting to his own home, Arvid Martineau strides about, wringing his hands and sighing these astounding words: "She is bringing it on herself—bringing it on herself! Oh, why did I not get her away in time—in *time*—in TIME? But the ball!—that must be stopped! *Nom de Dieu*, what shall I do?—what shall I do?" and tears trickle down his kindly face.

But, forcing himself to deliberation, the attorney goes to thinking calmly, and finally makes up his mind upon a course of procedure which brings about some curious occurrences during the following week.

CHAPTER VI.

"I DO THE ROMEO ACT!"

THE party at the Tournay house apparently have no fears of the future.

The young lady and gentleman are seated in the little *salon*. Pamela, still playing Creole propriety, is reading her Bible in the adjoining parlor, hoping to make up for the various sins of omission and commission of which she has been guilty this Sabbath day.

Miss Louise, however, upon whose conscience the Sunday's jaunt does not seem to rest very heavily, sits in an easy chair, her white hand playing with one of the tassels that hang down from its upholstery, and her blue eyes, which have grown dark with some latent emotion, gazing dreamily at the handsome cavalier, who is now laying out a programme of gayety for the coming week.

"To-morrow evening," suggests Covington, "supposing you and Mrs. Joyce go with me to Monsieur Placide's Varieties. We will see him in his great rôie of 'Corporal Cartouche.' What do you say to that, Cousin Lou?"

"Delightful!" assents the girl, to whom everything this gentleman now proposes seems agreeable.

"Then on Tuesday evening the French theatre. How does that strike you?"

"I'm afraid you and Pamela won't enjoy that very much," laughs Louise. "Neither of you speaks French."

"I shall! I shall obtain the emotions of the play from your vivacious face," remarks the gentleman confidently.

"And look at me all the time to do it?" cries the

young lady, playfully. "Act first, scene first: blue eyes, brown hair! Act first, scene second: brown hair, blue eyes! Comedy scene: blue eyes, brown hair, white teeth and snickers! Tragedy climax: blue eyes, brown hair, nervous twitching of the eyelids, lips tightly compressed, and rivers of tears. *Ciel!* My countenance would be very fatiguing before the curtain fell."

"Not to me!" whispers the Kentuckian, something coming into his face to make the young lady who has been gazing vivaciously at him, suddenly droop her eyes.

"The tragedy climax would indeed be a novelty to me," adds Bob, then murmurs sympathetically, even romantically: "You know I have never seen you cry."

"And you never will!" says the girl, impulsively. "Treat me as you have done to-day and you *never will!*"

But she checks herself and suggests: "If you can come to-morrow about two, possibly I may give you a cup of tea."

"My week is entirely at your disposal," remarks the young man.

"Only *this* week?" murmurs the girl, a latent coquetry in her manner.

"Only the rest of my ——!" whispers Mr. Ardent, but pauses here, his Cousin Louise having run away from him.

"*Au revoir,*" airily remarks the young lady who has found a chaperone convenient, and is standing by the side of Mrs. Joyce.

"Till to-morrow," returns the gallant, and takes his leave, but as he strides away communes with himself: "Of course, naturally I scared her. Hold your horses, Bob; don't make your running until you're in the homestretch;" then laughs: "We Kentuckians are impulsive fellows; we pay on sight, fight *on sight* and love ON SIGHT."

"What was Mr. Covington saying to you?" asks Mrs. Joyce, who has not forgotten her schoolmistress method of observing young ladies' faces. "You seem agitated."

"Agitated! Of course, I am! Who wouldn't be, at

the thought of a first ball and a first ball-dress? We'll see Monsieur Martineau to-morrow," cries Miss Louise, to whom finances have never been much trouble, perhaps because she has never spent a great deal. Her father's allowance to her had been liberal for a school-girl, and at the plantation there had been no way of dissipating capital.

But in the morning, financial trouble comes upon this young lady for the first time.

Indications of this are easily apparent to' Bob when he makes his afternoon visit, at two o'clock the next day.

He saunters in from lunch at the Orleans Club, and finds himself received by Mrs. Joyce and her pretty charge, both the ladies being seated in the courtyard, which as the sun shines on it, seems like a nook in the tropics. The old-fashioned house runs entirely around it, sweet-smelling flowers are on the verandas above, some plantains, bananas, and palms give shade; blossoming plants and trailing vines destroy the formality of its stucco walls; while the whole place is made picturesque by a little bubbling fountain, which does not throw its water very high, and an old-fashioned but romantic-looking awning of bright-colored stripes. This is slung from the rear wall and gives a very pretty effect, especially as Miss Louise, looking fresh and cool in a white muslin which is very sheer and permits glimpses of white shoulders and white arms, is sitting beneath it; a Louise Qu'nze table bearing some light refreshments and a smoking teapot and tea things in front of her.

"You see I'm ready for you," she remarks, as the gentleman is shown in by her maid; then cries: "Lorena! some more hot water—quick! Mr. Covington—I see by his promptness—is anxious for his tea."

"Yes," suggests Mrs. Joyce. "Mr. Covington is always at your behest;" then adds, grimly: "I wish all other gentlemen were."

"Well, all who know you are yours to command now," replies the Kentuckian, "and you'll know a good many more bucks and blades, Miss Louise, on Thursday evening. Here is your invitation for the

Pelican—and yours, Mrs. Joyce——" then pauses, astonished.

For there are tears in the bright eyes of his cousin, as she falters: "I—I am forever obliged to you. You have been very good to me, but—but I cannot go."

"Not go!" cries Bob, aghast. "Great Goliah! What will become of me and the rest of the boys?" then says, anxiously: "What is the reason? You're not ill? You haven't heard bad news?"

"Yes; but I have—*very!*" answers Louise, whose lips are trembling.

To this Mrs. Joyce adds, savagely: "That skinflint Martineau!" and goes away, as if she couldn't bear to discuss him.

But the young lady says: "I don't know that I can blame him. He has always looked out for my interests. He says, I—I can't afford it."

At this, even in her misery the Kentuckian makes the girl happy. "Always defending everybody, ain't you?" he cries—then says, rather commandingly: "Now tell me all about it."

"Well," replies the young lady, "this morning I went down to Madame Olympe and I picked out a— Oh I can't describe the dress!—the whole affair is too dreadful—I—I had it sent home to me. Afterwards we selected one for Mrs. Joyce—a robe of black velvet with lace,—something that would suit her. Then we went to Monsieur Martineau's office and he—he told me it would be impossible for him to pay for the dresses, and—and I'm going to send them back! Oh the humiliation! I'm—I'm very unhappy!"

"Well, you shan't be, long!" replies her cousin, "I'll step down and see Martineau. Don't send the dresses back! This affair is in my hands now!"

"Is it?" cries the girl, eagerly. "Is it, Cousin Bob? Then, if it is, I'm sure it'll be all right." And she gives him a glance of trust and admiration that makes him very happy and his heart beat very fast.

So he strides away, leaving his cup of tea untasted, in the excitement of his cousin's wrongs, for he is muttering as he walks along; "I wonder if her trustee, or guardian, or whatever he is, is a damned old scoundrel. I must take a look into Cousin Louise's affairs!" and makes his way to the office of the *avocat* which is on Custom House Street.

On announcing his name, he is very shortly shown in to the Creole attorney's private office, to have every suspicion of Arvid Martineau swept away as he gazes into that gentleman's precise yet noble face.

Though the lawyer has a certain nervous anxiety in his manner, Covington is very affably received. The attorney even looks pleased when the young man says: "I have called to see you about some business for my Cousin Louise. Please don't think that I wish to intrude either my advice or direction, but what seems to us men of the world a trifle, is a very great affair to a girl who is going to her *first* ball."

"*Going* to her first ball?" echoes Martineau. "She said that would be impossible without a new dress."

"Yes; but we must furnish it for her. You say, I understand, that the Tournay estate cannot afford it?"

"Not exactly that, "remarks the *avocat*," but——" He hesitates a little here, then goes on rapidly and earnestly, though Covington can see he weighs every word he utters: "I will take you into my confidence. There is a chance of a certain claim being made against the Tournay estate. In case it is made, I shall have to meet it, and Mademoiselle Louise's income and her sister's will——" The attorney hesitates here.

"Will be diminished?" suggests Covington.

"*Will be nothing !*"

"Great powers! You astound me!" Bob's face is very serious. "But of course you will oppose any such claim."

"Between ourselves," remarks the legal gentleman, "I do not think any defense *can be made*, if the claim is properly set forth."

"Heavens and earth! Then *of course* the claim will be presented!"

"That I do not know."

"Why not ?"

"Because I do not think that the party having the legal right in the matter is aware of his position. That is one reason—perhaps my best one—though I hope not," mutters the lawyer, a peculiar questioning expression running over his features as he gazes at the young Kentuckian.

"Miss Louise knows nothing about it?"

"No; I have not been able to bring myself to tell her. In case the claim is not made, *I shall never tell her!* That is the reason I have wished her to take her sister and go to Paris. In case the claim is made, the young ladies being here, would only bring trouble upon them, without doing them any good on earth. In fact, their presence would only add to my embarrassment in arranging the affair."

"And the party having this infernal hold upon the Tournay estate doesn't know it?"

"No!—and from my lips, he never shall!" says the Creole lawyer, determinedly. "It is not my duty, as executor of this estate, or trustee for it, to go about finding claims against it or claimants for it. Do you think so, Mr. Covington?"

"No, I'll be hanged if I do!" says Bob, though his face is very solemn. A moment after, he brightens up a little, and adds: "But, for that reason, we must not prevent the girl's having a good time—eh, Monsieur Martineau?"

"You mean with regard to ball dresses?"

"Certainly!"

"Under the circumstances," remarks the Creole lawyer, "I do not feel authorized in providing any more money than will permit Miss Louise a comfortable living. The estate must be kept up, and I—this is from a strict business standpoint—must be in position to make the proper accounting if the claim is made."

"This is a very ex—extraordinary situation," falters Covington. Then he suddenly says: "As Louise's nearest relative, make me your confidant in the matter —tell me all about it. Let us try to euchre any scoundrel who would rob a girl who can't be beat—this side of Jordan."

This suggestion seems to have a curious effect upon Martineau. His face changes color; he looks at Bob for one moment, as if almost about to speak, but finally mutters: "No! *Mon Dieu!* I cannot!" then adds, apparently, as if wishing to close the discussion: "The more who know this secret, the greater danger of its coming to the person who might use it. I have the greatest respect for you—the greatest admiration for you—Monsieur Covington; but you are young, you have the quick impulse—the hasty frankness of youth—I have the discretion of age. The secret remains mine—at all events for the present."

"Perhaps you are right," returns Covington, who has been thinking the matter over; then he suddenly says: "But Louise must have her ball dress. No cloud from this iniquitous claim must come upon her life, if I can roll it away. As her nearest relative, it is my duty—by Heaven, sir!—to stand up for her rights and her happiness, which have become—I am more confiding than you—very dear to me. I have been fortunate——" He sits down and, despite the protests of the Creole attorney, draws out a pocket check-book and writes hurriedly. "Here is my check on the Bank of Louisiana for five thousand dollars. Now don't go to preaching, my dear Martineau! I'm flush now; La Farge paid his bets to-day. This I authorize you to expend for the personal expenses of my cousin, sir, and —hang it—under the circumstances you can't refuse. Though, not one word to Miss Louise about it! You come to the Pelican ball and you'll see what a high old time we'll have, despite incipient claims and unknown dangers. Pay Madame Olympe's bill when it arrives, and, by Heaven! if you want more, call upon Bob Covington, of Lexington, who knows what it is to have the prettiest girl in Louisiana for a cousin!"

So the young buck goes away, leaving Martineau looking at him, admiration mingled with astonishment in his eyes.

But a moment after, the attorney almost wails: "My Heaven! His generosity will compel me to tell. They —they *must* not go to the ball! After the questions that sneaking police lawyer asked me to-day— that must be prevented! At the last I *must* speak!" next mutters, as if frightened: "No—no—not yet!

there must be some way to arrange this! *Think*, Martineau, THINK!" then jeers himself: "Is your brain paralyzed over the invitation of a young lady to a ball? Old man, you are becoming a dotard!—because this matter is—is—breaking your heart!"

And he sinks down and drops his head upon his desk, this man who is considered as hardheaded and subtle-minded a legal formalist as any of the Louisiana bar.

A few minutes of intense emotion, and the lawyer is a man of action once more. He rings his bell; one of his clerks comes in and gives him a report. Looking this over, after his assistant has departed, Martineau's eyes beam. He cries: "That was a very pretty ruse! That heads off for the present Mr. Kitson Jarvis. Now, while I have time, in a few days I must get those girls to Europe!" then thinks the matter over deeply, and gives vent to this extraordinary sentiment: "As GOD IS MY JUDGE, I DO NOT THINK HE WILL DEEM IT A ROBBERY!"

But this interview brings with it a curious decision to Mr. Covington. This young man's steps are by no means as rapid as those that led him to the attorney's office. He had come to discuss a bill for ball dresses; he has discovered beneath the small annoyance a very great calamity.

"Threatened with the loss of her fortune?" he thinks. "That makes no difference! Thank Heaven, that makes no difference! I've enough! God has been good to me. We'll have a high old time, any way, and if she——" His heart beats, so he does not finish the sentence, but murmurs: "I'll speak before she knows! Louise shall not think that pity has given her a lover! not by the soul of Daniel Boone!"

A resolution that brings about in the course of the next two or three days another and more fearful embarrassment to the Creole attorney.

Mr. Covington, in the course of a quarter of an hour, is back at the Tournay home on Dauphine Street. Louise rises eagerly as he enters the courtyard, for the sun is still warm and she is still making a pretty picture under the old awning. Looking into his face, she falters: "I can see! Monsieur Martineau refused!" for, despite his resolve of a "high old time," Mr. Bob has a very moody manner.

"No! Those ball-dresses are all right! Martineau is no longer a skinflint; he'll pay your bills. Only remember, you can't buy all of Olympe and Sophie's goods at once, my little lady," answers the gentleman, affecting a lightness he scarcely feels.

If Bob has ever had a regret for his five-thousand-dollar check, he thinks the money well lost as he gazes at the delight in the girl's face. She cries: "Of course! How foolish I was! I knew *you* could do anything!" then goes on in almost ecstatic happiness: "Cousin Bob, you must see it! Come up in the parlor and look at it—my first dress, for my first ball!"

There is a flutter of light skirts and flitting of pretty feet as she runs ahead of him up the stairs, clapping her hands, the joy of youth in her eyes—that joy which makes the little things of this world into mighty pleasures—that joy which comes to us but once, and for a brief season, in a lifetime.

But, arrived in the *salon*, this young lady, with feminine fickleness of purpose, changes her mind, and suddenly says: "No. On second thoughts, you shan't see Olympe's creation—*just yet!* Wednesday is my evening for entertaining you—a little surprise for my Cousin Bob," a new and, she thinks, enchanting idea having flown into her vivacious brain.

So, he going away, Louise tells the good news to Mrs. Joyce, remarking: "Haven't I a wonder for a cousin? He twists the stern Martineau about his fingers as if he were a ribbon! We must look out for ourselves, Pamela! This mighty man will soon be dictator of our household!—a merciful tyrant, I hope," and a little embarrassed blush flies over her charming countenance, though she doesn't know what a curious prophecy she is making.

And Mrs. Joyce, hearing the good tidings, rejoices also, for the loss of the black velvet and point lace robe had been a cruel disappointment, even to her; ex-schoolmistresses rejoicing in toilettes as well as those of less drastic mold.

In the evening, however, after an elaborate make-up under the hands of Mr. Cæsar, our young gentleman escorts Mrs. Joyce and Miss Tournay to the theatre, where they all enjoy Placide's performance very much, the Kentuckian being astonished at the intense amount of enthusiasm the young lady displays. From this they walk home, the night being very pleasant, and the distance not very great, and Miss Louise tells him that it is the fourth time in all her life she has been in a playhouse: three times from Miss Martin's establishment in New York, on certain gala occasions, and this evening; which has been much the most pleasant of them all.

"Yes; there were *no* young gentlemen on Miss Martin's occasions," remarks Pamela, with a grim laugh.

Though Mrs. Joyce is by their side, the two contrive to enjoy themselves very well, but after arrival at the Tournay mansion, Mr. Covington makes what, as he expresses it to himself afterward—is ."a very bad break."

The chaperone is standing at the head of the stairs in the little courtyard, waiting for Louise. That young lady at the bottom, is murmuring: "Good night, Cousin Bob," and extending patrician fingers.

As he takes the delicate hand in his, something flies into the Kentuckian's eyes. He mutters: "Why do you always call me *cousin?*"

"Because you *are* one!" replies the young lady suddenly; then continues, a wounded tone in her voice: "Do you suppose I would permit so many privileges of *tête-à-tête* to a   gentleman who was *not!*" next says, haughtily: "What do you mean, any way?"

"I mean," replies Mr. Rapid, who now loses his head, "just forget I am your cousin. Think of me as Bob Covington, just like any other young fellow."

"You were very anxious to assume the relationship, not much over two days ago," answers the girl, blushing hotly, then continues: "Your request is granted, Monsieur Covington," dropping a demure courtesy. To this she adds: "You are talking to me *alone*—my chaperone not in ear-shot. Permit me to suggest that Creole etiquette decrees this is not proper between gentlemen and young ladies who are not *relatives.*"

"Well, under those circumstances," answers Bob, biting his lips, "supposing we become cousins again."

"No!" cries the young lady, suddenly. Then she turns her blazing eyes on his and mutters: "We can never be cousins again! Good evening. Take your hand from my wrist! You know you have no right to such a familiarity to one who is not your relative, Cousin Bob. No, I don't mean that. Good night— good-bye. Forgive me. Don't be angry with me— *Au revoir!*"

And so she runs away, a mixture of blushes, embarrassment and charming graces, to the protection of her chaperone, who is grimly awaiting her at the head of the stairs.

But Miss Louise has not yet escaped the embarrassments of the evening. Mrs. Joyce turns inquiring eyes upon her, after they are in the parlor, and remarks: "Why did you linger at the foot of the stairs, Louise? It is hardly the proper thing to do."

"What! With my *cousin?*" says the girl, airily.

"Pooh! A fig for such cousinship!" cries Pamela. Then she utters these awful words: "Can't you see that young fellow is treating you like a girl he wants to marry?"

"Marry?" gasps Louise, her face growing very red and her eyes very bright; then she falters out this ingenuous idea: "How should I know? I—I have never been courted *before*," but flies from Pamela's comments to the solitude of her chamber, where she says: "The bold fellow! The idea!—and only two days!" next contradicts herself with: "I love a brave man!"

As for the "brave man," after another hard night at poker with La Farge and *confrères*, he remarks to himself: "By Jove! I play a bad game now! I've lost my nerve! Laid down three queens before a bobtail flush;" then says, reflectively, yet determinedly: "No, I have not lost my nerve! I've got the grit of wildcats! By the battle of Tippecanoe, within two days I do the darned fool Romeo act!"

BOOK II.

A Very Unfortunate Young Lady.

CHAPTER VII.

KITSON JARVIS SHAKES HANDS WITH HIMSELF.

ON that same Monday, filled with hopes, joys, and fears, for there are one or two of the latter connected with his "best stroke of business in the Crescent City," Mr. Kitson Jarvis, full of the remembrance of the pretty picture Miss Tournay and Mr. Covington had made the afternoon before, goes down to his offices on Lafayette Street, just off Peters, and therefore quite convenient, not only to the courts, but to seafaring and steamboat men, who are his principal clients. These consist of two rooms, over the doors of which the sign is conspicuously displayed:

KITSON JARVIS,
ATTORNEY AND COUNSELOR-AT-LAW,
Proctor in Admiralty and *Avocat Français.*

The larger of these apartments is devoted to the routine business of the office, and is adorned by volumes of "Blackstone," "Kent's Commentaries," "Chitty on Pleadings," the "Civil Code of Louisiana of 1853," "Code Napoleon," and various other works on French and American law, all tending to display the legal acumen of the gentleman whose sign is over the door.

This connects with a smaller and inner chamber which Mr. Jarvis uses as a private office; his particular desk and safe containing his more important and con-

fidential papers being prominent in the furniture of
the room.   The appearance of the place is brisk and
businesslike in both the main and the private office, the
usual legal documents and papers bearing general evidence of a bustling business.   For Mr. Jarvis has quite
a little practice up and down the river with smaller
planters, and is considered extremely effective in handling seamen's cases, legally bulldozing Jack Tars who
refuse to leave New Orleans in unseaworthy vessels, and
doing the general business of an all-round, rough-and-
tumble sea-captain's lawyer.

On his entrance he is greeted by a bow from a bright-
looking young Frenchman of about twenty years of
age, who is his only clerk, Monsieur Alfred Cotain.
This young gentleman, who has been industriously
plying a quill pen, sticks it behind his ear and answers
his employer's question, "Any new business this morning?" with a good deal of Gallic snap and vivacity,
apparently being about as brisk as his chief.

"Yes," says the young man, "Captain Jenkins of
the bark *Bonny Bell* wants you to take proceedings
against two seamen, Robert Bonehill and Jack Mur-
phy, who, he says, have accepted his advance money,
and now refuse to sail, on the ground that the *Bonny
Bell* is bound for the Gold Coast, and they are afraid
she intends to go into running slaves to Cuba—a voyage they didn't sign for.   Coffee & Judkins, shipping
agents, want them prosecuted also."

"All right!   Draw up a summons and get out an
application for an order of arrest," replies the attorney; then asks, sharply: "Anything else?"

"Yes, sir.   The first mate of the *General Pike No. 4*
is up for thumping a deck-hand until he jumped overboard."

"Is the deck-hand drowned?"

"No."

"Then that won't amount to much.   Deck-hands
don't count."

"But the *deck-hand* has retained us."

"Ah!   Yes!   Tell the deck-hand I'll get him heavy
damages for the infernal outrage.   Draw up a summons and complaint.   Get hold of that mate and see

how much he'll compromise for, *down!*　What next?"

"Well—Captain Coulson——" The clerk hesitates.

"Cuss it! speak quick!"

"Well, sir, Captain Coulson has come in once more to see about that property on Esplanade Street. He says you must either pass or throw out that title in twenty-four hours. His boat, the *General Jones*, leaves for the Red River to-morrow afternoon, and he *will* have the matter settled. Besides, Coulson says the Société Mutuel are pressing him; they only allowed him four weeks for the passage of title, and you have already taken six. He says he wants an answer, 'Yes' or 'No,' whether the title is good."

"Next time Coulson comes in show him in to me right off, Alfred," remarks his employer, and goes into his private office, shutting the door with a bang, and his clerk thinks he hears some low and deep curses, and wonders what the devil is the matter about Coulson and his property.

And there are some exceedingly deep curses, though very low ones, coming from the lips of Mr. Kitson Jarvis, who is muttering to himself: "By the Eternal! will that letter from California never come? I wrote immediately I had grasped what that abstract might mean. It should be here even now, if it comes by the Nicaragua line. I'll take a look at the darned thing again."

Then opening his safe he produces an abstract of title of property on Esplanade Street, near Calvez.

Running over the original grants of same, which had been in block from the French crown to the Jesuits and from the Jesuits to various settlers in the early days of Louisiana, Mr. Jarvis comes down to a transfer made June 23, 1833, by one François Contino and wife to Prosper Delaunay Tournay, of Assumption Parish, of a large frontage on this street for the sum of $1,500.

Next a deed, from said Prosper D. Tournay to Simon S. Jennings for one-third of same property, noted on the abstract as being passed as good, valid, unencumbered and *complete*, and carrying fee simple title, by Dubois & Merrill, *Avocats;* consideration, $700. The date of this is also the year 1833, August 20th, just two months afterward. There is only one more transfer of the property on record, that of August 19, 1835, when said property had been deeded by Simon S. Jennings to the Société Mutuel of New Orleans, a small investment company of that date, and passed also by the same attorneys, Dubois & Merrill; consideration, $800.

The property has apparently remained in the possession of the Société Mutuel, who are now about to sell the same to Jackson R. Coulson, captain of the Mississippi River steamboat *General Jones*, for $2,500; Jarvis being Coulson's attorney, the abstract has been placed in his hands to pass upon the validity of the title.

Looking at this record, Mr. Jarvis remarks: "It's all-fired curious how Dubois & Merrill, who were considered about the best real estate lawyers of their day in New Orleans, passed this title without the signature of the *wife* of Prosper Delaunay Tournay!

"The deed was made in 1833, and Tournay was married in 1832 to Eulalie Camila Poussin, so far as I can discover. There is certainly no record of renunciation of community of gains by Eulalie Camila in New Orleans, and no renunciation of common property rights by said Eulalie Camila in Assumption Parish, where the marriage was reported to have taken place." Here a hideous kind of grin comes over Jarvis's face.

"As far as I can find out," cogitates the attorney, "this Eulalie Camila brought no *dot* to her husband, but as he married her in 1832, one year before he purchased this Esplanade property, it became *common* property. And yet, with no renunciation of partnership and community of gains by this wife of Prosper Tournay, Dubois & Merrill twice reported Tournay's deed as complete and *unencumbered*.

"I have ferreted out," he thinks, "as much as I dared without giving any one a hint of what I'm driving after, and the thing would be pretty simple if either Dubois or Merrill were get-at-able. But Dubois is dead, and Merrill went to California, full of the gold fever of 1849. He is now an attorney in San Francisco, and—hang it!—for his own professional reputation he *must* answer my letter!"

Then he goes poring over the records of the Tournay family, obtained from Assumption Parish, beginning at Prosper Delaunay Tournay, born 1804—"That's the father!" mutters the lawyer—and his sister Isabel Laurey, born 1806. Prosper was married 1832 to Eulalie Camila Poussin and had issue by her, Louise Camours, born 1834—"That's the beauty of the race-course,"—Horace Jackson, born 1835, died 1836—"He's out of the way!"—and Nita Hortense, born June 4, 1841. Eulalie Camila Poussin Tournay died June 5, 1841.

"Apparently the mother died at the birth of the last child Nita, who is now at Miss Martin's boarding-school, No. 209 Lafayette Place, New York City."

Then he goes on: "Isabel Laurey Tournay was married, 1826, to Harrod Boone Covington, of Kentucky, and had issue Robert Boone Covington, 1827. That's our young buck of the race-course, the one who is going to be so darned lucky, *perhaps!* Oh, I've got the Tournay and the Covington families down pretty fine," chuckles the attorney.

This reverie is broken by his clerk, Alfred, coming in and saying: "Captain Coulson has called again."

But the river man has already announced himself. From the outer office comes a stern, terror-of-deckhands voice, crying savagely: "You tell your boss, youngster, that, darn his blind-fog optics, he can't snag me in that real estate deal, another day! If Jarvis doesn't open his jaws and give me some opinion about that title, I'll chuck him overboard and scoot the abstract to Sampson Ketchum in two minutes!"

"Very well, Cotain. Show the gentleman in," returns Mr. Jarvis, setting his jaws for a diplomatic combat; for Coulson is a man who does not take his hat off, even to pilots, and is considered more able at bully-ragging mates than any other freight boat captain on the river; which is saying all that can be said for any man. He is a short, stocky individual, very broad of shoulder, with long arms of apparently enormous strength. He has red face, red hair, red eyes, black teeth and bull-dog jaw, which he is wagging, grinding his teeth together, even as he enters,

"What the devil's the matter?" he shouts, trying to force himself to amiability. "Darn me, Jarvis, you're the slowest craft on the river! You must have run up a blind chute and got caught by falling water on this real estate deal. Are you left high and dry till next spring? Don't you know those Society Mutual chaps declare you could give a 'say so' on that title in two days, if you put a nigger's brains onto it? Bust my boilers, one would think you'd been blown up and become a hulk! The society agreed to give four weeks for you to look into the matter, and here it's nearly seven, and they'll be getting another customer. By the Eternal! If you don't put on steam I'll bust you up in business!"

The lawyer deems it unwise to interrupt this effusion, judging it best to let the riverman blow off superfluous steam. Then he raises his hand, deprecatingly, and says: "Captain Coulson, will you have a cigar?"

"Darn it! I didn't come for a smoke! I came for your gab on that title!"

"Yes, but have a cigar while I show you the *leetle* difficulty I am in. It is not a question of title exactly, it is a question of whether the deed carries *all* the property. You have heard, I presume, of community of gains?"

"*Damn* community of gains!"

"But community of gains may *damn* you. Well, perhaps you don't understand about transfers *inter vivos* and ——

"H—m!"

"And you are not entirely up in transfers by *mortis causa?*"

"By gad, sir!——"

"Listen to me. Are you aware of the difference between a residuary legacy and a contingent remainder? Can you define the variance between fee simple and a life estate?"

"By Jumping Jonah! I'm not up for examination for the bar!"

"Certainly not! But I am compelled to give you your title to the property, free and clear of everything, without any debts, rebates, contingencies, side-issues, sub-claims, liens, feoffs, emoluments, or peradventures. Remember that!"

"You don't say!" mutters the sea-dog.

"And furthermore, *in addendum; ab hoc et ab hac,* yet *ad arbitrium,* and *ad huc sub judices lis est, Festina lente; Fides et justitia!*"

"Quit that! Quit that jabbering!"

"Jabbering, my dear sir? I'm simply putting some of the problems of your case before you. Do you expect an answer on such questions in a moment? *Experentia docet stultus. Vexata quæstio! vinculum matrimonii* and *status quo!* Remember that! *Qui tacet consentit!*" During this compendium of legal aphorisms Mr. Jarvis has become very excited and vehement, and rattles off his last sally in apparently savage fury.

"If you love your life, quit cussing me in Latin!"

"I am not cursing you in Latin, sir. I am simply giving you a few of the difficulties of your case. Suppose I passed this title, and there came over to you, by referee duly appointed, a commission to determine how much of this land you hold, and they brought you in for heavy damages, sir—heavy damages!—after I had told you the title was good. What would you do in such a case?"

"*Do!*" cries the Captain, "DO! Why, darn my eyes, I'd lick the life out of you for having passed it!"

"Very well, sir. Under the circumstances, I request a few days more. When I tell you the title is right, it will be, and you can hold it to the day of judgment."

"By the Texas eagle, I *will* hold it to the day of judgment if I ever get onto that land!"

"Very well, sir. Do you expect me to risk my personal safety as well as my professional reputation on the drop of a hat? Remember, sir, I am working for a *summum bonum, multum in parvo,* and a fee simple *pro bono publico* that will permit you and your descendants, male and female, to hold this property *per se* in perpetuity by the *lex loci,* by the *lex non scripta,* by the *lex scripta,* by the *lex terræ,* UNTO THE END OF MAN! Remember that!"

"Well, that being the state of the case," says the

captain, humbly, "I s'pose I'll have to give you a leetle more time."

"Yes, sir. Always act slowly in real estate matters. Come in and see me about Friday."

"Friday? How the devil can I see you then? I'll be tied agin' the bank, up the Red River, Friday!"

"Quite right! Come to me when you get back. Your money is in the Bank of Louisiana, isn't it? That's not going to burst; now you know you've got something! If you went away and I passed this title hurriedly, you might wake up and find you hadn't anything. And permit me to tell you that a personal assault upon *me* for a bad passage of title would bring upon you an avalanche of civil and criminal litigation that would make you blow up your boat in despair. Remember, sir, the office of a member of the Louisiana bar is not the hurricane deck of one of your cursed river freight boats! Now let us have a cigar and take a snifter."

"Well, since you put it that way," remarks the captain, accepting the olive branch, "and your cigars being very good—— Have you got any corn-juice in yer private demijohn?"

This being produced, Captain Jackson Coulson, of the steamer *General Jones*, walks away, remarking to himself: "Hang me! I wonder if it was a game of bluff. Any way, I'll raise Cain with the deckhands this trip!"

"I think that'll keep him quiet for a day or two, curse him!" says the lawyer. Then he suddenly cries: "Alfred, run down to the postoffice! See if they can tell you exactly when the next California mail will come in."

Word being very shortly brought him by his clerk that it may not get in until Wednesday, Mr. Kitson Jarvis glumly thinks "I can't hang this thing up forever!" then suddenly mutters: "By Jupiter! I'll go over and see Martineau! He was Tournay's lawyer! Perhaps I can pump him a little about the matter."

This he does, producing somewhat remarkable results.

The office of Monsieur Martineau, is upon Custom House Street, near Chartres, and bears the sign "*Detaille et Martineau, Avocats."* Detaille has been dead a number of years, but the sign still remains, though Arvid Martineau follows his profession entirely upon his own account.

As Kitson approaches the entrance, he sees standing in Custom House Street, in front of the door, the same family carriage that had borne Miss Tournay out to the race-course upon the preceding Saturday.

"Ah! consulting with family lawyer!" thinks Mr. Jarvis. "There's no doubt Martineau still manages the Tournay estate."

With this he enters the office, which consists of three rooms. A large public one in which several clerks are engaged in a quiet, conservative, old style method of doing business. Another, opening both from the hallway and general office, is used by Martineau as his consulting room. In it he arranges the affairs of a number of the most prominent Creole families: families with great estates; families with hundreds of slaves; families who raise thousands of bales of cotton; families whose names were prominent in the colony, when it was French, when it was Spanish, and afterward when it was French again.

The office immediately behind this, originally had belonged to his former partner. Now it is scarcely used, except when some one of Arvid's lady clients wishes to see the gentleman who manages her estates. Above this, after the French custom, Martineau has his own private apartments, and lives in bachelor contentment, looked after by his aunt, a maiden lady of about sixty, and two or three devoted servants.

The whole place appears to Kitson Jarvis, as he expresses it, "infernally slow." "I'd rouse those lazy clerks up," he thinks, as he enters the outer room. "My boy Alfred could do the business of the kit of them." But looking upon the names on the various boxes of papers of the Martignys, Soulés, Carrolls, Polks and Mariés, even Mr. Jarvis feels himself impressed, and mutters: "A conservative, but respectable, and—hang me!—an infernally rich practice."

The next instant he is asking the head-clerk, Auguste Pichoir, if his principal can be seen. "In a few minutes, Monsieur," answers the young man, "I will take your name in. At present Monsieur Martineau is engaged with another client. Will you not be seated?"

"Of course," replies Mr. Jarvis, and, knowing very well who is in consultation with the lawyer, he goes to cogitating over the matter that is now upon his mind, to be roused from it by the brush of feminine draperies and the sunshine of beauty, as Miss Louise sweeps past him from the inner office, accompanied by Mrs. Joyce. The interview has been upon a no more weighty subject than the young lady's millinery bills, but as the attorney glances with admiring eyes over the radiant loveliness of the girl's face and figure, he gives a horrified start and gasps "By the Eternal, she *knows!*" for the appearance of the girl denotes disappointment, almost to despair.

Then Kitson is relieved. Miss Louise suddenly whispers to Mrs. Joyce: "He's simply *awful!* He—he—you do not understand, Pamela—he absolutely refused to pay for my dress for Thursday, and Madame Olympe has sent it home. Oh! what shall I do? What shall I do? He—" she gives a savage yet pitiful glance at the inner office— "he even commanded me not to buy any more costumes! I used to get a great deal more money before papa died; now, I have my own income and he won't let me spend it! I—I can't take his answer! I'll go in and see him again!" adds the young lady, stamping her little foot petulantly.

She leaves Mrs. Joyce standing outside, makes a tremulous dive into the private office of Monsieur Martineau, to emerge therefrom half a minute after, apparently defeated. For tears now veil Mademoiselle Louise's exquisite eyes, and she mutters to Mrs. Joyce: "He—he told me he had other people's interests to look after as well as mine! He *absolutely* refused! I—I shan't be able to go to the ball! You—you don't seem to understand!—I—*I can't go to the ball!*"

And scarely heeding some half-hearted attempts at condolence from her companion, the young lady goes out, the tears of bitter disappointment in her eyes, followed by her chaperone, leaving Mr. Jarvis gazing after and chuckling: "Great Taylor!" What a fright she gave me! I was afraid the fat was in the fire and she *knew*—when it was only old Martineau shutting down on the funds." Here a very cunning gleam comes into his eyes, for into the attorney's mind has suddenly flown this proposition: "The Tournay estates produce a very good income. Why the dickens should Martineau object to the young lady's spending her portion of it? Be gosh! *of course*—not a dollar of it is *hers*—not by a kibosh!"

This idea makes him a little more confident that he is on, as he expresses it, "the right trail."

As Kitson is ushered into the private office, his ferret eyes take cognizance of a small safe upon which he sees the name "Prosper D. Tournay."

"Good morning, Monsieur Jarvis," remarks the Creole advocate, with punctilious politeness. "Though I know you by sight, I have never had the pleasure of doing any business with you."

"Ditto, ditto!" responds the Yankee attorney. "It's only a very little matter that I'm going to trouble you about!" Then he goes on rapidly, for Kitson has thought out his questions as he has walked over, and rather hopes to take the more conservative legal gentleman by surprise. "It's that property oh Esplanade Street that Tournay made a deed of in 1833 to Simon S. Jennings and Jennings deeded in '35 to the Société Mutuel. I am passing on the title of same, and though Tournay was married in 1832, and purchased said real estate in 1833, his wife's signature is not on the deed, and I find no relinquishment of community of gains by Madame Tournay in the New Orleans records."

Even as he says this, Kitson Jarvis guesses that he has hit the man looking him so blandly in the face very hard.

Though Martineau's eyes have never left his, though his form still stands erect, there is a gradual paleness creeping into his face, and his moustache trembles very, very slightly, as he answers: "I was not Prosper Tour-

nay's attorney at that time.   His business did not come
to our firm till 1840.   Probably the renunciation of
community rights is upon the parish record where
Monsieur Tournay lived."

"Assumption?" answers Jarvis.   "I have had those
records searched.   There is no renunciation there."

"Ah, but you forget there is La Fourche.   Prosper
Tournay had a small plantation there, near Guidrys.
Probably, if you will search you will find it there."

This is a terrible and unexpected blow to Jarvis.   He
mutters: "Parish La Fourche? I never knew of that;"
and for a moment seems disconcerted.

"Anyway, the title has been passed upon," continues Martineau, his voice growing firmer, "as you
know, by a very excellent firm of older days, Dubois &
Merrill.   There can be no doubt about that title."

"No; I don't believe there is any doubt about that
title.   I'm sure there's no doubt about that title,"
answers Kitson, his tone becoming more confident, his
manner less dejected.   Then he goes on: "Don't you
think in looking over the old papers of the Tournay
estate—you handle it now, I believe—you could find
something that would elucidate why Madame Tournay's signature was not necessary to that deed? Could
you not overhaul the contents of that safe, as I want to
pass upon that title at once?"

"That safe?" falters the French gentleman.

"Yes, that safe!"   Here Jarvis's smile becomes full
of latent insinuation.   "The one towards which you
are glancing, the one marked 'Prosper D. Tournay.'
If you can find time in the next few hours, just see if
you can discover among the papers in that little iron
box, some reason why that title was passed as good
and unencumbered by Dubois & Merrill, and yet does
not bear the signature of Madame Tournay."

"I—I will try and accommodate you," remarks the
Creole lawyer, holding himself very erect as if he
hardly dare unbend, for fear he might falter.

"Thank you.   Good day."   And Mr. Jarvis walks
out, muttering to himself: "By Jove, Kitson, shake
hands!   I believe I've guessed right, even though
there may be a renunciation on the records of Parish

La Fourche. I'll send down a search; it won't take more than a day or two. But, whether I find it or not, there's some' Tournay skeleton locked up in that safe, or I'll forfeit my certificate to practice law."

Left by himself, Arvid Martineau, after a moment's agitated thought, mutters these curious words: "Thank God! He is a noble young man! But, *Mon Dieu!* What will it be for them at best? Oh, but it must not be! It must not be! I have feared that Esplanade property—I should have bought it long ago. It is the only title that Tournay transferred!"

Then suddenly he rings his bell. His clerk comes in, and he says: "Pichoir, go to the Société Mutuel at once," and whispers a few brief sentences.

And the young man going out, the old French lawyer closes the door of his outer office, locks himself in, and murmurs: "Should I not warn her? There's one who is not here—dear little Nita. I have dandled her on my knee." Then he breaks out: "Oh, may God forgive you, Prosper Tournay! God forgive you; I cannot! Procrastinator! Dreamer! Poet! Sensualist! Man of too refined sensibilities to face thy own miserable mistake, thou hast left thy crime to crush two poor innocents! *Grand Dieu! Aie pitié d'elles!—aie pitié d'elles!*"

Then, brave gentleman as he is—for in Arvid Martineau's veins flows the blood of those who have died for France in many a pitched battle—he bursts out crying like a child, wringing his hands and sobbing: "*Grâce! Grâce! pour les innocents!* Take the cup from them—Oh, Father in Heaven!"

CHAPTER VIII.

THE LETTER FROM CALIFORNIA.

RETURNING from this interview to his office, Kitson arranges with a French notary to run down to La Fourche and examine the records of that parish.

After attending to the usual routine of his office and

exacting thirty dollars cash as a matter of compromise from the mate who has beaten the deck-hand, Mr. Jarvis goes to meditating upon the Tournay affair.

"If I could get that letter from California," he thinks, "if my suspicion does amount to anything, the first attorney who gets the news to Mr. Bob Covington, will be the one to handle the pickings." Here he reflects: "By heaven! I can't be right! Martineau would have got his work in upon the Kentuckian before now, if there had been anything in it!" and, judging others by himself, becomes very glum.

But the next morning, Tuesday, Mr. Kitson Jarvis gets a sudden shock that knocks contemplation out of him and sets him going again. He has not been in his office more than an hour before he hears exclamations of surprise and dismay from his clerk, Alfred Cotain, mingled with a gruff, seafaring voice.

Rising, he finds himself confronted by Jackson Coulson, the captain of the *General Jones*, who has just swept away little Cotain from impeding his entrance. The river-boatman real estate speculator has a couple of papers in his hands and the light of battle in his eyes.

"By the Etarnal!" he screams. "You miserable shyster!—you legal slow poke! You're slower than the *John J. Roe!* You've grounded yourself on your beef-bones and me too!"

"What is the—the matter?" asks Kitson, his face growing anxious, for he sees the affair is serious.

"What is the *matter? This* is the matter! Your infernal dilly-dallying, *Multus in parvum*, deferential remainders and contingent attainders, has busted me all up in my real estate deal! Damn it! *Some one else has got the property, that's all!*"

"Got the property?" gasps Kitson, growing very white. Though he does not fear so much for the real estate as for the secret that may be hidden in the abstract of its title, which is worth a hundred lots like that on Esplanade Street.

"Yes; got the property, by heaven! Bought it over my head! Look at this letter! It was sold yesterday—and for a hundred dollars more than I was

to get it for. One hundred dollars more, you land-
shark! Twenty-six hundred dollars—that's what they
got for it from some sneak named Jules Errard. The
title was passed by a French attorney *as good* in twenty
minutes, and you took seven weeks and then—damn
it!—you didn't know anything about it. Oh, you're
only fit for trying niggers, you are, and I'd smash your
brains out, if you had any, if it was not for these!"
He flourishes two papers. "The Society Mutual, who
don't want any trouble with me, write that they have
returned my check for five hundred dollars as advance
payment on the title and also the hundred dollars extra
they received from Errard. But that doesn't square
me. That land is worth all of three thousand dollars,
and by every snag on the Mississippi I've got a good
mind to take it out of your hide!"

Here the attorney, in the agitation of the moment,
makes a remark that is unfortunate for himself. He
snarls: "Don't bother me with your miserable affairs!
I've got something more important to think of."

But he has not!

For, with a whoop of rage, Jackson Coulson leads off
with his right foot, and Kitson goes down over his desk,
and lies doubled up on the floor.

"Take that for your infernal *Vobiscums* and *Pater
nostras* and your Choctaw Latin! Take that for
dallying in real estate debentures and cross-bonds,
which are as much ahead of you as I'm over a
stoker, you infernal Jeremy Diddler, you nigger lawyer, you non-committal, compromise up-hill-and-down-
tide son-of-a-sea-cook! I've busted your biler, anyway!"

With this parting effusion, the man of the river departs for his boat, the *General Jones*, which even now
has steam up at the levee, muttering to himself: "Oh,
won't it be hell and blazes for my deck-hands this trip!"

Arising from this interview, not so much wounded
in body as in spirit, and showing no marks of the
fray—for Captain Coulson, being accustomed to tackle
"niggers," has not smitten him in the head, but has
kicked him in the stomach—Mr. Kitson Jarvis, after
he has recovered his breath and sunk into his chair, to

which he has been assisted by his clerk, who has looked upon the affray with a prolonged grin and several half-subdued snickers, tries to pull himself, mentally and physically, together.

After half an hour devoted to physical revival—the Captain's foot having been very heavy—he contrives to make his way to the Société Mutuel. For into his mind has now come the query: "Why the dickens did anyone buy that property in such a hurry? It is not worth over twenty-five hundred dollars at the most!"

At the office of that company Mr. Jarvis finds that the purchaser is, as Captain Coulson had stated, some one named Jules Errard. This individual had come into the Société Mutuel office and had asked if the property was for sale. They had, considering that they had given Coulson no less than three renewals of time for search of title, told him it was. Two hours afterward Errard had returned and said the title had been passed upon by his *avocat*, paid the money in full by a certified check upon the Citizens' Bank, drawn to their order, and that their deed to Jules Errard was now on record.

"Do you know what attorney passed on the title?" asks Mr. Jarvis, nervously.

"No," answers the officer of the company. "But it was probably one of the Creole *avocats*. They are better up in New Orleans real estate than you American gentlemen. The French lawyer only took two hours to settle what you have not determined in seven weeks—to tell you the truth, your delay frightened me about our title."

"Yes; I'm a little hazy about some of your New Orleans transfers, your seignorial rights in the days of the early colonies, and your crown-grants and church fiefs," remarks Mr. Jarvis, who does not mind if the Société Mutuel think him a fool as long as they don't "get onto," as he expresses it, the more important point in the case.

He is now, however, very anxious to find Monsieur Jules Errard. From him he can perhaps learn the name of the attorney who passed the title and judge what are the chances of any one else discovering a secret that he thought he alone had guessed, though these later developments make him inclined to doubt his sagacity. For here is another lawyer passing this title as all right.

To find Monsieur Jules Errard, Mr. Jarvis naturally turns to the city directory, and, after looking down the *E's*, stares in open-eyed amazement at the name of

" Errard—Jules Maxim, Clerk with Arvid Martineau, Custom House and Conti Streets, residence No. 139 Bourbon Street."

Then suddenly a great joy comes over the acute features of Mr. Jarvis. "Jules Errard—Martineau's clerk. Title passed by Arvid Martineau! Land bought in by Arvid Martineau to prevent further investigation of title. Undoubtedly a deed not on record from Jules Errard to Arvid Martineau. Ha ha, you French fox!" he chuckles. "You're not equal to the Yankee 'possum."

Then, despite a sickly feeling in the region of his stomach, Coulson's souvenir of his search of title of the Esplanade Street property, the attorney goes very jauntily to his lunch, and shortly after makes it his business to stroll into the *Magasin du Sud* of Monsieur Pierre Larost, who, as a matter of business, knows most of the Creole young men, as well as their revenues and credits.

From this gentleman he extracts a few words of information in regard to Jules Errard.

"Do I think Monsieur Jules Errard good for twenty-six hundred dollars?" jeers the keeper of the bazaar, with a deprecating shrug of the shoulders. "Do I think Monsieur Jules Errard good for twenty-six *centimes?* He receives a moderate salary from his employer, Martineau, of which he spends three-fourths upon the ladies, the other quarter upon himself, and now has come to grief upon the race last Saturday."

"Right you are!" assents Jarvis. "Then I'll not take him on Bolster's bail bond," and so saunters out.

Coming from this, Kitson laughs: "I have called your little game, Arvid Martineau, and it won't work." But here he ruefully scratches his head and thinks: "I haven't got the evidence; I've only the suspicion, and Martineau may bluff me off if I haven't got the proof dead to rights. Hang it, he's evidently working for the girls—of course—executor's big stealings—no one to call him to account! Oh, you old French scoundrel, you! Wait till I get my fingers in your pie!"

But the pie of the Creole *avocat*, though its odors are extremely savory, seems very far distant, and a little indistinct and hazy to the anxious Kitson.

However, joy cometh with the following morning.

Entering his office early on Wednesday, his clerk lays a letter in front of him, and says: "That's what you've been looking for, from California, is it not?"

Gazing at it, it bears the postmark of San Francisco, March 6, 1854. But Jarvis does not wait long in examination of the envelope; it is the inside that he wants.

And he gets it as follows:

TEHAMA HOUSE,
San Francisco, Cal., March 5, 1854.

Kitson Jarvis, Esq.,
    Attorney-at-Law,
        Lafayette Street, New Orleans, La.

Dear Sir: In reply to your letter of February 10th, in regard to property on Esplanade Street, New Orleans, the deed of which, from Prosper Delaunay Tournay to Simon S. Jennings, was without the signature of Eulalie Camila, title to which was passed upon as valid and *unencumbered*, by Dubois & Merrill, of which firm I was junior partner at that time, and which property was later passed upon again when deeded to Société Mutuel, of which we were attorneys, I can say that notwithstanding the absence of the signature of said Eulalie Camila, and the non-renunciation by her of community rights, that the deed of Prosper Delaunay Tournay was good, sufficient, and UNENCUMBERED by any lien as to community property, or partnership of gains.

I remember the affair very well, notwithstanding the long lapse of time, on account of the peculiarity connected with the transaction, and without wishing to do injury to any one, or to disclose any social secrets of the late Prosper Delaunay Tournay, for my professional reputation I will refer you to the Civil Code of Louisiana, Article 35, also Articles 175, 945, and 1462. A hint to a practicing lawyer of your State is sufficient.

Further particulars can be obtained of one Faval Bigore
Poussin, Notary, of Guidrys, Parish La Fourche, Louisiana,
who was living when I left the State, though of advanced age,
and whose affidavit I brought with me in my old papers to San
Francisco, having been petitioned by Tournay not to affix the
same to abstract of title. This paper was unfortunately destroyed in the fire of San Francisco, June, 1850.

I know professionally that said affidavit ought to have been
attached to abstract of title; but the pressure brought to bear
upon us by Tournay, who was a great personal friend of our
senior partner, Mr. Dubois, was of such a character that we hes-
itated, delayed the matter, and finally in the lapse of years
neglected to do the same. Even now I write upon the subject
with considerable regret, but since you choose to bring up the
affair, am compelled to give you the information you ask, on
account of the Société Mutuel. This I have done in a way perfectly plain to any one cognizant of Louisiana law, and the
articles of the Civil Code that I have enumerated.

Yours respectfully,
ASA J. MERRILL.

P. S.—I may also state that Tournay would never have made
said deed, had he known the questions he would have to answer
to make that title good and complete. I will further say, that
so far as I know, Tournay, who was a dabbler in science and
dreamer in poetry, never made another transfer of any other
part of the Esplanade real estate during the life of said Eulalie
Camila, fearing a deed with his single signature would cause
questions that would lead to the general knowledge of a fact he
wished to keep from public comment.   A. J. M.

On reading this, Mr. Kitson, who is pretty well acquainted with the Civil Code of his State, makes himself doubly sure by pulling down the volume, reads
over the articles noted in the letter, gives a prolonged
whistle, and mutters: "I've got 'em! Those girls' scalps
are in my hands! And by George, I've got Martineau,
too! Seems to me this gentleman has been running
very close to embezzlement! Aha! my representative
of the old *régime.*"
He rings his bell, and half an hour afterward a
messenger is despatched to the French notary who is
searching the papers in La Fourche Parish, bearing

certain questions to be asked of one Faval Bigore Poussin. This man is instructed to take relays of horses so as to catch Mr. Jarvis's agent, if possible, before he has left the county town of La Fourche.

This being done, Kitson turns the matter over in his mind, for he likes to look at propositions from all sides. After a few minutes' intellectual converse with himself, he ejaculates: "Poussin!—the name Eulalie was married under! I wonder if the notary Poussin played the father to the girl. By Jove! perhaps he was her father! You never can tell where these social complications in this part of the world are going to lead you to. But I must be moving! Should Martineau get a hint I know as much as I do, for his own safety he would disclose his secret before my jaws could wag and so cut me out of the best piece of business I've ever run against."

With this idea he writes a short note addressed to "Robert Boone Covington, Esq., St. Charles Hotel," asking that gentleman if he can possibly step over to his office, as he wishes to speak to him on a matter of important business. This Jarvis gives to his clerk, telling him to deliver it in person and get an answer, if possible, forthwith.

To him are brought back very shortly, the following lines:

WEDNESDAY AFTERNOON.

MY DEAR SIR: I am too busy having a frolic down here to bother myself with business just at present; but if you will call and see me at the St. Charles Hotel this evening, I can give you about a minute and a quarter of my time, a cocktail, and a cigar.

After next Saturday's race, however, I will contrive to call upon you, on the Monday following.

Yours in haste,

ROBERT B. COVINGTON.

"Yes, I suppose he *is* having a high old time. Kentucky blood, eh?" ejaculates the lawyer, and he mutters: "You darned fool! if you knew what is ahead of you you'd be jumping over to this office quicker than if you were on the back of a mustang. You lucky devil!"

"Any way, I'll have a go at my dandy to-night! No

one shall get their finger in this pie ahead of Kitson Jarvis. But it will be only *hints* of his mighty good fortune young Covington'll get, until I have his signature for my commission in the matter."

Acting upon this idea, Mr. Kitson Jarvis, arraying himself in his best black broadcloth suit, makes his appearance at the St. Charles Hotel early in the evening, and chances, to meet Mr. Bob almost at the entrance of that gorgeous establishment. To him he rapidly introduces himself.

"Ah, yes!— the attorney who wrote to me, to-day," answers the Kentuckian, genially but hurriedly. "But, I haven't time to talk to you now, and I have to defer my cocktail and cigar hospitality till next meeting. I am happy to hear, however, that you hint that there is some property coming to me." ' ,For the attorney's remarks, though very hasty, have been extremely guarded. "At present, you must excuse me; I have an engagement with my cousin, Miss Tournay," and Bob moves on.

"And afterward?" suggests the attorney.

"Afterward, I have some gentlemen to sup with me at the Orleans Club."

"Can't you give me five minutes there?"

"Yes; I presume I can," remarks the young man; "about twelve o'clock. Are you a member?"

"No," replies Jarvis, the delight of whose life would have been to have had entrée to that home of the young bloods of New Orleans.

"Very well; send up your name, and I'll try and see you. At present—I believe I'm late now. You will please excuse me—though I'm glad to hear you've good news for me. I cannot keep my cousin waiting."

"And the Kentuckian strides rapidly away, leaving Jarvis looking at him and thinking: "From his talk, I should judge he's very anxious to look into that gal's bright eyes. My commission goes up five per cent. !"

According to schedule, however, about midnight Kitson makes his appearance on Charles Street at the portals of the young-blood club of New Orleans of that day, here to receive shock, astonishment, and then—shock again.

On giving his name to the sable servant at the entrance, he is shown into the reception room; but a few moments after, the servitor makes his appearance, holding Jarvis's card in his hand, with a very solemn face and frightened manner, and remarks: "Mistah Covington begs to be excused. He has business of such 'portance dat he can't see yo', sah."

"Why, I've got an appointment with him!" cries the attorney; then suggests, slipping a quarter into the outstretched hand of the club flunkey: "He cannot understand! Tell him it's Mr. Kitson Jarvis, attorney and counselor-at-law and Proctor in Admiralty! Remind him I'm waiting for him!"

"I dahsen't remind him, sah!" remarks the colored functionary. "Mistah La Farge told me not to come into de room agin!"

"Very well. I will wait for him. By the Lord! I'll wait for this buck who thinks more of fun than he does of ducats!" mutters the attorney, and sits there for an hour, glumly cogitating: "The idiot! The dashed fool! The blanked run-away, high-play scapegrace! I suppose he's at poker now, that's the matter with him! He don't guess what I've got to tell him! He doesn't know he's the darnedest fool for luck this side of Canaan!"

So, filled with rage at Covington, the attorney waits until two o'clock in the morning, when that gentleman comes hurriedly down, accompanied by Talliaferro and La Farge. In the hall Jarvis steps out to meet him, but is greeted with these discouraging words: "You'll excuse me; but I can't see you, my dear sir."

Then the young man for an instant leads the attorney aside and whispers: "I would not disclose it to any one else, but perhaps, Mr. Jarvis, I owe an explanation to you, who have waited for me. Not a word to anybody. At present I am engaged in a duel—— Coming, La Farge!"

Bob steps into a waiting carriage with his friends and hurriedly drives off, leaving the lawyer struck down by his awful words, for he is muttering to himself: "If they *kill* him—if they kill *my client!* Holly Jerush! what will become of my commission?"

Then Mr. Kitson Jarvis goes to praying—something he had never done before: "God save him! Don't let his young blood knock him out! Mercy—mercy for *my client!*" but here he begins to meditate on who is Covington's next of kin, contemplating immediate letters to them on the news of his demise.

CHAPTER IX.

JULES DELABORDE, THE FIRE-EATER.

THE news that Mr. Covington has imparted to the attorney is unfortunately true, for events have been running along pretty fast with the Kentuckian since the Monday evening on which he threatened to make a Romeo of himself. Some have been brought about by Monsieur Martineau's extraordinary course; some by his own dashing impetuosity, one or two others by Monsieur La Farge, the Creole exquisite and Louis-iana beau.

The next day, Tuesday, after Mr. Covington had threatened to do his Romeo act, he strolls over in the afternoon to Dauphine Street, thinking he will get tea from the fair hands of his cousin.

Here, to his dismay, he receives word by Mrs. Joyce that Miss Tournay is too indisposed either to see him or to go to the French theatre this evening, as she promised. "Louise excited herself too much yes-terday over the disappointment that would have come to her had it not been for your good offices about her ball dress, dear Mr. Covington," says the chaperone.

"Please give Miss Tournay my—my heartfelt re-grets," mutters Bob; then says, anxiously: "She—she is not *very* ill?"

"Oh, no; she will be well enough to see you to-morrow evening. She left that message for you. You won't forget Wednesday at eight?"

"Forget it?" ejaculates Covington. "Not while my head is on my shoulders!" and going away somewhat cast down in spirits, wonders if his "awful break" about cousinship had anything to do with Miss Tournay's not receiving him.

Therefore this gentleman does not—as per contract with himself—do his "Romeo act" this day, but, getting to his club, kills time with billiards till evening, then sends a box of bonbons, big enough to make a well girl sick, to his invalid charmer, and goes to playing poker to while away the night.

The next day, though it is a difficult matter to keep from the bright eyes that are now running in his imagination, our young gallant strolls from his hotel to the Orleans Club, where, in that establishment which is the headquarters of all the bloods of New Orleans of that day, he contrives to keep his *inamorata* from his mind for three or four hours by dawdling away his time; a portion of it being spent in discussing horseflesh in general and Lexington's chances for next Saturday's race with Colonel Talliaferro, Poindexter, and several other well-known turfmen, and the other portion in company with Monsieur La Farge, who has stepped into the dining room.

Here the two young men discuss one of *maître d'hôtel* Santini's far-famed lunches, the excellence of which is driving the great restaurateurs of New Orleans, Messrs. Victor, Moreau, and Miguel, to despair. In easy conversation over their oysters, crabs, terrapin and game, the young Louisianian tells the Kentuckian of some of the troubles that have come upon him on account of his being on the Invitation Committee for the approaching ball of the Pelican Club.

"You will present my compliments, I hope, to your cousin, Miss Tournay," says the Creole, "and say that I had the honor of leaving my card for her yesterday. It was rather early in the afternoon for a formal call, but my duties on the committee have been so great that they compelled me to take the only opportunity that presented itself. What I had supposed would be one of the most agreeable occupations of my life, trying to make my friends happy by invitations for Thursday evening's *fête*, has become to me at last a matter of annoyance, and in certain respects quite disagreeable."

"Why, I had supposed it would be just the reverse," laughs Covington. "Importuned, petted, and made much of by the ladies for those little cards that are now the most valuable things in the world in their eyes, and delicately requested by your gentlemen friends for similar favors."

"That is my trouble," remarks La Farge. "The invitations have reached their limit, but the people wanting to go to the ball have not. Besides, application has been made to me by parties who cannot be considered eligible to the honor. Some rather distressing affairs have happened with ladies whom we would not invite and yet it was difficult politely to refuse—also one or two serious matters with gentlemen whose applications for entrée we did not regard as worthy of consideration. I'm afraid I've made more enemies than I have friends in the matter. The extreme exclusiveness of the ball has been my difficulty; to dances at the St. Charles nearly everybody goes who wishes ; but the ball of the Pelican Club is a different thing. Even now I expect some trouble with Monsieur Jules Delaborde."

"What! That professional gambler ?" mutters the Kentuckian. "Did he suppose that *he* would obtain entrée?"

"Whether he did or not," replies the Creole, "I am told he has made threats against me because his name has been ignored by the Committee. But you'll excuse me—I see Major McBurney, who wishes to speak to me—probably about some other of these annoyances."

"Certainly!" answers Bob, "only don't forget my supper this evening, eleven o'clock—here!"

"I shall not forget," answers the Creole, and steps over to Major McBurney, who is apparently anxious to see him.

Left by himself, the Kentuckian dawdles over coffee and cigar. The dining-room is gradually becoming deserted, its hum is dying away; voices come to him

from the next table.   Two men are speaking in under-
tones to each other.

"*Nom de Dieu!*" says one man, "I shall insult that
dandy of the old *régime* to-night.   He will not dance
at his Pelican Ball; his carcass shall be adorning the
St. Louis cemetery."

"*Diable!* Don't speak so loud!" whispers the
other.   "I don't owe La Farge any good will myself."

A few moments after, the two leave their table, and
Covington, contriving to turn around, notes that the
one making the threat is Monsieur Jules Delaborde.

Though not particularly acquainted with the man,
he is very well aware that he bears a reputation for
being a dead shot and also a perfect master of the
small sword.   For Delaborde had been *a maître
d'armes* in a French cavalry regiment and has to a
certain extent *fought* himself into society.

Though making some pretensions to style, birth and
breeding, it is rumored Delaborde's living is gained by
a surreptitious connection with a well-known gambling
house of the Rue Royale.   Turning this over in his
mind, Bob knows the matter is a serious one for La
Farge.

These rather morbid considerations of his friend's
chances are broken in upon by Talliaferro joining him
at his table.

"What the dickens is the matter with you, my boy?"
says the genial Colonel.   "You look morose enough
to be in love."

At which Bob gives a tremendous start, but answers:
"It's not the *game* of love I'm thinking of, but the
god of war."

"Humph! You're in trouble with some gentleman?"

"No; but I'm afraid a friend of mine will be." And
Covington, knowing very well the Colonel's reputation
as a past master of the art and etiquette of the duello,
tells him the conversation he has just heard at the
neighboring table.

"Good Lord!" mutters Talliaferro.   "This affair
is a serious one!   That Delaborde is just enough of a
gentleman to make it practically impossible to ignore

a challenge from him. But he is as dead a shot as any man in the pistol gallery, and even more accomplished with the small sword. Still—" here the old gentleman reflects — " I think I may be of advantage to your friend;" then adds: "Look here, my boy! If the difficulty comes to a head, induce La Farge to ask you to be his second."

"I think he intends that; otherwise he would not have spoken to me about it," replies Covington.

"Very well; in that case come immediately to me."

"You think you can be of assistance?"

"If you act as I advise—yes! Only, get word with your man and tell him in case of a difficulty to so deport himself that he *must* be the challenged party."

"That he may select his weapons?"

"Of course! Take care and give your friend this counsel at once!"

"I will!" replies Bob, and a few minutes after, getting chance of word with La Farge, he relates just what he heard at the neighboring table, and gives him Talliaferro's advice.

"Which I will take!" mutters the Creole. "I'm not going to throw away my life if I can help it. Besides—hang it!—I'm a very poor hand with the *coliche-marde*, and between ourselves, by no means a good shot. But just the same," adds the young man, " I will meet any man, big or little, if necessary for the preservation of my good name, the honor of my kindred, or the fair repute of any lady whom I hold in esteem."

"My sentiments, also!" says the Kentuckian. "And if that scoundrel puts you *hors de combat*, he shall have to do with me!"

The two young men's hands clasp as they voice the sentiments of the chivalry of the South and West of that day—mistaken, foolish, bloodthirsty, if you will— but still regarded by them as embodying the highest principles of manhood, courage, and honor.

But thoughts of war are soon knocked out of the Kentuckian's head by a note brought to him from the St. Charles by Mr. Cæsar.

Dainty, perfumed, and bearing evidence of lady's

handicraft, apparently it has been written in a hurry, on a card and under great excitement.   It is:

Wednesday, April 5, 1854.

DEAR BOB :

Monsieur Martineau wishes Nita and me to go to Paris *immediately*.   Please come and see me *instantly*, and give me your advice.

Yours,

LOUISE C. TOURNAY.

P. S.—*I don't want to go.*

Inspecting this, Mr. Covington mutters in dismay: "Go immediately to Paris? Great David! Go to Paris? Not by a jugful! I suppose it's something about that infernal claim Martineau seems so frightened about."

These considerations tend to make Mr. Covington very anxious to do his " Romeo act " this day; a resolution that is perchance quickened by the extreme beauty of the young lady as he walks into the parlor of the Tournay mansion, where he is delighted to find Miss Louise alone.

She has apparently been waiting for him, for she cries: "I knew you'd come as soon as you received my note. You can always be relied upon when I'm in trouble."

"Tell me all about it !" says Bob, eagerly.

"Well, it is very little, but still very important," replies his charmer. "Monsieur Martineau sent for me to-day and told me that he thought it best for my interests for me to leave by direct steamboat for Paris as soon as possible. Nita will join me in the French capital from New York, as soon as word can be sent to her and proper arrangements made."

"Is not this very sudden?" asks the Kentuckian, who now fears the *avocat's* suggestion must have been prompted by the impending claim.

"Yes; just at present it is," replies Miss Louise. "But this is not the first time he has suggested that I

pack my trunks.   Monsieur Martineau advised immediately after my father's death that both my sister and
I should go direct to Paris.   You talk this matter over
with him and tell him that I don't want to go—that I'd
sooner remain here—that I know I shall like New
Orleans society."

"Why don't you speak to him?   You could per-
suade any man!" mutters Covington, as indeed he
thinks she can; Miss Louise looking very persuasive to
him, in a simple white muslin gown.

"But *not* Monsieur Martineau!" replies the young
lady.   "I think he has a horror of my entering society.
Every time I mention ball or ball-dress to him I seem
to give him a fever and ague—chiefly the ague.   Even
now he has sent for Mrs. Joyce, I am sure, to induce
her to use her influence with me to make me pack up
and get away to Paris."

"All right! I'll settle him!" remarks the Kentuckian, complaisantly.

"Will you? Thank you!" answers Louise. "I didn't
mind it once; but—but now' I—*I won't go*—that's all
about it!" and she stamps a little foot.

"And you shan't!" cries Bob, and perchance would
stay longer did not the lateness of the hour make
him hurry to Custom House Street.

Fortunately, the Creole lawyer is in.   He is just dis-
missing a lady from his private office.   Pamela is
coming out with faltering steps and a dazed look on her
prim face.   Meeting the Kentuckian, she gives a sudden and startled "Oh!" and scarce returning his bow,
seems to shudder as she brushes hurriedly past him.

A moment after, Covington is shown in to the Creole
attorney.   Martineau, after shaking hands with him,
remarks: "Mrs. Joyce was here a few moments ago,
on, I imagine, the same errand that brought you.   She
came to tell me that Mademoiselle Tournay wished to
defer her trip to Paris."

"You've struck it!" replies Bob.   "My cousin
Louise is going to have a high old time in New Or-
leans society.   She knows *that!*   She is wild about the
Pelican ball, as what young girl would not be—and
I'm going to see her through with it."   Here the at-
torney's serious face stops him.

"You know as well as I, Monsieur Covington," says Martineau earnestly, "that I only wish to act for the interests of Louise and Nita. These seem to me best guarded by the young ladies living in Paris."

"It is that infernal claim?"

"Yes."

"There's danger of its being set up?"

"I am afraid so. Certain things that have come to me in the last day or two make me think another lawyer has suspicions of the affair. I can put it no more definitely to you at present, but believe me when I tell you, as God is my judge, if that man discovers a secret I have guarded—sometimes, against my own interests—that it will be better that the two girls are away from here. Then no papers could be served upon them; I—I could make a better compromise."

"Well, I'll be equally candid with you," answers Bob. "At present I shall not oppose your wishes in the matter; but certain things may occur that—that may give me the right to dictate in this matter."

"How—how so?" whispers Martineau, in agitated voice.

"I may find I have a claim myself!"

"*Mon Dieu!* What do you mean?" The *avocat* has bounded from his chair.

"Tell you perhaps in a day or two," laughs the Kentuckian. "If so, I shall not permit the young lady we are speaking of to go to Europe. By the by, do you know anything of an attorney here called Kitson Jarvis?"

"Kit—son Jar—vis?" The words come out of the Creole's mouth slowly, his face becoming flushed, then deathly pale.

"Yes, Kitson Jarvis! You don't know anything to his discredit? He can be trusted?" queries Covington, noting the peculiar expression on Martineau's countenance.

"No; I—I know nothing to his discredit."

"Glad to hear that," replies Bob. "I had a note from him to-day, saying that he had discovered a claim to certain property I had in Louisiana. But I will say good day; you do not look well, Monsieur

Martineau. Is it that old trouble you complained of on Sunday evening?" and the Kentucky beau takes his departure.

Gazing at his retreating form, Martineau gives a low, broken sigh, and murmurs: "*Miséricorde! Miséricorde!* The hand has fallen!"

———

CHAPTER X.

PARADISE AND THE PERI.

ABOUT eight o'clock on this evening Mr. Covington, after having achieved an elaborate toilet at the hands of Mr. Cæsar, raps on the door of the Tournay residence, and there is a little tremble in his voice as he asks the answering servant if the ladies are in.

The servitor having shown him into the *salon* and taken his card, the gentleman mutters to himself: "Bob, keep your spunk up!" for this is the evening he has determined to "do the Romeo act." Nothing can stop him now; he is bound to speak before the girl knows she will be dependent upon him, the attorney's conversation this day having impressed him with the idea that the claim that is hanging over the Tournay estate will very shortly be made.

"I must get ahead of that," thinks the generous fellow, as he looks about him and sees, somewhat to his surprise, the room is more brilliantly lighted than usual.

A moment after, he receives a little sensation. Mrs. Joyce comes in to him, her face pale and eyes startled and falters: "Mr. Covington, Louise asked me to—to excuse her to you for—for a few moments. She has a little surprise for you. I think she promised it to you some days ago. This is Wednesday evening—the evening she asked you to let her entertain you. I—I hope you won't be angry with her for keeping you waiting."

"Angry?" cries Bob quite surprised, not so much at these remarks—though the last one seems to him rather curious—but at the manner in which they are given.　Pamela's face and movements are as prim and precise as ever, but there is a nervous flutter in her gestures and a peculiar pleading look in her eyes that somehow make him think she is frightened of him.

This unfortunately is the case.

For Martineau, driven into a corner, has sent for Mrs. Joyce this afternoon and being compelled, has made to her, under Pamela's oath of absolute secrecy, certain revelations that have caused that lady to first think she must be crazy and then wonder if she is alive.

To these he has added: "You are on no account to permit Mr. Covington to take Louise to the Pelican ball to-morrow night."

She now gazes at the young man's smiling face as if he were a mixture of Basilisk and Blue Beard, and as-tonishes him by faltering again: "Yes; you—you will not be angry with Louise," adding, faintly: "Please don't—please don't."

"Don't do what?" asks Bob.

"N—n—nothing!"

"Don't do nothing!　That's bad grammar, Mrs. Joyce," laughs the young man; which is a very unkind observation to make to an ex-schoolmistress.

Then he goes on: "Is anything the matter?"—for the appearance of the lady suggests trouble.　"My heavens, is Louise ill?　Why doesn't she come down? What does she keep me waiting for?"

Remarks that tend to add to the agitation of the chaperone, who says meekly: "No, *please* don't be severe with her; she's getting dressed as quickly as she can.　She is going to amuse you by appearing in the new ball dress—the one you were so kind as to get for her.　At first I opposed it—I didn't think it was quite the proper thing; but finally—I deemed it was best that she should do everything in her power to make you pleased with her, and I said I would come down and talk to you so that you would not be impatient—or angry—or——."

"Oh, yes; I'm a terrible fellow!" cries Bob. "You should see me in a tantrum, Mrs. Joyce.　You isk Mr. Cæsar, my man, if I'm not a wild Injun when I've got the harum scarums!"

These suggestions do not appear to add to the lady's serenity, and she would perhaps make some astounding revelations to Covington in her agitation, did not at this moment a vision of beauty glide in to him that knocks every other consideration out of Mr. Romeo's head.

With a muttered "Great Pocahontas!" Mr. Bob stands looking at Miss Louise, who trips up to him, a little blush upon her face and the excited happiness of a girl who knows that she looks — *her very best*.

"Behold the surprise, Mr. Covington — I mean Cousin Bob — Well I mean Bob — you — you told me you liked that best — " murmurs the young lady, "but I did not know how to entertain you — I have done so little for you and you so much for me about getting Mr. Martineau's consent for this dress, that I thought I would let you have the *first* look at it. Besides," pouts the young lady, "You have seen all my other evening gowns. I have so very few of them; but I hope in a few days to be better off." This last, quite complaisantly.

"By George!" thinks Bob, in astounded self-commune, "If she orders a few more of these clippers from Madame Olympe there won't be much left of that five-thousand-dollar check."

But all the same he is very happy! For his sweetheart — at this moment he has made up his mind he will call her that, and that no other man on earth shall — makes about as pretty a picture as has ever gladdened the eyes of lover.

Before this night he had thought Louise Tournay as graceful a creature as any in the world; but now art has made her ethereal.

The *toilette de bal* — according to the custom of the epoch — is plain as to corsage, which simply outlines a figure that under the Southern sun is no longer immature, but nobly though exquisitely developed. From out the glistening satin of the bodice gleam shoulders, arms, and bosom of purest snow; each graceful contour made warm by budding life, each beauty line made brilliant by vivacious youth; and over all there is the

blushing face and laughing eyes of her he loves. For
the young lady is very happy this evening.

Were it not for the draperies of the costume, perchance Louise might appear too much like breathing
marble; but these, in many falling skirts of softest
gauze, each of some delicate but differing tint, float
from the zone that girdles her lithe waist over the sim-
mering satin of her robe, and as she moves take color-
combinations varying with each pose—all light, all
graceful, and all charming.

Besides, these skirts have a wavy motion as Miss
Beauty glides before him; some trick of modiste Bob
has never seen before.

"Ah! You like it?" laughs the girl, her eyes becoming very happy. Then she cries: "Do you know I
feel light as the breezes—Pamela, play me a polka! and
I'll show him a dancing lesson at Miss Martin's establishment for young ladies."

"Would you like it?" asks Mrs. Joyce, appealingly.

Getting word from Covington that he would like it very
much, she goes meekly to the piano, and to her strains
the young lady cries: " *Bon jour Mesdemoiselles! Attention! Position!* " imitating a French dancing-master.
" Mademoiselle Tournay, pray keep ze head erect! Remember your foots must point not in—'*Voilà! Un—deux
—trois—Jêté! Assemblez!*'" and the girl gives the daz-
zled Bob a most coquettish and alluring courtesy, next
ejaculates: "Presto, Mrs. Joyce! Don't play the Dead
March from Saul; make it a lively polka, *à la Julien!*"
Then, catching the rhythm of the merry air, Louise
dances with all her soul before Mr. Covington's fas
cinated eyes.

But as Mr. Bob looks on, his brows slowly contract!

The dress, which has just arrived from Paris, con-
tains the latest novelty—a hint of the coming crinoline
that is just becoming the rage of woman, the scoff, yet
the allurement of man. This dazzling ball gown, being
one of the earliest imported, is the first Mr. Covington's
eyes have ever seen; and he does not like crinoline effects.

The graceful wavy movement of her flying skirts
attracts   his   notice,   there   gleams   a   sight   very

pretty, but somewhat disturbing to Mr. Bob; Louise's fairy feet, in satin slippers, and gracefully moulded ankles, dazzling and rounded, in tightest silken web, so light that the white skin gleams beneath, appear too often and too generously—not for his own delight; but as he looks he thinks: "This will be for the delectation of other admirers of beauty to-morrow evening."

And this young man has a jealous soul.

"Don't you think it's very beautiful? Don't you think it's very becoming? Don't you think I'll look very well in my *toilette de bal?*" asks the young lady, eager for his praise.

To this Mr. Covington answers: "Yes; you are very beautiful in it—too beautiful;" then adds, severely: "But it is too much of a ballet costume for you to wear to-morrow evening."

"Not wear it at the Pelican?" cries the girl, scarce believing her ears.

"Certainly *not!* I do not think it is quite the proper thing for a young lady."

"Not the *proper* thing? Goodness! It is the last conceit! This is a duplicate of one the Comtesse de Soissons wore at the last ball at the Tuileries. It created a *sensation!*"

"Too much of one, I expect. But it *won't* create a sensation at the Pelican. You'll—you'll excuse me— you cannot wear it there."

"And who will prevent me?" The young lady's tone is icy and haughty.

Here Mrs. Joyce suddenly rises from the piano shuddering: "Oh don't—*don't* contradict him, Louise! DON'T! He might be angry with you."

But this pours anything but oil upon the troubled waters. "Angry with *me?*" cries the girl, her eyes dazzling, her cheeks red. "It is I who should be angry with him. Because—I have permitted him the intimacy of cousinship and because he has been very good to me—I'll admit that—and obtained this dress for me through his influence with Monsieur Martineau, and because—I suppose he's my only gentleman relative on earth, he assumes an authority I will not permit."

"I am sure your trustee would agree with me in the matter," suggests Covington, glumly.

"Yes; Monsieur Martineau does not wish her to go to the ball!" cries Mrs. Joyce.

Then the storm breaks forth!

"Monsieur Martineau doesn't *wish* me to go to the ball!" sneers the young lady, her piquant nose very high in the air; then says haughtily: "Pish for Monsieur Martineau! I am my own mistress! I do what I like! You hear me—I DO WHAT I LIKE! I go to the ball in this dress and in no other, Mr. Covington—NO OTHER!"

"Under these circumstances—I shall not take you," mutters the young man, biting his moustache grimly.

"You won't take me?" Her dainty nose is higher in the air, her coral lip curls in disdain. "I believe there are other gallants in New Orleans. Monsieur La Farge—he left his card yesterday—I'm sure he would accompany Mrs. Joyce and me. Yes, and glad of the chance, even with this *outré* ballet ball-dress. Quick, Mrs. Joyce! A note to Monsieur La Farge!"

But something in the young gentleman's face stops the young lady here. Mr. Covington, says: "I beg you will not write Monsieur La Farge. It would not be the proper etiquette of Creole society for a gentleman who knows you so slightly to accompany you to a public function, notwithstanding you have a chaperone."

"And how will you stop it, Cousin Bob?" jeers Miss Louise, mockingly.

Then Mrs. Joyce gets sight of Mr. Blue Beard in a tantrum, and it makes her shudder.

"How?" says the young man, his voice very low, and very deliberate. "How? In case La Farge does not accede to my view of the proper etiquette of the transaction, I shall tell him that though he is my very good friend I will prevent his taking you to the ball to-morrow *night*, by meeting him on the dueling ground of New Orleans to-morrow *afternoon*."

"You would—risk—your life?" gasps Pamela.

"To keep her name in high respect? Yes!" answers Bob, and he points to Miss Beauty, who is gazing at him with blazing, brilliant eyes.

Then the nobility of the girl flashes up! "You would do this for *me?*" she falters—and is very much pleased to find he would.

"Do it?" cries the Kentuckian, brushing the curls back from his broad forehead. "Do it? I'd do it like a quarter-horse! Is not your good repute dearer to me than my own honor?"

"You—you must be right," shudders Louise, or you would not look so awful and so noble!" then adds impulsively: "Forgive me, Cousin Bob!" next murmurs piteously, "The Pelican ball is a thing of the past for me. Pamela, we need not have thought so much of our dresses for the occasion." And the girl begins to look like a Peri outside the gate of Paradise; for this *fête* has been very much to her, like the opening of the portals of social Heaven, and it is very bitter to see them close, even though Archangel Bob seals them up.

But, noting the tears of despairing loveliness in his sweetheart's eyes, Mr. Covington throws out the white flag and mutters: "My God! You're crying! Forgive me! Go to the ball! Go to *fifty balls*, but—but *don't cry!*"

"I can't. I have got no dress!" is the despairing moan.

"Go to the ball! Ransack every modiste in New Orleans! Find as beautiful a gown as you desire! But don't wear—this thing with the jigging skirts."

"But Monsieur Martineau will object to the expense. He scolded me last time," murmurs Louise, archly, brushing the pearls from her eyes and pouting very prettily.

"It will be *my* affair to arrange that matter for you with your trustee. If *he* says no, come to *me!* From now on I will look after your finances," answers Bob, thinking of the claim to the Tournay estates.

"Oh, what a cousin you are!" cries Louise, suddenly. "You've known me but four days, and now you dominate the household and twist me around your finger." And the young lady droops her eyes, turns away her head, and, sitting at the piano, plays abstractedly, with one white hand, the air of a little Creole love song.

"Dominate the household? That's a thundering fine idea!" remarks Bob. "Apropos of that, Mrs. Joyce, was not Miss Louise to give me a cup of tea this evening? Could not you kindly arrange for it?"

"Yes, sir," replies that lady, meekly, and goes away, shuddering: "He must *know!* Oh, Heaven, will he tell her *now?*"

"No, don't run after her," whispers Covington, for Louise has started up.

"Wouldn't you like me to dance for you again?" says the girl uneasily.

"Very much; but not *now!*"

"Then I'll play for you."

"No music," mutters the young man. "Here! Sit beside me on the sofa."

"You wish me to sit—*there?*" falters Louise.

"Yes; right beside me."

"Oh, what a tyrant you are! There! What do you want next?" but this ends in a subdued but plaintive scream.

"You!" whispers Bob, coming to his Romeo act with a plunge, and gathering in all this beauty, laces, and gauzes, straight to his heart. "You! Your love! Your hand in mine through life—your heart beating against mine through life—you to call me husband; I to call you wife. That's what I want of YOU !"

"O—o—h!" falters the girl, fluttering to get away.

"No, you don't—never out of my arms—till you have spoken."

"What would—you have me—say?" and her blushing face is hid upon his stalwart shoulder.

"I love you, Bob!"

"I—love—you," comes faintly from the buried head.

"And now," says the Kentuckian, mad with rapture, "I have never kissed you as a cousin."

"No; you've been very unkind to me," falters the girl.

"By the Lord Harry! You shall never accuse me of that again! Let me look at your eyes."

"I can't. I'm crying."

"Crying?"

"Yes; but—but happy tears. Cousin Bob—no I

forgot you don't like that. Oh goodness! *Mon Dieu!* Bob—how—how impetuous you are!"

"Now, by Heavens! you'll never accuse me again, Miss, of not kissing you!" whispers the enraptured Romeo, looking into his Juliet's lovely face.

But after a little the girl starts from him and remarks roguishly: "This is not Creole etiquette! You should bow before me and say: 'Mademoiselle, may I have the honor of requesting your hand from Monsieur Martineau, your trustee?'"

"No; but this is what I *will* tell Martineau," cries Bob, striding up to his will-o'-the-wisp and gathering her in once more. "This girl I love doesn't go running over to Paris, without me by her side. And that will take place after we have clasped hands in Christ Church up on Canal Street, in not over a month from now."

"A month? So soon?" falters his *fiancée*, Mr. Covington's wooing seeming to her very rapid and impetuous; though perchance this makes him all the more dear to her.

"Of course! Short engagements—long marriages! Then we run away to Paris, after your sister. You don't object to Paris on general principles? No girl does!"

"No," whispers his sweetheart, bashfully. "I should love Paris. But I did not want to go there after—after——"

"After what?"

"After I had seen you!" and the girl puts her fair arms round his neck and her coral lips up to his, trustingly, lovingly, and he receives what he afterward calls "an angel kiss." But it is not—though as near it as earthly mortals get; for it is the first outpouring of a girl's pure heart.

So it comes to pass that Mrs. Joyce returning, finds the two seated at antipodal ends of the sofa and conversing very confusedly. A few minutes after, Mr. Covington, rising to take his leave, says: "Don't forget a new ball dress for to-morrow evening!" and so goes away, the happiest young blood in New Orleans.

A few seconds after, the young lady, turning to

her chaperone, laughs: "What *is* the matter with this toilette?" and shakes the skirts out, inspecting it with critical eyes.

"Why, don't you know?" returns the ex-schoolmistress, blushing.

"No. I have been wondering what Bob meant—but didn't dare to ask him."

"Very well; just fly round a few times in front of that mirror, and look at yourself."

Which Miss Tournay does, and gazing upon her reflected self suddenly cries: "Oh, heavens and earth! No wonder! I had no idea! I was like a ballet girl."

"Pretty near it," remarks Mrs. Joyce, grimly.

"Well," says the young lady, blushing divinely. "I'm glad it was no worse."

"No *worse!* — how do you mean?"

"Well, I mean—Oh well—Oh, Mrs. Joyce, I'm the happiest girl on earth!"

"Happiest girl?"

"Yes. A month from now I marry my cousin Bob, in Christ Church. Isn't that joy enough for one girl?"

And she runs away, leaving the matron gazing after her with frightened face and muttering with very pale lips: "My God!"

An exclamation that means very strong emotion with women of Mrs. Joyce's prim propriety.

CHAPTER XI.

THE DUEL BEHIND THE CEMETERY.

FROM this interview of love Bob goes away, too happy to quarrel with any one, and valuing his life very much more than he did an hour before. Sweet kisses are on his lips, and he wants a great many more of them before he dies. The world looks very pleasant to him as he comes in at the open portals of the Orleans Club.

Here in a private room are grouped a number of the best known men about town—Messrs. Poindexter and

Zyminski, of turf fame; Baldwin, of Mississippi, celebrated for his anecdotes; young Soulé, La Farge, and
Martigny, of Creole blood; also, Colonel Talliaferro of
his own State. These, with half-a-dozen others—
kindred spirits, jovial souls, and dashing fellows—
make up the party that Mr. Covington has the pleasure
of entertaining this evening.

A moment later and they are seated at one of Santini's exquisite suppers, magnificently served on a flower-
bedecked table covered with handsome china and cut-
glass, La Farge, to whom the supper is practically
given, occupying a chair on one side of Bob and
Talliaferro one on the other.

"You've heard nothing more of Delaborde?" whispers the Kentuckian to the Creole.

"Not yet," answers the New Orleans exquisite,
"but I doubtless shall soon. At present, I am only
thinking of your hospitality."

So are the rest—for oysters, fish, game, and wines
of rare vintage, together with much sparkling Moselle
and champagne, engross the attention of the *bons
vivants*.

It is nearly twelve o'clock. The conversation is becoming hilarious. Repartee, badinage and good stories
float about, mingled now with the fumes of the finest
Havanas, luxuries much more common at that day in
the United States than at present under our new revenue laws.

Baldwin has just told his great anecdote of the
Knoxville exquisite, who visited New Orleans and ate
pineapple out of his finger-bowl in the dining-room of
the St. Charles Hotel, to such guffaws of waiters and
merriment of guests as made him fly the town. And a
young doctor has related the well-known story of
"Cupping on the Sternum."

The laughter at this has hardly finished when a card
is brought to La Farge.

"Very well," replies the young Louisianian. "Tell
him I will be down to see him in a minute," and he
holds the card for Covington to see.

But catching sight of the name before the servant
has left the room, Talliaferro cries: "Hi, boy! Stop!"

and turning to La Farge, whispers: "Permit me to suggest that you do not go down unaccompanied; or better still, see him here."

"I think you're right," answers the Creole, and calls to the waiter: "Tell Monsieur Delaborde I will see him in this room."

Then, the servitor having gone on his errand, the Colonel whispers: "Mr. Covington delivered my advice to you? You will pardon the liberty I, who am a man of more experience than you, took in sending it. But, if what my friend Bob says is true, for your own protection, my dear young man, follow my advice. Be sure and force this fire-eater to challenge *you*! Don't throw away a chance!" To this he adds some deft advice, catching which Mr. Covington bursts out laughing.

A moment later Jules Delaborde, rigged up in the extreme of fashion, enters the apartment and closes the door. If there had been any doubt as to the fire-eater's hostility of intention his countenance destroys it, for he has a very nasty scowl upon his face as he gazes across the table at the young Creole.

"I have called to see you, Monsieur La Farge," says the man, "to demand of you here, in the presence of your friends, how you have dared to erase my name from the invitation list of the Pelican Club."

His manner and voice have such omen in them that the rest of the party, who have paid very little attention to the card incident, being laughing and talking among themselves, swing round in their chairs and gaze at him astonished.

"Dared!" remarks La Farge, and Covington notes the young man's tone though very low and quiet is very steady—"to erase your name from the invitation list of the Pelican Club? I can answer that very quickly. Your name, Monsieur Delaborde, never was on the invitation list of the Pelican Club. The Pelican Club doesn't invite *niggers!*"

There is a shout of amazement, almost horror, at this, the most atrocious insult that in those days and that city, could be put upon a man. Then there is a little laugh, as unfortunately the dark, crisp hair and black waxed bristling moustache of the French fire-eater as he scowls about, give some color to the Creole's assertion.

"*Nigger?*" shrieks Delaborde. "*Sacré!* you call me 'NIGGER?'" And he would advance upon the Louisianian.

"But Talliaferro cries: "Throw the fellow out!" and probably not caring to have their conviviality disturbed, and at all events acting upon his commands, the rest of the party spring up, seize and expel the bellicose and frantic Delaborde from the apartment.

But as he disappears he grinds out between his white teeth: "*Nom de Dieu!* For this, Henri La Farge, I must have your heart's blood!"

"By the Lord Harry!" remarks Talliaferro complaisantly, "now he'll have to challenge *you*. If he doesn't, Monsieur Fire-eater can never enter a club-room or parlor in New Orleans again."

As for the rest, they sit down to their wine and cigars once more, though Soulé whispers to the gentleman next him: "I don't think La Farge can avoid meeting the fellow, however; there's no proof of what Henri said."

This also seems to be the Creole's idea of the matter, for a very few minutes after, when a card is brought up bearing the name of Monsieur Albert Montant, representing Monsieur Jules Delaborde, La Farge steps out to meet the gentleman and refers him to Mr. Covington, who will act for him in the matter.

There is no talk of compromise between the seconds; the insult has been so flagrant. Mr. Covington accepts the challenge on behalf of his principal, and, acting upon Talliaferro's advice, immediately names sabres as the weapons; time, six o'clock the coming morning; ground, just beyond the old St. Louis Cemetery.

"Sabres?" mutters the fire-eater's second. "They are curious weapons."

"But within the strict letter of the Code," replies the Kentuckian; "and, representing the challenged party, absolutely in our discretion."

"Very well," returns the representative of Delaborde. "Though had we not better say *colichemardes* or pistols?"

"Neither!" answers Bob. "Sabres!" And this matter being arranged, he returns to the supper-room, where he, Talliaferro and La Farge go into consultation about the matter. It is during this time that Mr. Jarvis's card being brought up to him, the attorney receives the intimation that Covington is too busy to see him, even on business.

Likewise also when they come down to drive to Colonel Talliaferro's house to get the weapons and make further preparation, though intercepted in the hallway by Jarvis, Bob gives him the answer that drives Kitson to such anxiety as to his client's safety.

For Covington does not think of property now; he is thinking of saving his friend's life, which Talliaferro and he both conclude will not be a very easy matter, as they soon discover that La Farge knows nothing about any weapon whatsoever.

"How any man could have lived in the South, and be as ignorant as you, is more than I can understand," growls the colonel, shaking his head. "A man that walks on gunpowder down here, as you Creoles do, ought at least to be able to fire it off."

Finally, he says: "I think here's your only chance. Fight him as Skerritt* did the fencing master in Texas; that's the reason I chose sabres!" And he tells him about the duel that had made that young Englishman famous in the Southwest, when he had met a French *maître d'armes* and cut him down in twenty seconds. "You know nothing about weapons: that's your advantage, perhaps. Assume the upper guard—so!" the colonel explains: "Yes; do it in that awkward way. He'll see you don't know anything about the weapon; and think he has an easy thing of it; he'll make the right cut, which is utterly unprotected by your guard. Then just jump aside one foot—you're light on your feet—

---

*This duel, fought by a young Englishman in Texas, with a French *maître d'armes*, was a matter of notoriety at that time. This gentleman, having planted his opponent in the soil of the Lone Star State, lived afterward in San Francisco, and became so famous on account of this singular and sanguinary affair, that he was offered the position of second in command of the Walker filibustering expedition to Nicaragua.—ED.

with your left hand grab his weapon!—run it under your arm—and give him your point straight in the stomach!—perform the hari-kari on him—don't trouble yourself about his heart or his lungs, just rip him up! No—darn it!—Don't rehearse! You'll get to doing it too well," continues Talliaferro, "and he'll perhaps guess your little game. Then, mark me!—you'll have no more chance with this instructor of French cavalry than a 'possum with a nigger. Take a cup of .coffee and a glass of cognac. I should not advise the liquor if you were to use pistols; but activity is more important than accuracy in what is ahead of you this morning, young man. Now, good-bye, boys, and God bless you!"

Then he whispers in Covington's ear: "Take a couple of revolvers. Don't forget that, in case of any trouble with the second, because this is a rather *outré* performance on the field of honor, though perfectly correct. You know I would not counsel anything else. Do the best you can for La Farge; remember he has a mother who loves him."

"I'd do that, without," replies the Kentuckian, and turns to follow his friend who is already in the carriage.

But Talliaferro motions him to stay, and adds: "If La Farge does his work right his opponent is sure to die; so both of you had better get out of New Orleans for a few weeks."

"But the Louisiana Legislature repealed the law against dueling," mutters Covington, "three years ago."

"But they have not repealed the law against homicide. A wounded opponent would be a matter of little moment; but a slain one——Well, even that will blow over in a few weeks. Still, in case of Delaborde's death, both you young men had better leave town for a few days."

"What! and miss the Pelican ball?"

"Shucks! you would not dance at it. You might do a *pas seul* on the floor of the jail over there; though, probably they would bail you out. Still, you'd better be away."

"I presume you're right," says the Kentuckian very

glumly; absence from the young lady on Dauphine Street not seeming pleasant to him at this moment.

The sun is just rising on New Orleans as La Farge and his second, accompanied by a surgeon, arrive at the old dueling ground behind the St. Louis Cemetery, the place on which Creole youth have been accustomed to report themselves about this hour in the morning with their *colichemardes* or small swords and spit each other for the many insults that chanced to pass in that fiery society, when treading on a gentleman's corns sometimes produced serious results.

Here they are promptly met by *Messieurs* Delaborde and Montant, accompanied also by another gentleman who carries a case of surgical instruments.

Both parties being apparently anxious to get to work, the affair is settled in a short five minutes.

The weapons are measured, positions given, Covington looking out that his man does not get more than half the sun; in fact taking note of the direction of that luminary, he succeeds in giving Delaborde a little the most of it in his eyes and furthermore whispers to La Farge to edge still farther to the left and give his opponent a little more of the sun's rays.

"Of course you can't do it for more than a few seconds," he says, "after that, this master of fence will move you about the field at his pleasure. Remember, you must settle it at once or it goes against you!" and he wrings La Farge's hand.

"I understand," mutters the young man, and Covington is delighted to notice that his principal is very alert, yet as cool and collected this morning as he was at the supper table of the evening before.

"I think he'll perhaps do the trick," cogitates Covington, grimly. "La Farge comes of a fighting race, even if he does not know how to fight."

A moment later, the men are in position. As the Creole puts up his guard, Bob sees his opponent sneer and a little hope comes to him that Delaborde will think it a very easy matter.

This he apparently does, for this is what Covington sees:

Two quick, sharp feints, and then the expert's sabre

flashes in the air to cut the light-limbed Creole down. But, even as the blow descends upon him, he sees La Farge make a quick move to the right, dodge the cut, grab the naked blade in his left hand and guide it under his arm; then giving point with his own weapon, spring straight at the expert's abdomen. Then Laborde is lying on the ground, gasping faintly: "*Assassiné!* He held my blade!"

"It was not fair!" cries his second, coming up menacingly toward La Farge.

"Perfectly fair!" says Covington, stepping in front of his principal. "The practice has been recognized by the Code for a hundred years, ever since men who could not fence have been challenged by men who could. Declare this *en regle*, Monsieur Montant, or step off ten paces with me! I have here two revolvers. I won't take my man from the field branded as you would brand him! Announce you are satisfied, or take your distance!" The Kentuckian produces two murderous looking weapons.

To this, Montant, after a moment's consideration, replies: "I spoke in the heat of the moment. Upon consideration, I remember the affairs of O'Brien and Skerritt. I believe you are right, sir. I am satisfied."

Meantime, the two surgeons have been at work on the combatants; one bending over Delaborde, who lies upon the ground with no chance of recovery; the other binding up La Farge's left hand, some of the fingers of which have been cut to the bone, also a slight wound in the extreme point of his left shoulder, for he had not been quick enough to save himself entirely from the fencing master's cut.

A moment after, Covington is assisting Henri to the carriage, for his friend has lost considerable blood. Suddenly the young Creole remarks:

"We're dogged! Who is this intercepting us?"

And Covington bursts out laughing: "By Jove! It's my attorney!"

For Mr. Kitson Jarvis, unable to restrain his anxieties, has followed his precious client in a cab and hovered around and kept watch over him all this night, at Talliaferro's and, afterward pursuing him to the field of honor, has chuckled delightedly when he finds his man was not a principal in the affair.

Jarvis now says: "I *must* see you, Mr. Covington!"

"Impossible! We'll have to get out of town! That man is dying over there!"

"Well, homicide ain't much in this place. You'll be all right in a few weeks. I know the sentiment here."

"Yes; but I leave on the first boat for Louisville," replies Covington. "Now I must get my man away."

"What boat are you going on?"

"The first one that sails."

"That's the *Eclipse!* She starts at nine this morning," says Jarvis. "I know all about the river."

"Very well. If you want to talk to me, meet me at the boat. At present I must get my friend home;" and putting La Farge into his carriage, the duelists drive away.

So it comes to pass that Monsieur Martineau receives a shock this morning, for he has scarcely dressed before the Kentuckian is shown into his breakfast-room.

"I've got to leave town," remarks Covington, hurriedly. "There was a duel about the invitations to the Pelican Ball."

"*Mon Dieu!* As I feared!" mutters the *avocat* with a frightened face.

"What! Did you know of Delaborde, the fire-eater's, intention to insult La Farge?"

"La Farge?"

"Yes, it wasn't I who killed the man."

"Oh, it was Monsieur La Farge," mutters the lawyer. "I had feared—— Then why do you have to go?"

"I was the second, and La Farge killed his man."

"Ah! Then you *had* better leave for a few weeks!" And Martineau's tone becomes easy. A moment after, his eye brightens. In the Kentuckian's absence he sees at least a respite from the fearful embarrassments that have been upon him. Covington away, Mademoiselle Louise can hardly go to the Pelican ball. Besides, this young man, on his travels, may be useful in another manner.

The *avocat* becomes now quick, brisk, and alert. He says: "You are going to Louisville? You can do me, and also Miss Louise, a great service. Continue your journey as far as New York. That will not be difficult. A fast steamboat up the Ohio to Wheeling or Pittsburgh, a short stage over the mountains, and then you have the railway."

"And in New York, what then ?"

"Here is a check for two thousand dollars," remarks the attorney, filling one out. Handing it to the Kentuckian, he continues: "With this money pay all necessary expenses of Mademoiselle Nita at Miss Martin's boarding-school; then obtain passage for her for Paris, where the child will be placed in the *Convent de Dames du Sacré Cœur.*"

"But Miss Martin may not recognize a cousin's authority."

"My messenger will meet you at the boat with the necessary credentials to Miss Martin, also a letter to my agent in Paris, who will make all arrangements about the young lady. The schoolmistress will obtain a lady to take Nita to Paris; the child is too young to travel alone. Now you will not have more than time to get ready and take the boat."

"By George! you're right!" ejaculates the Kentuckian, who, looking at his watch discovers that it is now a quarter past eight, and he has another and much more important adieu to make. But this puts another matter into his head, and he says, even as he leaves the apartment: "Yes; it will be best for Miss Nita to go to Paris direct, especially as Louise will remain here. But good-bye—I have no time to lose."

And though the lawyer would call him back for further explanation, the young man hurries away, remarking to himself: "Holy Poker! I forgot to tell him *the news*. But Louise can tell Martineau her own story, if she is not too bashful. Any way, I have no time for explanation."

For Mr. Covington is now in a great hurry. Jumping into the cab that has been waiting for him, he drives along Dauphine Street at a tearing pace.

At the Tournay house he fortunately finds his sweetheart ready to see him, but greatly agitated, Mr. Cæsar having preceded his master with a note; that sable and voluble valet's inaccurate explanations of the duel having created consternation in Louise's mind.

Even as he enters her *salon* the young lady, hastily arrayed in pretty morning robe, comes hurriedly to meet him. From out its floating sleeves two white and tender arms fly round his neck; two teary eyes look into his; two trembling lips whisper: "*Dieu merci!* You have escaped alive! But still you have to fly. You killed—your friend—La Farge in mortal combat?"

To this Bob listens, astounded, then cries: "Who told you that?"

"Your man Cæsar. He said you had stabbed La Farge to death with a sword and were now flying the country. He knew it, because when you came in and told him to pack for his life, you had blood upon your shirt."

"Yes. From assisting in binding La Farge's hand—that's where the blood came from." Then Covington bursts out, angrily: "That nigger-brain! To frighten you with such a yarn!" next adds gloomily: "It's bad enough as it is. I was La Farge's second in a meeting he had with the fire-eater, Delaborde. La Farge killed his man, and our friends think it best, as the duel had a fatal ending, that we both leave New Orleans for a little time."

"How long?" whispers his sweetheart, faintly.

"Well—perhaps a month—until the matter has slipped over. It doesn't amount to a great deal, but I'm afraid we'll have to miss the Pelican ball."

"The Pelican ball?" *You*—you will be away from me," and the girl is round his neck once more.

"Well, I would have had to leave in a few days, any way. You see, I've certain arrangements to make up in Kentucky—matters to settle, so I can stay here until after our wedding——"

"Oh! Bob!"

"Yes! Arrange my house so that I can bring a bride to it! Besides, I've a little errand for Martineau in New York; he thinks it well your sister should go to Paris at once. I agree with him. There's no need of her waiting to accompany us; three would be too big a honeymoon crowd.   We'll run over to Paris and see Nita, together!"

"Delightful!"

"And do the French capital!   Oh, this wedding-trip of ours, Louise, is going to be a very dandy affair!"

"What do I care where we go—what we do—so long as—as——"

"As what—sweetheart?"

"As we are together!"

"Great Cupid! I must kiss you for that!" whispers Covington.

"Of course! I thought you would, my Bob," says Miss Louise, looking archly through her tears; and finally getting her lips to herself once more, goes to making "my Bob" very happy, giving him some bashfully entrancing evidences of the love that is in her fair young soul as she murmurs trustingly, innocently: "I prayed last night to God that I might make you as happy as—as you have made me."

"Prayed!—when I was scheming to kill!   My heaven!   I'm not worthy of you!   But——"

"Oh my Heaven! you're—you're going away!" and the girl, giving him a despairing glance that sets him on fire, the two go into a combination rapture of joy and sorrow—of joy, for they love; of sorrow, for they must part.   Then Louise cries, faintly and suddenly: "Not *yet!*   Don't leave me YET!"

"I must!   I shall miss the boat.   Remember it's only for a few weeks; and then—Christ Church— the minister—rice and old slippers, and away we go *together!*   Don't forget my New York address, St. Nicholas Hotel.   And now your dear little third finger, left hand!"

"My mercy!—What *are* you doing?—Kissing my fingers so!"

"Putting on the engagement ring, of course."

"Oh, Bob!—Good Heavens, you—are—going!"

"Yes."

So with a long, last, good-bye kiss he runs down into the courtyard and jumps into his cab; and, looking back as he drives away, sees fluttering from the balcony a little handkerchief of lace.

A moment after, this is wet with tears—happy ones! Looking at the sparkling thing on her finger, the girl kisses it very tenderly, and murmurs: "My Bob!" then bursts into the dining-room, where Mrs. Joyce, who apparently has not cared to meet Mr. Covington this morning, is seated over her breakfast. Flashing the bauble under the ex-schoolmistress's eyes, Louise cries: "Engagement ring! And now *trousseau!*—TROUS-SEAU!" for the joy of shopping, as well as the joy of love, is in her soul.

At these words of happy girlhood Pamela springs up, and, gazing with affrighted eyes upon Bob's souvenir, falters: "It—it is very pretty;" then goes away by herself, and commences to tremble and cry—this stern old Yankee schoolmistress.

Arriving at the levee Bob boards his steamer, that is puffing black smoke from her two big funnels, to find he has scarce five minutes before the gangplank will be pulled in, but has plenty of business awaiting him. One of Monsieur Martineau's clerks comes hurriedly on board after him, and gives him two letters of introduction for himself; one of them to Miss Martin, the New York schoolmistress; another to Miss Nita, his cousin; also one to be given to that young lady herself to present to Monsieur Commenfaut, 35 Rue Lafitte, Martineau's correspondent in Paris.

The clerk has hardly presented these and gone away before Kitson Jarvis comes down, bringing with him the extraordinary creature that Covington had tipped upon the races; the one who had handed him his card at the field of Chalmette. The attorney, who is out of breath, remarks: "I picked up this notary and brought him with me. I want you to sign some documents before you leave; they are of vital import-ance."

"Let me read them first," says the Kentuckian.

"You have hardly time."

"Well, I read *first*, any way!"

Looking over them, Covington discovers that they are both very brief. One is an agreement to pay Mr. Kitson Jarvis ten per cent. of any properties he may recover for him that may come to him through his mother, Isabel Laurey Covington, *née* Isabel Laurey Tournay.

"That's a reasonable price, seeing, without me you would never have known anything about the property," remarks Jarvis, eagerly.

"Yes; I think under the circumstances it is. It's only ten per cent. of what you *get*," returns Bob, who is generally pretty easy and liberal in money matters. "You are to bear all expenses of the suit, I see."

"Yes; that will be easy. They won't come high," adds Kitson.

"And this other," continues Covington, "is a power of attorney from me to you, to bring all necessary action in the matter in the courts of this State or the United States to enforce my claims, and also gives you power of attorney during my absence to hold any money you may recover for me, subject to my order, in the Bank of Louisiana, where said funds are to be deposited."

"Yes; subject to your own personal check—not to mine," says the lawyer. "You see I can't get away with any of it. I have protected you in the matter thoroughly."

"Also," reads Mr. Covington, "to hold for me, subject to my order, any property, real or otherwise, you may recover. That's all right, I guess!" Then he asks: "What is this property?"

"Couldn't tell that, till you've signed these papers. I had too much trouble nosing out the goods to let another counsel in to take half my commission. Tell you when you've signed."

"All right," answers Covington, after a second's hasty thought, for the time is very short now.

They withdraw to the cabin, where the Kentuckian places his signature to both documents.

"These will require a notary's acknowledgment," remarks Kitson. "Just put your seal on it, old man," he says to the weazened individual at his side.

"That's the allfiredest curious notary you've got. That's my race-course tipster," laughs Bob.

"Well, he's all right. I picked him up in a dickens of a hurry, on Front Street, on my way down."

"Monsieur, I am perfectly *en regle*, perfectly legal. My attestation and stamp are as good as anybody's," asserts the dried-up old man, and puts his signature and seal upon the two papers.

"Now, where can I communicate with you, Mr. Covington?" asks the lawyer.

"St. Nicholas Hotel, New York."

But here the notary interjects suddenly, "Please, your—your last information about the horse-race, Monsieur Covington? The Alabamians and Louisianians and the people down here tell me that Lecomte has a good show with a light track."

"Then I'll probably not lose much money by going away," replies the Kentuckian. "By the by, what is the amount of property that you expect to pick up for me here? Five hundred dollars? Eh, Mr. Jarvis?" he cries jocularly. For the attorney, having got the papers in his pocket, is making a hurried rush for the levee, as the cry is now: "All ashore!"

"About two hundred and fifty thousand dollars!" yells back Jarvis, and flies over the gang plank, which is just being drawn in.

Then the boat shoots out into the river, having on its deck an astounded young man, who is muttering: "Two hundred and fifty thousand dollars! Great snakes! Whoop! If I get it what a wedding spree Louise and I will have. Ju-peter! My darling and I can do the grand on that!"

CHAPTER XII.

POUSSIN THE NOTARY.

COMING from his hurried interview with Covington, Jarvis, in the privacy of his office, goes to chuckling over the papers he has received from the Kentuckian, remarking: "I'm almost ready now to give Martineau hot shot. Just one or two more *leetle* things, and all the Tournay estates, goods, chattels, live stock "—he chuckles horribly over the last item—" will be in my hands, to turn over to my client when he comes back after that duello affair blows over. I reckon I'll get the evidence I want this morning. That man I sent to La Fourche should be here to-day, Thursday, sure as boilers will burst."

In this Mr. Kitson's predictions proved correct. His agent sent to search the records comes in late in the afternoon, but brings partial disappointment with him. No record of renunciation of community of gains by Eulalie Camila is in evidence in La Fourche parish, yet he has been unable to discover the old notary Faval Bigore Poussin, the people there stating that the man had removed to New Orleans about three years before; and some of them think him dead, he being very old, dried up, and weazened at the time he left Guidrys.

Jarvis's agent, however, brings a description of Poussin, stating that though French on his father's side, he was Spanish on his mother's side and had lived at Guidrys for nearly forty years. Furthermore, Faval Bigore Poussin was an inveterate gambler, and had dissipated a fortune backing every cock-fight and every horse-race held in the district.

"Just the man to aid the aristocratic, dreaming, poetic, romantic Tournay in his social deception," cogitates the bustling attorney, though he makes a wry face over the fact that the man whose affidavit he wants is probably dead.

His face is still longer when, after inquiry from Pierre Larost, he finds that gentleman knows nothing about any one of the name of Faval Bigore Poussin. Queries among the legal profession also give no further revelation.

"Poussin, the notary, is apparently not in New Orleans, unless he is in one of the cemeteries," cogitates Kitson, his face growing long as he thinks of this alternative, for Poussin's affidavit is necessary to a perfect case, and some information which has been brought him by his alert clerk, Cotain, tells him speedy action is vital.

From the moment the news had come that Poussin had left Guidrys to live in New Orleans, Cotain, under his master's instructions, has been trying to get track of the notary. He has made his inquiries chiefly in the offices of lawyers who would be apt to require the services of such a functionary.

Monsieur Cotain now comes in to make further report. He says: "I have inquired of a sufficient number of lawyers to be reasonably sure that Poussin is not known to the profession, certainly not to the more reputable portion of it."

"Whom did you ask last?" queries Kitson, sharply.

"The French *avocats*. I dropped into Selliers & Content's; none of the clerks there had heard of him. I pumped Messrs. Jordan & Labiche; they did not know of him. So likewise at the offices of Duval et Fils, Robain, Patineau, Jobert, and Martineau."

"Martineau!" cries Jarvis, aghast; then says, suddenly: "What did they say there?"

"Well, I asked the head clerk, Pichoir. He did not know of the man, but said possibly his principal might be able to tell, but at present he was out, at the office of the Havana Line of steamboats."

"Great Powhattamie! I will go down there and see Martineau myself; he is probably at the Havana Line now. It's only a step," mutters Kitson, and takes his departure hurriedly, thinking: "By the Lord! I'll have to move quick. Martineau'll do it in a hurry if he hears any inquiries made about Poussin, the notary. That was an unlucky step of Cotain's, though not his fault." For Jarvis has taken no one into his confidence in this matter, and simply told his assistant to see if he could find the whereabouts of a notary named Faval Bigore Poussin.

At the offices of the Havana Steamship Company, Kitson does not find Martineau, but discovers the *avocat* has just engaged a cabin with two first-class passages for France, via Cuba, Martinique, and the French line of steamboats from that island.

On looking over the ship's list of passengers he finds no names are registered for the berths engaged by Martineau, and goes away, meditatively whistling: "By Jove, I've struck the old fox's last dodge! But, jumping jingo! I must get that evidence *in time!* The boat sails to-morrow. If I can't get it, I'll have to bluff without it!   Any way there shan't be any stealing from my client when I've his power of attorney, ready *for use.*"

Going back to his office he looks over this paper very carefully, to be sure he has given himself all the power necessary.   It being nearly evening, he lights the gas and by it reads the documents that young Covington had signed this morning.

"Yes; that's straight enough and strong enough for me to hold anything that may come to him—real estate, merchandise, goods, chattels, bonds, securities, live stock, and personal property of any kind.   The acknowledgment is also in perfect form," he mutters, then suddenly utters such a war-whoop of astounded joy that Cotain flies in from the outer office to ask what is the matter.

"Nothing, nothing, Cotain, only we've spotted our notary!   I had him acknowledge two papers this morning, and by the Holy Poker! I never looked at his name!   Yes; Faval Bigore Poussin; he s down on Fulton Street somewhere.   I don't wonder reputable attorneys didn't know of him.   I reckon all the documents that fellow acknowledges are agreements for sporting events and sailor affidavits.   It's mighty curious I didn't run across him some time in the course of my practice."

With this uncomplimentary allusion to his clientage Kitson says: "Now to clap hands on him!" and takes his way to Fulton Street.   After hunting about a quarter of an hour in semi-darkness he finally discovers the notary's sign, and reading it, chuckles: "He must be a curious fellow.   Down on his luck a little— so much easier for me."

The place is lighted up, and one or two people have just gone in ahead of him, as Jarvis opens the door, which he notices indicates exit or entrance by the ringing of a bell attached to it.   Behind a little counter the man, he is in search of, is apparently doing a business, anything but notarial.

"Ah!" remarks the little dried-up individual with sharp eyes.   "Monsieur has come for tickets for the cock-fight to morrow evening at Rodriguez."

" No, I'll be hanged if I have!"

"Pardon! Then Monsieur wishes the latest information of the horses for Saturday's race. I have just
received a very curious and valuable tip with regard to
it. Can tell you the exact time of Lecomte's trial this
morning."

"No; I'm not a sport," mutters Kitson.

"Ah, then, Monsieur, will you please wait for these
gentlemen?" and Jarvis sees him sell a couple of tickets
for Rodriguez' cock-fight to some Spanish-looking individuals, telling them it will be a grand main, Cuba
vs. Louisiana; the finest birds have just arrived on the
Havana steamer.

"You don't remember me?" says Jarvis, as the
jingling bell announces the two men have gone out.
"You acknowledged a couple of documents for me this
morning, on the steamboat."

"Ah, *oui, Monsieur*, you wish my services as a notary?
Those papers were acknowledged correctly?'

"Yes; but I want to talk to you about another
matter."

"*Certainement!* Ah! you do want information about
the race. I can make it very valuable to you, Monsieur.
Step into my private office, for this is a secret that is
worth a great deal of money. *Parbleu!* If it were known
the betting would change immediately in New Orleans.
This way, Monsieur!" and Poussin shows Jarvis into a
little room that is behind the more public part of his
establishment. Here there are writing materials, pens,
ink and paper, one or two notarial stamps, two or three
dilapidated chairs, a rickety table, and a rusty old
safe—the whole illuminated by a single gas-jet.

"Monsieur, I am at your service," says the little
man, with a profound bow.

"I did not call about the races, but on legal business," returns the lawyer, who has been occupying his
time by mentally measuring the individual he is addressing. "Your name is Faval Bigore Poussin, once
notary at Guidrys."

"Yes; for over forty years. But, Monsieur, you
will pardon me—What may you wish to know, before
I answer any questions? *Voila!* the bell—Excuse
me a moment!" and Poussin runs out, apparently to

sell more tickets for the cock-fight, for Jarvis hears him in excited voice, crying: "Six magnificent combats to-morrow evening! Chickens of the finest breed! Four pound, eight-ounce cocks—two-year-olds!"

During this, the lawyer thinks the matter over and determines that Poussin must not know the real object for which he wishes his affidavit. "That would be expensive with that fellow," chuckles Kitson grimly.

A moment after, the notary returns to him and says: "Now, Monsieur, your answer to my question?"

"Well," remarks the attorney, consideringly, "I am looking up the title of a piece of property on Esplanade Street. You made an affidavit in regard to that title twenty years ago; do you remember it?"

As the lawyer speaks he thinks he sees a start of recollection in the shrewd yet monkey face. Then to his dismay Poussin says stupidly: "No, monsieur; I remember nothing about it—You will excuse me—the ring at my bell again!" and goes out to sell more tickets to Rodriguez' cock-fight, or a tip upon some of the races, or something or other. At all events, he does not return again, while Kitson sits cursing him under his breath. Finally the lawyer looks out and sees the notary busy counting up his day's receipts.

"Look here! I want to see you!" calls Jarvis, sharply.

"Monsieur, I have told you that I remember nothing."

"I have got something here that may quicken your memory."

"*Bien!*" cries the little Creole, and coming in to him once more, laughs: "Monsieur, what quickens memory in a poor man?"

"Ten dollars!"

"I can remember very little for so poor a sum."

"Well, I can't afford to pay more."

"Monsieur, I have been very unfortunate. I have lost a great deal upon the last races. Cannot you say more?"

"That's my price!"

"I can remember only a little for ten dollars."

"Well, spit it out!"

"Well; you have not given me the ten dollars."

"And by the Lord Harry, I won't!" cries Kitson firmly, for he now knows that if he raises his terms he will probably get very little and have to pay a good deal for it, and by this time has become aware that if the man guesses his real object for wishing the affidavit it will be a matter not of tens but of hundreds of dollars to stimulate his memory up to the proper point.

"It ain't altogether important," continues the attorney, nonchalantly: "It's only a *duplicate* of an affidavit I wanted of you—just the same as you made for Dubois & Merrill. It will expedite my search of the title; but I can easily get the information from Mr. Merrill in California. If you cannot remember——" and Jarvis seems about to leave.

"But Monsieur—my mind seems clearer now! Perhaps I can recollect."

"For ten dollars?"

"A *little* for ten dollars."

"A little is of no earthly use! Ten dollars is my figure *for all*—the affidavit in full!" and Kitson goes slowly to the door.

But the Creole calls him hastily back and says: "*Monsieur*, if I receive, as notary, my fees for registering my own affidavit, in addition to the ten dollars, I will make the deposition that you wish."

"Very well;" assents the attorney, and goes to questioning rapidly: "You were notary at Guidrys forty years ago. You sold a slave——"

"Yes; I sold many slaves. In those days I was very rich," says the man dreamily. "I was—permit me to tell you; you are not the kind to be shocked—I was the agent for Monsieur Jean Lafitte, fought with him at the battle of New Orleans, and with him received pardon from the United States Government for any acts of privateering or smuggling we had done. That victory that gave us the thanks of General Jackson and the American Government destroyed my great prosperity. Under promise of pardon the band divided their spoils, and a great many of them settled down and became planters. It was the end of a great company!" This last, very sadly. "I perceived what would be the effect of the clemency of the United States, and struggled against it; but it came. Where now are Jean and Pierre Lafitte and that gallant band? GONE!"

"I'll be gone in a minute, too," says Kitson, savagely, "if you don't get to your point! Quit romancing! Now come to business! You sold a slave, one Eulalie Camila——?"

"Eulalie Camila?" the man starts.

"Yes, Eulalie Camila! Therefore it was not necessary for her to put her name to the deed of Prosper Delaunay Tournay, though some kind of a ceremony or reputed marriage—of course not legal—took place between them."

"Ah! *Oui*, monsieur, I remember—the marriage was——"

"Of no account! All I want is your affidavit. A duplicate of the one you made before Messrs. Dubois & Merrill would pass that title as good and complete. Now do you want to give it or not, for ten dollars and no more?"

"And my notary's fees?"

"And your notary's fees, but not another red cent."

"Monsieur, I will make the affidavit." Then Poussin goes on, dreamily: "Yes, I sold her in 1832. To be sure let me consult my account book." He hurriedly unlocks and opens the dilapidated safe which stands at the back of the apartment, then, after examining and rummaging over a number of dusty papers, old documents and time-stained memorandum-books, he cries: "Yes; it is here!" and, producing an old ledger, shows to Kitson's gloating eyes the following entry:

"1832—March 21st.

Sold to Prosper Delaunay Tournay, this day, Eulalie Camila, aged 19, also the mulatto girl Dorcas, age 16, and negro boy, Jumbo, age 17, for $1,500 cash, and order on Dobson & Cartwright, New Orleans, for two hogheads of plug tobacco and six bales average cotton. Delivered goods same day."

As he sees this record of faded ink, the paper yellow from age, by great effort Kitson keeps the joy out of his face.   Then he contrives to mutter: "Yes; that—that settles the date; now for your affidavit," and, sitting down at the table Jarvis draws up the deposition he wants, in a form, as he remarks to himself, "strong enough to chain the Goddess of Liberty."   .

"There! Sign your name to that," says the lawyer, and Poussin, putting his signature to the same, is about to affix his notarial seal, but is suddenly stopped by the attorney's suggesting: "That might not be quite regular. I rather guess it is of questionable legality for a man to administer oath to himself. Now, don't shake your head that way at me. I'll pay you your fees just the same, but we'll have this acknowledged before another notary."

Therefore, he takes Mr. Poussin away with him, that worthy leaving his establishment in charge of a mulatto boy who has come in and seated himself behind the counter during his absence in the inner office.

It is now so late, that Jarvis leads the little man with him into the French quarter, where notaries generally have their offices and homes together. Here, finding one, the oath is administered to Lafitte's ex-agent, and the proper stamps are put on the document. Then Kitson pays both notaries and settles his account with Poussin, the latter begging him for "a few—just a few more dollars."

But the attorney is as adamant and gives him only the sum specified, saying: "It's too much, any way! This is only a duplicate—just saves me a leetle trouble, that's all. Good night. Much obliged," and goes on his way, his feet light and his heart happy, cogitating: "Now, I'll make things almighty taut this very night."

He goes up to his office, adding: "I'll make things all straight *in New York* also! I'm a virtuous lawyer! I work for my client, and by Heaven! no man's ever labored harder than I have to-day for my young Kentucky blood. I will get *everything* for him! That invention of Mr. Morse is going to make things real easy for me here." With this he sits down and writes a telegram—something very unusual to him, as to most business men, in those days; for messages by wire were rare and expensive luxuries, and the telegraph had not been very long completed between the Crescent City and the metropolis of the Empire State. This is what Mr. Kitson writes:

"To Robert Boone Covington,

St. Nicholas Hotel, New York City.

Very sick. Return to New Orleans immediately, bringing Nita with you. Important. Don't telegraph but come at once.

LOUISE.

To be left until called for.

"I reckon that's no forgery by the law of this State," chuckles the attorney as his clerk departs to the telegraph office. "Now to put a stopper on Martineau!" He looks at his watch. "It's nearly eight o'clock. Shall it be dinner first and the *avocat* afterward? No, I'm prepared, and by Heaven, I do my duty! No one can ever accuse Kitson Jarvis of not doing the square thing by his client."

So he starts from his office, humming a merry tune, chuckling to himself at one moment, laughing out loud at others and snapping his big fingers gleefully at each step; to bring such misery as even lawyers seldom bring to suffering humanity in the pursuit of their daily bread.

CHAPTER XIII.

"THIS MAN MUST BE MAD!"

On arriving in Custom House Street, Kitson sees standing in front of Martineau's offices a carriage. Inspecting this, as he crosses the street, he notes it is the Tournay equipage, recognizing the driver who sits upon the box and the cross-matched team of horses.

Then his eyes catching the gleam of gas-lights on the lower floor, which is still faintly illuminated, the attorney communes with himself, even as he raps on the outside door: "By Jupiter! my guess was right! That French fox is getting the bird ready to fly away. Miss Tournay is with him now—probably receiving money for her traveling expenses and ticket for the

Havana boat. I was just in time! Nebuchadnezzar! Won't young Covington thank me for putting my hands upon this beauty before she flitted!"

Rapping on the portal, he is admitted by a negro woman, who, on hearing he wishes to see her master on business, says: "Yes, M'sieur Martineau down stairs, but 'gaged. Yo' gibs me yo' card and I'll tell him yo' heah," and shows him into the main or outer office, in which one gas-light is burning, and from which the clerks have departed hours ago.

As Kitson sits waiting, he thinks he hears a man's and a woman's excited voices coming to him from the next room, then a hasty, frightened, masculine ejaculation in French, apparently as the servant presents his card; next a few more whispered words.

A moment after, the colored girl entering, says: "M'sieur Martineau see yo', sah!" and shows him into the second office, where he stands gazing at the Creole *avocat* and Miss Louise Tournay, who have risen as he steps in.

Never has the girl seemed to Kitson Jarvis so lovely, though he has noted her several times : once at the race-course, once at Spanish Fort, once at Placide's Theatre, and each time she has looked, as he has expressed it: " Almighty exquisite in design." But as he gazes on her,—perchance with freer glance taking in a little more detail—never has he seen her so exquisitely brilliant. Mayhap it is because of the· very plainness of her costume, for Louise is not now in a gala toilette, but in a plain traveling dress or walking costume of dark cloth of light texture. This, without furbelow or trimming save some velvet bands, displays her noble figure without distroying the justness of its symmetry or marring its graceful contours by puffs or flounces.

Her face, even as he gazes on it, has a somewhat startled expression, which adds to its loveliness. Upon her head is a hat, which scarcely conceals the slightly curling locks upon which it is perched. Her delicate hands are gloved; from out the dark folds of her skirt peeps a little foot, perfectly booted. The only relief of the costume are plain lace ruchings at throat and wrists—emphasizing the whiteness of her neck and arms.

"Perhaps it's kinder lucky I found her here," cogitates the attorney. "I can settle up this business in one whack. Though—darn me!—I hate to do it; she looks so proud and chirpy."

Which in truth she does! Though surprised and perhaps slightly nervous even now, the girl is still supremely happy.

For this is what has happened to Miss Louise Tournay this day!

Mr. Covington having departed this morning, leaving his sweetheart sad at his parting, yet happy in his love, and filled with the ecstasy that comes to most girls but once in life—that of making preparations to mate with the man of her heart—Louise has cried to Mrs. Joyce: "I must be worthy of him! My Bob must think me the most beautiful bride in Louisiana! My wedding dress! My trousseau!"

Gay and excited, she has dragged with her Mrs. Joyce, who has a white, startled face, in a long round of nuptial shopping, inspecting the stocks of Mesdames Olympe and Sophie, remarking to her companion: "My trousseau shall be worthy of the gentleman I wed!"

This has occupied her pretty well into the afternoon. Then, after dinner, she has gone to figuring and cried out: "Oh, how extravagant I have been! I must see Monsieur Martineau quick! Oh, he must be liberal to me in this my hour of happy triumph!" and laughed. "How he'll scold me until he learns the good news! Gracious! I wish Bob had told him!—It—it is so embarrassing!" giving a coquettish *moue*.

This has made her very well pleased to receive a note from Martineau, asking her to call upon him this evening. To this interview she would have brought Mrs. Joyce, but that lady has an ague shudder and has pleaded indisposition. For something has been wearing upon Pamela's mind, to the destruction of her nervous system. Two or three times, as she has looked at the girl, her spectacles have been dimmed.

Therefore, accompanied by her maid, Lorena, Miss

Tournay has been driven over this even.ng to Monsieur Martineau's combined office and residence, to be received by the old gentleman in his private consulting room, he thinking it well his speech to-night shall be far from the listening ears of servants. Somewhat to the astonishment of Miss Tournay, he has curtly directed Lorena to step upstairs and wait for them in his kitchen.

Then the old *avocat* has motioned Louise to a seat, and with a very serious look on his face, has said: "My dear child, I have sent for you to speak to you on a matter of the gravest importance. I have tickets for you and Mrs. Joyce to leave here to-morrow by the steamer to Havana, then to Martinique, then to Paris, where you will meet your sister."

"Impossible! I cannot go!" cries the *fiancée* suddenly.

"You must!"

"Not now! Afterward——" she laughs. "And apropos of that, you dear old Monsieur Martineau, I want to ask you for six thousand dollars."

"*Mon Dieu!*" gasps the *avocat*. And he suddenly breaks out upon her: "You don't understand! Poor child! You do not know!"

"Ah, it is *you* who do not know; it is you who do not understand," returns the girl, mockingly. "But I will enlighten you." With this she blushes hotly, but looks archly at him, then droops her head, and murmurs: "Don't look at me while I tell you *my* secret."

"Don't look at *me*," whispers the guardian of the Tournay estate in sorrowful voice, "while I disclose to you *my* secret."

And they would each tell the other astounding and shocking things, did not at this moment, after a hasty knock, and being told to enter, the negro woman who has admitted Kitson Jarvis come courtesying in and say: "A gem'man to see yo', sah."

Looking at the card, Martineau reads on it, hastily scribbled: "Imperative, important business! can't wait!" and beneath in Roman type is the name of "Kitson Jarvis, Attorney and Counselor at Law and Proctor in Admiralty." He gazes at Louise.

But she is impatiently whispering: "Now what were you going to say? Shall you tell your secret, or I tell mine *first?* Mine will, I hope, meet your approval and make you happy." This last in laughing archness.

But her words die away as she sees Martineau's awful face. He says, slowly, to the servant: "Show the gentleman in at once!"

The colored woman going out, he looks at Louise with eyes so sad, so frightened that they startle Miss Tournay, as he mutters: "Perhaps — *Mon Dieu!* — he may tell it to you. Perhaps — Oh, God pity you—*it has come!*"

But Jarvis, unaware of what has preceded his entrance, after a nod to the attorney, which is slightly returned, says rapidly: "I would like a few words with you in private, Monsieur Martineau;" for even he shrinks from telling his tale in the presence of so beautiful a victim. To this he adds, with great significance: "Do you think she had better hear *just at present?*"

His tone, his look, tell the Creole attorney the errand on which Kitson has come. His next words drive home the truth and put the iron into Martineau's tender heart, for the man continues: "The action you have taken in regard to those tickets for the Havana boat makes it necessary I protect my client at once. Yes; those tickets lying on your desk!" For the Creole has made a gesture of dissent, though he has said nothing.

"For whom do you act?" mutters the *avocat*, "and what do you mean?"

"I act for the heir of the Tournay estate—the gentleman who gave me this power of attorney." And Kitson produces the document signed this morning.

Glancing at the signature, Martineau does not answer, but sits at his desk shading his eyes with a hand that trembles slightly. A moment after, he says hoarsely, "What do you claim?"

"*Everything!* Real estate, personal property, live stock—EVERYTHING! Prosper Delaunay Tournay died intestate; he *dared* not make a will!"

"*Dared?*" cries the girl haughtily, for Louise has remained standing, gazing on these men, surprised, not knowing whether to go or stay, their words having taken but a few brief moments. "Dared!" she repeats; then adds, haughtily: "You are speaking of my father, sir!—Prosper Delaunay Tournay was *my father!*"

But Kitson goes on, in the cold tones of a lawyer: "I am speaking for my client, whose interests I must protect. I have here the affidavit of Faval Bigore Poussin, stating that he sold the slave-girl, Eulalie Camila——."

Though this last is addressed to Martineau, Louise breaks in again in sharp astonishment, crying: "Monsieur Martineau, tell him he lies! That is my mother's name!"

"Unfortunately for you, yes!" returns Jarvis. But he pays little heed to Miss Tournay and still continues to address Martineau in rather laughing triumph: "That little deed without the signature of Eulalie Camila to that Esplanade Street property gave me the hint. I worked it up. I have Merrill's letter—of the firm of Dubois & Merrill—from California, stating the facts. Here it is! I have the affidavit of Poussin, who sold Eulalie Camila to Prosper Delaunay Tournay. I make claim for the next of kin and true heir to the whole Tournay estate—to everything. Acting under his power of attorney, I shall not permit you to ship or run out from the country *any* of his goods or chattels! You know what I mean—you know what those Havana tickets mean. If you dare let that girl move, I will arrest, detain and put her in the calaboose, as fleeing from her master. You see what Merrill writes! Read it!—as sound a lawyer as ever practiced at the Louisiana bar—' Article 945 Civil Code, Louisiana: " *Slaves* are incapable of inheriting or transmitting property;" Article 1462: "*Slaves* cannot dispose of or receive by donation, *inter vivos* or *mortis causa !* ' "

" *Slaves !*" screams Louise, taking up the strain in a higher key. "You—you are speaking about my mother?"

Jarvis, looking on her now, notes her face has grown

very white, and her lips, that were red as coral, have
become parched and gray.

"Yes, of course. *Your* mother and *your sister's*
mother!" he answers, his voice hoarse but triumphant. To this he adds in horrible impressiveness:
"Civil Code, Article 183.—'All their issue and
offspring, born or to be born, shall be and they are
hereby declared to be and remain forever hereafter
absolute slaves, and shall follow the condition of *the
mother.*'"

And, looking at the *avocat* he laughs: "You
can't deny it, Martineau!" then turns and addresses
the girl in tones that seem to her insane: "You are not
Miss Louise Tournay—it's just as well for you to know
it now—you are Louise; you and your sister Nita are
part of this estate, and, as such, *belong* to my client!"

"BELONG?" echoes Louise, in hoarse whisper, her
lips white, her frame trembling at this dire but incredible suggestion. Then, turning to Martineau, who
still sits, his head in his hands, she cries: "What does
he mean? Why don't you answer? Rise up and look
him in the face as I do, and tell him it is not true!"

But Martineau does not answer, though Kitson does:
"He don't tell me it isn't true, because he can't!"
chuckles the claimant.

Up to now this horrid interview has been as unreal
to Louise as an opium dream. Suddenly the appre-
hension of what this man is proclaiming gets into the
girl's mind, though it seems to her as incredible as if
she were told she were a beast of the field, chewing
the cud. For here she sharply cries, with white lips:
"God of heaven! YOU MEAN I AM A SLAVE?"

"That is exactly what I *do* mean!"

To this the girl makes no answer, but tearing the
gloves off her white hands, looks at her patrician fingers and beautifully tinted nails. Then, with one
hasty sweep, she whips up a sleeve to show, to the el-
bow, an arm, white, dazzling, as beautifully proportioned and as exquisitely moulded as that of Grecian
goddess. Gazing at this with all her eyes, she holds
it in Kitson's face and cries: "Impossible! Who will
dare to say that there is one drop of tainted black

blood within my veins?   Monsieur Martineau, the man is mad!   Call for the police!—he must be put in the madhouse!"

Then, the attorney not answering her, she mutters: "Get up!   Look him in the face and tell him he lies— as I tell him!"

And the *avocat* rising, she catches his eyes, then murmurs, brokenly: "*Mon Dieu!*   There is despair in your face!" next shrieks: "My God! YOU BELIEVE HIM!"

"He can do nothing else!   No lawyer in this commonwealth could," remarks Jarvis dryly, his pencil rapping on the desk a funeral march for her heart as she listens.   "Think for yourself and you will perceive that Martineau knows and has known, and keeping it quiet for your sake, has tried to ship you off to Paris."

Here suddenly, Louise cries: "*Mon Dieu!*   That's what you meant by the tickets!   That's the reason you wanted us to go away as soon as my father died! Ah, now I know!"

"Yes, and he knows, too!" chuckles Jarvis.   "I have enough evidence here to prove my case in any court in Louisiana.   This power of attorney from the heir of the estate entitles me to take and to hold everything that is his—even you, young lady! Besides, I have this document!"   He holds before Louise's horrified eyes a copy of the transcript taken from the ledger of old Poussin that night, crying: "See!   Your mother's bill of sale—March 21st, 1832—two years before you were born!"

But the girl screams out, in awful jeer: "'For fifteen hundred dollars *cash*, two hogsheads of plug *tobacco* and six bales of *cotton!*'   Yes! I am indeed merchandise!"   then mutters hoarsely: "Who — who claims me in servitude?"

"Why the heir to the estate of course—the next of kin—Robert Boone Covington, of Lexington, Kentucky, whose power of attorney to seize and hold you I have within my hands.   *Here!* LOOK AT IT!"

As she sees the signature of the man she loves, to this thing procured for her degradation, her eyes glaze with horror; one gasping, shrieking wail of anguish comes rasping out from the tortured lips: "My God! THE MAN WHOM I AM TO MARRY!"

"The man you are to MARRY?" cries Martineau, starting up at this new revelation, upon which Kitson even looks aghast.

But with one soft sigh, nature having mercifully stolen thought and sentiency from out this suffering girl in her extremity, Louise sinks down like a beautiful statue thrown from its pedestal and falls at their feet, inert as marble, and for the moment—thank God—as senseless.

CHAPTER XIV.

"FOR MY SISTER'S SAKE!"

MARTINEAU, looking on her face, murmurs: "*Pauvre—pauvre chérie!*" then stooping down, sobs: "*Viens dans mes bras!*" and takes to his heart as a man, this beautiful but stricken creature whom the laws of his land had made him unable to defend as a lawyer. Gazing at the triumphant Jarvis, he mutters: "*Miserable!* You are satisfied?"

And though Kitson does not answer, his face says that he is, *very much!*

"Help me to revive her—if you have pity in your soul!" mutters Martineau.

On this Jarvis runs into the back office and brings water to dash it on her face, which is now pale as ivory, and lifting Louise to a sofa they strive to bring sentiency and memory back to her; though the Creole mutters: "Better she were dead."

"Even Kitson would pity her—as he sprinkles with water the fair forehead of the girl from which the clustering locks of soft brown hair are brushed away, disheveled now; for one great mass—bronze in the light, dark in the shadow, falls even unto her waist—did he not note the wondrous beauty of this chattel personal. Even as he looks on her he thinks: "She's just the primest goods!   My client, Covington, will be almighty kind to her!   The gal will forget all this, when she finds what a loving master he'll make to her," and chuckles, though silently: "Oh, Hankey Pankey! ain't he lucky!   How Mr. Bob'll thank me for what I've done for him!"

A few minutes after, Miss Tournay comes to her un-happy senses.   She is reclining on a sofa, her hair dis-heveled, her hat fallen to the floor.   Martineau is chafing her hands; Mr. Jarvis is fanning her.

She murmurs in dazed tones: "Did I faint?" then staggers up and screams: "No! no! I can't believe! It is impossible! It is not true! I, Louise Tournay, educated — taught to believe myself one of the elect! — I who, to-night, would have danced with the man I love amid the proudest ladies in all this city— claimed as a slave by my affianced husband! — my Bob — whose kisses I still feel upon my lips — I, IN SERVITUDE!"

Then brushing her tangled hair off her brow the girl confronts Kitson, and the intensity of her glance frightens him.   "Tell me," she says sud-denly, "ONE THING! *Answer!* as you must answer at the seat of God!   The truth! — don't trick me!   Did Robert Boone Covington, the man who said he would wed me in Christ Church next month, that we should go through life hand in hand, heart to heart, *husband and wife* — did he *know* that you were in his name to claim me as his bondmaid?"

At this Kitson hesitates!

"THE TRUTH! *as you hope to see God!*"

And Kitson tells her the truth!   "No!" he says, impressively.   "Covington gave me his power of at-torney, knowing I had property to claim for him; but— as the Lord is above me! — he did not guess it was property that was considered yours or you were a part of it."

"That is enough!   Thank God!" cries the girl. "Now I can live until I see his face!"   But here, catch-ing a significant glance in Jarvis's eye, she suddenly falters: "No — no!   Of course — I know by the laws he can't marry me!" then adds with dignity: "Oblige me by withdrawing, sir, till I can confer with Monsieur Martineau."

Here a shock—the first of many which are to fall upon this exquisite creature—comes to Louise. Mr. Kitson says deprecatingly: "You will excuse me, but I have my client's interests to protect. There must be no chance of your running away—escaping—don't you see!"

"You have my word on that. Mademoiselle Louise will remain here!" returns Martineau, sharply.

"You will excuse me, but—you would have run her out of here to-morrow if I had not interfered. Under the circumstances you will not blame me," dissents Jarvis, though his tone is apologetic.

"If you will wait in the outer office, it will be impossible for this—this young lady to leave without your seeing her. She sits here! Permit her a few words with me!" Then the French lawyer cries savagely: "*Hors d'ici!* if you don't leave this room I will drive you from it."

"Under these circumstances I will withdraw for a few minutes," remarks Jarvis, and leaves the two together.

Then the faltering girl comes to Martineau and whispers: "Is this true? No prevarication!—tell me the legal truth. Am I a slave of Robert Boone Covington, or any man? Am I part of the Tournay estate? Am I not my mother's legitimate daughter? Was she not the legitimate wife—or was she the slave of my father? That's what he means, doesn't he?" pointing to the outer office, where Kitson sits on guard, but rubbing his hands and very happy.

"The cold legal truth of the matter is this—something I would have kept from you all your life, if possible—something I tried to shield you from, but now— *pauvre chérie*, something that is before you and your sister," murmurs her adviser, with choking voice.

"My sister—Nita?" shudders Miss Tournay, a new horror coming into her face.

"Your father—curse him!"

"No—no!"

"Curse him, I say!" continues Martineau. "Simulated marriage with Eulalie Camila, your mother, his slave, bought from this man Poussin. You saw the documents, or copies of them. Your father did not manumit your mother; neither did he free you or your sister."

"Oh, cruel!" falters the girl.

"Prosper Tournay," says the *avocat* bitterly, "kept by a false pride from acknowledging his sins, could not bring it to his paltering, sensitive heart—" there is a sneer in the lawyer's voice—"to placard for forty days on the court-house of La Fourche Parish his intention to manumit you, or to obtain permission from a police jury for the same. He attempted to do this once, not giving your names, but merely stating two slave girls, one ten, one seventeen. His application was refused by the jury, because the statement was too indefinite. At last he made up his mind to do the thing as prescribed by law. I drew up for him the papers for your enfranchisement and your sister's. He was about to come to New Orleans to sign them, when death overtook him by the accident."

"No! no! Impossible!" moans the girl. "It cannot be!"

Here the attorney's voice strikes her hard as a death-warrant; he mutters: "Your manumission papers, also your sister's, both unsigned, are in that safe marked 'Tournay'; also the bill of sale of your mother, Eulalie Camila, to your father."

"Yes! for fifteen hundred dollars, two hogsheads of tobacco, and six bales of cotton," jeers the girl, in such unnatural voice, that Jarvis starts up, thinking she has gone mad. Then she whispers: "I curse my father also!" next mutters: "No—no! God forgive him! He did intend to do me and my sister justice at the last." Here, suddenly, a shudder runs through Louise; she moans: "NITA! We *must* save her!" and the noble soul of the girl commences to shine through all the anguish in her face, and continues to shine while she makes sacrifice of herself to save, as she pitifully hopes, her sister.

She says: "Send for this man. Make compromise with him, so that Nita may escape. I know Mr. Covington will be good to me—but—Oh! Arvid Martineau

—will he regard me as he did before—before he knew? and what may he not decide as to my sister, she is young—she may anger him. Do something for Nita!"

And the *avocat* whispers: "What can I do? *Mon Dieu!* What can I?"

"Make some compromise!—some way to save her! You know she was always your favorite—you dandled her on your knee. Save Nita! Call him in—save Nita some way!"

Then Martineau thinks with all his might, but cannot solve the problem until Louise says, suddenly: "This man told me Mr. Covington did not know the claim to be made in his name was for the estate and included us two poor girls."

"Yes; I heard that," answers the lawyer.

"Then Bob—Mr. Covington—doesn't know yet that Nita is his—his—I cannot say it, but you know what I mean. If he is not communicated with, then he will send my sister, as he promised you, to Paris; there she can protect her rights—if she *has* any. I am here; I cannot escape—I must see him—this man I love—and know what fate he has prepared for me. Then shall come to me what to do with my poor body and my poor soul."

With this, rising, with face of martyr going to the tigers, and voice made strong by self-sacrifice and sister's love, Louise Tournay stands proudly erect, and says commandingly: "Mr.—— I do not know your name—the attorney for Mr. Covington—please come to me."

Jarvis enters, and is pretty well aware his battle is his own, the property his client's, and his commission is as good as in his pocket. Something in the girl's face tells him this as she speaks slowly, considerately: "You have told me Mr. Covington, your client, doesn't know of this claim, or what he claims through you."

"Quite right," says Jarvis.

"If I—who am over eighteen—agree to make no contest in the matter as regards myself, will you agree not to communicate by telegraph with Mr. Covington, or tell him the details of his claim until he returns? Mon-

sieur Martineau will telegraph him to come back—you
to see the dispatch."

"The covenant of one in servitude has no legal
weight!" says Jarvis.

"No—I know that; but if I give my word to make
no opposition—to place myself subject to Mr. Covington's control——"

"If I agree to do this, you will place yourself in my
hands?" asks Kitson, "and Monsieur Martineau will
account with me and hold any moneys, any property or
estates for the order of my client?"

"Yes!" answers the girl, suddenly, desperately.

"Under the circumstances I'll take your word for
it!" answers Jarvis, with sudden urbanity.

"Will you make oath of it, solemnly—as you hope to
meet your God—that you will not communicate with
your client by word or deed—especially by telegraph
—until he returns to New Orleans—until I have spoken
to him?" falters Louise.

"Humph! Your sister's in New York?"

"O—o—h, yes."

"Do you want to plead her cause before she
knows?"

"Yes!"

"You wish to plead in person to the man who has
asked you to marry him—the man who you think
loves you—the man who——"

"No; I know he could not marry me now!" breaks
in the girl, bitterly. "The laws here forbid that. But
I want to save the agony that has come to me this
night from coming to my sister. Do you agree? If
not, Monsieur Martineau, let the law take its course;
let them claim me, if they can get me; let them drag
me into court."

"Oh, that wouldn't take long. The laws are too
well settled on this point. Martineau is too sound a
lawyer not to know that as well as I do," cries Jarvis,
triumph in his eye. Then he goes on: "But I don't
wish any scandal; I don't believe my client would,
and if you will put yourself in my hands I will agree,
under bond of ten thousand dollars, if you want, not to
communicate from this moment—mark the time—8.50

P. M., Thursday, April 6, 1854—with Robert Boone
Covington in New York," replies Kitson, who cogently
thinks he has already telegraphed enough to ensure all
of the estate.

"Then—dear Monsieur Martineau—draw up the
bond," mutters the girl, her eyes blazing at the thought:
"My sister will be free!"

"Do you know what will be your condition under
this agreement?" asks the old lawyer, with dismay in
his voice.

"Yes; after he has signed I am under *his* control."
She turns piteous eyes on Kitson. "He will be the
agent of—of my owner. Draw up the agreement."

Here Martineau, rising, cries: "I forbid you to do
this!"

"But my sister! Think of my sister!" falters Louise,
tears dimming her sparkling eyes.

"If you don't give up and do as you agreed," interjects Kitson, a menace in his tones, "I will telegraph
to the United States Marshal in New York to take possession of and hold your sister Nita, under the Fugitive
Slave Act. I'll——."

But he gets no further. Louise cries hastily, desperately: "You shall not! Nita shall not suffer the agony
I feel!" and wringing her hands, gasps: "I agree! I
am in your hands;" then mutters hoarsely: "In that
safe—the one I point to—the one marked 'Tournay'—
you will find the bill of sale of my mother, Eulalie
Camila, and the papers of enfranchisement for me,
drawn up for my father's signature, but unsigned by
him! Have I kept my word?"

"Yes. You have done the trick this time, surely!"
chuckles Jarvis, adding as the *avocat* turns away with a
sigh: "I serve notice on you, Arvid Martineau, not
to destroy those documents that are the property of my
client. I reckon the papers are there for the sister
Nita's manumission also."

"But you will keep your word? You won't telegraph
Bob—No—no I—I can't call him that now—my *master*,
Mr. Covington!" screams Miss Tournay. Then turning to the Creole, she says determinedly: "I have kept
my word. Draw up the papers for this man—see that
he keeps his oath and bond."

"Very well," sighs Martineau, "if you insist upon it, Louise." Then he says sternly: "Only I warn you, Mr. Jarvis, beware how you treat this—this young lady. Mr. Covington will hold you answerable for her. You know how he loves her."

"Yes; answerable that she doesn't get away," retorts the other, "and of that I shall take mighty good care, but in a way that will bring no open scandal She will be at her own home. She will live as she has lived; only, in the interests of my client I shall see that she shall not escape to Paris, as you would have aided her to do."

Then the necessary agreement being drawn up, and Mr. Jarvis having signed the same and satisfied Martineau that he will not communicate with his client, the girl rises, an unnatural calmness in her voice and manner, and says: "Mr. Jarvis—I believe that is your name—I am at your disposal."

"To hold as a slave of my client, by my power of attorney."

And the iron enters into the girl's soul. She bows her head and does not answer.

And now one of the conditions of servitude comes to this refined creature, who is from the moment no more her own mistress. Mr. Jarvis remarks: "I will not be able to make the arrangements I wish for you for half or three-quarters of an hour. Please step into the back office while I transact some other business with Monsieur Martineau." He leads the way, and Louise, following him, sits down in the retiring room, but shudders a little as she sees Kitson turn the key in the door leading to the hallway, so she cannot pass out without coming through the private office, in which he will be.

"You'll excuse me," says her captor, pocketing the key, "but I have a duty to my client."

"Oh, he will thank you for it," gasps the girl. "Mr. Covington will thank you for it."

"I have no doubt he will!" remarks the attorney, going out without closing the door. Then, as Louise sits there, another little pang—though she feels it slightly, she has suffered so much—comes to her; she notices the two lawyers do not seem to mind whether she hears their conversation, and she shudders. "I am becoming a thing—something they don't regard as a human being."

For they are talking to each other about the Tournay property, and Martineau is explaining that he has sixty thousand dollars in the Bank of Louisiana and the Citizens' Bank to the credit of the estate, and showing how he has nursed the finances and has paid out as little as possible.

"But your keeping it from the rightful heir," chuckles Kitson, who is in exuberant humor, "has been a pretty plum for yours truly."

"As trustee of the estate," says the old attorney, formally but politely, "I beg to remind you that it is not my business to *find* claimants for it. It is only my duty to keep the property intact."

"Yes; I see you've done that very well. So if you'll simply give me an order to the officers of the banks saying the moneys can't be drawn out without our joint check—or, if you object to that, your check with Mr. Covington's signature attached, I am satisfied."

To this the Creole attorney, looking at his brother of the law, says sharply: "I shall turn over no money until Mr. Covington arrives, though I am perfectly willing to give you a stipulation agreeing that the bank accounts of the Tournay estate shall remain intact until I personally have word with your client; otherwise you must obtain an order from some judge in chambers for me to make accounting."

"That course you know I won't take," remarks Kitson.

"Yes," sneers Martineau, "the servitude of that beautiful creature would make every man in New Orleans turn his back upon you."

"Well, the law wouldn't, and I'm only doing the square thing by my client. However, it's all right. Give me the stipulation. Two or three weeks more doesn't make any difference in this matter. And while you are writing, just let me send this note; it's in a hurry!" Then Jarvis, who has been scribbling rapidly, says to the servant whom Martineau has summoned:

"Tell the Tournay coachman to drive with a rush round to this address and bring back with him the lady to whom this letter is directed."

As the wheels of the carriage rumble over the 'pavement, Mr. Covington's attorney goes merrily to work again, running through the details of property real and personal, the number of negroes on the plantations, the list of house-servants in New Orleans, adding to this last another name: "Louise, seamstress." "I reckon I'd better put her that way," he chuckles.

Then he discusses with the trustee of the estate, other things that seem to please Jarvis very greatly — money matters, bonds, mortgages and growing crops.

All this seems a hum to the girl's ears as she sits drearily in the next room. She hardly notes it; shock and suffering have stunned her.

Once though, she springs up, and would stride to the door, with blazing eyes. Jarvis is saying: "What do you reckon is the market value of Louise? Twenty-five hundred dollars? You know I receive ten per cent. commission."

But the attorney's quick ears have caught her light step; he comes to the door and says sharply: "Sit down! I am not ready for you yet." And she, obeying him, wonders if this is not all a nightmare from which she must soon awake—awake and be happy.

Suddenly there is a rattle of horses' hoofs outside.

A moment after, the servant coming in says: "Dere's a lady to see Mistah Jarvis."

"Yes; very well! Tell her I will speak to her in a minute." Then turning to Martineau, he whispers: "I want you to see that I do everything properly and genteelly. These are simply my precautions in regard to the girl you were going to run off."

The next moment Kitson, stepping into the outer office, goes into conversation with a woman of determined face and medium height, but figure square and strongly built, her age about thirty. She answers to the name of Mrs. Hannah Combes. She is stewardess of a river steamboat, but at present is enjoying a run on shore: as such, Mr. Jarvis has known her to be absolutely honest, reliable, and perfectly capable of carrying out the instructions he gives her. She has also been matron of an industrial school for girls. To this woman he explains her duties, her authority and power, very carefully and very accurately, ending by saying: "You think you understand me?"

"Thoroughly! If the terms are right the person placed in my charge will receive my whole attention. I will be answerable."

The woman's wages being settled, Mr. Jarvis says to Martineau, who is still looking at his accounts, though his eyes are too dim to read: "Now this is what I propose. All I want is to know that when my client arrives in New Orleans, the estate will be intact. For this purpose I have engaged Mrs. Combes, who is absolutely reliable, to take the place of Miss Tournay's maid whom you mentioned was upstairs when you gave me the schedules of the house-servants. This mulatto gal, I have no doubt, like most of her race, has a tongue in her head. Neither you, nor I, nor Mr. Covington care particularly for this affair to be noised about, and I think it wise for Lorena to be returned to the plantation Beau Rivage, there to remain for the present at least. The person I have engaged will take her place, and be known as Miss Tournay's maid. I have given her authority over her charge amply sufficient to prevent any evasion or flight. She had better return with Louise in the place of Lorena, whom, if you will be kind enough to send to Assumption, you will confer a favor, I know, upon my client, Mr. Covington."

To this Martineau cries impulsively: "I offer you a personal bond for ten thousand dollars that Louise remains here till she sees him."

"Could you give me a bond she might not make away with herself?" answers Jarvis, impressively. "Louise knows according to the laws here she cannot marry him—that thought may make her desperate. I won't take the risk! I know my client values that girl like thunder!—I have seen the way he looked at her. I won't take any bond whatsoever, and that settles it."

This suggestion startles Martineau. What may the agonized girl not do in some wild frenzy, some sudden desperation? "Perhaps it is best," he murmurs.

And Mr. Kitson, stepping to the door of the third room, says: "Louise—come here!"

Addressed thus, by this man who has never spoken to her before this night; this commonplace calling of her first name smites the captive even as if it were a blow; but she rises and coming to him answers quietly: "I have placed myself in your hands. What do you wish?"

"I shall send you home this evening with a lady who will appear to act as your maid, but really will boss you —that's all—a lady to whose authority you must submit yourself. She will dominate your actions sufficiently to insure your not escaping until I can place you in my client's hands. I shall probably not see you until Mr. Covington arrives, provided you are subservient to her control."

"Yes; I would prefer never to see you again, Mr. Jarvis," falters the girl. "Not that I think you have been more unkind than—than the very innate cruelty of your mission compels you to; but your face will always be in my mind as the most cruel, cruel thing this earth has shown to me." And the tears start from her eyes. But dashing these away with her hand she bravely mutters: "I will go; only—only let me get my hat on."

Here Mr. Jarvis calls: "Mrs. Combes, please come to me!" and the woman joining him, he says: "Louise, this is the lady who will act as your maid, see to your comfort and safety, and control you."

To this Mrs. Combes, seeming to know her business very well, adds: "Let me help you with your dress!" And, pinning the dainty bonnet on the girl's head, she buttons Louise's jacket carefully up, the night being slightly damp and misty.

She is about to lead her forth when Martineau, suddenly rising, comes to Jarvis and says: "Permit me a few words with Miss Louise!"

His tone is so imperative that Kitson replies: "Certainly!"

He and Mrs. Combes walk to the outer office, near the door of which they stand waiting for their charge, to whom Martineau is saying, in low voice: "Had you not sacrificed yourself, I might have put off this evil hour."

"But only for a day or two," murmurs the girl, "and by it I have saved Nita."

"Perhaps!" replies the *avocat;* then goes on, savagely: "If Jarvis doesn't keep his convention with me in regard to your sister, I will——" but he checks himself here and whispers very sadly, with tears of pity in his eyes: "I pray God the young man who holds your fate in his hands, my poor child, may be very wise and very noble," then sinks down at his desk, sighing deeply.

A moment after, there is the noise of wheels outside; the patter of horses' hoofs dies away, and the *avocat* murmurs to himself: "God help her! *In extremis !*"

CHAPTER XV.

IN EXTREMIS.

Noting that Martineau has gone back to his desk, Mrs. Combes raises her voice and says incisively: "Louise, come here!"

A moment later, followed by Kitson and her directress. the girl, though her limbs tremble a little, contrives to walk quite firmly down the steps leading to the street, and from the very force of habit stands, as mistress of the equipage, waiting for the others to enter the carriage in advance of her.

From this pose she is sharply aroused by Hannah's saying: "Step in at once!"

A second later the *gouvernante* sits beside her subject, and Louise suddenly hears Jarvis say to the driver: "Home quick!"

Almost at the same moment Mrs. Combes promptly whispers: "Give me your hand," and Louise finds her wrist taken and very firmly held by strong and nervous fingers.

A few moments after, as they drive across Bourbon

Street, another carriage, with ladies in light evening dresses and accompanied by their esquires, passes very close to them. From it come light laughter and careless words. One of its occupants is babbling: "It's a pity Monsieur La Farge and young Mr. Covington will not be present at the *fête.*"

"Yes," adds another. "The reckless fellows killed some one in a duel this morning."

At this, Louise starts up, shuddering and moaning.

"What is the matter with you?" whispers her startled monitress, for the captive has been very quiet until now.

"I—I was going to that ball to-night—to dance with the man of my heart—and now, *what am I?*" gasps the tortured girl, and wrings her hands and sobs so bitterly that a little pity comes into the heart of the woman beside her, as she says: "That's right! Tears'll do you good. Anything is better than moping."

On reaching the Tournay residence, Hannah Combes steps out first, and then assists her charge to alight. Together, they go up to the *salon,* where, the night before, this girl had been clasped in lover's arms, and Mrs. Joyce, meeting them, sees that the blow has fallen. She gasps: "You know?"

"Yes—in all its horror, present and—to come!" shudders Louise; then chancing to see in the apartment some articles that have been sent to her from modistes—things pertaining to her nuptial trousseau— things that drive her frantic—this tortured one throws herself into Pamela's arms and sobs as if her heart would break.

Upon this scene her attendant does not immediately intrude, but after some ten minutes, enters and says firmly: "I think it well, Louise, you should retire for this evening."

And Mrs. Joyce looking at the woman with inquiring eyes, Miss Tournay falters: "Pamela, this is Mrs. Combes—I think that is the name—who will act as my maid and my—my *keeper*—that's what it is!—that's what it *means!*—until Mr. Covington comes, if I have the heart to remain alive until that day."

"It shall be my care to see that you *do* remain alive!" remarks Hannah with significant determination.

But the girl breaks from her and runs to her chamber, where she goes about wringing her hands and shuddering: "Slave of the man I was to marry! This will break my heart! My God! will it break his also?"

But to Louise's astonishment she finds that this woman who has accompanied her, soothes her and is tender to her and says: "Poor thing! Cheer up!" and gives her something that makes her sleep; for among other avocations—and she's had a good many—Hannah Combes has once been a hospital nurse.

A few minutes after, Miss Tournay's *gouvernante* returns to the little *salon* and explains exactly how matters stand to the prim schoolmistress, who has an astounded look upon her face.

"Monsieur Martineau knows of this?" asks Pamela anxiously and sternly.

"Of my control of the girl Louise? Yes! I brought her direct from his office."

A few minutes after, a note arrives from the *avocat*, reciting to Mrs. Joyce the facts and ending with "I pray you to remain with Louise until Mr. Covington returns. Do what you can to cheer her—to make her forget the sad fate that has come upon her."

This being shown to Mrs. Combes, she says: "You see the house will be in my charge, under the control of Mr. Jarvis. But you can do a great deal to help me, in preventing this shock producing a brain fever in my ward. Louise plays and sings?"

"Yes."

"Encourage her to do so, and let her dwell as little as she can on—on her master. She has a romantic affection for him, I understand. Now, good night—for I have lots to do. My trunk will arrive very shortly; would you kindly order it up to my rooms?"

With these words Hannah goes away, and coming to her charge, who is sleeping, though uneasily, this woman mutters: "My laws! No wonder they value her! She's the prettiest thing I ever saw!" Then looking at the delicate, transparent complexion, and ivory whiteness of her ward's shoulders and arms, she mutters: "If there's negro blood in that body, Venus was a Hottentot!—Nonsense!—But that's none of my business!   I can see I'm going to have a terrible time; she's one of the kind that will take to the high strikes mighty easy."

Mrs. Combes's prognostication is true.   The next morning there is a terrible awakening—an awakening that tells of despair.

"Louise rises in her bed, puts both hands to her fair brow, upon which some dead weight seems pressing, and says suddenly: "What horrible thing happened to me last night?" then looking around and seeing Hannah, she screams : "I know! My Heaven—*I know now!* Bondmaid to the man I love! Slave to him who would have been the husband of my heart!"   And springing up, she goes striding about the room like one possessed, turning upon her guardian and muttering: "Yes—yes! The woman—*my keeper—I know you!*   I recollect it all!   You are to hold me in bondage and *alive* until my master comes!" and struggling from her, will allow no change of toilet from the light night-robe that she wears.

After a few minutes, however, Louise murmurs, sadly: "*But I must live until I see him!*" and in this thought permits herself to be persuaded to take a cup of coffee, and curiously feels stimulated by it, our mental depending so much upon our physical being. Then very shortly, under her *gouvernante's* deft hands, Louise finds herself dressed, and comes to breakfast in a way that wholly astounds and partially horrifies Mrs. Joyce, who is waiting anxiously.

For this girl is now a different being from the fairy maid of happy yesterday—from even the crushed and broken thing who had sobbed out her heart in Mrs. Joyce's arms last night.   There are no tears; the beautiful eyes are dark with despair, but shine with haughty pride.   Exquisite archness has left the mobile face, and the graceful playfulness on the sensitive lips has been superseded by a wild, yet piquant sarcasm.

Miss Tournay sweeps in, as lovely this morning as she has ever looked.

Dressed in a light morning wrapper, a mass of lace, and furbelows, she takes her place at the head of the breakfast table, and gives her orders to the waiting maid as if she were still the mistress as of yore. Mrs. Joyce notes also that Louise answers to the name "Miss Tournay," though in an absent manner; for in truth the appellation seems very far away to the girl, back in the hazy past.

Oftimes, this morning, she has jeered herself by repeating Mr. Jarvis's observation of the night before: "You are not Miss Tournay now; you are the slave-girl, Louise."

Under the circumstances, the conversation is disjointed—at times imbecile—they even talk of the weather! Neither Mrs. Joyce nor the young lady eat very much.

Soon, the maid having left the room, Miss Tournay rises and says: "An hour at the piano!"

"Why?" asks Pamela.

"Why? Because I'm *ordered* by my *gouvernante*," breaks out Louise. "Oh, don't think Hannah Combes —that's her name—has not her eye upon me every moment! She is sitting in the hall there now, to prevent escape. Don't I know the meaning of this dress? Look at this bouffant robe, open all the way down the front, and tied only by a girdle at the waist! See how liberally it displays the short under petticoat—these thin slippers and weblike stockings." The girl pokes out a little foot piquantly and jeers: "This half undress is to prevent my running in the street to flit away! Lace fetters—butterfly chains!" Then continues in sad tones: "It is not she who keeps me here to await the man I yesterday, as his affianced, kissed farewell; it is my love and trust in him! But, o–o–h— I pray, God, I love him not too much! That thought makes me fear—that dread makes me want to hide myself from him! But how?—where?" Then she looks round, despairingly, and whispers: "The woman has taken everything from me—money, jewelry—even my engagement ring! But what matters it? The law will not permit us to wed—why should I hold the symbol of the plighted troth of *my master*? Oh God!" and

she wrings her hands, "How happy I was yesterday!
—wedding rings and wedding bracelets—and now—
manacled for my master's coming! That's what it means!
But I must play! My *orders* from my *gouvernante* are to
play to prevent brain fever."

Then she goes to the piano and bangs it in a wild,
excited way that makes Parmela shudder, but does it
for an hour.

"I'm going to Monsieur Martineau's. Have you
any message for him?" asks the ex-schoolmistress,
who has remained, anxiously watching.

"No, except to tell him to see that Mr. Jarvis keeps
his word about that telegram. My sister must not experience my lot! That is the reason I made no defense.
But it would have been unavailing," and Louise whispers, with white face and set lips: "Martineau himself
acknowledged it! He has the bill of sale of my mother
for fifteen hundred dollars cash and—two bales of *plug
tobacco*—and six bales of *cotton! O—o—o—h!* That
brought the fact that I was merchandise home to me.
He has also papers drawn up for my manumission and
Nita's—*unsigned* by a *sensitive* father, who could not
bear to brand his children as slaves, *yet made them
such!*"

Upon this rhapsody of despair Mrs. Combes breaks
in, saying: "Louise, calm yourself—don't be foolish.
You'll make yourself ill!"

"What are your orders, Madame?" asks the girl,
and, on hearing them, she sneers: "Ah, I am to
have a drive for my health!—fresh air to keep the
chattel personal in good marketable condition!"

So, about half an hour afterward, Louise goes out to
drive in the close carriage, the *gouvernante* sitting grimly
beside her, though trying to amuse this captive of Mr.
Jarvis's legal bow and spear.

Half an hour after, Mrs. Joyce, in consultation with
Martineau, tells him the occurrences of the morning,
and he says: "Probably it is well for her she has some
one to look after her. God knows what Louise might
do in her despair! We must bring Covington back.
the whole issue lies in his nobility or vileness!"

Therefore he sends a telegram to meet Bob in New

York, though he dares not say more for Nita's sake than

"For God's sake return. Imperative that you be here quickly."

Returning from this visit Pamela finds Miss Tournay has come in from her drive in an awful humor.

Louise is striding about and muttering: "No more upon the streets—for me! Every person's face I look at tells me they know I am a chattel!"

"Why, it was only your beauty, you foolish girl," laughs Mrs. Combes, impatiently, as she takes off her ward's cloak and hat, puts her in negligee house-garb and locks up every article of street apparel. In truth, Hannah's charge has worried her greatly during carriage exercise—having at times haughty airs and saying: " Remember you're my maid, outside my chamber!" and afterward, perhaps within the minute, laughing: "What are your commands, Madam?" or—jeering " I see it in your eye—chastisement for the slave girl who does not bow the head."

In this Louise has guessed quite closely. Hannah, grimly, once or twice would have liked to have had the power, for Miss Tournay has been a thorn and a vexation unto her. But the woman has done her duty by the girl. She has seen there has been no chance of her charge's evasion or escape, and further than that has striven to her utmost to keep Louise from thinking of her lot; for that purpose assuming authority that perchance has been a sting unto her charge. For a very fiend of pride has sprung up in this captive's soul, who yesterday was susceptible to every softening influence of life and could not have used an unkind word to even her own careless maid, Lorena.

So the day goes on, and it is a long one for poor Mrs. Joyce as well as Mrs. Combes, Louise even bringing tears to dear old Pamela's eyes by saying, sarcastically: "Why don't you go away from here? Do you not fear companionship with a girl of mixed blood will degrade a proud Caucasian Yankee schoolmarm?"

"I stay with you!" answers Mrs. Joyce, sadly, wiping her dimmed spectacles. "I stay with you! Do you think I'd desert you in such a strait, you poor darling?"

But the girl rises at this and cries, hoarsely: "No pity! Besides"—here she suddenly extends her exquisitely proportioned arm, white as the driven snow, and asks: "Do you believe, Pamela, there is one drop of tainted blood within those veins?"

"No!" cries her companion, impulsively.

"Ah! so glad to hear that!" sneers Louise, bitterly. "Mr. Covington, *my master*, doesn't admire negro blood. I've often heard him call his jabbering Mr. Cæsar 'Nigger-brain!' and 'Hottentot-tongue!'" Expressions the long-suffering Bob had sometimes used in speaking of his sable valet. Next she scoffs: "But perhaps our master will be more tender, more considerate of my feelings; I am more valuable than Mr. Cæsar—I'm scheduled 'Louise, seamstress, twenty-five hundred dollars!'"

Then suddenly this creature, whose emotions lash her to despair, cries: "Here, Mrs. Combes!"

And that alert matron coming in, she queries: "You're an expert in valuing human flesh and blood; don't you think I'm worth more than twenty-five hundred dollars? In the auction mart I'd be called a *fancy* article!" With this she strides to her room, followed both by Mrs. Joyce and the matron, for both are mortally afraid their charge will do her beautiful self some injury.

"I've got my patient quieted now!" whispers Mrs. Combes some half hour afterward. "I had to give her another opiate. Now, I'll put it plainly to you, as I want your assistance and advice. If this thing goes on, I must have some way of controlling these frantic outbursts. Can you give me a hint? Who does Louise love best in the world?"

"Mr. Covington, I think."

"Pshaw! He's the trouble!"

"Nita—her sister!" cries Mrs. Joyce, suddenly, and is almost sorry for it.

For the matron says: "Much obliged! I guess you've hit it! Nita is the ticket!" and goes away to consult with Mr. Jarvis.

The next day, some threat Mrs. Combes has used in regard to her school-girl sister in New York tends to

make Miss Tournay much more pliable. She takes her
carriage exercise without a murmur; she plays with
Mrs. Joyce by the hour on the piano; she does not
even scoff at her fair self, and explains this all by saying: "I am waiting—waiting to see that my sister's
fate shall not be as cruel as my own. Were it not for
Nita, I'd end it all quickly!" Then the tortured one
wrings her hands and mutters: "But no! I cannot!
Hannah always has her eye on me. I must live—live
to bring happiness and joy unto *my master!* But I tell
you, Pamela Joyce, that though I love him—Heaven
help me!—as much now as ever!—as *my master* he shall
not so much as touch my hand! Oh, there are rare
times coming for Mr. Robert Covington, of Lexington,
Kentucky, and me, *his bondmaid*, whom he left as *his
affianced bride!*"

So things go on until the next Wednesday.

The previous Saturday the great race has taken
place, unheeded by Louise, in which the jockey John
has won his freedom by riding Lecomte to victory over
the Kentucky colt.

Returning from her Wednesday drive, Miss Tournay
comes in to Mrs. Joyce and laughs uproariously but not
merrily: "Pamela, this is fun! That Combes woman
thinks I'm trying to escape. See how nervously Hannah
goes about now! A man stepped up to our carriage,
while she was out of it, making some purchase in Canal
Street, and said, taking off his hat very politely to this
poor chattel: 'Miss Tournay, I believe? I owe you some
money; shall I send it to your house?' And I, embarrassed by this sudden address, answered, 'Yes; send it
anywhere you please.' But on being questioned and
rated by my keeper for having held secret communication with some agent of Martineau's for my abduction,
when I stated what had happened, she took the liberty
of doubting my word. Why shouldn't she? Who would
believe such a *likely* story?

"You should have seen Hannah's look," Louise
goes on, "as the horses flew and she rattled me home.
Now, both doors to the courtyard are bolted, and I—I
am to be locked up myself. The little dressing-room
will be my cell; it has no windows, only a high sky-
light from which I can't make escape."

This, to Mrs. Joyce's horror, proves to be the truth, for Hannah, coming in, says, sharply: "Louise, step with me!" And the girl, putting up her piquant nose and drawing the air through her dilated, clean-cut nostrils like a thoroughbred under curb, goes with her.

Half an hour later, passing out for consultation on this matter with Mr. Jarvis, Mrs. Combes is confronted at the street door by a man who says: "For Miss Tournay, from Jobson & Johnson," handing, to the astonished woman, an envelope containing bills for a hundred and fifty dollars, with a slip marked: "Lecomte, 60 to 90."

Now this curious incident has come about as follows: Mr. Covington, ever anxious to do something for the girl of his heart, had the week before put two bets for her, paying cash for both, one on each horse, so that his sweetheart must apparently win any way, and Jobson & Johnson, not finding the gentleman, and being square sporting people, wished to make immediate settlement of the same, and so had forwarded the wager to Miss Tournay.

Therefore Louise, after an hour's incarceration, comes back to Mrs. Joyce, and says, with blazing eyes: "I have been under lock and key! It is a curious feeling Pamela, hearing the bolts click on you and being sealed up from the outside world; but one which I should get used to. Am I not always in bondage?—fettered by law,—but most of all fettered by *my love?*"

And Hannah Combes approaching, with some words of apology for having doubted her statement, Miss Tourney says, calmly: "I do not blame you. It was a most unlikely story that I, who can have nothing of my own by law, should have money *owing* to *me*. Preposterous! Bob's love, that produced it—is also *preposterous!*" then falters, brokenly: "And that is the simple truth—he loves me—that is my *agony!* Each day my Bob's generous thought for me brings me more misery!" Suddenly her eyes blaze despairingly, she screams at Mrs. Combes: "Doesn't each morning a boy deposit at these doors a gorgeous bunch of orange blossoms and white rose-buds, to tell of coming nuptials

that shall never come ?   Bouquets you *dare* not let me
see for fear *I shall go mad.*   And now a little present
that his generous heart wanted to make me—some
glove-money, under pretence of a bet—has given to
me *incarceration!*   So it must always be; the more he
adores me, the greater my despair—growing deeper
the nearer he comes to me.   For then there will be
nothing, except to bless him for his goodness and *to
die*—that's what it means!   FOR I WILL NOT TAKE
DEGRADATION FROM HIS LOVE!''

And for the first time since that awful evening this
tortured girl breaks out and sobs the blue eyes almost
from out her head, and throws herself despairingly on
a sofa of the room, as the two women look at her
aghast; but Mrs. Combes whispers: ''It's a good thing
for her!   If she had held in much longer she'd have
gone crazy.''

Seemingly it does her good.   After this Louise,
though she goes about haughty as a goddess and disdainful as pride itself, does not now have the rhapsodies
of despair that at the first had stricken her down.

So it comes to pass that one day, nearly two weeks
after, Miss Tournay, sitting in her chamber, suddenly hears in the courtyard a voice—merry and
laughing, but one that makes her tremble and shudder,
and her face grow white with a strange dread, and looking out, the girl gives forth an awful cry: '' My God!
Betrayed! Nita—Nita HERE!   Oh, Mother of Misery!
My sister in bondage like myself!''

For there is a rustle of short skirts and a child of
about thirteen years is running up the stairway and
laughing: ''Is that you, dear Mrs. Joyce?   Cousin
Bob brought me.   What makes you look so white?   How
is Louise?   We hear she is sick; is she better?   We've
lots to tell her!''

As she looks on this, Louise moans to herself: ''He
must have *known!*   This man of my heart—would not
let ONE of us escape!''   Then a moment after, she
falters: ''No—no!   My God!   *My* Bob—I'll not
believe until I look into your honest face and hear
from your own lips that you have lured my sister to
this land of bondage, to make us both your THRALLS
AND SERFS!''

BOOK III.

How He Loved Her.

CHAPTER XVI.

OMINOUS evidences on this point come to the captive very soon.

Louise rises and falters: "Good Heavens! How can I tell Nita? I haven't the strength, but still—I must! Better from my lips than another's!" With this she staggers to the door to open it and greet the coming bondmaid—her sister.

To her dismay, the door is locked upon the outside, and though she struggles and fights and tries with all her strength to force it open—for now she hears Nita's voice crying in childish petulance—she cannot succeed, and perforce is compelled to await the pleasure of her *gouvernante*.

Tears pour down her cheeks as she thinks: "Not permitted to kiss my sister! not allowed to speak to Nita, when I have not seen her for over a year! Oh, this is bondage!" and Louise flies about the chamber like a caged bird beating at the bars.

But chancing to glance out on the court yard, the captive pauses, — starts and looks again, then sudden coldness comes in all her limbs, shudders run through her trembling frame and she has to clutch a chair to hold herself erect. For Mr. Cæsar, Covington's sable valet, is coming in at the archway of the residence, and with him are men bringing not only her sister's trunk but the baggage *of his master!* — hat-boxes, valises, canes, and all the other impedimenta of a travel-ing dandy, who is coming to his house and home.

A moment later, these are all taken into one of the lower rooms, the mulatto whisking his cane and tapping his lacquered boots and following after them as if he had reached his resting place.

"Oh, Heavens! He is coming here *to live!* He has assumed possession of his house! God help us both— hemust have *known*, and brought my sister back with him *to bondage!*" And Louise's eyes have horror in them and her proud head droops.

A moment after, the door is opened, and Mrs. Combes confronts Miss Tournay.

"Let me pass!" says the girl. "I want to see my sister!"

"That's impossible — you can't see her now!"

"Why not?"

"Why? She was saucy to me, and I locked her up. Besides I've got to get you ready for your master's eye."

Then, Mr.—Mr Covington *knows?*"

"Why, it looks as if he knew everything. He sends his trunks here—he's in consultation with the lawyers —he has brought that minx back with him. It looks as if he knew."

"And Mrs. Joyce?" falters the girl.

"I'm with you here—I don't leave this house," ex-claims the Yankee schoolmarm from the hall, "until I give that cruel, sneaking brute a piece of my mind!" And Pamela, though she has already arrayed herself for the street—for it is evident she will not remain under the rooftree of this villain-slaveholder—shakes her um-brella savagely, and strides about as if eager to express herself to the scoundrel, Covington.

"Now," says Hannah, "step this way, Louise; I am going to fix you up right smart to greet your boss."

"Yes," cries the girl, desperately. "Make me as beautiful as you like—you lady's maid to a slave!"

And driven frantic by misery, Louise jeers with bit-ing words and cutting sarcasm, the woman as she decks her, until Hannah looks at her grimly, and mutters: "Oh, lawdy, if I only *dared!* I'd take the highfalutins out of your proud body! I'd smack your white skin till ye knew ye were no better than a field hand, and kissed the ground I walked on!"

But the girl pays no attention to the mutterings of the woman who dresses her. There is but one thought in her heart: "I pray God I may be lovely in his eyes! I pray Heaven I may be fascinating to this man who calls himself my master, so that I can break his cruel heart—if he has any."

Under Mrs. Combes's hands, Louise permits herself to be robed so that she may find favor in her owner's sight, and prepare a welcome for the man of her heart such as he recks not of—nor guesses with wildest guess—though he has been in New Orleans these two hours.

For this is what has happened to Bob since his arrival in New York. He would have made arrangements to send Nita to Paris, but on his appearance at the St. Nicholas Hotel he had immediately received Kitson's telegram signed "Louise." Filled with anxiety, he had presented his letters to Miss Martin and obtained her permission to take his little cousin with him to New Orleans. While making preparations to return, comes Martineau's telegram. This hurries his departure, and accompanied by Miss Nita—a teacher of the school going with them as far as Pittsburgh— Mr. Covington, journeying by rail through Pennsylvania, places his pretty charge on boat upon the Ohio River.

At Cairo, they board the *A. L. Shotwell*, and come as rapidly down to New Orleans as current, steam, and a lightning-boat will bring them. During this trip, Mr. Covington treating the child of thirteen with the deference he would give a young lady of more advanced years, and with the impulsive generosity of his Western nature showering bonbons upon her and pretty things to make her journey pleasant, Bob and his cousin Nita become the greatest of friends.

But, all the trip, the little lady wonders what makes the big fellow, as he paces the deck of the great steamboat, sigh so deeply. For these telegrams have given him an awful anxiety for the loved one of his heart, and he is counting each revolution of the mighty wheel, and each high-pressure-toot of steam as they sweep past island, and point, and snag, and river town, until one fine morning, the great crescent of steamboats along the levee comes into view, and the *A. L. Shotwell's* lines are cast ashore in New Orleans.

The gang plank is no sooner over than Covington, eager to learn of his sweetheart's welfare, springs off the boat. Almost immediately on landing he finds himself approached by a policeman who chances to know him by sight. This man says very respectfully: "There's a warrant out for your arrest, on that Delaborde duel. You're my prisoner, sir."

"Oh that's all right," remarks Bob. "I expected it. I'll go with you immediately; you're only doing your duty; but just let me make a few arrangements. Here Cæsar!" he cries.

"Yes sah!"

"Take Miss Nita home to the Tournay residence and get yourself and my baggage on to the Verandah! I'll be after you very shortly."

"Get yo' baggage onto de veranda?" says the black scratching his oily wool.

"Certainly! That's what I said—and be quick about it," shouts Covington, as he steps on the boat to bring his charge on shore.

Bob does not dare to tell his valet why he is detained, fearing the knowledge of his arrest, as magnified and embellished by Mr. Cæsar's vivid imagination and love for sensation, may cause Miss Tournay uneasiness on his account.

A moment later, Miss Nita trips along the gangplank and is assisted by her cousin into a carriage. Here she pouts her pretty lips and says: "Not coming with me, Cousin Bob? Louise will be expecting you!" then laughs: "And you pretended to be so anxious about her."

"As I am! Tell her I'll be with her almost within the hour. Tell her that unexpected business of moment keeps me from her—that it's impossible for me to see her just at present."

"Very well. *Au revoir!* I'll tell Louise what a fine

cavalier you've been to me on the trip! I'll sing your praises, Cousin Bob, until you come to toot your own horn. That's the way you express it, I believe." And the child, using one of his own phrases, smiles at him very sweetly as she is driven away, Mr. Cæsar sitting on the box, surrounded by the baggage.

But Nita, who is a dark-eyed witch, of piquant face, quick temper and loving heart, has no time to sing the praises of this gentleman, who has obtained a very warm place in her heart by his attentions of the journey. On arrival at the Tournay mansion and encountering Mrs. Joyce, that lady on seeing the child has burst out into vituperation of Cousin Bob, saying: "Good Heavens! You must not see your sister!—this will break her heart! The coward-villain—the sneaking slave-owner!"

"Break whose heart? What coward-villain?" asks Nita; then suddenly says: "Louise? you mean *her* heart? What do you mean? I never could understand you at school in my lessons! What do you mean?"

"I mean, you foolish child, that your coming will strike down your sister who loves you! She has made for you such sacrifice as sister never made before—her own liberty, to keep you from being enslaved—enslaved by this cousin of yours, who has sneakingly brought you from New York to make you his bondmaid; I mean that you, Nita, are one of his slaves!"

"Slaves? Rubbish!" cries the child. "Why, you crazy old abolitionist, what are you driving at? My Cousin Bob has sickened me with bonbons, and treated me as if I were a princess in a fairy book!—I'm Cousin Bob's slave? Why, you are crazy!"

"Sometimes I think I am—sometimes I think I should be—that such injustice should exist upon this earth. You poor lamb, you don't know what you're talking about. You are Mr. Covington's slave, I tell you! I'll save Louise the agony of doing it. You belong to Mr. Covington—can't you understand that? Your mother was a slave before you; you have not been manumitted, he is the heir to your estate—to the Tournay estate—and you and your sister are part of it. That scoundrel lured you here so that you may be more fully in his hands—you poor little manacled girl!"

But the little manacled girl, growing very savage at such remarks, inserts her tiny tongue into the hollow of her pretty cheek, hits it a deft smack with school-girl hand, and making saucy report of bursting toy balloon, cries out: "Nixy, you idiot! You don't know what you're talking about!"

But suddenly this is broken in upon by a stern voice saying: "Here! Quit your noise!" and Hannah Combes stamps her foot. "You're Nita?"

"I'm Miss Nita Tournay! What do you want with me? What do you mean by flying at me, you old thing!"

"What do I mean?" cries Hannah. "I mean that I'm mistress of this house at present. I take charge of you, as well as your sister—*I* know my duty. Come with me, you slave brat!" For Mrs. Combes for three weeks has been bottled up, and now noting the arrival of Mr. Covington's baggage in the house, and that he has brought back another bondmaid, thinks she will have it all within her hands.

"Slave brat!" cries the outraged child, "what do you mean—you old ape ?"

Here suddenly Nita discovers what Mrs. Combes *does* mean. Despite her tears, entreaties, struggles, she is rushed by this lady to a vacant room and put under lock and key, that matron grimly determining on an awful vengeance for the saucy words as soon as she has time to work her will.

But at present Hannah has a duty to perform. She has received instructions from Mr. Jarvis that on Mr. Covington's arrival, Louise must look her very best to greet her coming master.

.   .   .   .

Bob has taken cab with the officer who has made the arrest and gone to the Court House.

From there he sends a hurried massage to Martineau, thinking: "While he arranges my bail I'll hear from him news of my sweetheart. By this time he must know we're engaged."

Soon after, the *avocat* coming to him, the Kentuckian,

hardly waiting for greeting, says hurriedly: "In New York I received a telegram from Miss Tournay, stating she was ill. How is she now?"

"She is, I think, as well as can be expected," answers the Creole, slowly.

But there is something in his voice that makes Bob whisper: "You—you mean she is *very* ill?"

"No; I think she is in reasonable health. I have not seen Louise for some week or two," returns Martineau. Then he asks, suddenly and anxiously: "You received a telegram from her—Mr. Covington?"

"Yes; asking me to bring Nita with me."

"You—you did it?"

"Certainly! Her sister was sick; Nita should be with her. Less than an hour ago I sent the child up to the Tournay house under charge of Mr. Cæsar. Now bail me as quickly as possible, so I may go there myself! It doesn't seem to me you've given much attention to my *fiancée* during my absence. I presume Louise told you that next month she becomes Mrs. Covington," returns Bob, by no means pleased at the lack of interest the *avocat* apparently has taken in his sweetheart and her coming nuptials. "Still, she can't be very ill," he reasons, and stands impatient while the bail bond is made out.

It is not for any excessive amount, and Martineau informs his client, as they leave the court-room, that the affair need cause him no great anxiety.*

"Oh! I have another that causes me much more—the health of the woman I love!" says Bob, and calling a cab, directs the driver to the Tournay residence.

But Martineau, as they are about to step in, whispers: "No—to my office first! I'll explain as we drive."

"All right!" says Covington, hurriedly. "I'll drop you there—but for me, a sight of my darling!" In the cab he cries: "No legal business for me to-day! Woods-afire! haven't I a claim for two hundred and fifty thousand dollars in another lawyer's hands, and

---

* The law of Louisiana against dueling of 1848 had been repealed in 1854, and the much more severe enactment of 1856, of course, had not as yet been passed by the Louisiana Legislature.—ED.

do I run after him to learn if he has bagged it?   Dauphine Street and Louise's sweet face for me!"

"*Mon Dieu!* No!" stammers his companion; then whispers, with trembling lips: "Not till I have told you!"

"What?" falters Bob, and, looking on the Creole, an agony gets in his voice; he gasps: "Good God, man! Louise is—is dead!—and you don't dare to tell me! Has the yellow fever of last year broken out again—and stolen my heart from me? She was well—happy—joyous when I left her arms—— And now—*now*—NOW!" The strong man is trembling.

"*Grand Dieu!* You love her so?"

"Love her—as my life!—speak!—don't you see—my God, she's dead!"

"No—No! It is not that!" cries Martineau.

"Not dead?—then what's the matter? What has been the matter with you ever since you met me this morning?—There are tears in your eyes now—What's happened?"

"Step into my office and I'll tell you—the cab's at my door. You must come!—it were a crime if I let you go to her until you knew!"

Impressed by the Creole's manner even more than by his words, Bob follows Martineau. In the lawyer's private office, he says, commandingly: "Speak!"—then mutters falteringly once more. "You—you say Louise is well?"

"Louise is as well as can be expected, beggared as she is in fortune and happiness."

"Beggared!—by whom?"

"By *you!*"

"WHAT?"

"The claim I told you of—the one that hung over the Tournay estate—the one I said could not be resisted—the one I said meant ruin—the one I suppose I ought in common honesty to have disclosed to you—is *your* claim. You are the master now of the Tournay estate! Your attorney, Jarvis, has done his work too well! Stay here!—Don't leave until I've told you *all!*" for Bob is striding toward the door.

"No—let me go to her!—I must explain that this

legal robbery was without my knowledge—my consent.'

"*You cannot explain!*"

"I can—I can tell Louise how I love her!"

"That will be worse!"

"What do you mean?"

"I mean it will break her heart the *more!*"

"You're crazy!—she loves me!"

"That is what will break her heart."

"I marry her next month! What difference does it make as to the money?—then it is hers again!"

"You cannot marry her!"

"Then she must be dead!"

"She can no more become your bride under the laws of Louisiana than if she were."

"Are you mad or am I?"

"Neither of us!—I wish to Heaven we were!"

"I think—I begin to understand," says Covington, slowly. "It is some legal trick or irregularity in her mother's marriage—some slur upon my sweetheart's legitimacy of birth. That's what it must be! That's why I've turned her out of her possessions—her and her poor little sister." Then he goes on rapidly: "But, Martineau, I'm not that kind of a man! I love her! I don't turn my back for any accidents of birth on this girl I adore—on this girl who loves me—who accepted me as her husband when she could be proud—when she thought she was rich. In her day of despair I do not abandon my sweetheart! Bob Covington isn't built that way! By the Lord Harry, I'll marry her the sooner!"

"You cannot marry her—you do not understand. Louise Tournay and her sister are *part* of the estate that to-day I shall be compelled to make over to you."

"*Part* of the estate?"

"Yes! They are now—your—your SLAVES, Mr. Covington."

But Covington does not answer. He stands staring fixedly in Martineau's face, struck speechless. Then, with a muttered, long drawn out, gurgling sigh, he sinks into a chair and still gazes at the Creole *avocat*, though his strong hands clench themselves together and once or twice he makes a motion of unbelief.

After a moment, however, he rises rather tremblingly, dashes the hair from his brow, seizes Martineau by the shoulders, looks wildly in his eyes and mutters: "You don't mean to tell me that my—my affianced bride is *my property?*" then bursts out: "Good Heavens! She's white as I am—whiter! You're mad!"

"Sit down and listen!"

With a gasp Covington obeys, wiping the perspiration from his brow and shivering sometimes as he hears the tale, as the Creole attorney gives a succinct but accurate statement of the case, also a report of Mr. Jarvis's action in the affair, and unlocking his safe produces the documents that had brought destruction on Louise.

Getting these in his hands and reading them over Covington turns very pale and falters: "The bill of sale of her mother—and—the papers drawn up for the manumission of Nita and my—my love!—For I tell you, Martineau, even this—this slur upon my darling has not diminished my love for her—my *respectful* love, which this day I shall prove—as God is above me—I shall prove! And I ain't bragging!" Then he goes on: "I see now why you wanted Nita and Louise in Paris! I understand why you've kept this secret from me—why you tried to place them beyond my grasp! God bless you for it, Arvid Martineau, God bless you!"

"And God bless *you!*" cries the attorney, "For I see—*Dieu merci!*—they have fallen into the hands of a noble gentleman!" And with Creole emotion the old gentleman embraces the younger, and after the fashion of the French, kisses the big Kentuckian on each cheek.

This is broken in upon by a jovial voice crying out: "Here's another of the happy family!—Shake!"

It is Mr. Kitson Jarvis, who has heard of Covington's arrival, and having told the clerks that he is expected, has received immediate entrée.

"Didn't I do the thing up for you in prime legal style, Mr. Covington? You're as good as in possession of the property now. Brought the other little chattel down with you from New York—estate *all* here," continues the attorney in affable joy, for he thinks Bob has been embracing Martineau, enraptured at getting so easily all the goods and chattels, real and personal, of the Tournay estate, especially the beautiful Louise.

He might go on, however, with dangerous remarks about the fair captive of his legal acumen, did not his client turn upon him, the veins standing out like whipcords from his forehead, and mutter savagely: "By Satan—you're the cuss!"

"Of course I am," answers Kitson, laughingly, "and no lawyer in New Orleans could have done it slicker! Didn't I nose out that old Esplanade deed of Prosper Tournay? Didn't that give me the hint? Didn't I get the affidavit of Faval Bigore Poussin? Didn't I send that telegram signed "Louise" to New York——."

"In contravention of your oath!" cries Martineau. "When she sacrificed herself to give her sister freedom."

"There you're out!" replies Jarvis. "I kept my word. That telegram had already been sent. I don't let the grass grow under my feet while taking care of my client! You'll find that out, Mr. Covington—money, cash, plantations, goods, chattels—everything—right here under your hand. You ought to be the happiest jim-dandy in New Orleans to-day!"

"I suppose you did your work after your legal lights well enough. But—do you see these arms—good, strong ones aren't they? By the Eternal!—I'd sooner you had torn them both out of their sockets than have put chains on her pretty wrists! That's how happy I am!" mutters Bob, regarding his successful attorney with an evil eye. Then he shudders: "By heaven, you have tricked me into bringing Nita here to bondage! Louise will think I have betrayed her sister, and that it is by my will and command she has been made my *slave!*"

"Well, the girl's knowing you're her master won't do you any harm in your courting," chuckles Jarvis, then gurgles suddenly: "Gol darn it, what are ye doing!"

For Covington has him by the throat and is whispering: "Another word, and,—by Daniel Boone!—I'll dash your brains out against that safe!"

"That's as—assault and b—b—battery!"

"Yes, and homicide too; but you won't be alive to claim damages!" jeers the Kentuckian. Then he cries: "Pish! She's breaking her heart while I'm making a fool of myself!" and drops the breathless Jarvis into a chair.

"What are you going to do?" asks Martineau eagerly, for Bob is picking up his hat from the floor and placing it on his head.

"Do?—By all I hold sacred, I'm going to *un*do the wrong that has been done my angel—if all the laws of Louisiana stand against me!"

From now on, the Creole *avocat* notices that there are no more spasms of emotional fury from this young man, who now knits his brows as if thinking very deeply on some mighty problem.

"And—and my fee?" pants Jarvis—who has recovered a little of his breath.

"It shall be paid to the last picayune! Meet me at eight o'clock to-night, here. But mark me—as you love your miserable life—not one word of the degradation of the woman I adore to outside ears! My God! If she's been illtreated by that woman you've put in charge of her, look to yourself!"

"I only acted as agent, to be sure she wouldn't run away. You're her master!"

"I'm her master to protect, to ennoble her, to raise her up against the world that would pull her down—to love her better now than I ever loved her before!"

And Covington strides about the room looking like a grizzly in a den of rattlesnakes; impressing Jarvis so much that the attorney whispers: "At eight o'clock I will call for the cash!" and departs, apparently wishing to let the Kentuckian work off his quixotic ideas.

For as such Kitson regards them, cogitating as he goes away: "Wait till my young spark puts eyes on the loveliness that is now his property—By Jerush! He'll be shaking hands with himself and me too—this evening at eight!"

But Jarvis does not know Bob Covington as well

now as he will a few hours later. For this day the
young Kentuckian does a few things that make not
only the cute Yankee attorney, but also the more dig-
nified Creole *avocat* open their eyes and roll their heads
astounded.

CHAPTER XVII.

"THE RASHEST PROMISE MAN EVER MADE."

ALREADY he commences to bring astonishment on
Martineau, for the moment Jarvis has left, Covington
says, a strangely guarded tone in his voice: "Don't
you think we had better call upon Miss Tournay? She
may be anxious as to the position I may assume to
her."

"Had not you better go alone?" remarks the *avocat*,
hesitatingly. "Louise might not like to express herself fully in the presence of a third party. You know
she was engaged to marry you——"

"Is engaged to marry me! Miss Tournay *is* engaged
to marry me! Pardon my correcting you—but my
dear Martineau—Miss Tournay *is still* my affianced
bride. Though, of course, my relations to her are
now so delicate, my intercourse with her must be most
guarded."

Then for the last time until he sees his love, Bob
Covington breaks out, faltering: "I'm going to beg
her pardon—my angel that unwittingly I have injured
—my darling, with chains upon her wrists—my chains!
But by the Heaven above me! I mean to put no touch
of shame upon my sweetheart's brow! Come on! I'd
sooner face the fire of a battery than this interview;
but it will be worse for her. I expect the poor girl
will break down when she sees me."

But Mr. Covington does not know Miss Tournay!
Though he gets evidence of what his reception in
Dauphine Street will be from the skirmish line in Mrs.
Joyce.

As they enter the little *salon*, the ex-schoolmistress

swoops down upon Bob. She is dressed for departure, carrying an umbrella in her hand and the fire of battle gleaming through her spectacles.

With no bows, or how-d'ye-dos, or glad-to-see-yous, she opens fire. "Don't you guess," she cries, in indignant scorn, "you're a little, the meanest sneak upon this earth? You miserable child-kidnapper! You creature, who would degrade the girl you once promised to make your wife, and not content with her slavery and humiliation, you seize her unfortunate sister and lure her down here to despair also!"

"You are laboring under a misunderstanding," mutters Bob shamefacedly. "I brought Nita here under a mistake—a false telegram sent by that infernal attorney of mine!"

"Oh, yes! Put your sins upon your myrmidon! I haven't long to stay in this house, thank Heaven! But before I go I'll tell you what I think of you!"

And she would go on, unheeding Martineau's deprecating gestures, but Bob breaks in: "Doesn't Nita say I treated her with all the respect due any lady?—that, child as she is, she has had every delicate attention and courtesy from my hands?"

"Oh, yes; that's your cunningness! You did not want a scene upon the boat, when every man's hand would have been raised against you; but now——"

"What has been done to her?"

"She has been locked up!"

"Good heavens!"

"She has been seized by this woman, Mrs. Combes!"

Here Hannah comes in to take her own part. She says: "Acting under Mr. Jarvis, your attorney's, authority, I have taken such precautions as I deemed best for the safety of your property; that's all. Nita was saucy to me, and I locked her up. The girl Louise is now ready to see you at your convenience."

"Let Nita out at once!" cries Covington. "Martineau, you settle with this woman—I can't look at her complacently—Get her out of the house as soon as possible! Give her a hundred dollars to hold her tongue—only get her out!" Then he turns to Mrs. Joyce and says: "Will you please have the kindness to inform Miss Tournay, with my card, that I beg her to see me.   It would also be my wish, if you can bring yourself to remain here."

"Not in your service!" snorts Pamela. ·

"No!   As Miss Tournay's companion, as you were before—if *she* wishes it."

"Very well; I'll give her your message."

And Martineau having settled with Mrs. Combes, and given her enough money to insure that matron's silence, telling her, in addition, that Jarvis will never forgive her if she does not keep her tongue very close, that matron comes in to Mr. Covington once more and says: "I thank you very much, sir, for your liberality to me.   You will find the girl Louise has received much kinder treatment at my hands than she deserved.   She is very beautiful, and I hope you'll be kind to her."

This kind of talk drives Bob crazy.   He mutters: "Yes—only please go away—please go away—Hang it!—get out—Don't you see——"

"Of course I see you're very anxious to look at your beautiful slave," adds the woman, with a farewell shot, for she has noticed that every time she has mentioned "the girl Louise" her master has given a shudder.

Then for a moment Bob has a chance to speak to Martineau.   He says: "I reckon you'd better get Mrs. Joyce into the other parlor.   That will preserve all the convenances, and—perhaps Louise—Miss Tournay—may say some bitter things.   Heaven pity me —there seems to be some horrible misunderstanding of me."

Just here he gets an additional evidence of this. Nita, released from confinement, comes out, her black eyes sparkling with rage, and stepping up to him cries: "My master, I am told!   O-o-o-h how I hate you!"

"Wasn't I good to you all this week?   Haven't I done everything for your comfort—your happiness?" falters poor Bob.

"My happiness?   Mrs. Joyce says you've stole my money—and are going to make me work myself!   Oh, yes; you've—you've done a great deal for me, Cousin Bob!   Go and blow your own horn and toot your trumpet to Louise—see how she'll love you! They tell me you asked her to marry you—when she was *rich*— Now bossed by that awful woman, who has whipped her!"

"Whipped her?" screams Bob, adding an awful oath.

"Well, I don't know whether she did or not. But that woman threatened to whip *me*, and I suppose she did the same to Louise. Just wait! you'll see how much she loves you! Oh, we've both got lots to thank you for!"

"For Heaven's sake! don't strike a poor fellow when he's down," mutters the unfortunate Covington, hanging his head.

Then a hush falls on them all, as Mrs. Joyce enters and whispers nervously: "She's coming!"

And it seems to awe them, this approaching meeting of man and woman who parted as betrothed, and who now meet, the man as master, the woman as his slave, forbidden by the law to wed, but not forbidden by the law to love.

In obedience to a muttered word from Martineau, Mrs. Joyce withdraws with him into the second parlor, taking with her the unwilling Nita, though she is whispering, savagely: "Let me stay—I want to see Louise give master *fits!*"

The *avocat*, as he draws the child away, gives a glance of sympathy to Covington, who, taking a long-drawn breath, stands, his tongue dumb, his eyes speaking— this master who is trembling as he looks upon his bond- maid.

For Louise now stands before him, and his sweet- heart, in her new serfdom, seems more lovely to him than she had ever looked in pride and glory.

And she is more lovely!

Suffering has made the exquisite face more spiritual. A wondrous grace pervades each sweeping pose, each vivid gesture. In her willowy figure there is a strange mixture of shrinking bashfulness and stately hauteur, punctuated once or twice in this strange interview by mutinous yet piquant sarcasm, as if this chattel mocked her lowly lot and sometimes even the dictator of her destiny.

Louise is only slightly thinner, but her eyes have in them a pathetic beauty that had not been theirs before. Yet, even with this sadness of the violet eyes with latent tears behind them, this shrinking of the mobile figure, Covington as he gazes at her, knows this woman, who is his chattel, is the proudest being, in her humiliation, he has ever seen upon the earth.

As the girl comes in, a mighty blush of modesty, perchance of embarrassment, flies over neck and bust and face. Louise droops her eyes, for she now feels, brought home to her for the first time in all its hideous reality, that she is not her own. *She is property.* THIS MAN OWNS HER FLESH AND BLOOD. She belongs to him; his will must be her will; his command her law; by his hand she may be corrected and chastised. Against this, her spirit flies up in agonized rebellion. She longs to be beautiful and haughty—beautiful to make him love her, though she is his serf—haughty enough to break the heart of this man, she now thinks, holds her and her sister as his chattels—and glories in it.

With this idea Louise has let Mrs. Combes do her will upon her, and Hannah has done her work very well. She is dressed quite simply, in one of the light gowns made for her to prevent all excursions upon the street. It is a simple white muslin, trimmed with a little lace, with a few white ruchings. From out its snow, her arms, shoulders and maiden bosom gleam like ivory in that extraordinary delicacy of tint which marks the purest Castilian blood. The soft draperies give to her a fairy-like appearance; but, oh, she is the haughtiest fairy that ever tripped a cloud.

Covington, forgetful of all but love and pity, steps forward hurriedly to meet her. But she, divining that he will take her to his heart, stays him, and shocks him with an awful shudder; then sweeps to the floor in haughty courtesy, and murmurs: "My master."

It is the word that can give him the most pain her lips can utter.

He whispers excitedly: "Call me any name but that!"

"What title do you wish, sir?"

"My heaven, how unjust you are!"

"Unjust?" cries the girl; and her white hand points to her little enslaved sister. Suddenly, she breaks out, her voice sad with destroyed hope: "Oh, how I have loved and trusted you! On that fearful night when they proved to me I was your chattel, all I asked, was: '*Does my Bob know?*' And when they told me you were ignorant, I said: 'Then, I can live to see him.' That is what has kept me alive, looking for your coming face, listening for your expected voice. But now——"

"Now you condemn me unheard!"

"Unheard? Your actions speak!" And her eyes blaze. Then, curiously, she begins to beg: "This very day, please—please send Nita and me to your plantation at Beau Rivage. Oh, you can do it safely!" for Bob has made a sudden gesture of dissent. "Mr. Jarvis can easily find some trusted agent to take us poor girls safely there—Mrs. Combes, for instance." This with a little shudder. "A line to your overseer or housekeeper at Beau Rivage will ensure a sharp eye and strict hand being kept upon us—your slaves!"

"Send *you* to an overseer?" shrieks Bob.

And she, mistaking him again, grows very pale and desperate, and falters: "You—you surely do not mean for—for *me*—to stay here in this house as your *slave*, when you occupy it as *your home?* Ah, that were too great an infamy!"

"What makes you think this monstrous thing?" gasps Bob indignantly.

"Monstrous?" echoes his chattel, in disdainful unbelief. "Is not your valet, with all your trunks, within this house?"

"Eternal curses on his darky brain!"

But she doesn't head this, and goes on: "Why should I expect mercy from your hands, who have given Nita none? Why should I hope for truth from you who have, despite your promise, brought my sister back with you to a slavery as cruel as my own?"

"Have you finished?"

"If it is your will, sir!"

"Then listen to me!" says Covington, sternly.

And growing very calm, half with indignation, half with despair, he tells her *all* the truth. Of Jarvis's lying telegram about her health, that he should bring Nita back to her sick sister ; how he had journeyed as rapidly as rail and boat could bring him, and paced the deck of the steamer each night as she swept down the Mississippi, anxious for the welfare of his love, "Now," he says, "I come here, within my hand a trinket, bought at Tiffany's in New York, to prove I never for an instant knew your fate; that I still regard you as my affianced bride. This ring—" He holds up a flaming diamond.

"Oh, yes; I need another! The one you last placed on my finger was taken from me. So everything else. Your agents took good care I had no chance of flight."

"But I did not know that! By Daniel Boone, how could I tell that ?" And Bob breaks out with fearful imprecations against Jarvis and the woman Combes, then mutters hoarsely: "How have they treated you ?"

Looking at him, the girl knows if she says the word, in his anguish this man she is now lashing to desperation with her loveliness and her contumely, will doubtless kill his attorney and perchance make short work of the woman who has guarded her so carefully in his interests.

Then by God's fortune and her generous heart, Louise does not speak of confinement, of lock and key and threatened chastisement, but simply says: "They treated me as if they thought I were very precious in your eyes—as if I were to be the crowning glory of your triumphant coming back, my master."

And gazing at her, Covington murmurs, his soul in his voice: "Precious you are to me, dear one! I love you heart and soul, despite what the law has made you, despite everything that stands between us."

"Then while I—I have my own self-respect, let me fly from you!" whispers the girl, with white lips, who now, knowing the truth of this man of her heart, loves him more because of the injustice she has done him—ay, even perchance because of the barrier that is betwixt

their love; next droops her head, and murmurs, hopelessly, despairingly, blushingly: "But I am a slave—
fallen below the world's pity—even beneath its
scorn!"

" But not beneath my love!"

"Pardon me. *My chains make me above it!*" And
rising to her full height, Louise looks to Bob's ardent
eyes as dazzling but as cold as ever vestal Virginia
looked to Appius Claudius.

But here sudden inspiration coming to him, he
whispers: "Behold another ring that was purchased
for your finger in New York!" and drawing from his
pocket holds up to her a glittering circlet of pure gold
—that symbol of the greatest honor man can give to
woman—the ring of holy marriage—then says, in indignant pride : "Miscontrue this if you dare,
Louise!" next mutters hoarsely: "No more insults to
my love."

"You—you would make me your wife?" falters the
girl. "Chattel as I am ?—Bondmaid as I am ?—Your
own serf ?—you would make your honored wife?"

"By the Deity, I would!"

On this there is a faltering cry: "My Bob! Have I
been unjust?"

"Unjust? Do you think it is happiness to me
to see the woman I adore — my promised bride —
the woman I wed or do not wed at all — cast down before the world — sullied by my hand? Ah! I suffer,
even more than you."

" Do you, Bob?" says the girl, tenderly. "Do you,
Bob?" For she is wavering now, and commences to
tremble in every limb and look at him with something
of the old time glances of his betrothed.

Seeing this, he steps forward to get an arm round
her and hold her up, and perchance would kiss her; for
he is very hungry for her lips.

But she, steadying herself, puts her hands before her
as if to keep him off, and smites him with these awful
words: "No kisses for *my master!* My lips are for my
affianced husband! Remember the law forbids us
marriage!" Then seeing how she has wounded him, for
he has staggered back, she falters: " Forgive me!

There is no hope for us. I love you, Bob —. I hoped to wed you. Oh, dear one, how happy I was when I thought within the month — you — you would join me at the chancel and make me before all the world your happy and your honored wife."

And he, driven mad for the moment by the beauty and loveliness of this fair creature, who is quivering before him, the love in her face shrouded by despair, whispers: "*I will do it yet!*" then cries: "Martineau, come here and listen to my words!" and turning to his bondmaid says: "The law has thrown you, my angel, *down;* my love shall raise you UP! I will take you up the aisle of the proudest church in New Orleans — Christ Church, I believe, was the one we talked of — and there make you my bride, I swear to Heaven, despite the law!"

But he gets no further. For with a faint, sighing scream of joy, or despair, or of unbelief, or all, Louise has fallen fainting into her master's arms, as senseless as when she first heard she was his slave.

And Martineau, gazing on them, whispers with white lips: "*Mon Dieu!* That was the rashest promise love ever brought from man's lips to a woman!"

CHAPTER XVIII.

KITSON JARVIS TAKES ANOTHER FEE.

"THAT afterward!" says Covington, desperately. "Now help me to bring life and recollection to my loved one."

Raising Louise in his strong arms, he carries her to a sofa, and implores: "Send for a doctor, quick! Mrs. Joyce—aid me! Nita—run for water!" and all the time he is fondling Louise's fair hands and kissing her white brow. A moment later he sighs: "God can't intend to curse forever such beauty and such goodness." Gazing at her, he suddenly cries: "Do you think there is aught but Caucasian blood in this fair body?—aye—blood of the purest and noblest? I don't care for your documents! I don't care for your proofs! I don't care for your law—but the one law of Louisiana that declares that no white person can be a slave—and that I will prove her to be!"

Then he turns to Mrs. Joyce, who is whispering to him: "Forgive me; I did not know how noble you could be," and says: "Take care of her. Manage the house as if it were *her own*—as I will make it yet! Treat her tenderly, for my sake. For, heaven help me, I will see her face no more so long as the law says I am her *master* and she my *bondmaid!*"

Soon after this, a physician being in attendance on Louise, with one last kiss upon the pale lips that are even now regaining their color, Covington whispers hastily to Mrs. Joyce: "Keep me informed of my darling's condition; I stop at the Verandah Hotel," and turns to go away, followed by Martineau.

But even as he reaches the head of the stairs, two pretty little arms are round his neck and a sweet little face is put upon his shoulder, and Miss Nita says: "Kiss me, cousin Bob, and forgive me. You're the best cousin in the world! I ain't afraid of you, even if you are my master."

As they step down the stairs together, Martineau, who has been turning the matter over in his mind, remarks: "My poor boy, you have made two rash promises."

"Both I will keep!"

"Impossible!"

"Why?"

"The law will prevent your doing the one; and the young lady herself will prevent your keeping the other.'

"I can manumit her."

"Of course. After forty days' notice, posting her name up in the Court House and obtaining permission of a jury. It will be a terrible blow to your pride and it will break Louise's heart."

"There's another way out of this," mutters Bob, who is young and has not yet learned that love and pluck don't always win the battles of this earth. "But first, a word with that infernal scoundrel sitting up there on the bannister." He turns an evil eye on Mr. Cæsar, who is calmly smoking on one of the balconies with Mr. Covington's luggage about him and, the day being warm, an umbrella over his head.

"What are you doing up there?" cries Covington sternly, stepping into the middle of the courtyard.

"I'se waiting for orders," answers the sable valet, withdrawing a big, strong and succulent cigar from his lips.

"What were my orders?"

"I was to take Miss Nita home and get your luggage out on to the veranda."

"On to the Verandah *Hotel*, you crazy imp of Eblis —you darky-brain! Let me get at you!"

"Not at present, Mistah Covington. We'll argue dis point from a distance. Why didn't yo' say the Verandah *Hotel?* I s'posed yo' wanted to stop at the St. Charles."

"No, I said Verandah, you nigger-brain! I wanted to be quiet and retired; I wanted to get away from the bloods. Let me at you!"

But Martineau puts his hand upon Bob's arm and suggests smilingly: "It was a curious, though not so unnatural, mistake; and produced, I imagine, a little uneasiness in your——" he checks himself, then says: "your affianced's mind." For Martineau, under the circumstances feels he can now call the beautiful girl, who is recovering consciousness above, by no other title. "But come on to the Verandah yourself," he adds. "My poor boy, you've had nothing to eat since you left the boat this morning."

"Very well, I'll go on to the hotel and act like an ordinary human being, if you'll get me one paper."

"What is it?"

"I think it can be obtained to-day. It is simply an appointment by the proper court to act as guardian for Nita Tournay, a child under age. Do you think you can do it?"

"Yes."

"Without bringing Nita into court?"

"Certainly! Though, of course," says the Creole

avocat, "under the circumstances, Mr. Covington, the document will be an empty form. Children of Nita's condition have nothing to protect. As her master you have full control of her."

"Don't call me that," whispers Bob, "because that means despair to me. It is through Nita I hope to guard the interests of my affianced bride. Can you get me the paper?"

"Certainly."

"Very well; give it to me when I meet you at your office. What time does Jarvis come?"

"Eight o'clock."

"Let me meet you then at seven. Think over everything connected with Prosper Tournay's life and Nita's mother. I can discuss that with you in the hour before Kitson Jarvis—my sharp attorney, who has taken such good care of my interests—comes to get his settlement."

With this Bob goes away, and forces himself to eat a sombre meal at the Verandah, that magnificent hostelry at the corner of Common and St. Charles Streets, the most quiet and probably the most aristocratic in its day in New Orleans.

Then to the astonishment of Mr. Cæsar, who has arrived with his baggage, Bob goes up to his apartments, and refusing all offer of change of raiment, paces the room, thinking, pondering, and sometimes putting his hands to his brow. Suddenly he cries: "I must have some more subtle, certainly a calmer mind to work out her salvation!" and strides to the office on Custom House Street, with a very throbbing brain in his head and a very heavy heart in his body.

In his consulting-room he finds the Creole *avocat*, every paper bearing upon the case in front of him. These are simply the bill of sale from Poussin of Eulalie Camila to Prosper Tournay, the papers for the manumission of Louise and Nita, drawn up ready for execution but unsigned, and a few notes from the *savant* to Martineau in regard to the matter of making his daughters free and providing for their future welfare.

"Why didn't you destroy all these cursed things?" mutters Covington after looking them over. "Why did you not wipe out all evidence by which that infernal lawyer has brought destruction upon these two poor girls and upon me?"

"I kept these," answers the Creole attorney, "for the very purpose I use them now, to show them to you, these young ladies' owner—for what is the good of mincing a matter you have got to look in the face, I have got to look in the face, Louise has got to look in the face—so that you should know what Prosper Tournay's intentions were regarding his children."

"You mean that I can see he wanted to free the girls and leave them his property? That I shall do of course *at the last.*"

"Yes; if a jury appointed for that purpose in New Orleans, or a police jury in Assumption or La Fourche Parish permit you to; but only after giving public notice of the same for forty days."*

"But these children have not been claimed in slavery, and the law says—at least I have been so told—

---

* The method of procedure for the emancipation of slaves in Louisiana was in some respects different to that of any other State. *Vide Stroud's Slave Laws.*

Civil Code of Louisiana, Article 184. A man who wishes to emancipate his slave is bound to make a declaration of his intention to the judge of the parish where he resides; the judge must order notice of it to be published during forty days by advertisement posted at the door of the court-house; and if, at the expiration of this delay, no opposition be made, he shall authorize the master to pass the act of emancipation.

Ibid. Art. 185. "No one can emancipate his slave unless the slave has attained the age of thirty years, and has behaved well at least for four years preceding his emancipation," except (Art. 186) "a slave who has saved the life of his master, his master's wife or one of his children;" for such a one "may be emancipated at any age."

Under the Civil Code of Louisiana slaves under thirty years of age may be emancipated by their masters with the *consent* of a jury. The tribunal to act upon this petition consists in New Orleans, of the recorder and council of the municipality, and in the other portions of the State of a police jury, composed of a president and eight or twelve members, who hold their offices for two years and are elected by ballot. Three-fourths of either of these tribunals, in addition to the respective presiding officer, determine upon the merits of the claim set forth in the petition. After consent of jury he must proceed by usual course.—ED.

that any slave unclaimed for ten years, is a slave no longer," observes Covington, a gleam of hope in his voice.

"That is if they had been resident in Louisiana all the time, and furthermore, if they are *over thirty years of age.*   Besides, these deeds of manumission show they have been claimed. It will not apply, you see," returns Martineau.   "Neither was their mother treated as a slave by Tournay after he married her; but she died after nine years of married life, and besides she was also *under* thirty.   There is no way that you can free Louise and Nita unless you manumit them according to law, and with public notice."

"And that would crush Louise's heart with shame and prevent my keeping my promise of marriage to her," mutters Bob. Then he goes on: "Tell me all about the father of these girls."

"As far as I know, these are the only facts that will interest you about your uncle, Prosper Delaunay Tournay. He was a student, a *savant,* a poet, a selfish sensualist, an immense egotist—a man of tremendous false pride—one who would rather keep his shameful secret than do justice to his offspring."

"Do you know, I rather think it must have been this matter that made my mother turn her back upon her brother?" suggests the Kentuckian.

"Perhaps," returns the lawyer, "though there was undoubtedly some sort of a ceremony between him and the mother of these young ladies—performed, I imagine before a notary—probably the Poussin who apparently gave Eulalie his name, the Poussin who sold her, Faval Bigore——"

"Oh, yes; don't repeat the name of that miserable whelp!" mutters Covington, "by the Lord, he's the sharp who sells tips on the races, the one who gave me his dirty card—the dispenser of cock-fight tickets!" and laughs bitterly: "He once had the mother of my sweetheart as his bondmaid? Rather a curious sort of pauper to own anything!"

"Not at all. This man you speak of was once very rich. He was a trusted agent of Lafitte, the pirate, in early days, and amassed considerable property, all of which he has lost through gaming. At one time he had many slaves. Perhaps Eulalie Camila was in some illegitimate way entitled to bear the name of Poussin. God knows! she may have been his own offspring by a slave mother. It was a wild, reckless country in those days; plantations miles apart, each man a feudal baron on his own estate. The country is becoming closely settled now. Thus it happens that no one in New Orleans has the slightest suspicion of the true status of these two young ladies."

"You've kept mighty good care of that, I hope," mutters Bob, brokenly.

"Yes; even the house servants do not guess. To keep expenses down, these have been very few. Mamon, the old cook, who is deaf as a post, Jacques, the aged gardener and man of all work, who answers your knock, and Manda, the dining-room girl. The coachman sleeps away from the house. Mrs. Combes was supposed to be the maid of Louise, while she had charge of her. Nothing has come up in the courts."

"And nothing shall, if I can prevent it!" returns Covington. Then he says meditatively: "Tell me all about this man Jarvis—this cunning attorney. How did he nose out the affair and bring destruction on me?"

And Arvid Martineau telling him, Bob suddenly astounds his listener by saying: "I rather reckon Mr. Kitson Jarvis is my man! You have the order of the court appointing me guardian for Nita Hortense Tournay?"

"Yes," answers Arvid, handing him the document; and would ask further questions, but Mr. Kitson Jarvis is announced.

This worthy comes in, genial, happy, glowing all over and chuckling: "Ah, my dear client. No hard feelings now. I calculated when you saw *all* I'd captured, you'd pray for me this evening. Guess you've been shaking hands with yourself most of the time lately. You young bloods are impulsive, enthusiastic and romantic, but when it gets down to solid comfort you know a *particularly* good thing as well as anybody. Now as the Tournay estate is as good as yours and in fact in your possession—for Martineau daren't hold it one minute after you say you want it— we'll all go out and pop a champagne cork.   Then I'll make the demand and get the property all turned over, and with your permish—I'll take my fee."

But here Covington horrifies his attorney.   He says shortly: "Martineau may admit that I'm in possession of the Tournay estate, but I won't!   I believe Prosper Tournay's daughters should be as free as you and I— free to inherit their father's wealth—*free*——"

As this oration has proceeded, Jarvis's eyes have given one wild, astounded roll, his jaw has dropped. Now, the lower one flies up with a sudden, startling snap.

"Under these circumstances," he interrupts, in cold determination, "I warn you, Martineau, to hold that property.   I bring suit to-morrow morning to put you in possession, Mr. Robert Covington; and I also bring action for my fee, ten per cent.—the estate is worth $250,000.   Do you suppose I'm going to be euchred out of my money when I've won it, because you've gone crazy and romantic and willy-willow- ish?   An inquiry *de lunatico* is what I'll get out for you, my client; and, hang me, if I think the jury will be long in adjudging you *non compos mentis* and—as crazy as a March hare!"

Here his client astonishes the attorney again.   He says, coolly: "You need have no fear of your fee. I'm going to pay that out of my own pocket to-night. I will give you my check for ten thousand dollars on the Bank of Louisiana, also my note at three months, payable at the same institution—Martineau will indorse it—for fifteen thousand dollars.   Will that be accept- able to you?"

"Certainly! with Martineau's indorsement I can negotiate that note in five minutes at the bank to- morrow."

"Under these circumstances—having nothing more to do with my claims to the Tournay estate—you will please surrender my power of attorney."

So the necessary papers and receipts being made, and the note and check being given, Mr. Kitson Jarvis deposits them in a long, black pocket-book, and carefully buttoning this up in his inner pocket, turns to go, saying: "I'm much obliged to you. No hard feelings, I hope. You'll change your mind, my buck, in a day or two—you'll take the good things I and the Lord have given you. Of course, this highfalutin sentimental jamboree is kinder to grease your feelings—as it were—a leetle practical joke on your conscience. But, for all that, you're not quite a lunatic and—— Supposing we go out and pop that champagne cork. You won't?—Very well—I'm gone."

But here the greatest astonishment of his life comes to Mr. Jarvis. Covington says: "Don't go! I've got another case for you."

"Another case?" As good a one as this ?"

" Perhaps."

"The Lord be good to me!" And horses could not have dragged Mr. Jarvis from out that office.

" "I'm the guardian by this paper, of Nita Hortense Tournay, a minor. As her guardian I employ you to protect her interests and assert her lawful claim to freedom of life, limb and body, and her right to inherit from her father direct, as next of kin."

"Humph!" mutters the lawyer, and sinks down in a chair and begins to whistle softly, then says words that make Covington's heart like lead: " I won't take the case!"

"Why not?"

"Not on a *contingent* fee, any way! There's not one chance in a million of my winning it!"

" *Why not ?* "

" Because this is all poppy-cock—fiddle-de-dee—no 'count, nonsense. What kind of a case could we bring into court? The collateral evidence of those deeds of the Esplanade property, twice supported by the affidavit of Poussin, is all against Nita Hortense! The record of the bill of sale of the mother, the father's own deed of manumission—*unsigned*, prove that Louise and Nita were his slaves, and that he wished to *free* them. That knocks Nita Hortense sky high! We can't attack the fact that these children were their father's property. Still, I'll take Nita's case, but *not on a contingent fee !* "

"How much?" says Bob, hoarsely, eagerly.

"I want two thousand dollars in cash and three thousand dollars to be paid if I win, though I don't regard that last as cutting any figure. I'll sell it for five dollars now! Still, you've been pretty square and liberal with me in putting you in, and I'll be light on you in trying to turn you out. But Lord! This hotspur frenzy of yours won't last, Mr. Covington! You'll be coming to me in a day or two and suggesting 'Can't I have some of that retainer back? You'd better tear up these papers!' This document ain't any 'count any way; a girl in Nita's condition doesn't need a guardian —can't have one. You're her boss—her owner."

"Will you take the case?"

"Yes!—for the two thousand dollars I'd take most anything—and work for it!—for I'm an honest lawyer! I saved a cotton-press man's life once, when I knew he'd committed an up and down freeze-your-blood murder! I always do the square by my clients!"

"Very well," remarks Bob. I'll pay your fee!"

And he does so, drawing a check; though the appearance of his bank balance afterward, makes the young man look rather glum. "Now, Mr. Jarvis," he says: "give me your best views of the matter!"

"Well, my best views on the matter are that you tell me to tear up this check, and quit making a darned fool of yourself."

"I mean, your best views for your client, Nita Hortense Tournay!"

Mr. Kitson guffaws, puts Covington's last check in his pocket-book, beside the other one, buttons his coat up and says: "Do you mind ordering up a little of the right stuff and having a few cigars, Martineau?" I always think cuter when I'm fuming, but ain't thirsty." Then, with the whisky before him, and a lighted cigar in his mouth, Mr. Jarvis blows out the following suggestions: "There is still one chance, one leetle chance, in my client Nita's favor. We can't attack 'Prosper Tournay's title to the girls; our only hope is to attack the ownership of Faval Bigore Poussin to their mother, Eulalie Camila."

"Ah, that's the idea! Now you're talking!" cries Bob, excitedly.

"Yes, but I'm only *talking !* Bombarding that title is shooting at a very long range. You have to go back, not to the transfer of Eulalie Camila to Prosper Tournay, but to the time when the girl came into Poussin's hands — away back into the Dark Ages. May even have to go as far into the wilderness as Jackson's time — the battle of New Orleans. You see, Eulalie was about nineteen years old — so the bill of sale says—in 1832; that would make her born in 1813. It isn't so distant to go for documentary evidence, but for *viva voce* proof — personal deposition—it is like trying to get the affidavit of Pocahontas, as to whether she was ever married to Captain John Smith. Thirty years ago we would have had a much better chance of attacking Poussin's title; but every day this world rolls round, rubs out forty-year-old parole testimony like blazes!" Then he continues earnestly, addressing Martineau: "Tell me all you know about this fellow, Poussin."

And the *avocat* informing him, Jarvis remarks: "It's all against us! The fellow was rich at that time; he had plenty of slaves!"

Here seeing how Covington's brow lowers, Mr. Jarvis gives him a word or two of hope. He observes: "There's one thing I can tell you to chivvy you up a bit. Mrs. Combes told me this afternoon that she had no doubt that Louise had purer blood and whiter blood than any of us—regular blue blood—thorough Castilian, Hidalgo, keep-your-hat-on-in-the-presence-of-the-King-of-Spain article. She said she became convinced of this when she had charge of Louise." "There has probably been some deviltry somewhere back—about the time of Cleopatra—but how are we going to find, much more prove this, by satisfactory evidence? Mr. Covington, to all legal intents and purposes you might as well have kept yer two thousand dollars. You'd better look the thing right in the face and have papers made out to free these two girls before you change your mind."

"I shall never change my mind!" returns Bob. Then he says sternly: "Will you or will you not do your duty by the client whose money you now have in your pocket—Nita Hortense Tournay?"

I'll do my duty by little Nita, as I would if she were the Queen of England or Venus di Medici, or a nigger-wench! The minute I finger my retainer, I'm square. Watch me!" And he goes to the door, but suddenly turns back, a flash in his eye, and remarks: "You say, Martineau, that this chap Poussin was once an agent for Lafitte and his band of buccaneers, pirates, smugglers and patriots down on Barataria Bay ?"

"Yes!"

"All right — I'm going to work!" And without further explanation Kitson disappears, whistling softly; leaving Martineau and Covington gazing at each other.

"What do you think of the matter?" asks Bob.

"That you have probably engaged the best man you could have found for your purpose. By the by, how are you off for ready money?"

"Pretty flat after the last payment," mutters Bob.

"I have sixty thousand dollars for the Tournay estate in bank at present. Do you want any of it?" says Martineau. "That shows what I think of the matter!"

"Not a dime!"

"Understand me," remarks the *avocat*, "that when you paid Kitson Jarvis his commission for obtaining you the Tournay estates, you practically acknowledged that they were in your possession. You might as well look the matter right in the face. All this Nita business is nonsense."

"It is my one hope of making my promise good to the woman I love," cries Bob. "Good night!" And, Covington strides away.

Looking after him, Martineau shrugs his shoulders and mutters: "Most of his ready money gone! $60,000 in bank for him—two fine plantations and city property—an exquisitely beautiful slave whom he loves and who loves him! *Parbleu!* There is a very great temptation ahead of my young gentleman!"

But the Tempter has not yet quite come home to Bob Covington. He strides off to the Orleans Club, wishing to forget the matter, but does not.

The rooms of that brilliant establishment are not very

full   It is now well along in April; a good many of the *habitués* are either flitting to the soft gulf breezes at Pass Christian or to Northern watering places.   The racing contingent have all gone away; a great many of them, Kentuckians principally, having dropped all their winnings of the first race, and more besides, upon the last one, when their colt suffered defeat.

However, Mr. Covington meets young Hector Soulé and McBurney, and sits down to talk to them, the Major chatting to him of the fearfully bad luck of his friend Talliaferro on the fatal Saturday on which Lecomte reversed the verdict.

Soulé telling him that La Farge is now in Havana, and suggesting: "Your trial as a second won't amount to much.   You didn't kill Delaborde, whose death is regarded here as a public blessing.   But shove your case along, so Henri can judge whether it is best for him to return immediately or send for Alma."

"Alma?   Who is she?"

"Why, didn't you know," remarks Hector, "that Henri had *placéed* to him about six months ago Alma de Careno?   She was not a slave.   In fact old Careno is quite a rich man; still there's a tinge of African descent in the family, which, of course, permits no other union.   The girl adored La Farge, and according to the old Creole custom it was the only thing that permitted her happiness—a practical marriage, without the ceremony.   Henri is very anxious, if he is compelled to remain away from New Orleans, that she should join him.   They've a very pretty little place on Ursulines Street; old Careno settled that upon the young lady, and gave her a grand ball as the usual send off.   I was there; so were nearly all the bloods of New Orleans; but, of course, Henri's mother and sister, though they knew of the affair, were not present."

"Do you think Henri loves her?"

"Devotedly."

"And the young lady?"

"She will be as true to him as if fifty priests had said service over them."

But this talk of a beautiful woman and love and devotion sets Bob's heart to beating.

He gets up, bidding his friends good night, and refusing offers of play wanders out of the club-house.

He thinks New Orleans is a deucedly slow place, as from the very force of habit his steps turn toward the Tournay residence. He sees no light in the *salon* windows.

Then suddenly a wave of anxiety goes over him and he thinks: "Great Taylor! I haven't heard how Louise is for—for four hours!" and would cross the street and make personal inquiry, but checks himself and mutters: "No—that infernal promise!" and strides rapidly back to the Verandah Hotel, where getting hold of Mr. Cæsar he sends him off with a hurried note to Mrs. Joyce. It is not very late; only ten o'clock in the evening—and receiving response that there is no fear of brain fever and that Louise is sleeping, Mr. Covington, worn out by the conflicting emotions of this astounding day, turns in himself and tries to sleep, but cannot.

About twelve o'clock he dresses again and goes to the Orleans Club and there spends the night in poker, with very bad financial results to himself; for it requires a calm mind and a cool philosophy to successfully dally with chips, red, blue and white.

At six o'clock in the morning from this game, he strolls out upon the streets of New Orleans   A flower-girl, with bunches of beautiful blossoms, puts an idea into his head; he goes to a florist in the French market, and orders delivered to Miss Louise Tournay each morning a bouquet of the same beautiful white roses and orange blossoms that had been sent by him during his New York absence, but had been kept from the captive fearing they would drive her to despair.

These blossoms have a different effect to-day.

While he tries to eat his breakfast at the hotel a note comes from Mrs. Joyce, which makes him very happy, and reads as follow:

You Darling Good Fellow:

I'd like to get hold of you to kiss you myself! Those orange blossoms have been a better tonic to Louise than all the doctor's medicines. She is now asleep, the flowers in her hand.

In a day or two she will probably be well enough to see you. Then I don't believe she'll let you keep that promise.

By the by, how about Nita? Am I empowered to get masters for her? The child should not lose her schooling.

Yours admiringly,
PAMELA JOYCE.

Comforted by this note, poor Bob turns in and contrives to get a few hours' sleep.

CHAPTER XIX.

TWO PECULIAR ADVERTISEMENTS.

NOTWITHSTANDING, Mr. Covington doesn't look very spry and cute; so Mr. Jarvis thinks when he meets him at Martineau's office in the afternoon.

"I have brought over," says the attorney, "some things that belong to ye." He hands Bob a box containing all Louise's money and jewelry that had been filched from her; also, a little pocket-book with "Nita" on it in silver letters, containing the poor child's wealth, that had been garnisheed by the keen Mrs. Combes. "Your property, I reckon."

"I suppose so—for the present," answers his client, with a sigh. Then he says: "Any evidence?"

"Nix!"

"Why don't you get to work?"

"Get to work? So I am! But when a man is groping about for a pin in a coal-hole on a dark night, and *there is no pin*, he's going to do some looking before he finds it. Still, I'm lighting a candle to blink about for it." And he goes away, leaving Covington looking glumly at poor Louise's and Nita's wealth, that is now his.

"You don't seem very well," remarks Martineau.

"No! My blood boils when I think of this business! See! what has been filched from them—poor little Nita's pocket-book, with a paltry twenty dollars that I gave the child in New York, and this ring I placed upon Louise's finger. I'm their robber—not Jarvis!"

"Not at all, my dear boy! It is the law," mutters the *avocat*. "And you are acting more nobly than any one I ever guessed would under such circumstances.

A sleepless night, eh? You'll have more of them. Now go off and get some rest."

"Not till I have returned these."

"You are going to the Tournay residence?"

"I have to! I must arrange about Nita's schooling."

Glancing after him, Martineau, with a French shrug of his shoulders, thinks: "Poor fellow! Nibbling round the bait now. I very much fear for his last promise."

And it is in danger!

As he raises the knocker of the Tournay house at two o'clock this afternoon, Bob Covington has but one thought: "*She* is upstairs!"

A servant answering his summons, however, he simply sends his card to Mrs. Joyce, and the man returning, announces that lady will see him.

A moment after, Pamela comes into the *salon* and beams on him through her spectacles, whispering: "You noble, whole-souled darling boy! I can't tell you what happiness those white blossoms gave to your—your fiancée!" Then she goes on: "I think you will have to forget your last promise—the one she did not hear. In two or three days, Louise will be able to see you; if you do not come, she will not understand, and will droop again. You caught her heart tighter, young man, in your last few words than you ever caught it before, much as she loved you."

This makes Covington hold up his head, which has been rather long-faced during the first part of the day.

"We will consider that last promise of mine when Louise—Miss Tournay—is well enough to see me," he answers. "At present, I have brought you these trinkets that were taken from her, and Nita's little pocket money of which that woman robbed the child."

"Which she has been in want of, I think," laughs Mrs. Joyce. The child has been anxious for bonbons."

Just at this moment, Nita, entering, lends embarrassment to the interview. She comes up in unaffected artlessness, gives Mr. Covington a confiding kiss, and prattles: "Won't you take me for a walk, Cousin Bob?

Mrs. Joyce doesn't know whether you would like me to go out alone. She says I must do everything you wish!"

"And why?" laughs Covington.

"Because you're my master, I guess. They don't want me to talk about it, but I know it. You needn't look unhappy—I'm not afraid of you. Louise is, though! Goodness! how she kissed your flowers this morning, and then looked scared. I love you, but I shouldn't care if you were angry with me."

"Tush!" cries Mrs. Joyce, breaking in. "You don't know what you are talking about!"

"Oh, yes, I do. He is our master." Then turning her big eyes on Bob she says in childish trust: "You're not going to be stern and strict and cruel with us, like the servants in the kitchen say some people are?"

"Great snakes! You haven't been talking to *them*?" asks Bob, aghast.

"No, but I have been asking questions; I was anxious to know."

"Then for God's sake don't think any more about this wretched business. Only when you want anything or have any favor to ask, come to me and I will do it."

"Will you?" cries Nita, taking him at his word. "Very well. In Canal Street I am told that they sell the finest *biscuit glacé* in the world. Will you get me some?"

"Lots of it—and bonbons besides! Anything else you want!" cries Bob, delighted.

And this hard-hearted serfholder takes his little chattel, who walks with him her hand confidingly in his, to the finest confectioner on the great thoroughfare, and loads her down with enough goodies—as Mrs. Joyce remarks after they get home—"to make her sick for a week!"

Then Pamela telling him Louise will be well enough to be up the next day, Mr. Covington departs.

But his condition of mind is still unfavorable to successful poker, and passing the night in playing, with more bad luck, the next morning, instead of going to

Martineau's, he walks into Jarvis's office on Lafayette Street and demands: "What have you been doing?"

"Well, look at the *Crescent*," remarks Kitson.   "Do you see those ads I have underlined?   Read 'em."

Examining the columns of the paper, Mr. Covington notes two curious advertisements, one reading:

A meeting of all who have sought for the buried treasures of Lafitte is called at the office of Wells & Burnham, No. 25 Conti Street, at 10 o'clock, April 25. Something of great interest to all who have sought for the buccaneer's lost treasure has been discovered.

The second, in another column of the paper, is:

PENSIONS.

It is expected the next Congress will pass a special bill for the pensioning of the survivors of Lafitte's band, who fought with such gallantry under Jackson at New Orleans. Immediate registration in advance will be of great benefit to any of the survivors of the once famous " Company of the Gulf." Please apply at the office of Bookman & Caldwell, pension agents, 138 Magazine Street, April 27, from 10 A.M. to 1 P.M. All failing to report that day must wait until after the act is passed.

"What the deuce do these mean?" asks Bob, astounded.

"These are in the interests of our little Nita Hortense," remarks Jarvis, contemplatively.   "I am now acting on the only supposition that will make her case a possible one; that is, that she has no negro or Indian blood whatsoever in her veins, and is absolutely descended from white parents, all the way down from Adam and Eve.   Now the question is, how a white child or white girl might become a slave; of course only through the villainy and rascality of some cuss who put her in that false position.   This, I'm sorry to say, has been done by unscrupulous speculators more than once, commencing with that fellow Turnbull* and his Florida land grant in 1767; when he induced five

---

* In 1767 Dr. Turnbull, obtaining a grant of land in Florida, paid four hundred pounds sterling to the Governor of Modon in Greece and received permission to convey sundry families from that country for colonization. He also brought a number from Corsica and Minorca, luring them from their homes with promises of gift of lands, provisions, and clothing.
Worn out by the passage of four months, many of them were

hundred Greeks, Corsicans and Minorcans and their families to take passage from the Mediterranean in his vessels and planted them in New Smyrna, surrounded by Seminoles, alligators, and rattlesnakes. Here he made them his slaves, working them under the lash and selling a number of their daughters of pure Greek and Minorcan blood into slavery in various places in the Soutn.

"Next there is the regulation, low-down kidnapping of poor white children, though this has not been very frequent, I'm happy to say. But Nita's only chance is on the Andalusian, Castilian, blue-blood theory, which bears out Mrs. Combes's idea in regard to the girls. Acting on that, I have been figuring out where and how Poussin might have obtained Eulalie Camila as a child. Being the agent of Lafitte, whose vessels scoured the Gulf of Mexico and captured many ships, some of 'em probably with white children on board, may possibly have put some girls of Caucasian blood into his hands; as children, they couldn't protect themselves, and perhaps he turned an honest penny on a few of them.

"Now, this was a long time ago. Going into the Dark Ages is a difficult matter, especially for personal evidence, and I want to see every human being that may by any chance know, if any such thing occurred. Those two advertisements will bring every critter

---

sick when they arrived on the American coast. These people, of pure white blood and many of them of former social ease—in all some fifteen hundred souls—were taken into the interior of Florida and settled at New Smyrna. They were to work for five years for Turnbull.

Here they were governed and harshly treated as slaves by Turnbull. Many who had been in affluence in their own country had to go barefoot through the year, and were worked in gangs under the lash, cruelties equal to those of the Spaniards of San Domingo upon the Indians of that island being inflicted on them. Among other outrages, Turnbull took scores of the most beautiful daughters of these people and sold them as slaves in the American colonies and Louisiana.

Finally, after a number of years they obtained their liberty by appeal to the English authorities of St. Augustine, but Turnbull's punishment was practically nominal.

Vide: "Sewall's Sketches of St. Augustine," *unexpurgated* edition, "Our World," etc.—ED.

around here who has ever dabbled in the Lafitte matter, one way or 'tother. I've put the dates of both of these meetings very close, for two reasons: First, you're in a hurry about the matter, I reckon. Second, I don't want anybody to write on to Washington and find out advertisement No. 2 is a hoax. Third, because death may sweep away at any moment the parol evidence that might be vital. These veterans of the battle of New Orleans are growing beautifully less day by day."

"Do you think anything will come of it?"

"Humph! When you throw a fishing-line into the water, do you know whether you're going to get a fish?"

"I don't often," remarks Bob. "I'm a poor angler."

"Well, say that you want to find a fish of a peculiar kind, of which there's only one swimming in the waters of the whole ocean, and that fish is *dead*—what's your chances? I have no doubt I'll get lots of fish with these advertisements; but the question is whether they'll be the fish I want. But you'll excuse me bidding you good-day, Mr. Covington. I'll see you at Martineau's office on the afternoons of April 25th and 27th, to tell you what turns up from these ads."

From this interview Covington comes away, a little more cheerful. At all events, Kitson is *trying* to do something.

But this waiting with no hope is dreary work. The club does not satisfy him; the city seems to him as forlorn as when it had the plague upon it the year before. Even his old *confrères* of the Orleans Club appear to him different, and he seems different to them. They notice that Bob Covington has grown meditative and is no more the dashing, reckless, light-hearted fellow of a month ago. What he wants is the sight of his bondmaid—his sweetheart—his love of loves, Louise.

So a little time runs along, each day Mrs. Joyce reporting to him Louise is getting stronger. Finally she writes Louise is well and makes him very happy, but with this news comes a shock.

He is walking along Canal Street, its *banquettes* thronged with people, its pavements crowded with carriages, some of them containing gay parties bound to the Lake. Suddenly he notices the cross-matched team of the Tournay equipage, and past him roll Louise and Mrs. Joyce.

Despite his promise to himself, Bob's eyes will turn to this being he adores; he doffs his hat, and she, seeing him, half rises in the carriage and waives a daintily gloved hand in recognition. Robed as she is in tight-fitting driving dress, Louise is patrician from the plumed hat that is perched upon her dark brown locks to the perfectly booted little foot that peeps out from beneath her skirt.

As Covington looks, for the life of him he cannot help thinking: "How marvelous, that this lovely, high bred creature is my *property!*"

Just then their eyes meet. For one moment Louise's are bright, almost radiant. Suddenly she blushes painfully; her head droops. The next instant, though her face is pale, her eyes gleam with mutinous fire and her fair head is carried very haughtily.

Mrs. Joyce, sitting beside her, whispers: "What is the matter, Louise? At first you looked so pleased to see Mr. Covington; now you seem angry."

"It is only with my fate!" whispers the girl, "not with him. When he first looked at me his eyes said, '*Fiancée*'; but afterward they said 'Bondmaid.'"

"You ought to be ashamed of yourself!" cries Pamela, indignantly. "After all he has done for you — all he is trying to do for you and your sister. No man was ever more generous!"

"Perhaps my pride makes me too sensitive ; but, oh!—it is a curious thing to feel you do not belong to yourself!" Louise mutters with a shudder. Then looking at her pretty glove, she says bitterly: "This hand is not my own—it is *his*. This foot," she taps the tip of her little boot with a parasol, "is *his* also." He has but to say the word, and all these fine things come off, and I go to waiting in his kitchen or working in his cotton-field, as he elects! The very bread I put in my mouth is *his*. The money I spend for gloves or bonbons, is *his* also. And though I love Bob Covington dearly,—very dearly!—more now than ever—still at times I can't help rattling my gilded chains." And she draws the breath in through her nostrils like a thoroughbred curbed too tightly.

As for the owner of all this beauty, something in the girl's glance has made him ashamed of himself. He mutters: "Every time she'll look on me, my sweetheart will feel the humiliation of her lot. I'm glad I made that promise not to see her!" adding doggedly, "I'll keep it, too!"

This he does; the Tournay carriage passes him again, but he doesn't glance toward it, though Louise's bright eyes are turned almost beseechingly to him! Seeing he will not look, the young lady laughs a little, then jeers to Mrs. Joyce: "Mr. Covington doesn't seem much interested in his *property*."

This evening, as luck will have it, Bob runs across another very beautiful young lady. He has finished a morose and dejected dinner at the Verandah, and wandered into the parlor of the hotel, which is not very crowded, wondering what he will do to kill time this lonely evening, when a very handsome, dashing and splendidly dressed girl comes toward him, followed by a gentleman of slouch hat and military bearing. "Dad, here's Mr. Covington!" she cries; then says, in easy intimacy: "What are you doing, Bob, in this hot city?" and the Kentuckian finds himself with Miss Johnson's hand in his.

"Why, Miss Sally!" remarks the gentleman addressed. "That's just what I was going to ask you. You've come from Louisville, haven't you?"

"No, from Texas. Father's got millions of acres there."

"Five hundred thousand, my dear child," corrects General Sam Johnson, then goes on: "I have a big ranch near Galveston, Mr. Covington, but land is the only thing that is not valuable in Texas." As he shakes hands, he continues: "They're going to run you for Congress next election in the Blue Grass district, I understand!"

"I hope so," says Bob, cheerily.

"Well, count on my support."

"And mine also!" says Miss Sally, enthusiastically.

Then she asks: "You've come from Lexington?"

"No, from New York."

"Pretty cousin in New York?" laughs the young lady, archly.

"No, pretty cousin is here."

"Ah, that's the reason you've come from New York?" says Miss Sally. Then she adds: "We shall be here for a day or two; supposing you take me to see the pretty cousin—Miss Tournay, I believe?"

In his excitement and agony Covington has scarcely realized the immensity of the awful social gulf that separates his love from women of his rank and class in life—that a social taint is on his sweetheart that he may ignore but cannot efface—that to introduce Louise to this young lady who is talking so easily to him would now be considered by her father and Miss Johnson's friends an act of which no gentleman could be guilty and an insult for which even his blood could not atone. His face shows the harrowing misery of the thought.

"You—you are not well, Mr. Covington?" asks Miss Johnson, anxiously.

"Yes—I am well—but Miss—Miss Tournay is not— at least not well enough to receive visitors," he mutters.

The girl looking at him and noting his embarrassment, thinks: "Aha! Refused! Dashing Bob Covington has met his Waterloo at last. But I'll take pity on him for a day or two," and suggests: "What are you thinking of doing this evening? Papa is going to take me to the Amphitheatre. Tony Denier, the celebrated clown, will perform, and Mlle. Seraphine will do her wonderful butterfly dance on *horseback*. The *steed*, if not the *lady*, should attract a Blue Grass man."

"It does!" says Covington. "Supposing I——"

"Go with us? That will be delightful. Dad won't bother us much," whispers the young lady, taking his arm.

So the two go off to the Amphitheatre, and "Dad" doesn't bother them much, for practically it is a *tête-à-tête*, Gen. Sam Johnson walking to the bar with great regularity between acts and permitting his charming daughter and Mr. Covington plenty of opportunity for confidential chat, which, of course, drifts into a petite flirtation.

Afterward, they have a very pleasant supper at Moreau's restaurant, Mr. Baldwin, of Mississippi, joining them, together with his sister, a fragile-looking Vicksburg girl. The consequence is that a party is formed to go to the lake the next afternoon, and Mr. Covington, looking into the beautiful eyes and under the influence of the persuasive tongue of a very pretty girl, and mighty happy to get some respite from his own anxieties, consents to escort Miss Sally Johnson.

The next afternoon they all drive to Spanish Fort, where the rest of the party have a delightful evening, and Bob kills time, though his heart would be nearly broken did he but know the effect his excursion has produced.

Just before dusk, as their big, open carriage has turned into the shell-road, a closed vehicle containing Louise, upon her second drive of renewed health and strength, accompanied by Mrs. Joyce, has passed it. Bob's eyes being on the beautiful Miss Johnson, who sits beside him on the box, he has not noticed his bondmaid *fiancée*—but Louise has seen him.

Suddenly, Pamela wonders at a little muffled, plaintive cry and a slight ringing of fair hands, for the girl is murmuring to herself bitterly, hopelessly: "Is it his promise that keeps him from me ?"

"The cruel villain!" thinks Mrs. Joyce. And eyeing through her specs viciously the back of the departing Covington, she takes the sufferer to her heart.

Next morning, the "cruel villain" is interviewed in the parlor of his hotel by an irate Yankee lady whose specs flash fire, and Bob Covington discovers there is decided latent force in Mrs. Joyce's prim face when the ex-schoolmistress thinks occasion calls for it.

She thus addresses him: "Look here, young man; do you think you are doing your duty?"

"What duty?"

The answer that comes from this old abolitionist lady takes away the slaveholder's breath: "The duty of exercising your authority as *master* over those two girls."

"WHAT?"

"I know you, in your generous heart, have told Martineau that you will hold him harmless for letting them have all the money they require. But that is not everything. Nita is perfectly uncontrollable. She says you are her only boss—nice word for a little girl to use—picked up in the kitchen—and she runs around in the streets just as she pleases."

"But cannot Louise control her?"

Here Mrs. Joyce shocks him a second time, by saying: "Can a *nothing* control a *nothing?* Nita says that you are as much her sister's boss as you are hers. Only yesterday I heard her tell Louise: 'We've both got to skip the line when Cousin Bob swings the rope.'"

"Hang it, Madame, I'm not running a nursery!" cries Bob, excitedly. "I give you the authority! You make Nita skip the rope!"

"And who will make Louise skip the rope?" laughs Mrs. Joyce, then she adds: "She will do it for you very gracefully and very docilely."

"I don't want to control her—I only want to guard and protect her."

"As Louise is placed, to guard her you must control her!"

"Great Lord! Boss my sweetheart? I ain't built that way, Madame!" mutters Covington, rising as if to conclude the interview.

"Oh yes, you are; but you don't want the trouble. With you it's heroics at your lawyer's and poker at your club," says Pamela savagely. Then she rises, too, and whispers in his ear: "Besides, you're breaking her heart by your neglect."

"Breaking her heart?"

"Yes. This morning I thank God that your white roses and orange blossoms came as usual, otherwise I think Louise would have been sick again."

"Sick? You astonish me! Why so?"

"Last night she saw you riding with that beautiful Miss Johnson of Louisville. Louise cannot command your attentions—think of that! If you're the generous fellow I believe you, prove it by giving them to her. Boss the Tournay house—take personal direction of Louise and by your care of her show that you love her. Will you?"

"I'd—I'd rather not try it?" says poor Bob, nervously.

"You must! Read this letter and see you must!" And Pamela hands him this:

My Dear Bob:

I *don't* want you to keep your promise—I mean the last one. The first is my glory and sustenance—the last is my despair. I know your generous reason, but I must write this, even if you chide me for it. You have a duty to me as my *master* just the same as I have to you as your *slave*. I demand you fulfill your duty.

Something that occurred last night shows me I not only must have your guidance, but protection. I don't mean because I, lonely and deserted, saw you in the society of a young lady of your own rank—though that would have broken my heart had it not been for those dear white flowers that came as usual to remind me of your other pledge that makes me happy, even in my trouble.

I know the underlined words in this letter are those that you forbade. But come to me, even if you chide me, even if you punish me; your sternest government would be better than your neglect, which is despair to

Your loving, devoted, and helpless

LOUISE.

"Why—how—does she need my protection? Hang me if I can understand!" ejaculates Covington with knit brows.

Then, to him Pamela tells a little incident that occurred the night before, at which he utters muttered anathemas and looks very serious. "Louise will explain it to you more fully," continues Mrs. Joyce. "But you can see that you have a duty to perform. Will you do it?"

"I will!" says Bob, determinedly. "You tell my darling I know my duty now and that I will do it."

And as Pamela goes away, Mr. Covington walks about the room with anguish in his eyes and uncertainty in his demeanor, the prerogatives and power of his

proud station not seeming to come very easily to this
fly-away Kentucky politician and club man of a month
before.

BOOK IV

How He Ruled Her,

CHAPTER XX.

"ISN'T IT WONDERFUL?"

BUT Bob Covington has some of his legal heroics, as Pamela terms them, to do this day before he assumes the reins of government.

Even now he feels glad that he has determined to "bust that promise!" The sun seems brighter to him, the town more cheerful, as he goes down to Martineau's office to see Jarvis in regard to the effect of his advertisement for Lafitte's veterans of the battle of New Orleans; the one for the seekers after the pirate's treasure having been a miserable fiasco.

On the afternoon of the 25th, Jarvis had come into Martineau's office, his coat torn and one or two suspicious bruises on his face.

"Did many of the treasure-seekers of Lafitte turn up at the office of Wells & Burnham?" Covington, who has been awaiting him, has asked.

"Yes. Gol darn it! I acted *Wells*, and I'll never do it any more. I hired the room for the day."

"Were there many there?"

"Many? Good lord, every nigger in New Orleans and the adjoining parishes came *en bloc!* I think most of the 'coons round here have done nothing on moonlight nights but hunt for Lafitte's treasure. Any way, there were enough of them to mob me. When I told 'em I wanted their *secret* information, they thought I was a spy to sponge the knowledge of the pirate's treasures out of 'em. Well, here I am—I'm alive, but that's about all. However, we'll hope for better results from the other cusses; there weren't many niggers in Lafitte's band any way." And Jarvis had gone away.

This afternoon, the 27th, he comes more cheerfully into Martineau's office, and says to the eager Bob: "The pension business to-day worked a leetle better than the other. I had a thousand liars, perjurers and villains call on me, and six *genuine* survivors of Lafitte's band; besides quite a delegation of widows and daughters and offspring of the late lamented pirate. No less than ten of his widows turned up; Jean must have been a hummer! And among the six veterans was our friend Poussin himself."

"That's great!" mutters Bob, triumphantly.

"Why? It's natural enough for Faval Bigore to turn up for his pension. There's no doubt he was one of Lafitte's band. That don't have any bearing on this case. Poussin turned up for his pension, and I tried to pump him — that's where I made a fool of my-self!"

"Did he disclose anything?"

"Well, all he would disclose, was fighting the big gun at the cotton-battery and performing prodigies of valor under Jackson. No — nothing out of Poussin. But I did get a drop of information from one of the late members of the 'Brotherhood of the Gulf.' It isn't at all curious those fellows don't care much about blabbing of what they did in those days; though they've been pardoned for it. A fellow named Jack Goslyn told me that in the three months before the battle of New Orleans, they captured several vessels bound from Spanish ports and one English bark. All these they were compelled to burn, and run their cargoes rapidly up into the interior, on account of the coming of the English squadron. Furthermore, that Poussin was one of the agents to whom these goods were entrusted, and that he believes Poussin never made full returns for the property put in his hands and is the biggest liar, scoundrel and sneak thief unhung. At all events, all the veterans, except Poussin, hate Poussin and think he robbed them.

"I made some guarded queries as to what might have been the fate of any passengers or crews of these vessels, but Goslyn didn't seem to care to talk much about them.   He, however, told me that any niggers on board were always sold up the country. "

" And the whites? "

" Reckon the regulation business — men walked the plank, and the ladies were made pirate-brides, etc."

" This doesn't seem to lead to anything," mutters Covington.

"No.   So far not one millionth as much evidence as that which let you walk out of court to-day, charged with being an accessory before the fact to the killing of Jules Delaborde.   Two nigger coachmen's evidence weren't good against whites.   A near-sighted German surgeon, who couldn't see anything but the wounded man, and Monsieur Albert Montant, Delaborde's second, who perjured himself after the usual manner of gentlemen.   Judge, as usual, took occasion to strongly condemn the barbarous practice of dueling— that's formula! This ought to be good news for your friend, the principal, La Farge."

"Then you don't think you can do anything for little Nita, I suppose," mutters Bob.

" Well, I never say die, as long as the cash don't run out."   And Mr. Jarvis goes into a brown study, from which he awakes in about two minutes, and says: " I want you to get me all the information Miss Louise can give you about her mother."

" I—I fear I can't accommodate you immediately," remarks Bob, hesitating.

" Oh that promise of yours not to see her as long as you are her master!" jeers Jarvis. " That's bosh! You'll have to see her some day and you'll *be* her master this month—next month—and a *year from now*. In this case I want every scrap of information I can get.   Not that I think there is any, nohow.   Reckon, if any deviltry did take place, we'll never see the witnesses to it till the Day of Judgment.   Now you get me the information, or, if not, by Coke upon Lyttelton I throw up the case!"

" Very well; I'll do it," says Bob, delighted at an extra reason for breaking his promise.

"Right you are! Now give me five hundred dollars!"

"What do you want them for?"

"Expenses! You bring your information to the Havana steamer at four o'clock to-day; I'll meet you there. There's a chance, your report may just send me cracking off to Spanish parts. Get me a miniature if you can—though I don't suppose there's anything of the kind—of Eulalie Camila—— But where's that five hundred?"

With almost a groan, Covington writes a check; for between poker and Jarvis and his payment of commission for a great estate of which he will not take possession, Bob is coming very close to mortgaging his Blue Grass farm about this time, and he knows it.

But Louise's eyes, shining pure as stars in winter still beam on him and keep him to his purpose.

The thought of seeing her, takes him along Dauphine street quite rapidly.

Ten minutes after, he is at the Tournay residence; Mrs. Joyce comes to him, and he tells her, hurriedly, his errand.

"You will be here this evening also," she says, " and assume the reins of authority?"

"Oh, mine will be a kid-glove government," remarks Bob, laughingly.

"Yes, but put a steel hand into the kid glove," suggests Pamela, whose experience has given her some pertinent ideas as to the best way of managing girls. Giving him a moment to digest this idea, she adds, cheerily:

"Now, young man, if you will take a little hint from an old schoolmarm, listen to me! Louise will probably this very day offer to you her full subordination. Then, mark me!—do not laugh it off with a Pish! and refuse it! Accept it as your right, assume it as your prerogative, impose it on her as her duty, and, if necessary, compel her obedience even in little things. Then she will obey when it comes to great ones."

"What great ones can there be between us?" asks Bob, somewhat astonished at these suggestions.

"Well, I understand you're spending a great deal

of money in trying to give Louise a freedom that even your lawyers pronounce impossible. She in some wild frenzy may in a moment destroy your last hope, unless you control her."

"I think I understand you," mutters Covington. "But, hang it, Madame! this is out of my line of business."

"Oh no, it is not. You're afraid she won't love you so much if you control her. But let me tell you something about women that you have never picked up yet: she won't love you unless you *do* control her."

"By Heaven, Madame! she doesn't need control!"

The answer that he gets astounds him. "Miss Louise Tournay perhaps did not! She had the right to guide and the power to protect herself. You have now no more Louise Tournay to deal with; you have a girl who has by the law no *right* to control herself, no power to defend herself, whose only hope is in your guidance and authority. Martineau told me that you would soon have to assume public ownership of her, in order even to free her. Look the thing squarely in the face! Do you think it is too much to give a little time and a little self-control to directing the destinies of the girl you love, who, by some law made by the devil, is now compelled to look to you both for government and defense? Please put that in your brain! Now step into the other parlor, dear Mr. Covington, and I'll send Louise to you at once."

The portières between the rooms are drawn.

Opening these, Covington's heart gives a mighty throb. Louise is standing before him!

Dressed in some simple morning gown of white, despite a suspicion of invalid negligée, the girl looks, though very slightly paler, fresh as a daisy and as blushing as a rose-bud. Bob notes the pathetic expression that was in her eyes when she first stood before him on his return, has nearly left them.

His thoughts are, however, vague. At present all he knows is that his goddess is before him—beautiful, piquant and charming as in the old and happy days.

"Louise—Miss Tournay—" he gasps, and for a moment would bow and take her hand to give her formal greeting.

But she, looking up at him, murmurs: "Are we not affianced? Do you repudiate your nosegay?" and gracefully rests on his shoulder one white hand, holding the bunch of rose-buds and orange blossoms she has received this morning; then, trustingly, lovingly, puts up the prettiest little mouth in the world for him to kiss.

What man could refuse such greeting? Not once but many times, the two rose-bud lips held up to him are kissed with true Kentucky ardor. Then his arm goes round her as she seems weak and totters a little, and she murmurs archly to him: "That's right! I'm not *very* strong yet. I—I think I need this hand to—to lead me through the world," then half laughs: "Oh, you needn't carry me! I'm not so extremely weak."

For Bob, in his plenitude of youthful love and strength, has borne Louise very tenderly but like a little child to a sofa and placed her on it.

"Won't you sit down? No! near me—by my side!" whispers the young lady, blushing as he takes her at her word.

"I—I haven't much time to stay," mutters Covington, who feels his resolutions of formality flying to the four winds of heaven, with his sweetheart beside him, looking love, trust, and gratitude, all in one. "I—I came on a matter of business."

"On business? Oh!" murmurs Louise, then adds in disappointed archness: "I—I had presumed it was my note."

"I—I intended to come this evening in answer to that," returns Bob.

"Did you? Then I hold you to that promise. But what business?"

"Very important—for you—for Nita."

"Ah, you have hope?"

For one instant the brightest sunshine he has ever seen floats about her face, then dies away as he answers: "It wouldn't be justice to you if I said I had. But I have a very astute mind working for you. And in that regard I am here to ask you to tell me all you can remember about your mother."

"My mother? Oh—I see," remarks Louise.

"Well, I was such a child, even when she died, I can recollect but little, and that only in a hazy, dreamy way. You see I—I didn't know that my mother's status would—would make me your—your——. Oh, I don't mean to reproach you!" for Covington has turned away his head. "You're the best, the dearest, the kindest master—No, I don't mean that, Mr. Covington!—*Bob!*"

He turns to her.

"Bob's the best name, I think, after all," she says, nestling on his shoulder, then goes on: "I'll tell you about my mother. She couldn't have been very well educated; I have just a faint suspicion, now I think of it, she did not read and write. That's bad news for you, isn't it?" for her listener has been unable to repress a sigh. "But she played exquisitely on the piano and harp and sang divinely, and was very, very beautiful. She was treated with the greatest respect and love about the plantation; though I don't think she ever left it. I'm sure my father never brought her to New Orleans."

"Very beautiful—of a Castilian type?" asks Bob, eagerly.

"Yes; but I can show her to you; you can judge for yourself. A strolling artist, some friend of my father—who—who was a poet and *savant*, you know," sneers the girl bitterly, "was once upon the plantation and painted a little miniature."

Louise runs away and returns in a few minutes with a portrait on ivory that justifies what she says of her mother's beauty. Gazing at this, Mr. Covington is delighted to notice that the face is of a pure Spanish type; though it indicates a lack of intellectuality. The eyes are very bright, the lips sensitive, the whole face wondrously vivacious, but without culture. Altogether, the picture indicates a woman of tender soul, loving heart, and bright, but uneducated mind, probably for lack of advantages in childhood.

"That is all you know?"

"Yes."

"Did your mother ever use any Spanish expressions?"

"Never!"

"Did she ever speak of her past life?"

"Yes."

"Ah!—in what way?"

"Well, she—I remember—she once said sadly to me that she had never been happy until she saw my father."

"That is all?"

"Everything."

"I must go," remarks Covington, rising and looking at his watch, for he remembers his appointment with Jarvis.

"So soon? Ah, it *was* business that brought you!" she pouts, "and you have talked of nothing else," giving him an arch but veiled glance that sets Mr. Bob's heart beating very fast.

"Yes, but it was your business—your freedom—your sister's welfare."

"Then I suppose I must forgive you. Forgive *you?*" she cries apologetically; "Ah! I have *nothing* to forgive!" then smiles: "Only I shall have *something* to forgive if you do not keep your promise and return this evening. But you *must* come!" she adds very seriously. "I have something to tell you that you must know," next falters: "For the last two days I—I have thought you were forgetting me—forgetting me, Bob—though each day came the bouquet to give me assurance of your love."

"Your—your health. My—my promise," stammers the young man.

"I won't think of any promise," cries the girl, her big eyes full of love, "but the great one you made me about Christ Church!" and grows red and blushing and takes his hand and falters: "The one I bless you for each morning as I wake, each night as I close my eyes, for by that I know the grandeur of your love, whether it ever comes or not." And she grows very tender to him and mutters: "If—if at the last you can't keep it—what—what shall we do?" and, blushing like a rose, quivers and sways, and somehow grows more tender to him all the time, and, putting her fair arms around his neck, nestles to him as if he were her only resting place on earth. Then she pleads: "Don't go *yet!*" but murmurs: "Well, if you must—I suppose the steamer will not wait—let me run down stairs with you," and, taking his hand, says: "Come into the garden with me; you can give me two minutes."

Here, walking by his side, she astounds and confuses him by murmuring: "Is not it wonderful that I, who used to be so proud, am now so humble? I try to make myself realize it. I say: 'This dress is *his*—this hat is *his*—this glove is *his*—this hand is *his*—*I am his!*'"

"Haven't I begged, entreated, commanded you not to talk that way?" mutters Bob, who has been hanging his head during this oration.

"Yes, but Mrs. Joyce tells me you are going to assume personal direction of me." She looks shyly at him, but goes on, very sweetly: "I am very glad of this; when you come this evening, I'll tell you why. I shall try to be obedient to you, but if not—" she adds archly yet nervously: "I—I suppose you'll have to make me skip the rope."

"Very well," says Bob, laughing. "I shall commence now. "You have several times called me 'Master' to-day, for which I shall inflict a penalty."

"Yes, dear—what penalty?"

"Five kisses, when I come this evening."

At which she droops her head and murmurs blushingly: "Then I'm afraid I shall be very naughty," but runs up the stairs, kissing her hand to him; and when again in the house laughs: "I believe he *will* come to inflict that penalty."

From this interview Bob goes hurriedly to the Havana boat and meets Jarvis.

On hearing Louise's account of her mother and seeing the miniature, the attorney says: "I'll take that with me to Cuba."

"You're satisfied you'd better go?"

"It's about the last chance; though slimmer than a shadpole."

In Havana you may meet Monsieur La Farge," remarks Covington, trying to get the affair out of his mind. "Would you tell him the result of my trial and that it's perfectly safe for him to come back ? "

"I'll do that with pleasure," rejoins Kitson. "I'll take his case for fifty dollars, and guarantee that he shan't be under arrest over two hours."

"Thank you. La Farge's address is Fulton's Hotel."

"Thank *you !* Shouldn't wonder if I make a double stroke of business this trip. I'll acquit La Farge and open up a Creole practice," remarks Jarvis, cheerily, and the gangplank being drawn in and the steamer's lines cast off, proceeds very happily on his way to the Havana.

CHAPTER XXI.

"FROM HIM ALL THINGS MUST COME."

COVINGTON, gazing after the departing boat, thinks gloomily: "That last five hundred dollars! By Heaven, if I play at poker again and lose, I'll have to sell Mr. Cæsar."

This idea is still in his head when, at half past seven in the evening, he stands in front of the Tournay residence, a box of bonbons and an exquisite bouquet of roses and orange blossoms in his hand. Even as he grasps the massive bronze knocker he cannot help thinking, though he despises himself for it: "This house is mine, and everything in it—save Mrs. Joyce— and only protected from me by my love for one of them !"

In the hall he is met by Nita. The child kisses him very sweetly and says, looking at the box: "Bonbons for me, Cousin Bob ? "

"Yes!"

"You're the best cousin in the world! And the flowers for Louise ? "

"Yes. Where is she ? "

"Oh, Louise is having it out with Martineau. Gracious! Hasn't she been high and mighty with him !"

says the little girl, adding with juvenile instinct: "With you she'll be as meek as a kitten," and runs away with her sweets.

Evidences of the child's social diagnosis come immediately to Covington. As he enters the first *salon* he hears the *avocat's* voice, in the other parlor, in vigorous and almost pathetic French expostulation.

He hesitates to interrupt him, but Louise, catching sight of her sweetheart, cries: "Mr. Covington, I beg you to come here," and Bob going to them, she says haughtily: "Monsieur Martineau, I will accept no criticism or dictation in regard to my expenses or personal conduct from you. The only one from whom I will receive chiding or correction is my *owner*, Mr. Robert Covington."

With her words, she takes Bob's big hand in both of her little ones, and, placing his arm over her shoulder, stands holding it convulsively, and this man—her master—can feel her tremble as she announces him as such, and in Louise's quivering limbs can discern that she knows her pretty knees must bend to his will— and at his word.

"You—you are legally right, I—I am grieved to say," remarks the *avocat*, sadly. "For ever since you, my dear young lady, placed yourself in Mr. Jarvis, his attorney's, hands you have under the law been Mr. Covington's absolute *personal property.*"

At these words Bob can feel the girl's hands grip his again, as though she felt, "Here is my dictator, but also my comfort and support."

"I was only speaking to you," goes on Martineau, "in Monsieur Covington's interests. I am sorry you are angry with me, Mademoiselle. I bid you *bon jour.*"

And the old gentleman walks out in quiet dignity, for Louise has said some cruel things to him this evening, her humiliating position making her nervously uneasy, and at times desperately anxious to assert herself.

"I am afraid you've wounded Arvid," Mr. Covington says, deprecatingly.

"Shouldn't wonder!" laughs Louise, saucily, then pouts: "He criticised me!"

"What is the trouble?" asks Bob, uneasily.

"Oh, Monsieur Martineau.thought I was too extravagant."

"In what?"

"Dress, furbelows, footgear!" and she puts out a
very pretty little slipper, "these gloves," and she holds
up *gants à la mode*, and remarks, bitterly: "I have not
yet learned the economies of a slave-girl; but, of
course, Bob," here she faces him, "if you say the
word I've *got* to do it! I know," her eyes seek his,
then droop, "that you are going to make me walk the
chalk line."

Here Covington perchance astounds and certainly
confuses her by saying determinedly: "You are
right!" He has pondered over Mrs. Joyce's hint and
has made up his mind that for this young lady's interests
he must control her and, if necessary, compel her obedience. For he now sees her cruel fate has made
Louise—from very nervousness—unequal to control
herself.

"Yes, I can see," she says, attempting archness,
though her lips tremble. "Tips of slippers always up to
the line!—eh, Bob?—just as at Miss Martin's. You
must get Mrs. Joyce to give you her academic manual."

And she stands before him, smiling saucily, though
her eyes are appealing, and, coming to position, drapes
back with her hands the white skirts of her robe, showing two delicate feet in weblike stockings and tiny
black slippers, which are fastened with thin crossed
elastics, school-girl fashion, over her high insteps that
gleam like ivory under the open work of the hosiery.
As she gives him an *enfant gâtée* expression, she
looks like a mutinous school-girl, but Bob mistakes her
for a fairy.

She is dressed exquisitely, in plain white muslin, so
very sheer that her white shoulders gleam through its
tissue. Its sleeves, made in juvenile fashion, are
drawn up by ribbon bows, displaying her superb arms,
bare to the shoulders, and without jewelry. So likewise her hands, except upon the third finger of the left
is the diamond of his troth. The whole toilette is
without ornament of any kind, save a little lace and
ribbon, and would appear, perchance, plain, were it not
for the beauty-curves it drapes.

Though her figure is exquisitely developed, still its proportions are so symmetrical that it has all the lightness and grace of girlhood mingled with the charms of Venus. Over all this is an excited, nervous agitation, emphasized by shy, appealing glances of the eyes, and sometimes by little quivers of arms or figure, that indicate Louise feels in every fibre of her sensitive body, "I stand in the presence of my ruler."

"How exquisitely you are gowned!" cries Bob, anxious to show he is also her lover and admirer.

"Ah! Delighted! I hope I shall always dress to please you!" she says, essaying an uneasy frivolity. Then, seeing the white flowers in his hand, the token of their troth, her eyes grow luminous, she murmurs: "For me? How good of you!"

As he gives them to her, she puts them to her lips, and the blossoms seem to soothe her; she looks at him diffidently over the superb bouquet, yet says archly: "You came, I—I presume, to inflict the penalty."

He steps to her. Louise surrenders her lips to his and receives immediate and plenteous absolution, the gallant Kentuckian remarking: "Now, darling, you're free to run up another little bill."

As his caress leaves her lips she turns and stands full in front of him, and he looking on her knows their fate has come upon them!

Suddenly a spasm of pride, not humiliated but destroyed, agitates her delicate features. She blushes till her ivory shoulders gleam pink as coral, then cries: "Bob, I—I CAN'T STAND IT! Even though I love you with all my soul, it is too—too bitter, too humiliating to think I am your *personal property*—YOUR CHATTEL!"

With infinite pity in his heart, the gentleman bows and mutters brokenly: "Miss—Miss Tournay, my presence, I fear, is an embarrassment to you this evening. With your permission I—I will take my leave."

He is stepping towards the door—but an agonized, convulsive clasp is on his arm, and Louise is begging wildly: "No—no! I didn't mean that! Bob, forgive me—Bob, I apologize! You must not leave! Don't punish me by *deserting* me—anything but THAT! You—you cannot go! you *must not go!* you SHALL NOT GO!"

Then she pleads: "Sit down by my side," and murmurs, with a half-choked sob: "You—you came here, Bob, this evening to assume my absolute personal direction, did you not? Mrs. Joyce told me you would."

"Yes;" says Covington firmly, "I came, Louise, to take direction of you as your master. I trust I shall always use my authority for your own welfare and your best interests. I think I have proved that by my action in this miserable matter, up to the present time—But if you think it ungenerous——" and he starts up.

"Ungenerous?" she cries. "It would be most *ungenerous* if you deserted me in my extremity!" then says, in tones that awe him: "To protect me you must rule me. Something will happen to-night that will show you without your defense I am indeed helpless to my enemy. I had supposed I was beneath the notice of the world; but now I find I am not beyond its persecution."

"Ah! You mean that infernal Mrs. Combes!" he mutters, savagely. "Tell me the whole unfortunate transaction."

"Yes, Bob!" whispers the girl—then falters: "But, oh! I'm afraid!"

"Afraid of what?"

"Afraid you'll—you'll be so angry with me."

"Not unless you've done wrong— Tell me!" His tone seems like a master's tone, and Louise trembles a little; for now she knows since this man has taken her government upon him she will be judged according to her merits and corrected according to her faults.

But she goes on as if she had made up her mind to an unpleasant incident, saying: "You know, dear, since you would not assume authority over me you sent me no pass, permitting me to go out of the house after night-fall."

"Great snakes! Who would have thought," cries Covington, "that you would be stopped in the street any more than—than Miss Sally Johnson?"

But unheeding this unfortunate simile, save by a piteous glance of the eyes, Louise continues: "Hannah Combes stopped me last night."

"Yes?"

"I was out in the evening. Mrs. Joyce wanted to make a purchase. She did not think I had better go—but I — I was so lonely. I stood at the door of a little shop on Royal Street. That woman, Mrs. Combes, chanced to be walking by. She came to me and said: 'Louise, have you a pass permitting you to be out after night?' 'That is not your business, Madame!' I answered. 'It is the right of any one to question a girl like you,'* she said. 'Perhaps you're trying to run away.' She has a mania for thinking I'm trying to escape," adds Louise, bitterly.

"Well?" says Bob, chewing his mustache.

"Well, she said she would take me to an officer, Bob. You know what that would have meant. I could not have denied that I was your—your servant; I should have been compelled to stay there until released by you."

"My God! She didn't take you to the calaboose?" screams Covington.

"No; fortunately Mrs. Joyce came out, and said I was in her charge, and then Hannah Combes went away, declaring that I had made an assault upon her, and she should look to you as my master for my punishment and damages."

"Made an assault upon her? What do you mean?"

"Well, she tried to take hold of my wrist, and lead me to—to an officer, but I pulled my hand from her."

"I'd like to wring her cursed neck!" mutters Bob, striding about the room. Then he asks: "Anything more?"

"Yes; Mrs. Combes was here at six o'clock this evening. Mrs. Joyce saw her. She said if you did not punish me to-night, she would sue you to-morrow morning. Pamela told her you would probably be here at nine o'clock; she said she would return then. Bob, she declares I struck her; but it isn't true—believe me, it isn't true!" This last is uttered despairingly.

For he has suddenly cried: "Good Lord! If the woman brings action against me—my Heaven—the whole town will know your—your servitude!" and is looking very serious.

---

*See Slave Regulations, Revised Statutes, Louisiana, 1852—Ed.

"You think I did wrong?" whispers Louise, and says, hopelessly: "I—I forgot my station."

"Eternal Powers! no! It is not any money damages I might have to pay—because your evidence would not be heard in a court of law, my poor darling—but it is the *publishing* to the world that you are my bondmaid! That I won't have—until Jarvis says there's no hope. I must get Jarvis!" Here he suddenly mutters, aghast: "Great Taylor! Kitson has gone to Havana!"

A moment after he discovers how serious the affair is. Mrs. Joyce comes in with a frightened face and says: "Mr. Covington, the woman—Mrs. Combes—wishes to see you."

"Very well. Have her shown into the next room." Then he remarks to Louise: "I do not wish you drawn into this matter in any way."

"I don't think it's money damages she wants—it's my humiliation and punishment this woman will demand," whispers the girl, desperately. "She—she has not forgiven me for some remarks I made to her when she had me in charge."

"It is for that reason I do not wish you to see her. Please remember, you must stay in your own room, dear, until I have sent the woman away." And Bob, brushing the hair back from his brow, goes in to meet Hannah Combes, while his sweetheart turns to leave the parlor for her chamber.

But, even as she goes, chancing to hear a word or two, she turns and listens and begins to tremble, then listen again, with clenched hands and desperate eyes.

"I have come, Mr. Covington," says Mrs. Combes, looking at Bob angrily—for this gentleman's unceremonious treatment of her on their first interview has made her vindictive to him—"to demand the punishment of your girl Louise."

"For what reason?" says Bob, affecting calmness, as he notes traces of whisky in the breath of the irate matron, Mrs. Combes having stiffened herself up on Bourbon and water for the occasion. She knows moreover, that Covington wishes the servitude of Louise to remain a secret, and in this view thinks she has got the whip hand of the gentleman and also of his beautiful bondmaid, whose cutting speeches have left their sting in her ignoble soul, which has been added to by one or two sneering remarks the young lady had made the evening before.

"For what *reason?*" cries Mrs. Combes. "Why, your girl Louise struck me last evening in the street!"

"I beg your pardon," remarks Bob. "Her description of the affair is entirely different."

"What! You would believe *her* instead of *me?* Well, we'll just go to court and see if her evidence will be taken in the case at all."

"We can arrange this matter outside of the court. How much money do you wish in liquidation of the damages?"

"I don't believe I want money at all," answers the woman, savagely. "At all events, I've got to have something else besides money! Louise struck me, and if you don't give her a right good, thorough dressing down, I'll go to court, money or no money!"

Here Bob's appearance is so frightful Mrs. Combes stops her tongue and gazes at his eyes.

"Hell and blazes——" he has broken forth.

But before he can say more, Louise has flown out of the next room and is standing in front of Hannah. "You cruel woman!" she shudders, "who would degrade me by the hand that loves me!"

Suddenly she feels Covington's firm grasp upon her shoulder.

"I will speak, Bob! I will tell her what I think of her!"

The next instant she is drawn to his breast, his arm goes round her and holds her firmly to him. He says: "Louise, you forget!" in a tone that compels her silence. And under his arm the girl gives a sudden thrill and throb, not quite of fear but still of servitude, for he has whispered sternly to her: "I punish disobedience!" and she knows this man holding her so strongly that she cannot move, will rule and govern her.

"That's right!" jeers Hannah. "Put the baggage in her place! Let her know you're her boss!"

"I will—*to protect her!*" And Louise feels the arm

round her lifting her up, as Bob Covington stands towering over her enemy, and she realizes though it is her dictator's arm it is the one that will shield her against all this world—even *herself*.

"Now," says Covington, to whom has suddenly come a lucky inspiration, "if I remember your infamous face, Mrs. Combes, you are a stewardess on the St. Louis line of steamboats. I have seen you on those boats."

"You have!—I'm layen off now—what of it?"

"Very well. The president of that line is my intimate. Its treasurer is my friend. I know four of its captains and two of its pilots. Kitson Jarvis knows every steamboat man on the river, and if you dare open your miserable mouth to say a word of this to any human being, I will see you never sail on another Mississippi River boat again!—Never!—so long as you or I live! Now will you take twenty dollars, and go in a hurry?"

"You ain't fighting this thing quite fair, Mr. Covington."

"Are *you?* Here—take the money and go!"

"I'll—I'll take the twenty dollars," says Mrs. Combes, then commences to beg: "Don't—don't use your influence against a poor, down-trodden woman!"

"I will!—if word comes back to me of this affair. I don't mean through the courts, but by rumor or scandal or any other way. Now, here's your money—leave!"

And he handing her a bill, Hannah would slink out of the parlor. But at its very door, the whisky getting into both her brain and tongue, she can't hold herself, and turns, gibing the defenseless one: "Sewing-girl in the parlor! Ho!—ho! Fixed up to beat creation! Ha!—ha! 'Taint whippens, but kisses, you get, I reckon. Who'd get justice on a fancy-gal mistress?"

As these words smite, Louise slips, with a shuddering cry, from her sweetheart's arms. She sinks upon the floor, and hides her face that burns with shame, then chills with horror.

With muttered imprecations and blazing eyes, Covington makes one step toward the woman, who, having struck down the defenseless, flies from him. Then he turns, and looks with pity and dismay upon his love, that even he, her master, cannot protect.

"It was to keep you from such infamies as this, dear one," Bob whispers, "that I had determined not to look upon your face. When your control was forced upon me, I—I feared this woman's tongue, that's the reason, Louise, I directed you not to see her. But you listened, and despite my command, came in—to be insulted!" he adds both bitterly and sternly.

To this the girl says nothing; but her eyes never leave his face—sometimes falteringly, sometimes pleadingly, but always adoringly. She looks at him as if he were her bulwark and defense; for now she knows from this man to her must come *everything*—whether of good or evil—in this world.

Then Covington goes on quite calmly: "To avoid any chance of such unpleasant incidents, I shall not permit you, Louise, to go out in the evening except in my charge."

"Yes, sir!"

"That I say to you as your *master*. As your *lover* I tell you I am always entirely at your service, to take you by day, by night, whenever or wherever it is my sweetheart's pleasure to go."

"Thank you, dear Bob!" and the girl beams love upon him, adding quite docilely: "It is so easy to obey you;" then cries with flaming eyes: "To the rest of the world I am twice as proud as before."

"And in this regard, had we not better write a little letter to Monsieur Martineau?" suggests Covington with a slight smile.

"Ah, you think I've been too extravagant?"

"Oh no! I don't care a continental for the money! Your pleasure first—but——"

"Oh, Bob, you want me to apologize?"

"Not apology, but explanation. Just to show Arvid that you still regard him as the good friend he has always been to you."

But she says, pride coming back to her: "As Miss Tournay, I could have written a note of apology as humbly as any lady on this earth. As Louise, your slave-girl, I am too haughty, or too ignoble, to do it!"

Then Louise finds she has a master.

"You don't know how happy it will make Martineau," Covington pleads. "Think over the matter. If you cannot bring yourself to write it to-night, write it to-morrow."

"And if not?" The piquant nose is in the air.

"If not, to-morrow morning," he says, quietly seating himself and gazing somewhat sternly at the girl, as she stands haughtily before him, "I shall take you to Monsieur Martineau's office. There you will make your *amende* in words. It is no degradation to acknowledge a fault."

"And if at Martineau's office I will not say the words you want me to?" she answers, defiantly.

"Then I, in your presence, shall apologize for you."

"Ah! By my humiliation you will prove you are my master!" she cries, and tears are in her eyes.

"You—you reproach me again with this accursed authority that has been forced upon me." He shudders, then mutters sadly: "This is what I feared! that my darling would forget my love—in my dominion."

Suddenly another gust of passion sweeps the fair creature. "Reproach *you?*" she cries, then makes him in his misery proud, ay, almost happy, for she whispers: "I bless Heaven *you* are my master, for you are the only man I could think of as my absolute owner—whose will must always be my will—and *live!* Every night I thank God that He in His mercy—since He has given me a lowly fate—has placed me under the hand of the one man in all this world to whom I could bow my head and say—'MY MASTER'," and, sinking at his feet, the girl places her head humbly on this, her autocrat's knee, and sobs as if worn out by conflict.

From this obeisance he would recoil aghast, but, remembering the schoolmistress's words: "When Louise offers, do not refuse her submission!" he places his hand tenderly upon her fair neck and while caressing it, dominates it. He says, and his voice seems very stern to her: "You will write this evening to Monsieur Martineau as I directed!"

"Yes, Bob! He deserves it, and you're a dear good fellow for making me do it."

This is sighed out penitently. Even as she does it, Bob can't help noting the exquisite grace of this girl, who in her·humility is perchance as beautiful as in her pride.   The pose of her kneeling figure indicates subjugation without abasement; withal there is an abandon in the attitude that makes it very graceful. A tress of her hair, which has become unbound, flits down over the white shoulders. Altogether Louise is a picture of penitence and loveliness.

Then comes to him very softly in contrite tones and little sobs: "Bob, dear, say—say that you for—forgive me."

In a mighty wave of tenderness he lifts her up, places her as he would a child upon his knee, pets her, and caresses her and thanks her for her docility.

And she, breaking into a rhapsody of mingled tenderness, obedience, and love, puts her arms round his neck and clinging convulsively to him, as if he were her support, pours out her soul, sighing: "Bob—*Bob*— Bob! You are all I have to look to on this earth. When you held me so sternly in your arms and told me you would chastise my disobedience, and yet protected me and held me up against that woman's persecution —and the world! then dear master," here she hides her head shyly upon his shoulder, "I felt I was your slave-girl for I feared the correction of your hand— feared it as thoroughly as if I were wincing from your rod," then whispers in his ear: "Bob, I know myself! You must hold me most strictly in your grasp, you must bind me to your slightest wish, with stern severity and rigorous chastisement or I shall be the *most rebellious slave· on earth!*" Her head flies up, her eyes blaze! But as they catch the glance of this man 'who now she feels is her dictator, she droops on his shoulder once again and begs: "Forgive my petulance," but affirms: "It's the truth, Bob! To protect me you must rule me! I feel—as I am by law— less than a little child!" then laughs with piteous archness: "And sometimes children are naughty," next murmurs: "But you must pet me and forgive me when I'm good."

And now she begins to show him she feels : he is his

bondmaid, for she begs him to give her his directions, so that she may walk under his will, in little things as well as large ones.

She pleads "Show me how great your interest is in me—by your care of the smallest matters of my life."

But this is a task of which Bob Covington knows but little. Finally, she laughs: "Your commands are *very* hard to do. I am to love you very much! I'm to go driving with you to-morrow at the lake! I'm to take awful good care of my—my precious self! I'm to go with you to the theatre in the evening, and I'm to love you all the time—ain't I, Cousin Bob! Oh! You're the hardest master that ever an unfortunate girl had who loved him to—distraction—that's what it is, Bob—distraction!"

"Now," she says, archly, but oh so wistfully: "Listen to my commands to you. You are not to go riding with that Sally Johnson any more, or you'll break my heart—that's all! Because, darling, I can't command your love, I can only beg it—Oh, mercy!"

For her cruel master has her in his arms, and is very tender to her, his bondmaid.

A few minutes after, she asks: "What must I do to-morrow morning? You hinted a drive to the lake."

"Yes; the sea breeze will do you good. Mrs. Joyce will go with us, of course."

And he going from her to the door of the room, she runs after him, and says: "See—what I—I made for you when I was ill!" and puts into his hand a little pocketbook beautifully embroidered, and bearing on it, in letters of white flowers: "Bob," then laughs: "I've been an awful bad girl; I must deserve a great many penalties of—of five kisses each."

Over her he sighs, and tears are in his eyes as he clutches her to his heart, and murmurs: "My own— by the blessing of God I'll win your battle yet! I will make you my *equal bride!* Dear one, you shall walk through life *beside me*—not beneath me! Never forget —though now I must control you—you are my AFFIANCED AND MY BELOVED!"

CHAPTER XXII.

WHAT SHALL HE DO?

FROM this Mr. Covington goes away, muttering: "By the Lord Harry, I feel like a backwoods teacher who's kept his best girl after school!" At his usual poker, worse results than ever come to him; this interview having been distracting even to a man of strong Western temperament.

On his bondmaid it has a more soothing influence. In the privacy of her chamber, Louise looks archly at herself in the glass and says: "I think this has stopped Bob's driving with that Sally Johnson!" Then suddenly her complete subjection to this man's will, even in the slightest things of life flies into her mind. She shudders: "Oh, merciful goodness! if *any one else* had owned me —" then thinks: "I know it — he is not going to permit me to have any will of my own; not only that — I have got to anticipate his wishes even in little things."

And suddenly remembering that Mr. Covington had, during the evening expressed himself as to her personal attire, that not being thoroughly well she should wear on out-door excursions, good, stout walking boots, she thinks: "If I didn't, I don't believe I should be permitted to leave the carriage at the Lake, and that would mean no breakfast—" then laughs: "Pooh! I could have my Bob's heart for breakfast, if I wanted it. But still—just the same—" and she makes her preparations.

The next morning, getting up bright and early, Louise goes down, a picture of youthful vivacity, and finding in the parlor her master, who has brought for her a beautiful bunch of white roses and orange blossoms, she seizes the typical flowers, gazes at him, salutes him military fashion, and says: "Inspection, sir!" putting under his view a pair of very high, tightly laced little French bottines, but of serviceable texture and make — and blushes delightfully as he gazes.

To her he laughs: "Inspection over! Salute!"

This she does with her whole soul. Then she hands him a little open note, saying: "Please read it, Bob, and if you approve, give it to Monsieur Martineau."

"Oh, it's all right, I know!" cries Covington, and sealing it unread, places it in his pocket.

Then she runs down by his side chatting quite brightly, and he putting her and Mrs. Joyce in the carriage, they drive towards the shell-road. Half an hour after, he is delighted to notice that the fresh air from the Gulf, at Spanish Fort, puts more roses on her pretty cheeks. Miss Tournay chats unembarrassed to him on subjects of the outer world, and altogether Mr. Covington feels much more comfortable.

At his suggestion they breakfast quietly at Monsieur Miguel's restaurant by the lakeside, there not being many people in the dining-room at this time in the day.

However, it chances that young Hector Soulé, being out for morning horseback exercise, comes in almost as the party are sitting down, and Bob finds himself compelled to introduce this gentleman, who is an intimate, to Louise and Mrs. Joyce.

This he does, mentioning the young lady as his "cousin, Miss Tournay." After some little further converse, this Creole beau jumps at a half-way invitation from Covington, and impressed with the beauty before him, sits down to breakfast with them, devoting a good deal of his time to looking at the exquisite face of the young lady and listening to her pretty speeches; for curiously enough, Louise has grown very laughing, arch, piquant, and qnite like her brilliant self of a few weeks ago.

The meal being over, Monsieur Soulé gallops for some distance beside the carriage, conversing with the fair creature who sits opposite Mr. Covington, and seems loath to doff his hat and bid her adieu.

Coming in from the drive, Bob spends the remainder of his afternoon at the Orleans Club, with a few of his companions who still remain in town. In the evening he takes his sweetheart to the theatre with Mrs. Joyce.

But his bondmaid makes him very happy, for as he

bids her good-night, the beautiful creature puts her arms around him, and murmurs: "Thank you, dear Bob! You have made the first day of your personal authority over me very pleasant."

"You have not felt it?" mutters Covington, nervously.

"Every moment—*firmly!* And, I thank you also for your mercy to me last night. When I deserved punishment you spared my disobedience." Then she utters a little plea: "Bob, please can't I be taken out to drive to-morrow morning again?"

"Why, certainly, dear one! That's what I was going to propose."

So, morning carriage exercise and breakfast at Miguel's become part of their routine, and two days after, Monsieur Hector Soulé happening to meet them at breakfast again, Miss Louise, obtaining a convenient opportunity, strolls with Covington out on the veranda. and looking first at the lake and then at the tip of her little boot, says anxiously: "I have a favor to ask of you, Bob. Monsieur Soulé has begged the privilege of calling; have I your permission to receive him?" She looks at him with downcast eyes, as her master thinks the matter over.

"Oh, you're—you're going to refuse me?" she murmurs piteously.

"Come this way," answers Covington, and, leading her to a retired spot, ceremoniously places a chair for her.

"Please—please don't think I'm rebellious," whispers Louise nervously, for once or twice in the last few days her master has disciplined her quite sharply.

"Not at all!" replies Bob. "I was just considering our future in this matter." Then he says tenderly: "Dear one, you know I wish you to have all the happiness possible. Now the moment Jarvis says there's no hope, I manumit you! That must be done in this State on account of the settlements of property I propose making upon you and Nita; otherwise, Martineau says, your enfranchisement might be questioned.*

---

*In the case of *Hinds vs. Brazealle*, reported in 2 Howard's Mississippi Reports, 840, the main question was whether a deed

Your names must go to a police jury in Assumption, as you are under thirty years of age, to obtain its permission to emancipate you and Nita.

"And if they—they refuse?" gasps Louise.

"Human beings could not refuse such a plea!" mutters Covington. "Afterward, I shall have to placard your name on the court-house of Assumption Parish for forty days as my slave, before I can enfranchise you."

"Yes, dear."

"Well, it will be undoubtedly some weeks before the jury gives its permission, and forty days thereafter; and in that time—I have thought over the matter carefully—I shall have to seclude you."

"Im—imprison me?" Her lips are trembling, her blue eyes are frightened.

"No, not exactly that; and it is for your sake I must do it. Your servitude would excite comment. When you are publicly known as my—my bondmaid there can be no more drives out here for you and me; your appearance in public would be embarrassing to you. Therefore I have decided during the time in which application is made to the jury to keep you very quietly and privately in the Tournay house. Of course you will see Mrs. Joyce and Nita and myself, and Monsieur Martineau, if necessary; but I do not think it wise to permit you to be seen in public. After that, when your name is posted up, I shall send you and Nita to Beau Rivage or the other place near Guidrys— whichever I think will be the most retired and therefore the pleasantest to you. Of course, as my publicly proclaimed bondmaid, gentlemen cannot visit you: if Monsieur Soulé should dare to call upon you,

---

of emancipation executed in Ohio was valid, and it *was held not to be so.*

"The consequence is," says Chief Justice Starkey, "John Munroe and his mother are still slaves, and a part of the estate of Elisha Brazealle.

"John Munroe, being a slave, cannot take property as devisee; and I apprehend it is equally clear that it cannot be held in trust for him. 4 Desaussure, 266.

"It follows, therefore, that the heirs are entitled to the property."—ED.

I should consider it a personal affront.   Now, if under these circumstances it will give you any pleasure or happiness, or brighten your life, tell Hector to come as often as he likes.   He is a very fine gentleman and a first-rate fellow."

"Thank you, dear Bob," says Louise, "I should like him to come very much.   Of course, no gentleman would call upon me after I am known as your slave."

And though Louise doesn't take Covington at his full word and tell Soulé to come as often as he pleases, in the restaurant she says very cordially to Monsieur Hector: "Mrs. Joyce and I are at home nearly every afternoon."

"Thank you! I shall avail myself of your kindness," replies the Creole beau.   Which he does once or twice within the next few days, and perhaps a little oftener than Mr. Covington thinks is altogether judicious.

But Bob has other things on his mind just at this time besides jealousy. The Havana steamer is now due; with it will come Kitson and his news—if he has any!

That afternoon Covington goes down to the levee to meet his attorney, and also is delighted to find his friend young La Farge has returned on the same boat.

Encountering Jarvis at the gangway, that worthy shakes his head at Bob gloomily, but a moment after, says cheerily: "I've bagged La Farge's case; he's on board with me now.   I'll tell you just what happened to me, over at Martineau's office, in two hours.   I'm going with my new client to get him bailed out.   Do you want to put your name on his bail-bond? You can if you want to, you know.   Won't take an hour to put you in possession of plenty of real estate here! Might as well do it now as any time."

Bob shakes his head to this and walks off to Martineau's office, but the temptation has grown stronger. His finances are getting in a desperate condition. True, he has not lost much at poker for the last week, but he has been what sporting-men call "chipping out" on Nita and Louise. Bonbons, presents, and other little things eat up a good deal of money,

and this young gentleman has not learned to econ-
omize.

Two hours afterward Kitson comes into Martineau's
office, full of his new case. He says triumphantly:
" I've just bailed La Farge. Two of the best names
in New Orleans on the bond—Soulé and Martigny—
could have had a dozen. You watch my speech if the
judge, when he acquits my client for lack of evidence,
puts in the usual formula about the barbarity of dueling. I'll make La Farge out a public benefactor, in
cutting off the fire-eating, bloodthirsty Delaborde—at
whose name mothers trembled for their sons."

" But my case!—the one in which you took my
money to go to Havana?" interjects Bob, savagely.

" Oh, you mean little Nita. Well, Nita is in the
broth."

" You did nothing?"

" Everything that was possible! I overhauled as
far as I was able all lists of vessels sailing from the
Havana for Mexico and Western Gulf ports from the
year 1812 to 1815 inclusive—that had never been heard
of since they left harbor. I picked out that route
because it was most natural for Spanish vessels to be
taken on that course by privateers from Barataria Bay.
For Lafitte always pretended to sail under a letter of
marque, from France or the Columbian Government,
to prey on *Spanish* commerce; not that I doubt he
picked up any other vessels that were convenient. But
I had to take some line of investigation and this seemed
the most likely. If the age of Eulalie Camila was 19
in 1832, it struck me the years 1813, 14 and 15, would
be about the proper time. I have here a list of vessels
that left the Cuban capital, and also similar ships that
sailed from Mexico for the Havana. They may have
gone down in storms; they may have encountered hur-
ricanes; they may have struck reefs. But this is the
list." And he holds up to Martineau and Bob a record the length of which makes both drop their jaws.

" We can't investigate all of these," remarks the
avocat.

" No. I've tried to find out in this list all who carried
white passengers, especially women; that generally

predicates children.   Of course, I can't find out much about any of them at this late day.   It's forty years ago, and most every thing had gone to the bow-wows in those days with Bony and Johnny Bull a fightin'; but these are the vessels that I have picked out as being the ones that there's any chance about at all."

Then he reads:

Barque *Huaca*, left Havana with four white passengers and one Chilean lady, bound West, probably for Vera Cruz.   Don't know whether any children.

Brigantine *Mercedes*, from Tampico.   Had three ladies on board, Mexicans, I reckon, and four children, two girls—one about the right age.

Schooner *Susan and Mary*, English.   Three white male passengers, two women and two children, both girls.   Bound for Vera Cruz.

Brig *Santo Espirito*, passengers Don Hernandez de Balboa de Rivera, wife, infant, and two servants—two other white males.

"This was the only one I could get the names of passengers," Jarvis explains.   "Don Hernandez was secretary of the Captain-General of Cuba, and was sent by him on a special mission to the Viceroy of Mexico, Calleja, who was having a tough time himself with a revolution about that year.

"With this gentleman went his wife, Dona Maria Magdalena de Rivera, and an infant daughter, one year old, so far as I can find out from the Spanish papers, called Carmelita Mira Estrella.   There were also two Englishmen on board, but they don't count. Besides, no one knows anything about what happened to any of these vessels; they simply disappeared. Here we are at the stone wall again!"

"You give it up then?"

"Well; might as well, I reckon."   And Jarvis goes away.

"I might as well, I reckon, too," sighs Bob.   Then he turns to Martineau, who has been listening, and says: "What do you advise?"

"The same as Jarvis."

"Any way," replies the young man, desperately: "I've got to ask you for financial assistance in some way.   Look here!   Glance over my accounts!" and he produces a memorandum book.

In addition I've a note falling due in two months, which you've indorsed, for $15,000. I'm overdrawn at my Louisville agents also. Crops won't come in till next Fall, but they won't be a drop in the bucket!"

"Here I can assist you," remarks Martineau. "That $5,000 you advanced for Louise and Nita's expenses, in any event is yours."

"Very well! Give it to me. All the same," he adds gloomily: "I'll have to put a mortgage on my Blue Grass stock farm—the 3,000 acres my father left me—the farm he fought the Indians off! It's a pretty nice place, but——," he sighs deeply.

"You need not place that mortgage," answers the *avocat*, writing a check. "There is $55,000 more here. You heard what Jarvis said. He can make a demand and get an order of the court in chambers. I shall make no opposition."

"My Heaven, I'll—*I'll do it!*" cries Bob, with a snap of his jaws; but suddenly falters: "No—no! Everybody will know my sweetheart is a——" and mutters, hoarsely: "Not yet! Something may turn up. I'll give the girls one more little chance—and MYSELF ALSO!"

"Yourself?"

Then Bob astounds the *avocat*. "Myself, *of course!*" he says, brokenly. "Whether I marry Louise Tournay, a white young lady, peer to any one in this land, or whether I marry Louise, my manumitted slave-girl, *I marry her*—my sweetheart and my love!"

"You know what that will mean for *you*—a marriage with a girl who is proclaimed by your very manumission as of mixed blood?" says Martineau very seriously.

"Don't I?" groans Bob. "Don't I know it means the destruction of my career?" then laughs, bitterly: "They talk of running me for Congress in the Blue Grass district. Do you think a man who has made a legal connection with an enfranchised slave would get any votes in my town of Lexington, Kentucky? Nary a one! This is an affair in which a man cannot raise his wife to his own level; he must fall down to hers! Do you suppose I could dare to go into the Orleans Club after the ceremony, which is not permitted here,

had taken place in a Northern State? Do you reckon
the ladies would receive me? Do you imagine my
chums and my companions would permit me their
fellowship? But, by Heaven, it is *her* sacrifice or *my*
sacrifice! and in this case it is the *master*—not the *slave*
—that goes to the wall!"

"*Diable!*" remarks Martineau, dryly. "We have
a custom down here, to fit just such cases. Did you
ever hear of a lady being *placéed* to a gentleman?"

"*Placée* Louise?" gasps Bob. "You—you advise
that?"

"I advise nothing. Only, perhaps you had better
investigate the custom," rejoins the *avocat*, his lips
trembling and his eyes a little moist.

"By—by Heaven! you break my heart," mutters
Covington, and flies from the office.

But he does not turn his steps toward Dauphine Street.
He cannot bring his lips to tell Louise that her last
hope—which never was a hope—is gone; that there
is no escape for her until he puts brand upon her by
manumitting her with public notice.

In a reckless, devil-may-care mood he wanders to the
Orleans Club, and meeting a number of boon companions, who are celebrating La Farge's return, he
drinks with them the health of his friend, time and
again.

After an hour or two of this, Henri, who is present,
draws him aside and says: "Covington, my boy,
Talliaferro's advice and your handling saved my life in
that duel. I want to talk to you about the evidence
that will come up in my case. I'm afraid they'll succeed in making it a little stronger than it was in yours.
Besides, I wish to ask your opinion as to Jarvis. He
says he is acting for you in some matter."

"He didn't tell you *what?*" gasps the Kentuckian.

"No! Otherwise I would not have engaged him for
my own case."

"Well, he's about the best man you can get, I think.
I'd sooner trust him with a difficult affair than any man
in New Orleans."

"*Bien!* come with me. I want to talk to you, and
I can't stay here. I've promised Alma to spend the even-

ing at home. I only take to my little domicile my very intimates—my chosen ones; but you've got very dear to my heart, Bob."

So the young men go away a little closer friends, for La Farge's words, than they were before.

A few minutes after, they step into a pretty residence erected in the old French style, though not nearly as large as the Tournay's, with its usual courtyard and garden—a house which La Farge enters as his own home, saying: "I have not introduced you to Alma."

In the parlor, an extremely handsome girl, with the very slightest traces of mixed blood in her beautiful face, exquisitely dressed, rises as La Farge enters, with a murmured cry of love; but seeing Mr. Covington, moves to receive him with the distinction of a lady.

"Alma, *ma chére*, this is my friend, Mr. Covington. Bob, permit me to present you to Madame La Farge," remarks the Creole.

"Monsieur, Henri has told me of your practically saving his life by your advice in that duel—which nearly broke my heart," says the lady, bowing cordially. "It was your message to him at Havana that has brought him back to me so soon. We shall always welcome your coming into this house." Then turning to La Farge, she asks: "Couldn't we, *mon cher*, give a little dinner to your friend next Sunday evening and Colonel Talliaferro? But I understand he has gone back to Kentucky. However, I will invite Adele Marchael, if Monsieur Covington will do us the honor."

Reasoning that he is seeing Louise altogether too much for even his own happiness in this unsettled state of their engagement, Bob Covington accepts.

After a few minutes' general conversation; and the lady, who is apparently highly accomplished, having sung a pretty little Cuban air La Farge has brought with him from Havana, Alma goes away and leaves Covington and his host to discuss the evidence in the latter's coming trial.

"We must get the thing over as soon as possible," remarks the young Creole in conclusion. "It's getting too warm to remain in New Orleans, and I want the affair off my mind, as I think of taking Alma for a flying summer trip to Europe and Paris.   My mother and sister remain on the plantation this year, and it permits me to travel with her without any chance of a *rencontre* with my immediate family, who, of course, are supposed theoretically to know nothing about my *placée*, who is practically my bride—whom I love and to whom I intend to be true, and who will be true to me."

."But about your children, if they come?" asks Bob, quite eagerly.

"Ah, their career in life is all planned. The money settlements are arranged, both for the boys and girls if they come.   The boys—well they have their own careers to cut out.   The girls—I suppose they—well, I hope their lives will be as happy as I intend to make their mother's.   I presume this Creole custom of ours is a little astonishing to you, a border-state man, but it is no more than the morganatic marriages of Europe; and a girl like Alma, who has been brought up in every refinement of life, prefers infinitely such a connection—which is the only one the laws permit her to a man of equal refinement and education—to a legal union with one of the race that claims her as its own, but with which she has practically naught in common except what the laws have forced upon her.   I suppose you're going back to the Orleans Club," he adds, as Covington bids him adieu; "tell my friends I'll not play poker with them this evening, and don't forget Sunday, which is to-morrow, at four o'clock."

From this inspection of the domestic happiness of La Farge and his beautiful *placée* bride, Mr. Covington goes away meditatively.   He has noted the respect with which Alma has been treated, not only by her servants but by the gentleman who is her husband in everything but name.

This matter getting into his head, at the Orleans Club he makes a good many inquiries incidentally in regard to this extraordinary Creole rite, discovering that Alma de Careno is spoken of very respectfully as Madame La Farge, by any gentleman who happens to mention her, and that Henri is regarded as having done the proper thing with the beautiful girl who loves him, but who could not wed him.

Coming home from poker this night, the young man gets to thinking: "I've got to do something myself, soon. Nita must be manumitted, and she also. Putting their names up in the court-house as my *property!*" he shudders. "But I've got to do it *soon*, because if—anything happened to me, their fate and their children's fate might be as cruel as theirs is now. No—much more so! for, thank God! according to my lights I mean to do the right thing by my darling, and a little more!" Then he suddenly stops in his walk, and a shiver, cold as ice, runs through him. He mutters: "*Placéed* to me!" and utters a horrible, mocking, despairing laugh.

The next day he does not go to see the beautiful young lady who is waiting and longing for him at the Tournay residence. For now a terrible problem—perhaps even a fearful temptation—is on Bob Covington. Not the temptation of money, but the temptation of love. The law forbids him to marry the woman of his heart. He will not give her up; he cannot bring his mind to think of that. That is despair for them both. What shall he do?

CHAPTER XXIII.

"A LITTLE JOKE ON MONSIEUR HECTOR!"

IT is in this mind that Mr. Covington arrays himself for the family dinner-party of his friend La Farge, and at four o'clock presents himself in Ursulines Street, to be received by the Creole and his *placée*.

Henri and Alma are alone in their parlor when Bob enters.

As he is being welcomed, a young lady makes her appearance and he is presented to Mademoiselle Tessa de Careno, Alma remarking: "I expected my friend Adele Marchael with us, but Monsieur Gaston Marchael has gone to visit his mother at Pass Christian and she did not like to accept my invitation without him. Tessa is my younger sister, Monsieur Covington, a little girl just from the convent, and it is difficult to get Mamma to trust her youngest one away from our family rooftree, even under my wings."

Both the ladies are in full evening toilet; their light gowns *chic*, fashionable, and lacy, indicating Parisian manufacture and French genius for costume.

A moment later, dinner is announced, and Bob, with Alma on his arm, enters the dining-room, preceded by La Farge, who laughingly says: " 'Tis thy first dinner party, little Tessa, and to it you go in with only your brother, *pauvre enfant.*"

The table is very prettily set with fresh flowers, china, crystal, and silver; and Bob, looking at Mademoiselle Tessa de Careno, who sits on one side of him, perceives she is in strong contrast to her sister Alma who is on his other hand. The younger is of slight, undeveloped figure and has big, dark eyes, as yet untinged with passion. The elder is a picture of luxuriant womanhood, and every glance of her magnificent orbs shows she loves Henri La Farge. The two sisters are the beginning and the end of a system. They both have the same skin tinted by one little drop of mixed blood; the difference between them is, that one has not begun to love—and the other is passion personified.

Mademoiselle Tessa, with her partially developed figure and trustful eyes, seems quite bashful and even at times ill at ease in his presence, for she answers Covington's remarks at first by "*Oui, Monsieur*" or "*Non, Monsieur*," but finally gets to telling him childish anecdotes of her convent life, in a naïve and simple manner that indicates her knowledge of the world is of the slightest. Intellectually she has not half the grasp of little Nita.

However, the conversation is very pleasant, the hospitality, Creole hospitality, which means the limit of cordial welcome and polite attention.

After the coffee, the gentlemen accompany the ladies into the drawing-room. Here Mademoiselle Tessa plays several duets with Alma, and sings one or two morceaux of Verdi and Bellini quite charmingly in a fresh, youthful voice.

Her musical technique is very fine, and Mr. Covington making a remark on this subject, Madame La Farge says impulsively: "Our little Tessa dances better, Monsieur, than she sings. You should see her polka! She has been at two balls already, one at the Circle and the other at Monsieur Tiebideau's, and at the convent she received medals for history and French poetry. I think Tessa is destined for a brilliant future. At her last dance Monsieur Jacques de Bonville was presented to her, and it is the gossip that her bright eyes will make him come to my father about her. You like Monsieur de Bonville, Tessa?" says her sister, laughing.

"Oh—very much!" replies the young lady, "though I have not spoken to him. He only bowed to me at the ball, but conversed about me for a long time with papa."

"Yes," says La Farge. "*Ma petite chérie* Tessa is going to make a grand match. De Bonville is a man of large property—a nice fellow—and I think will make Tessa very happy."

"If he does half as much as you do me," laughs Alma, putting a caressing hand on Henri's shoulder, "my little sister will be a very fortunate young lady."

"You know him, Covington. You played poker with him the other night," says Henri, taking the hand upon his shoulder in his own and kissing the little fingers ardently.

"Yes—oh, I remember him," mutters Bob, with a mental groan, as he thinks of the check he sent to this De Bonville, whom he has heard spoken of as a widower with six children.

But Bob does not talk a great deal this evening. He is doing, as Westerners say, a "heap of thinking." He has observed the elegance with which the dinner has been served. He now notes, in a dreamy kind of way, the exquisite fittings and furnishings of the parlor, and finally his imagination running riot; in his mind he sees Louise and himself in some such residence in the French quarter of this old city receiving La Farge and Alma at a family dinner like this.

But, on making his *adieux* to his host and hostess and their young lady sister, and getting out upon the street, Mr. Covington, as he walks along, shakes himself, like a big water-dog leaving the ocean for the land, and mutters: "No—my God!—no! Not for *her!* This kind of thing may do for children of undeveloped minds, or women of tropical passions and educated to the custom. But for my darling, with her noble intellect and haughty pride—my heaven!—it would be degradation and despair."

He has not seen Louise since Jarvis has practically thrown up the case. He has not been able to bring his courage to the point of telling her. But now, though he hesitates, his steps lead him to the Tournay house.

It is only seven in the evening, and the night being warm, from open windows come to him the sound of the piano and the voice of her he loves singing one of his own favorite melodies.

He must go in!

The servant, answering his knock, gives him entrée as a member of the family.

Unannounced, he enters the *salon*, to find Louise at the piano, still singing. He is perhaps rather startled to see young Monsieur Soulé seated not so far from his sweetheart and listening to her voice in about the same attitude in which he himself had sat when first Miss Tournay sang to him.

His bond-maid stops her melody, rises from the piano and gives her master her hand frankly. As he looks at her Bob smiles grimly, for he notices there is a faint blush of consciousness in his sweetheart's face, and perhaps the slightest embarrassment in her manner.

Soulé rises also, greeting Covington as an intimate quite cordially; but a few moments after, makes his bow to Louise, remarking, as he takes his departure: "Miss Tournay, please present my regards to Mrs. Joyce."

On this, Bob throwing eyes into the other parlor, to his shock, sees no Pamela and her ever present embroidery; embroidery that had not often been absent even when he, the potentate of the establishment, was here.

He glances at Louise, then says, a slight sarcasm in his voice: "Had you not better summon Mrs. Joyce, so that we may observe Creole *convenances*, now that Monsieur Hector has gone?"

"Mrs. Joyce is—is angry with me," pouts the young lady.

"Ah! Without just cause, I hope."

"It is about Monsieur Soulé," observes Louise, nervously and blushingly, yet frankly. "Pamela thinks he comes *too* often and stays *too* long."

"Ah! Then I—I presume you enjoy his society?"

"Quite well," she replies, a trace of bitterness in her voice. "It is pleasant to converse with a gentleman who doesn't know me for *what I am*. Soulé thinks me Miss Tournay, the heiress. A—a little joke on Monsieur Hector."

But the "little joke on Monsieur Hector" makes her pretty lips tremble and her delicate form quiver from humbled pride.

To this speech Bob answers nothing. He is wounded, but he pities her too much to chide her.

"A little novelty also to myself," Louise continues, "to look a gentleman in the face and not think he *knows* I am a chattel."

"You—you reproach me again for that?"

"No—no! I don't reproach you! You've been everything that is good to me," whispers the girl. "Only I've—I've been trying to *forget*." Then suddenly her eyes grow red, her hands flutter, her bosom throbs and pants; she breaks out despairingly: "Martineau was here yesterday and told me Mr. Jarvis had returned from Havana; that I must—forever and unalterably—consider myself your slave." With this tears come from the poor girl's eyes, but really from her heart—those bitter drops that are like drops of blood.

Her master would take his bondmaid in his arms to give her comfort, but she motions him from her, and grows very calm—so calm she frightens him, as she murmurs, "I have always guessed there never was any hope—that it was only your noble, generous self-sacrifice—which tried to rear a plant with no seed and no soil—a plant that should make me walk the earth, proud as I once was—and permit you to fulfill the promise that has made me love you so greatly—perhaps more than ever now, because I know it will not be always *your* sacrifice, but soon *my* sacrifice—that is, if you so decree."

"Martineau told you?" he says, hesitatingly.

"Everything! How you've sacrificed your own estate—how you've jeopardized your own fortune, trying to do my sister and me justice—how you are to-day in absolute want of money;" then she cries out: "Oh, don't try to deny it! Isn't Mr. Cæsar down in the kitchen, going about distracted, saying you've been talking of selling him? Listen! he's sobbing now, that he's going to lose the kindest master on earth."

"Oh, he'll soon get a better one!" ejaculates Bob, affecting a lightness he does not feel, "I've spoken to young Soulé; he'll take the dandy if necessary."

"Ah, you'd sell your clothes off your back for me, and jest about it, Bob," cries Louise, then coming to him, she murmurs: "You do so much for me, I—I notice when you neglect any *little* thing. You—you were not here yesterday."

"I—I couldn't bear to tell you."

"Nor *to-day!*—though of course I have no right to ask my master. You did not come—that wounded me; little things wound me now, dear. You know I —I can command nothing." She has got upon his knee—she now hides her head upon his shoulder.

"Oh, there's no particular secret about my whereabouts," says Covington, pleased that she has felt his absence, and pleased also that he can explain without wounding the poor girl, who is clinging to him. "I had a domestic dinner with La Farge."

"At the Orleans?"

"No; at his own house."

"Oh, his mother and sister are in town again?"

"No; at his own *home*." And practically compelled in the matter, he tells Louise of La Farge's domesticity, his love, his happiness.

Mayhap he is a little enthusiastic about the last, for Louise says suddenly: "Yes; I've heard of girls with a little taint in their blood—girls whom the law says shall not be married to *white* gentlemen—girls like ME —being *placéd!* "then adds, perchance pointedly: "Tell me the details of such domestic arrangements."

Whereupon Covington very delicately explains to her how La Färge has been made a happy man, how a grand ball had been given by the father of the young lady, Señor de Careno, and that afterward, all proper money settlements having been made to secure the financial safety of the new rooftree, Henri had been blessed by the woman of his love. "It was a marriage of the hearts, without a ceremony," he adds.

"A marriage of the hearts?" falters Louise, "*without a ceremony?*" Then looking at him she blushes crimson—droops her head and bursts out sobbing on his shoulder as if her heart would break.

He looks at her sharply, then mutters: "Martineau?"

"Y-e-s, Bob."

"Did he tell you what I said to him?"

"Yes, dear—that proves how much you love me. But, Bob, I—I want to prove how *much* I love you!" Then she startles him with: "Some day, perchance, I shall do it!"

His hand turns her face to his, and as he gazes, her violet eyes grow deep with passion, even her neck burns with a mighty blush. He kisses her tenderly but silently; for a little time neither of them speak. Then she rises from his knee, goes quietly to the piano and plays very softly Bellini's *Casta Diva*, and Bob wonders if she is thinking of the Druid Priestess and her sacrifice. But a subject has been broached between them that will now burn in both their minds.

This is very shortly again forced home to them. Nita comes in, her eyes big with excitement and her generous little heart on fire. She walks straight up to Mr. Covington and says: "*I hate you!*"

"Hate *me?* Why?"

"Oh, because you are *cruel!* You are going to sell poor Mr. Cæsar who loves you,—brought up on your plantation too!" Then indignation changes to dread. Nita shudders: "I'm afraid of you!"

"Afraid of *me?* Great powers! Have I not been

good to you all the time? Haven't I squandered bonbons on you?" mutters Bob, reproachfully.

"Yes; but you might sell *me!*" and her eyes growing big at the thought, the little girl suddenly asks an
awful question, then follows it up with a more horrible
suggestion. "He could do it, couldn't he, Louise?"
she asks. "He could sell *you* too!" then utters contemplatively: "He'd do it if he lost enough money at
poker—gamble us away!" adding: "Mr. Soulé would
give a good deal for Louise; I know it by the
way he looks at her!" next suddenly screams:—"Oh,
Heavens! are you going crazy!"

For Covington is striding about, muttering, "If I
thought that, I'd challenge him tomorrow!" and Louise
has sprung up and seized her and is whispering: "Tor-
turer—away!" as she drags the little sister to Mrs.
Joyce. Here she cries: "Nita, to bed!"—in such an
awful tone that the child obeys her for a wonder.

But Nita has planted a little germ of thought, ugly
thought, in Bob's mind.

"You see what is hanging over us," whispers Louise,
coming back to him, her face red as fire. "Something
must be done! My heaven!—if anything happened to
you, what—what would become of Nita?"

"You ask me to put your name up in Assumption
court-house as my slave?" he shudders; then mutters
savagely: "That only at—the *last!*"

"When will the *last* come?"

"When I can find it in my heart to take my idol
from her pedestal—not *before!*"

And she, catching his hand, fondles it, and sobs:
"Generous one! You will find that I can make a
sacrifice as well as you—some day."

"When?"

"Whenever you ask it." To this she adds, tremblingly, but pointedly: "I think you had better save
Mr. Cæsar."

"You mean——?"

"I mean that you take your legal own—the Tournay
estate, its bank account, property, real and personal,
its live stock—which of course includes Nita and myself." She is very calm and brave now, though very

pale, and her blue eyes have great unshed tears behind them."

"Only at the *last !* "

"This is the LAST! Have not both your lawyers told you there is no hope ? Is not Nita's one chance of ultimate freedom and mine also hanging upon your action ? TAKE US TO MANUMIT US." Then an agony comes in her voice; she shudders: "If you died, the estate would be sold! Bob—think of that! We would be sold at—at——" and cries out: "Put the chains on me, so that you can free me!"

"You know when the step is once taken," says Covington, very slowly, but he notes that his own hand trembles, "there can be no return. Then you will be branded as of ignoble blood, *forever !* "

"Yes."

"You demand it ?" His tone is solemn as death now, for this is the death either of his pride or of his love.

"I DEMAND IT !"

"Very well!" Then he says, almost pleadingly: "You—you will not reproach me for this, either now— or in time to come ?"

And she cries to him: "No! I will *bless* you!" then murmurs, clinging to him, her whole soul in her voice, as her white arms go round her master's neck: "Dear, noble Bob! You have done the best you can for me, and I will do the best I can for you."

But he dares not ask her what she means, and goes away from her horrified, muttering: "She begged me to publish her as my chattel! Good God! What must her anxiety be, to make her crave the brand of serfdom to get nearer to freedom by a *single* day!"

CHAPTER XXIV.

"THE WRONG END OF THE CIGAR."

IT is only nine o'clock in the evening. Covington, thinking the matter over, determines: "I must see Jarvis! He must demand the Tournay property for

me from Martineau. He is stopping at the St. Charles,
I believe."

For Kitson, with his twenty-five-thousand-dollar fee
in his pocket and increasing practice, has thought it
wise to place himself in greater social prominence, and
now occupies rooms at that gorgeous hostelry.

Bob has already sent up his card, when, strolling
into the bar-room he meets the attorney there.

"Ah! How-dy-do!" says Jarvis, enthusiastically.
"Come up and liquor, my client Covington!"

"No, thank you. I want to see you on a matter of
business."

"Very private?"

"Yes!"

"Jes so! Thought you'd be round in a day or two.
Shan't charge you anything; it's only part of the case
in which you paid me twenty-five thousand honest piastres. Come up to my room."

On arriving at his apartments, the lawyer locks the
door and says, sharply: "You want me to make the demand on Martineau?"

"Yes!" says Bob, desperately.

"All right! Have you all the Tournay estate, girls
included, to-morrow morning."

"Can't you find some way to give one little chance to
those poor helpless ones?" stammers the young man,
his face twitching.

"Oh, you mean the Nita case?"

"Yes! Isn't there any hope for her—the woman I
love?"

"Not a bit!" Then, noting that Bob has tears in
his eyes and his hands are trembling, Mr. Jarvis's tone
becomes sympathetic. He says: "I think I've gauged
you pretty square, young man. You want to do the
great—noble act, but I don't see any chance in that
highfalutin way. The best thing you can do is to take
the girls and manumit them according to law."

"Is there no other way?"

"There's no other way, except the Nita case, but
that don't amount to anything." And Kitson goes
about snapping his great big fingers; but suddenly, with
a tremendous, castanet report, he stops—whistles a

moment and says, earnestly: "Look here! You've not given my client Nita every chance she ought to have."

"What do you mean?"

"Well, Nita hasn't had a square deal, quite."

"Why not?"

"You're keeping this thing too darned *quiet*. You're not giving my little client any chance of *outside* evidence. Suppose a man was tried for murder, and nobody knew it; some one whose affidavit could clear him might be walking about the streets while the poor devil was being hung. Let me make the affair a *leetle* public."

"No; that's what we want to avoid. Louise would die of shame."

"Well, let me tell *one* man about it; it won't be much news to him, anyway."

"Who?"

"Faval Bigore Poussin."

"That broken down scoundrel—Why?"

"Well, watch me and *see!*"

"Do you think there's any hope?"

"Well, about as much as there is of my giving you back that twenty-five-thousand-dollar fee. Of course, I might go *crazy* and do it!"

"Then in that case, don't make the demand on Martineau till Wednesday!" says Bob, determinedly, and goes away, though he knows that it will involve an explanation to Louise.

However, after an uneasy night, the next morning about eleven o'clock he goes into the *avocat's* office and tells him he intends to take possession on Wednesday.

"You had better do it to-day," says Martineau, adding, rather sternly: "You gave a promise to that effect last night, and I tell you you are keeping in jeopardy the fate of two innocent and unfortunate creatures, if by any accident you died."

"Miss Tournay has been here?" replied Bob.

"Yes; she came and asked my advice."

"In regard to me?"

"Yes!"

"What did you tell her?'

"I gave her no advice. I simply laid the whole matter before her from a legal and social point of view."

Then he says, his voice growing stern: "Now a word of advice to you, my dear young friend. You have a certain duty to perform to those poor girls. Assume the responsibility the law puts upon you and make demand for the Tournay estate; then you can manumit Louise and Nita and——"

But Bob, remembering that Jarvis had snapped his fingers the night before, and recollecting that when Jarvis snaps his fingers he generally has a startling proposition in his astute brain, says, slowly: "I will not make the demand before Wednesday."

"Why not?—Doesn't Jarvis say there's no chance?"

"Yes;—still not till Wednesday;" then he adds, humbly: "I have a favor to ask."

"What is it?"

"I wish you'd advance me five hundred dollars on my body-servant, Mr. Cæsar, until that time."

"Certainly!" To this the *avocat* adds, sarcastically: "You're not playing poker very well, I'm afraid."

"No," mutters Covington. "I'm in mighty bad luck all round."

So Bob goes out with his check in his hand and a glum look on his countenance; for successful poker is impossible to a distracted mind, and this young gentleman has been losing lots of money in a desperate attempt to achieve financial equilibrium.

His spirits are not raised by the knowledge that he will have to explain his delay to Louise. In fact, Mr. Covington, as he walks toward Dauphine Street, makes up his mind that he will *not* explain, and agitate his sweetheart by a hope, when he has practically none himself.

On entering the Tournay *salon*, Mrs. Joyce comes to him and says: "You've missed her. Louise went out horseback riding."

"Any one with her?"

"Yes; a groom, of course. Louise didn't expect you so soon, and the poor girl needed fresh air, so I thought a little equestrian exercise would be good for her."

"You are quite right," assents Bob, rather pleased to postpone discussing his broken promise.

"Louise tells me," remarks Pamela, "that to-day you take publicly the full legal control of her and her sister."

"I suppose so," mutters Covington, who does not care to hear Pamela's comments on the matter.

"I'm glad of it!" cries Mrs. Joyce. "The anxiety has told upon Louise more than you guess, though she tries to be carelessly cheerful when you are present. Now you can free Nita and her. You are going to do it at once, of course."

"Certainly!" And he sits trying to chat with Pamela, but finally, looking at his watch, suggests, anxiously: "Louise has been out a long time. You're sure she rides well enough to control her steed?"

"Rides?" cries Mrs. Joyce. "Like an amazon! You should have seen her every day for the last year at *Beau Rivage*."

Just here there is a clatter of horses' hoofs outside, and Covington and Pamela step on to the veranda to meet a picture alluring to the eye and pleasant to the senses.

It is Miss Tournay, in full riding costume of that day, with dark blue habit—too long for safety, but not too long for grace—its bodice fitting her exquisite figure like a glove; her beautifully shaped head, decked with brown curls and crowned with hat of ostrich plumes; her pretty hands and arms gauntleted to the elbows, and her little feet cased in black, tight-laced riding boots.

She reins up her gray horse and calls quite blithely: "Bob, come and help me down!"

"With pleasure!" cries Covington, and hurries to her.

"You—you are not angry with me—for going without your permission?" she says, holding out her hand to him, yet looking at the horse's ears. "Mrs. Joyce advised it!"

"Oh, go as much as you like, dear one!" whispers Bob— "Only, next time give me a chance to go with you."

At this she looks embarrassed, but laughs: "Must I get down unaided? Ah, thank you, Bob!" as he lifts the beautiful creature from her saddle very tenderly, but with slightly more punctilio than if she were not his bondmaid.

"I was afraid you'd scold me," she says, shaking out her skirts. "The roads are very dusty, but I think that gallop by the Lake did me good." Then, looking at her watch—part of the jewelry that had been returned to her—she remarks: "Can I have been away three hours? I had no idea it was so late. Dear Bob, I hope I haven't kept you waiting." And placing her hand on his arm, goes up the stairs with him to Mrs. Joyce, easily and unaffectedly.

Covington, as he gazes at his sweetheart, notes there are two deep circles round the lovely eyes that beam on him in pathos and appeal; and, as she catches his glance, Louise shrinks from him a little bashfully, and her color heightens slightly. As they reach the head of the stairs the young lady's embarrassment seems to be heightened; she turns. Her riding habit is held up by one gloved hand; the other flicks nervously her little boot, with her riding whip. Twice she seems about to speak, and Covington, who has learnt to read his bondmaid's vagaries, witcheries and rebellions quite accurately, guesses she has some confession to make but is nervous—fearing reproof.

Louise, for the third time, is opening her lips, and now would doubtless speak, did not Pamela, whose social tact is not of very high order, suddenly interject: "My dear, Mr. Covington has just told me he has taken you as his property *officially* and *publicly*."

This announcement goes through the girl like an electric shock. She gives Bob one agonized glance, and grows deathly pale; suddenly a mighty wave of color flies to the very roots of her hair, she utters a faint, inarticulate cry, rushes into the parlor, throws herself on a sofa, and grovels over its cushions, but doesn't sob—at first!

Covington, cursing this sudden breaking of cruel yet untrue news, steps after the afflicted girl to give her sympathy and consolation.

Though she has demanded the cup, Louise finds it too bitter, now it is at her lips. She will not be comforted, and sighs, piteously: "Every one will know! People will point to me as your—your slave, Bob! Branded on my heart! If it wasn't for you, Bob, I'd—I'd sooner die than take this public degradation."

Probably she would faint, did not Covington and Mrs. Joyce bathe her brow and put pillows under her head, and she lies on the sofa quite pale, wringing her delicate hands from which they have taken the gauntlets.

"I will not permit you that shame! It shall not come to you, dear one!" mutters Covington.

She, misunderstanding him, replies: "Ah, yes; I know. You must now seclude me, as you decreed. That's right—that's kind, dear," she falters. "I could not go out riding again! People will know—Monsieur Soulé will know—everybody will know I am your chattel, Bob." And she wrings her hands and sobs: "The careless will point and laugh. The wicked will wonder if my master is *too* kind to me—the cruel, if they see tears in my eyes—and there will be lots, Bob—will jeer: 'This haughty slave doesn't take kindly to the whip.'" Then she goes on pleadingly: "But in your mercy, you won't keep me that long? My name goes right off, doesn't it, for manumission?"

"Of course!" gloomily answers this master, who doesn't know how to tell his bondmaid sweetheart that she has suffered all this agony—under a mistake; and takes to soothing her as a lover.

Under his caresses, she murmurs, attempting lightness: "Why, one would think *I* was the owner, *you* the serf, you're ministering to me so tenderly," for he is fanning her. Then she smiles piteously, and whispers bashfully: "Bob."

"Yes, dear."

"Bob, you—you haven't kissed me this morning."

This reproach Louise doesn't have to repeat, and soon after, getting his hand in hers, she murmurs: "Tell me."

"Tell you—dear one—what?"

"Well, first the arrangements you think of making for my sister."

Thereupon Bob, entering quite enthusiastically into the discussion of this affair, informs her that his purpose is to send Nita to Paris, to be educated in a fine convent, and that he proposes to settle half the Tournay property on the child.

"Ah, generous one!" cries his sweetheart. "You have made me very happy! Nita can have a career and live a happy life in a land where her present unhappy lot will not be known—or if known, not degrade her." After a little she adds: "We won't talk any more about these things at present—I'm—I'm worn out. Oh Bob, branded as a slave!" and her lips twitch.

After a little she grows calmer and remarks: "Come this evening and tell me what you intend my fate to be. Our love will make that problem harder than my sister's."

So Bob goes away without telling Louise he has postponed action to make her freedom and Nita's certain.

But like the moth about the candle, he returns at seven o'clock this evening, to be for the moment astounded.

His sweetheart is a different creature. Smiles have taken the place of tears. She is unnaturally gay—even to lightness.

Louise comes in to him, very beautifully but simply dressed in white—pure white; her arms and shoulders gleaming like ivory, her eyes sparkling with an impassioned lustre that he does not understand.

Mrs. Joyce does not even make pretence of embroidering in the next parlor. The two are alone together.

His bondmaid says to him quite calmly, though her lips and hands are trembling: "Now about myself! You cannot keep the promise you so nobly made; the law now forbids us that!"

"This is my proposition to you," returns Bob, coming to his point. "And mark me!—any wish or suggestion or resolve of yours in this matter shall be as free from my coercion as if you were in exactly the same state as when I first asked you to be my wife—my *honored* wife!" Then he says, love, tenderness, and determination in his tone: "THAT I ASK YOU AGAIN!"

"Marriage!" screams the girl in ecstasy, then falters: "The law forbids!"

"Not here, but in some other country! After you are manumitted I shall make the same monetary settlements on you as on Nita. You will go to Paris with your sister; there I will meet you; there the orange blossoms that are denied you here, shall linger upon your pure brow."

"Oh, Bob!" whispers his listener, "that is true generosity! Now I know how well you love me!" Then a gleam comes in her eyes; she says, proudly, yet fondly: "Listen to me, and *learn how well I love you*. I know all the sacrifices you have made for me—how you've risked your fortune, embarrassed your estate to give me here in this State the greatest honor a man can do a woman. But that is impossible!" and she begins to sigh, saying, slowly and contemplatively: "Bob, could you not take me to call upon Madame La Farge?" and hides her head upon his breast.

"I do not know La Farge's mother."

"Of course I don't refer to the Creole *grande dame*, I—I mean his—his *placée*—the one that in courtesy is called 'Madame La Farge.'" Her foot is tapping nervously, her face is very red.

"Good God! What are you driving at?"

"*This!* If you marry me, your manumitted slave, there will always be for you, in this your country, public contempt."

"But Europe!" says Bob, determinedly, "England!—where you can move in a society that will not cast you out—where your beauty and goodness might conquer for you a social recognition that is denied you here."

"You mean to make an exile of yourself for *my* sake?" she says, slowly, as if she can't believe his words.

"Yes! for your sake if necessary. But I can visit this country alone, if business calls me."

"Ah!—but would that be a *happy* life for *you?*" queries the the girl. "A year with me would be perhaps—love and sunshine," then cries: "I'd make it love and sunshine, any way! But afterward?" she sighs. "The

second year—a longing for your native land.   Three
years—the very fact—that I held you from your
country might make you cold to me.   Ah, Bob, that I
couldn't bear—that would be too cruel a reproach!
And I should be looking for it.   I am very sensitive;
you notice that I have grown so—ever since—Oh, Bob,
—ever since they told me *what I was!*"   Then she
whispers calmly but despairingly, "Let us end this!   It
is torturing your heart, it is breaking mine.   This is
what you must do to me! manumit me, make the settlement on me as on Nita, then *placée* me here to you as if
I were of the—the mixed blood the law decrees I am.
I shall not be alone then—I shall have society—though
not—not the society of a Christ Church wedding!—not
the society that—that you thought would be mine—
when you asked me to be your bride—when I thought
I should be your loved companion in this life—not—
not your petted slave."

But he springs up and paces the room, and says,
doggedly: "No!—By Heaven!—no!   Alma La Farge
and her sister are children in intellect compared to you.
They have been brought up to this custom; they have
been taught to expect it from childhood.   They see no
degradation in it; to them it is right, proper, and *usual*.
To you, a member of the Episcopal Church—to you
whose hanging head, whose teary eyes can't look me
in the face, because you are ashamed of the mere
thought, *it would be degradation unutterable.*   Your
humiliation would be my despair.   I should see you
droop—reproach in those eyes I love—would be my tor-
ment."   And he would take her in his arms.

But she draws away from him and cries: "You shan't
sacrifice yourself, Bob!   I tell you, for my sake, you
shall not destroy your career.   You aspire to the Congress of the United States.   Married to me, your—
your yeller gal—that's what they'd call me, who would
vote for you in your own town of Lexington, Kentucky?   Who'd not scorn you in your Orleans Club
here?   What ladies' *salon* would be open to you—you
would be as ostracised as me the bondmaid that you
stigmatize yourself to wed!"

Then seeing how he shudders at the mere thought of

contempt of friends, class and kindred, she continues, her voice ringing very clear: "*I* will make the sacrifice, which is *not* one, because I love you so much my life will be in you. You will have your career, I shall have my love! *I'm not ashamed!* See me—I can look you in the face!" and she tries to, but blushes and droops. "It will be nuptials of the heart—you said so the other night—a marriage without a ceremony, which is but a form between those who love." And this poor, despairing girl would falter out more words of persuasion, and by caresses try to prove to him that she will be happy as a *placée* bride.

Suddenly she pauses, gazing at him, astounded at the nobility of his love.

For he stops her sternly, and perchance for a moment shocks her, saying: "A little while ago I told you your wishes in this matter should not be controlled by me. Now I revoke the privilege!"

"Ah!"

"I exercise authority as your master to settle your future state in life! You hear that, Louise?"

"Yes, sir," and, sighing, trembles a little as she asks: "What fate?"

"*I marry you in Paris!* Prepare for that—THAT IS MY WILL!"

"No—no! You don't know what you're doing."

"That is my business! Now, do you intend to be my obedient one?" And he takes her in his arms, and, holding her fair face up to his, kisses her tears away and whispers: "Do you intend to be my wife in Paris, as I decree?"

"Oh, Bob, you noble one!" and she hides her head in his bosom, and clings to him. Yet, after a little, becoming arch, she laughs in his face: "Of course I do! I daren't disobey—my master!"

Bob knows that he has given her all the happiness he can in her cruel strait, and, fortunately, loves this beautiful yet helpless creature well enough to be happy for it.

"I'm mighty glad it's settled!" he says, taking a long breath.

So, after a little, he bids her farewell, and, coming

out of the house, sighs as if broken hearted: "It was either my pride or my love's chastity—and, thank Heaven! I did not degrade her," then mutters, bitterly: "By the Lord Harry! It was the master went to the wall this trip!"

But a little later in the evening, in his own room, thinking the matter over, he begins to throw his locks back from his brow and pace the room like a grizzly bear with poisoned arrows in him, giving out such sudden and violent paroxysms of rage and anguish that his valet, the faithful Cæsar, looking at him, says: "Oh, Mistah Covington! Shall I go fer a doctah? Has yo' got de jamborees?"

"Clear out you blarsted fool!" he cries, and expels the sable functionary from the room; then goes about muttering: "By the God of War, they'll call my children *niggers!* Oh God!—a Covington a *nigger!*—a *Bob* Covington a nigger!—that's what they'll call them round here—that's what the law will call them—*my poor little pickaninnies!* Though, by Heaven and earth, I know there's nothing but the grandest blood on earth within that beauty's veins!"

Just here he is interrupted by a bell-boy-knock, and, opening the door, receives a letter that astounds him. It reads as follows:

ROBERT COVINGTON, ESQ.
DEAR SIR :
I have lighted a fuse in that Nita matter that will be sure to blow up a bomb !—*if the bomb has any powder in it!* That's the point !
Get five thousand dollars in bank bills and put them where you can grab them *quick*—best in the safe of your hotel. Checks won't do ! See to this first thing in the morning.
Tell them at the office of the hotel to-morrow evening as you go out that you will be in by eleven o'clock. Then be sure to be in your room *at ten*, and don't—for the Lord's sake—try to see me or come near my office !
Yours hastily,
KITSON JARVIS,
Attorney at Law and Proctor in Admiralty.
P. S.—I don't think the bomb is going to have any powder in it ; so don't get flighty.

But Bob does get excited! It is no use to go to bed, so he walks off to the Orleans Club where he changes to hear something that agitates him more.

Young Soulé is at a near-by table.

A gentleman with whom Covington is chatting says to him, carelessly: "Hector has a new sweetheart, I imagine. He has the greatest eye for beauty in all New Orleans."

"Eye for beauty? Oh, you mean Soulé," remarks Bob following the other's glance.

"Yes; I saw him with one of the loveliest creatures in the world, taking a ride by the lake this morning."

"Glad to hear that!" laughs Covington, thinking that "the loveliest creature in the world" will probably prevent the gentleman under discussion calling so frequently at Dauphine Street.

"*You* may be glad," says his informant, "but, *sapristi, I* envied him! The young lady was a very fine horsewoman! A perfect example of grace—in dark blue riding habit trimmed with black braid, ostrich plumes of sable on her head, and rode a slashing gray saddle horse—But what is the matter with you?"

"N—n—nothing," stammers Bob. "Only, I've put the wrong end of my cigar in my mouth."

"Yes, that's a nasty accident!" says the other. "It happened to me once—but that was the night before I went out for my *first* duel—What!—are you going?"

"Yes. If I stay here it may be an omen for *my* first duel!" remarks the Kentuckian, rising.

For the little seed that Nita has planted has now grown big as a magic palm tree. But as he goes home he jeers: "I seem to be getting the wrong end of the cigar in every way;" then mutters, brokenly: "And she never mentioned it!"

BOOK V

How He Saved Her.

CHAPTER XXV.

"THAT OLD MAN LAUGHED AT ME."

But Louise gets bad news also this night!

Martineau comes, late in the evening, to ask her what arrangements she and Mr. Covington have arrived at, as to their future lives; for this old gentleman has a very tender spot in his heart for the unfortunate young lady.

So Arvid, though his gray eyes twinkle till he wipes his glasses, and his lip twitches as he listens, sits by the girl's side, his hand patting her beautiful curls, as Louise tells him of her noble Bob—his love and generous self-sacrifice for her. Her tale being ended, she asks: "What did the judge in chambers say when he decreed Nita and me to robbery and slavery?"

"Nothing. No demand has been made to-day."

"And the notice of my sister's manumission and my own has *not* been sent to Assumption Parish?"

"No; Mr. Covington did not demand possession of the Tournay estate."

"So Bob broke his promise and told me nothing of it!"

"I presume, my poor child, he cannot yet bring himself to placard your name as his slave," replies Martineau. "It is despair to him to inflict such humiliation upon you!"

"Don't I know that," she sighs. "But it must be done!" Suddenly she remembers how she has suffered for a degradation not yet put upon her. It makes her angry; she sits thinking deeply, then quickly says to the *avocate :* "Will you kindly send a letter for me ? Please!—It won't take a moment to write it."

Five minutes after, she places the letter in Martineau's grasp, and he notices her hand is feverish and trembles. But kissing her forehead, he murmurs: "*Bon soir.*"

The moment he has gone she runs to Pamela and says: "Dear Mrs. Joyce, I have a favor to ask of you. It's only a little ruse at which I don't think Mr. Covington will be very angry, to force him to recognize me as what I am. I know his delay is for some noble motive, and for my sake; but Nita is jeopardized on account of his pride for me that won't relinquish this useless struggle against fate."

"What is it ?" asks Pamela, anxiously.

"Oh, nothing very shocking. Something that will take place right here in the house, and if Bob objects, none of the servants need know. If he, by his silence, consents, they will see that I have been put in my proper place; that's all. Let me tell you about it." And she whispers, hastily, a few words into her companion's ear.

"He will be very angry."

"No, I don't think that, and if he is, his displeasure will fall on me—with whom he has a right to be angry if he chooses. You must let me do it."

Thus urged and entreated by Louise, Pamela consents. Next morning Mr. Covington receives a little note asking him to breakfast at the Tournay mansion. It is signed "Pamela Joyce."

Thinking of the fair arms that were round his neck last evening, and anxious to bring Miss Louise to book about that Soulé ride, Bob remarks to his attendant, Mr. Cæsar: "Get me rigged up in a hurry!" and shortly finds himself at the Dauphine Street residence.

In the little *salon* he is met by Mrs. Joyce, who says, striving by jauntiness to conceal embarrassment: "Just in time for breakfast, dear Mr. Covington. Flit into the dining-room."

"Louise; she is not ill ?"

"Oh, no! She—she will be here presently."

But entering the dining-room, Bob ejaculates: "Why, there are only covers for *two !*" then iterates, anxiously: "Louise is not ill?"

"Oh, no. Some—some careless mistake," stammers Mrs. Joyce. "We—we have a new waitress."

"Well, judging by the way this table is set," remarks the gentleman, critically, "I should say the wench must be a jim-dandy!"

"Yes; it is horrible!" cries Pamela, in dismay, for the table has been set in a very reckless manner, and is minus napkins, salt-cellars and a good deal of the *etcetera*, of a well-served breakfast. And she tries hastily to arrange the things, muttering: "The—the waitress is new—new to her work."

"Just from the cotton field, I reckon! By hookey! that's a nasty crash!" jeers Bob, as the sound of breakage comes from the butler's pantry; then mutters glumly: "You've—you've not a *new* cook also?"

"Oh, no. I can guarantee the cook," says Mrs. Joyce, nervously, and Mr. Covington, taking the chair assigned to him, finds himself at the head of the table; his back being towards the door to the butler's pantry, which connects with the downstairs kitchen by a dumb-waiter.

Some little time after, as he is impatiently remarking: "What a slow coach that new girl is!" an arm white as snow comes under his eye, arranging his breakfast in front of him.

He looks up with a start, as a sweet voice, agitated, but humble, is saying: "Monsieur, will you take tea, or coffee, or chocolate ?"

With a Kentucky whoop he springs up to see before him, Louise, shrinking, blushing, embarrassed, habited as the dining-room girl of the Tournay mansion. For she has a little maid's cap upon her fair head, a light black alpaca maid's gown with ruching round the neck, and sleeves reaching to the elbows, thus baring snow white arms for convenience of table service. The skirt for dining-room menage is short, displaying liberally balbriggan stockings and little slippers.

"You see I've arrived at last at my true status in the household!" she says with a tremble in her tones,

"'Will Monsieur have tea, coffee, or chocolate? After the omelet there is a steak.''

But she says no more; for the waiting-girl is suddenly gathered up in Mr. Covington's strong arms and deposited in his chair, as Bob remarks: "*I* do the waiting." Then imitating her humble tones, he continues: "Tea, coffee, or chocolate, Miss Tournay? There is also a steak after the omelet, Mademoiselle."

Louise makes an attempt to rise but he whispers, sternly: "You sit there, Miss and eat—I wait."

And he does wait, observing; "It's a pleasure to serve beauty! This is a picnic-breakfast; ladies first!" and other allusions of the kind. Once or twice his thrall makes effort to rise from the chair, but he commands quite sternly in her ear: "Louise, obey me! I order you to eat a good wholesome breakfast!" then bowing very low, asks: "Would you like waffles or buckwheat cakes this morning, *Mademoiselle?*—We have also maple syrup!" then entering from the butler's pantry suddenly, says: "But we *haven't!* the new girl broke the syrup bottle with her butter-fingers fifteen minutes ago."

Soon Pamela and Louise get to laughing despite themselves, and the girl pleads: "Bob, please come to breakfast with us. You don't know how unhappy you make me."

"You don't know how unhappy you make *me!* . Do you think I could eat with you standing behind my chair? This is foolishness! this is nonsense! If I hadn't objected, I suppose the cook would have discovered, or Manda would have come up, and then all New Orleans would have known there was a new and most lovely waitress in the Tournay dining-room, who stood behind Bob Covington, her master's chair, served him with great display of the prettiest ankles in the world, running at his beck and nod and trembling at his frown."

"But I can't eat with you behind my chair either," cries Louise, getting red, and tears almost gathering in her blue eyes, "especially when you're scolding me so."

"Very well. If I sit down with you," remarks Bob,

" will you stay by my side and do your duty by the breakfast ? "

Receiving a faltering " Yes," Mr. Covington, who, to•tell the truth, is very hungry and is not accustomed to seeing other people eat, yet getting none himself, and has surreptitiously stolen a bite or two and purloined a cup of coffee in the butler's pantry, sits down with Mrs. Joyce and his sweetheart, and soon they finish an *al fresco*, impromptu picnic-breakfast, for Manda, the dining-room girl, has been sent away to do other work this morning.

" Mrs. Joyce," he says, as he selects a cigar from his case, " where's Nita ? "

" I think studying one of her lessons."

" Would you be kind enough to see she keeps studying and doesn't come in ? "

" Certainly, dear Mr. Covington."

And Pamela going out, he thus addresses the new abigail, who is still seated at the breakfast table, nervously balancing a spoon upon her fork: " Louise, please come here ! "

" Certainly, sir." And Miss Tournay stands before him, looking most entrancing in the simple costume.

As he gazes his eyes grow very tender, though indignant, as he breaks out: " Do you suppose I'll permit you to make me blush to the nape of my neck by standing behind my chair ? You forget, Louise, you're my affianced." His arm goes round her and he takes her to his heart and kisses her blushing cheeks.

But she says: " Bob, you must acknowledge me as your slave to free me ! "

"Ah, some one has told you!"

" That you have not yet taken public title to me ?— Yes."

" Then—you—you insist on my treating this little escapade of yours from a serious standpoint ? "

" Yes, sir ! " with a curtsey.

" Very well," he says, glumly. " Have your way— exhibit yourself as the waitress of the Tournay mansion." Next, as though to frighten her from her resolve, adds sharply: "A light for my cigar—quick! And while you're about it, the morning paper!"

But she replies, humbly: "Yes, sir," and tripping daintily and gracefully about, lights his *perfecto*, and in a moment places the morning *Picayune* in his hand; then curtseys, asking: "Anything else, sir?"

"Not at present." He puffs away glumly, and casts abstracted eyes over the journal. Though she is the most beautiful and exquisite waiting-girl in all the world—though she is *his* waiting-girl—he seems ashamed to contemplate her. Suddenly a line in the paper catches his eye. He grows interested.

As he reads, Louise, standing behind him, awaiting his convenience, gets tired; a servant's pose fatigues her delicate limbs. She says: "Bob."

No answer.

"Bob!" pleadingly.

"Yes, dear," still reading the paper.

You mustn't call your waiting-maid, *dear!* and I wish you'd tell me to do something. Shall I wash the dishes?"

"And redden those pretty hands?—Certainly not! Jump up on that chair and dust those curtains well; a feather duster is more becoming than a dish-rag."

"But some one will see me. The window is open. This dress is awful short!"

"Not too short for a waiting-girl! You can stay up there till I tell you you can come down. You want people to know you're my slave——" he shivers at the ugly word—and goes to reading the paper again, eagerly, intently.

Then very bashfully, inspired by his jeers, Louise seizes a feather duster, jumps upon a chair, and, standing in the window in plain sight of the street, begins to fleck uneasily the summer dust from off the curtains. She peers timidly out. Joy and rapture!—nobody is passing in the dreamy, summery noon-day of the old French quarter. She goes to brushing desperately, every now and then flirting the feathers viciously about, hoping the cloud of dust will reach Bob's nostrils that he may give her permission to step out of the public eye. But now he seems to have no thought except the newspaper.

Suddenly the girl begins to blush and quiver and falters plaintively: "Bob, let me step down."

No answer.

"Bob—some one is looking! A horrid old man!" and she springs from the chair and stands before him saying, mutinously: "I don't care; I won't stay there!"

"Why are you not at work?"

"Oh, there was a horrid old man looking at me as I stood up on tiptoe in the chair and dusted. It was that awful creature who got a tip from you at the race, and gave you his dirty card. Why, what's the matter?"

For Covington has sprung to the window and is looking eagerly out. A moment after, he closes the blinds, returns, and says: "You're so ashamed of being seen as a slave! My poor darling it was your imagination."

"No, it was not! He went round the corner. He's a horrid thing!"

"Why?"

"Oh, well, this dress is so short. He looked at me and laughed, and then he glanced up and saw you— and seemed to jeer in my face. Oh, Bob—it's—it's awful to be *what I am!*" And with a despairing sigh she drops on her knees before him and puts her head in his lap, and sobs rack her graceful frame.

CHAPTER XXVI.

GAME-COCKS AS WATCHDOGS.

AFTER a little time, he says: "Now, a truce to this nonsense! You must let me manage the affair in my own way. Go to your room, put on one of your everyday dresses, appear as you have before, then come to me—I want to speak to you."

"You're going to scold me?"

"Yes."

"Well, I'd sooner you did that than be namby-pamby! Bob, I hate a man who is not determined!" Then, putting nose in air, she says, "As if I were afraid of you!" and runs off in better spirits than she has been before this morning.

He still sits reading this curious item—one he has

gone over half a dozen times—in the columns of the
Picayune:

BURGLARY PREVENTED BY GAME-COCKS.

Faval Bigore Poussin, the sporting notary, now swears by
Spanish chickens. The last steamer from Havana brought him
a large consignment of Cuban game-cocks, for use at Rodriguez's pit. He roosted them for the evening in his back office,
and in the middle of the night was awakened by the most tremendous crowing since the cock of St. Peter. Fearing that Men-
doza, the rival game-cock man, was stealing his roosters, Poussin flew in, pistol in hand, followed by his mulatto boy, but discovered that an attempt had been made upon his safe, in which
he stores only old papers. The burglars, to aid them at their
nefarious work had turned on a dark lantern, the light had
started roosterdom, cockadoodle-doo ! Poussin fired two shots,
probably without effect, at the miscreants, who would not have
obtained much if they had broken into or carried off hi s safe
Poussin's wealth being chiefly game-cocks, coupons for non-
winning Havana lottery tickets, cards for coming cock and dog
fights, and losing betting cards for horse-races. However,
Poussin now glorifies the Spanish rooster, stating, as a watchdog, he beats a terrier, and is equal to the goose of ancient
Rome.

What the deuce it means Covington can't guess. It
has something to do with Poussin, and he shrewdly
imagines—something to do with Jarvis. Poussin's
safe!—could Kitson think there might be evidence in
that ?

‘ Contemplation of this problem in broken in upon by
Louise, returning, dressed as Miss Tournay of old.
She says, a little anxiety in her voice: " Now for the
scolding!"

"Very well. Come into the parlor and sit by me,
so I can pet you if I frighten you too much."

" Oh, you *must* frighten me *a great deal.*"

"Why?"

"*More* petting, of course!" And she sits by him,
and puts her head on his shoulder, and looking up in
his eyes, droops hers and whispers: "Now, my dear
master."

"And in that authority I address you," remarks

Bob. "You must leave this matter in my hands, as to the time I take official ownership of you and Nita."

"But Monsieur Martineau says I have been your—your property ever since I surrendered myself to your attorney." And she hangs her head as she sits beside him.

But he goes on, uncompromisingly: "I—I have gone over this matter with you sufficiently. I now tell you that, since you will not conform to my ideas, I shall enforce them."

"Very well!"

"Now, stand in front of me—I want to look in your face." And his voice grows like a judge, as he says: "You were riding on horseback yesterday."

"Yes," faintly.

"Who was riding by your side?"

A sudden start goes through the girl. Her face grows red as a peony. Then she rises to her full height and says, firmly: "Monsieur Hector Soulé."

"And you never told me of it?" His voice is very sad.

"I—I was going to, Bob—but all we had to speak of yesterday put it out of my mind." Then she pouts: "It wasn't much. Soulé chanced to be riding too, and—meeting me at the Lake, rode by my side for half an hour."

"The groom at the regulation distance behind, I presume," returns Bob, savagely; and his brow grows very dark as he chews his moustache grimly.

But she startles him by saying, in that proud humiliation that always makes him pity her and yearn over her: "Do you ask these questions as my master, or as my betrothed ?"

"As both."

"Then I will tell you as *my* betrothed, that the suspicion implied in your question is unworthy of *you;* unworthy of *me!*" next sobs, "Bob, do you think for one moment that my whole heart and soul are not yours, after the sacrifice I offered to make for you but yesterday ?" and sinking on her knees, puts her head in his lap and says: "Forgive me as my lover."

"What man could doubt you, Louise ?" he cries, as he fondles her.

"Now," she continues, "to you as my master I admit I should have told you of Monsieur Soulé's attention! But. Bob Covington has forgiven me! Pooh for what Mr. Covington, my master, does about the matter!"

"Just the same," suggests her sweetheart, "no more horseback rides unless I'm at your side, eh?" And he playfully takes her little ear between his thumb and finger.

"Oh, you will go with me? Then they will be indeed a pleasure!"

"Also," Bob remarks, perchance a little moodily, "I think you'd better not be at home if young Soulé calls in the next few days."

"Do you order it?"

"No!"

"Then I will do it with joy. Don't fear—I'll be out to Monsieur Hector whenever you wish."

"And now," she falters, her face growing pale: "I have a confession to make to you."

"Humph! Another Soulé episode?" and Bob's eyes flash and his brows lower again.

"No—no more Soulé. He is finished for the present," she returns, airily, rather pleased that Covington, whom she loves with her whole heart, yet holds somewhat in awe, has a weak spot in his armor which she can probe at will.

"What then?"

"Bob, don't—don't be angry with me! Promise me you won't be angry with me!"

"What have you done?" he asks, anxiously; for her nervous manner has alarmed him, as in fact it has done all this day.

"I—I sent to the Clerk of Assumption Parish."

"What?"

"Notice of the registration of Nita and myself as your property. Forgive me! I wanted to save your love and pride in me that pang!"

"Louise, you haven't *dared?*"

"Yes, Bob; every breath of freedom you steal from my sister and myself seems like centuries."

Then his manner frightens her; he cries, hurriedly and hoarsely: "How did you send it?"

"I—"

"Answer me, Louise—I demand it!"

"As my master?" says the girl, proudly.

"No, as your lover, whose heart will break at your humiliation!"

"Then I gave it to Monsieur Martineau to post."

"Thank God!" falters Covington, and she sees him run from the room and fly down Dauphine Street, as she laughs: "He's too late! That letter was posted, if not last night, at least this morning!"

But Covington is not too late!

In Martineau's private office, the *avocat* says to him: "Here is a letter Louise asked me to post. I happened to glance at the address, and thought it wiser for her sake and for yours not to post it until you approved it."

"I thank you very much!" replies Covington. "Louise is getting into such a state of nervous agitation over the matter, she doesn't know what is for her best interests."

"Are you sure *you* do?" asks the old lawyer, searchingly.

Then Jarvis's instructions coming into his mind, Bob says, hurridly: "I must obtain from you five thousand dollars more."

"*Mon Dieu!* How badly you play poker!" gasps the *avocat*.

"No—not poker! I wish to use it in the Nita matter."

"*Ciel!*" my poor boy! You are ruining yourself for a chimera!"

"You have my farm as your security. It is worth a hundred thousand dollars. Besides, if it is a chimera, the Tournay estate is mine."

"Oh, very well. Sign your name to this note; make it at ten days—you will surely take possession in that time." And Martineau gives him a check for the money.

This he cashes at the bank, putting the bills in a big envelope, and buttoning it up in his pocket, returns to the Tournay mansion to find in its parlor a very mutinous young lady.

To her he hands the note silently, and she breaks out: "Even Martineau would not post a letter for—for the poor slave-girl Louise." then sneers, icily: "I thank you, my master, for your consideration in not putting upon me the humiliation of opening it." Next tearing the envelope open, she hands it to poor Bob, remarking: "It is my *duty* to let you read it—otherwise I may be whipped!"

"Great snakes! Louise! Don't—don't torture me by making me feel I am your tyrant !" begs Covington.

"Oh, yes; you ought to read it. You should read every letter that I inscribe. Some day I might write a little note to Monsieur Soulé!"

But this kind of conversation makes Bob look so savage that she changes her tone and bombards him with: "When are you going to take legal possession of the Tournay estate? To-morrow, as you promised?"

And he, thinking of Jarvis's note and the strange article he has read in the newspaper this day, shocks her by saying: "I do not know! I shall not take possession so long as there is the slightest chance for you. For your sake I have a little hope."

As the words leaves his mouth she screams: "*You have hope?* Oh, Heaven and earth, and mercy and goodness, you have HOPE!"—Her eyes beam, her face is illuminated as with the glow of a new sun. She dazzles him, yet shocks him.

"I have but little," he sighs helplessly, and sees the sunlight leave his sweetheart's face.

'Suddenly her eyes grow desperate. She cries: "For my sake have *no* hope! Take Nita and me as your chattels, so you can manumit us! It is your duty—*I demand it as your affianced wife!*"

"As your affianced husband I will not put shame upon you that cannot be taken off—until I choose!" he says, doggedly. Then rather awes this young lady who is looking commandingly on him, by taking her in his arms, seating her on his knee as a child, and telling her if she is disobedient he will punish her severely; but also kissing her and begging her to give herself one little chance.

Under his caresses she grows calmer, perchance

even more rational, and at last comforts him by saying: "Yes, Bob; I suppose I must consider you
right;" then looks into his face and murmuring: "Any
penalty?" puts up her lips to his and makes him as
happy as he can be in this strait.

After a little, however, she grows flighty again,
for the agitations of this awful waiting have made
this sensitive being high-strung, restive, almost hysteri-
cal. But her petulance and nervousness add to her
charm, and for half an hour she fascinates with
alternate tender love and pleading witchery, this man
whose pride for her has now become his torture.
Finally she jeers: "Bob, do you know you've got the
most rebellious bondmaid in the world before you?"

"The most charming!" he says.

"Compliments for a slave-girl? Pooh! Do you
know what I advise you to do with me to-day?"

"Kiss you?"

"No; lock me up in my room! If you don't I'm
sure I shall do something desperate."

"Nonsense! You talk as if you were a Fatima and
I a Bluebeard!"

"And did not Fatima get Bluebeard's throat cut?
Bob, I tell you that the best thing you can do is to put
me under lock and key."

But he doesn't; and laughs at her and caresses her
and says she's too pretty to be put out of sight.

Perchance he had better have taken her advice.

For when he has gone away she pouts: "He will not
take official charge of the estate to-morrow. He will
again delay Nita's manumission and mine, for some
poor, crazy, hopeless scheme of his to prevent our
being placarded as his property."

Then Satan, who has often been in the heads of
beautiful slave-girls before, gets into this one's, taking
position *au naturel* in Louise's fervid brain. She suddenly cries: "Soulé!" then jeers "Bob Covington,
I'LL MAKE YOU ACKNOWLEDGE ME YOUR SLAVE TO-
NIGHT! I SWEAR IT!"

Ten minutes after, a little blackamoor, bearing a
scented *billet doux*, departs for the Orléans Club.

CHAPTER XXVII.

"SILENCE, LOUISE!"

HER note has the desired effect. Monsieur Soulé, very proud and very happy, for this gentleman admires exceedingly this young lady, raps on the door of the Tournay residence about eight o'clock this evening.

Covington, who has become nervous, anxious, and fretful himself, perhaps on account of the freaks of his fair sweetheart, and more so, perchance, because of Jarvis's strange letter of the night before, eats a gloomy supper at the Verandah. Then, mindful of Kitson's instructions, he deposits the five thousand dollars in the hotel safe, also leaving careful word at the office that he will return at eleven o'clock this evening; *but not before.*

He turns his steps towards Dauphine Street, for his sweetheart, though she tortures him, fascinates him wondrously all this day. Coming near the Tournay house something like an hour after young Soulé, he sees lights in the parlor and hears the sound of Louise's voice and the piano. "Over her tantrums, eh? Poor, anxious girl!" he thinks.

But entering the *salon, he* gets the tantrums. Hector Soulé, with very ardent eyes, is bending over Louise, who looks lovely as an houri stolen from Paradise. Gazing at her, Bob gasps: "She's got on that cursed Pelican Ball dress!" and remembering, casts evil eyes upon the garment.

For his bondmaid is wearing the proscribed costume, and more dazzling and beautiful in it than perhaps she had been the night he asked her to be his bride. Both fair cheeks have hectic flushes on them, making the delicate ivory of her shoulders, arms, and bosom shine as snow under the waxlights of the room. Her bright eyes gleam like fire opals. In the many-colored gauzes of this sylphide dress she flits about, a rainbow queen, or rather a naughty fairy who is going to work a very bad enchantment this same evening.

There is within her eyes a sneaking, apologetic glance as she rises to meet her master. For she, even while she does this thing, is penitent. She knows she has disobeyed him; she knows she has wounded him; she knows she has even shocked him; for now it must be apparent she *deceived* him when she said she would receive the dashing young Creole, Hector Soulé, no more.

And Bob knows it too, and his heart grows heavier than it has been in all this month of troubles.· He stands before her, his breath half taken out of his body by astonishment and shock, by pain and anger.

Of the three, Soulé seems in much the best spirits, being quite good natured, as young beaux often are, when elated by a new and dazzling conquest. He rather laughs to himself, poor Covington looks so glumly at him.

But Bob, having the *savoir faire* of the man of the world, bows coldly but politely to this gentleman whom he now considers his rival, and the three sit down, conversing on the matters of the day. For Louise stops her music and perches herself gracefully on a little sofa with her two admirers conveniently in front of her on either hand, and they proceed to a triangular *conversazione* that makes Bob writhe upon his chair.

Still all would run along within the limits of conventional politeness, were it not that Louise has made promise to herself: " Bob Covington, my master, shall claim me as his bondmaid to this gay young gentleman who looks at me—so—so flatteringly."

And she would doubtless make Mr. Covington speak out and perchance sharply to her, did not he, making a shrewd guess at her idea, close his mouth and keep his tongue quite still, though sometimes his teeth will grind themselves together.

"Monsieur Soulé," Louise says, a touch of almost tenderness in her voice, "you were riding, I presume, to-day?"

"Yes, Mademoiselle; I had *hopes!*" This is emphasized by an ardent glance.

"Ah, thank you! So had I, *hopes* too." She returns the language of his eyes, then goes on, an uneasy snicker in her tones: "But I could not come; I was detained by domestic duties." And glancing sneakingly at Bob, murmurs: "We had a buttery-fingered dining-room girl this morning. Mr. Covington was at breakfast and criticised her service; he thought the wench must have just left the cotton-field."

Despite himself, Bob emits a horrid, uneasy, rasping laugh.

"You are amused, Monsieur Covington?" asks Soulé."

"You would not have been had you waited twenty minutes for your breakfast as I did," savagely mutters the gentleman addressed.

"Why, Bob had awful trouble with our dining-room girl. You know as guardian he is potentate of this house," cries Louise, giving an uneasy smile, then goes babbling on to young Soulé: "What would you do, Monsieur Hector, with a dining-room girl who sets the table horribly and breaks half the dishes in the butler's pantry at her first essay of table service? I told Mr. Covington she ought to be whipped."

"Oh, there's no telling what may happen to the new dining-room girl, *yet!*" laughs Bob, in jeering tone. It is the only ungenerous speech he has made under the torture and he despises himself for it as he sees his bondmaid color to the roots of her hair, then grow pale and tremble and bite her pretty lip.

"I'm sure I don't know, Mademoiselle Tournay," murmurs the young Creole. "My mother supervises all our old family servants, who are like members of the family itself. I—I suppose you had better sell her."

"Ah, *that's* the idea! Cousin Bob, Monsieur Soulé suggests you might sell the dining-room girl." Then Miss Tormentor adds, suggestively, as she glances at the ardent Creole: "You might not have to go far to find a purchaser."

To this Mr. Covington answers nothing. Once or twice his lips have opened, but his tongue has given no sound, though his glance is a very nasty one as he casts it upon the suggested new proprietor of all these fairy airs and graces; for Louise is most vivacious now.

"I *will* make him speak!" thinks his exquisite bond-maid, almost savagely. "Even if he chastises me;" and bites her lips. For she knows she has run up a pretty good score for herself and proceeds to add to it by being very tender with the eyes to her master's rival, and saying: "You like the Lake, Monsieur Soulé? So do I. What do you think of another morning's ride?" making as it were appointment with him.

But Covington holding the arms of his chair, says no word, though his eyes grow very cold, yet have flashes in them, and become those quiet, deadly eyes that are peculiar sometimes in Western men of long forbearance but very terrible when roused—the eyes of Davy Crockett, of Colonel Bowie—Kit Carson's eyes.

Then, finding words will not make this gentleman cry out, Louise takes more potent measures. The card of invitation to the Pelican ball lies upon an escritoire; it suggests a means.

"Monsieur Hector, you were on the committee who were kind enough to send me this invitation, I believe?"

"Yes, I had that honor. But you were not there."

"No; this was the dress I had prepared for it, but circumstances prevented my going. Monsieur Covington doesn't approve of the robe, though 'tis the latest fashion. These crinoline effects made Madame La Comtesse de Soissons the observed at a grand ball at the Tuileries. Monsieur Covington thinks it shows my twinkling feet too often and too much." And she gives the skirts a coquettish, wavy motion. "I will get your judgment on the subject." Then she calls: "Mrs. Joyce—Pamela! Come and play for me!" and cries: "*Un, deux, trois, Jeté! Assemblez!*—Dancing school lesson! Monsieur Covington has seen the little affair." And she seems full of gay spirits, laughing grace, and very happy—though her heart is like to break.

But she has won.

Mr. Covington, rising, says, stiffly: "Louise, you need not call in Mrs. Joyce to the piano." Then, bowing to the Creole, remarks: "Miss Tournay will not dance for you, Monsieur Soulé, this evening."

"Oh, but I will!" cries Louise, "and without

music!" and takes position, extending slippered foot and dazzling ankle, in a way that makes Bob grind his teeth.

"I forbid you to dance!" he says, sternly.

"And I forbid you to use that tone of insulting command to a young lady!" Monsieur Soulé remarks, rising also.

"And why not?"

"Because I will not permit any man to speak to a young lady, whom I honor and esteem, words of brutal command that are an insult!"

But the girl cries out: "Nonsense! Quarreling about a—" and would come between them.

But Bob says in such an awful voice that it stills even her tongue for a second: "Silence, Louise!"

To this Soulé exclaims: "I forbid you to use that tone!"

And Louise cries out: "I will speak! I will tell him——'

"Silence!"

"It is nonsense for gentlemen to quarrel about a—"

Before the syllable can leave her tongue, Covington's hand is clapped over her fair lips, which struggle to utter the word that will say she is his chattel. His arm is round her waist, in a flash she is picked up and borne through the second *salon*, through the dining-room, into the butler's pantry, and, with a whispered: "Silence, if you love me!" put down upon a dresser.

Before her astonished senses give her motion, she hears the click of key in lock; she is a prisoner. Covington, striding out through the other rooms, closes each door behind him to drown her voice, and, coming into the parlor, locks the door behind him, and, putting the key in his pocket, confronts the astounded Soulé.

Then the young Creole, stepping up to him, says: "Monsieur, you are no gentleman! I know not by what authority you act to this beautiful young lady as a brute; but you have my defiance, sir!"

The reply astounds Soulé still more. "You're quite right, Hector," says Bob, "under the circumstances I would say exactly the same as you."

"Ah, then, you have some explanation to make of this strange affair?"

"None! only I would suggest Miss Tournay's name shall not be mentioned."

"Certainly, sir! But you have my defiance and may expect to hear from me!"

And Soulé marches from the apartment, wondering if Covington, who has always seemed to him a courteous gentleman, has not gone mad.

Then Bob, unlocking the pantry door, releases his captive, and she comes out to him, a strange terror in her face. Not the terror of a slave who fears chastisement, but of a woman who fears danger to him she loves.

"You may come out now; you have had your way," he says, sternly.

"Ah, you have told!—Thank God, Bob, you have told him!" And her arms go round him, as she murmurs, sneering at herself: "Monsieur Soulé could better protect a bondmaid by his check-book than his sword."

At this suggestion, he shivers and unclasps her arms, then mutters: "I have told Soulé *nothing !* "

"NOTHING ?" Then seeing what he means, she bursts out in despairing sneer: "Oh, heaven! the Creole dandy is going to draw his sword for a slave-girl! He will be the laughter of New Orleans. And you, Bob, you will be thought foolish, too;" next falters: "I beg of you to placard my name to prevent a meeting with young Soulé.

"Humph! Bob Covington isn't built that way! I placard your name when I please—that I tell you as your master. As your lover, I tell you I will fight to keep you from being branded as my slave as long as I elect—that you will see when Monsieur Soulé sends his second."

And she screams: "My God, Bob! If he kills you!"

And he, mistaking the cause of her alarm, laughs: "Ah! That would destroy your chance of manumission."

"Oh, that's generous—generous to the woman who told him she would *placée* herself for his sake! Oh, Bob, that's *noble !* " she cries to him; then adds, sadly, and with reproachful eyes: "And yet, of course, you can say it to *me*. I am your chattel—that makes me to you defenseless."

"Pardon me," says Covington, hoarsely: "I am your master—that's the reason I am defenseless to you," then bursts out, indignantly: "But do not think when I face Hector Soulé's pistol, your fate will be in danger if I fall. To-night I make my will, leaving to Martineau, as trustee for you and little Nita, the Tournay estate and all else I have. I sign your papers of manumission; I direct Martineau to see that they are executed; I make every arrangement, *dead*, that I could make for your safety, your happiness, your future life, *living ;* save one—that is to show that you are *white and therefore free !*"

"No—no! You must not meet him!"

"And why not ?"

"Fighting for a slave-girl? Oh, Bob, the easy way is to put our names up, and take possession of the estate. Soulé would then understand that you were only chastising, too mildly, a rebellious slave. You've got to do it now!" she says in triumph. "You've got to acknowledge me as your chattel!"

"That would be to acknowledge myself a coward! The world would say: 'He did not brand her until his fears of a rival's pistol compelled him to assert the beautiful Miss Tournay was his bond-maid.' You don't suppose that I would be respected here for coming to this town and taking all the property of two poor girls and binding them to my triumphal car as slaves—even though the law says it is right and just! You know the sentiment of this community would respect even an abolitionist more than it would me. I keep silent!"

"And still let this thing hang over Nita and myself, keeping us one day *longer* from being free?"

"Ah! You know why!" he cries, despairingly.

"Yes, I know why— Yes, I *don't* know why! Sometimes I've thought to-day, Bob Covington, that you were tricking us poor girls; that you did not intend to manumit us at the last; that you loved me, perhaps, too well to tell me this, but not too well to take advantage of your authority as—as my master in *the end !*"

"Good God! You don't mean your words, Louise," he whispers. And throws back the hair from his forehead and gazes at her, awful reproach in his honest eyes.

But she, not heeding him, continues: "Oh, yes; it is easy to go on and make promises. You promised Sunday it would be Monday. You promised Monday it would be Wednesday! And now on Tuesday night you say, 'not Wednesday—Friday—some other day!' Oh—can't you see it's breaking my heart—breaking my heart—because sometimes I don't think you love me!"

"You know that is not true!"

"Well, whether you love me or whether you don't love me, perhaps I don't love you—perhaps I love Monsieur Soulé—THERE!" Then she screams: "No—no—no! Not that! My God!" For she has seen in Bob's eyes a glint that means if Soulé doesn't challenge him he will challenge Soulé—and kill him if he can!

"Listen to me!" says Covington. "I have at my own expense, and to my own sacrifice, kept you from putting the brand of slave upon yourself, because it would break my heart as well as yours. I wanted to give you the last living chance. That is the reason I have not said to the world you are my property—I am thy master. Louise! I had put you up on a cloud—a rainbow; I did it the first week I saw you—that happy week when you know, Louise, the sun was very bright to both of us, but——"

"But this is talk—which you are always making! If you love me, take me as your slave and manumit me! I demand it! You have no right to assume that it is your whim or pleasure when I shall be free. Every day of freedom you steal from me is a robbery I will not forgive!" she cries, angrily.

"Listen to me!" his voice is very stern now, and he looks to her like master to rebellious slave-girl. "This is my ultimatum! You remain quietly here in this house till Monsieur Hector and I have settled our affair."

"No—no! Silence might condemn both of you to death!"

"Ah! As I thought. You would send a note to

Soulé. I know what is in your mind! A letter to say you are my slave. I'll see that doesn't happen!" he says with flashing eyes. "I will give you one last chance, despite yourself!" then mutters, brokenly: "And if it does not come, humble my pride—call out to the world—this woman I adore—my pride—my heart—my love—my promised wife is slave to me—*to free her!*"

"That will be too late!" she shudders. "Then I may have your blood or Soulé's on my hands, for this mad freak. Forgive me, Bob—forgive me!" a tone of horror in her voice; next cries out to him desperately: "My ultimatum is that you come here to-morrow, early in the morning, before Soulé's second meets you—come here and I will stand behind your chair and as your slave, waiting upon you with Manda! Come here—scourge me into submission—it is your right by law—if I am rebellious. And I will think more of you than if you dawdle, dawdle with the chances of my life!"

"It is my will," he says very quietly, "that you remain here and send no more notes."

"If I refuse?"

"Then I, as your master, call to Mrs. Joyce and say to her: 'Take this girl Louise, lock her in her room, and see she communicates with no one.'"

"That is not necessary! Mrs. Joyce need not be degraded if I am! You have my word—I am your prisoner till you in your kindness, as my master, permit me to leave my chamber."

"You will write to no one?"

"Oh, let me tell him! It may save your life! My God—don't make me your murderess—or *his!*"

And he says, slowly, to her: "You shan't save *his* life! Give me your word to remain in your chamber and send no message by word or writing!"

"And if not?"

"I, thy master, shall put you in solitary confinement!"

"I will save you that ignominy," she says, haughtily. "Mr. Covington you have my word to keep my room and speak to no one without your permit," then curtsing to the ground, sneers: "I thank you for your kindness that you have not scourged me for my disobedient tongue!" and turns to go. But at the door she faces him. He looks at her as she stands posed, the gauzes of her robe floating about her loveliness ethereal; and she is to him as she was the night she gazed into his eyes and first said "I love you." But now with one white arm upraised, these awful words come floating from her lips: "A hint from me, my master. Whatever you do with me, for your own sake—*placée* me or marry me as you will—but *placée* me or marry me *before you free me.*"

"Why that?" gasps Covington.

"Because when the cage is opened the bird might fly away." Then her eyes blaze into his. Her voice grows harsh and strident. She says in words that grow bitter on her tongue: "*I am tired of looking on a face that always says to me I am a slave.*"

CHAPTER XXVIII.

"BOB COVINGTON ISN'T BUILT THAT WAY!"

STRICKEN by his sweetheart's bitter words, Bob, with a deep sigh, staggers silently from the house.

In his brain buzzes one thought: "She said: 'I'm tired of a face that always reminds me I am a slave!' Tired of my face!" he sighs, "But *not* of *his!*" then thinks: "I shouldn't have cared to see young Soulé before my pistol sights—but now, look to yourself, my Creole dandy!" and his eye grows cold and deadly. But as he walks the street his thoughts become more collected; he thinks: "If I meet Soulé to-morrow I must do my duty to-night! I must see Martineau and make the will I promised, and sign all necessary papers."

In this view he goes hurriedly to his room at the hotel, to obtain some necessary memoranda and receive — astonishment.

He enters to find his parlor lighted and Mr. Cæsar entertaining Kitson Jarvis.

"That's a right cute darky you've got, Covington," says the attorney, rising. "Better give him five dollars and let him go out and play poker for a while!"

So this being done, and Mr. Cæsar departing with joyous guffaw and rapid stride, Kitson says: "He's safe to be away all night, with a five-cent limit."

"You want to see me?" mutters Bob, gloomily; for he had forgotten Jarvis in his misery.

"Like a house afire!"

"Ah! You have evidence!

"None at all! but I can tell you this : that if you don't hear within twenty-four hours from Faval Bigore Poussin, you can be certain beyond an earthly peradventure that Louise and Nita can never be free—except by your emancipation. It's only one chance in a million; but Nita's got the chance. That I've been able to give her—that is, if you've got the five thousand dollars."

"They are in the safe below, obtainable at any moment."

"Well, that's business! Now I'll talk to you. Turning this Nita matter over in my mind, suddenly it struck me, as I snapped my fingers in your presence the other night, this cute idea. There's only one man living who can impeach Poussin's title to the mother of those girls, *that is Poussin himself ;*—and *he won't do it !*"

"Why not?"

"Because abducting, stealing, kidnapping, and unlawfully vending, and putting in bondage free white males, females, or children, is a state's prison offense. And Poussin would like to see a few more cock-fights in his declining years."

"But there was amnesty declared to Lafitte and his band for all acts, pirate or otherwise—"

"That was in 1815! Poussin sold Eulalie Camile in 1832! That amnesty don't work. Poussin knows it as well as anybody."

"Then if Eulalie Camila were not his slave, why did not Poussin tell Prosper Tournay when the father wished to free his daughters?"

"Poussin knew Tournay better than you. Tournay

would have said: 'My fifteen hundred dollars and my six bales of cotton and my two bales of tobacco, with interest at eight per cent.! Return them to me, and I won't have you indicted.' And would have very cheerfully, learning his daughters were not slaves, have put Poussin through a course of financial sprouts. No; under the circumstances, if he was not the owner of Eulalie Camila, Poussin has wisely waited to sell his information on that subject to *you!*"

"To me?"

"Yes, to you! And I have put him on the track of doing it. I approached him and said I was acting in the interests of Louise and Nita; that you had claimed and now had possession of the estate, and were holding both girls as slaves; and I offered him big money, if there was any flaw in his title to the mother, if he would reveal it, telling him I was sure they were of pure Castilian blood—not a trace of color in it."

"And he?" says Bob, suddenly, for he is forgetting his misery now in the excitement of Mr. Jarvis's communication.

"He said he had made one affidavit for me stating his sale of the mother of the girls; that he had traded her in the regular way of business, and that was all he knew about it. Furthermore he stated Eulalie Camila had been his legal property, and that nobody could prove she hadn't been. Then I knew that if there was any flaw in his claim to the girl that he sold Prosper Tournay, he would come to you and sell the information to you."

"To me! Why?"

"Because you, holding the Tournay estate and the girls, would be willing to pay him a mighty good price for it—*to destroy it.* No danger of your letting it get to the eye of a court of justice, eh?"

"And he thinks me such an infernal scoundrel?"

"Yes—he judges you by himself. He judges you'd do as he would do, and as a great many other men would do—buy the evidence and destroy it. Now there's still one thing," continues Kitson, "that can delay this matter—that is, if Poussin can really impeach his own title to Eulalie Camila."

"What?"

"His certainty that you are in possession of the Tournay estate, and hold Louise and Nita as your chattels."

"That I think was settled to-day," cries Bob; and hurriedly tells Kitson the incident of Louise at the window.

"By gum! That was proof enough, wasn't it?" chuckles Jarvis, "and Louise said he looked at you and grinned?"

"Yes."

"Then I can tell you that if you don't hear from him to-night you can make up your mind there's nothing to the Nita case, and that *I have given you absolute proof that there's nothing to it!* Now, what I came here for is to tell you how to act. This is a matter that's got to be juggled by you, and if you can't play the villain, and handle this little affair in a right down cold-blooded, heartless, scoundrelly manner, I don't think he will dare give you the evidence—that is if he's got any—*even for money!*

"Listen to my instructions. In case Poussin comes to you, no matter how he reflects upon your honor, no matter whether you want to dash out his infamous brains, you must treat him as I direct.

"You must appear infernally surprised at seeing him. Any suggestion that he has evidence in the case, you must treat as if you thought it worthless! State your position—that the girls' mother was a slave, sold by him, and that his own affidavits are to that fact; that the girls' father thought them slaves and was prepared to manumit them, but *didn't.* In fact, you must play him as you would a fish. Then he will tell you that he has evidence that will disprove that. To this you must answer, 'Give me proof—not only by your own affidavit—which won't be worth much, considering you have made another—but also by collateral *facts!*'—suggest to him to show—by evidence out of his old safe, or something that he's got—that his testimony would be fatal to your holding the Tournay estate. Tell him if he proves that and furnishes you the papers, you will give him the money you agree upon. But, until he gives you *evidence* that would, in a court of justice, free the girls—nary a red!"

"You think there's something in that safe in his office?" asks Bob, eagerly.

"Oh, the one on which the game-cocks played the watchdog? That wasn't a real attempt to steal; that was just a bit of a ruse of my clerk, Alfred Cotain, to give Poussin a little fright and make him move in a hurry in the matter. Poussin's old—if he died—good-bye the last chance! The papers, if there are any, wouldn't be of much use without his explanations. I don't think there's much show in the matter; but if there is any show, my client, Nita has got it!"

But even while he speaks there is a bell-boy's rap upon the door, and Convington, opening it, commences to tremble, and looks at Kitson and holds under his eye a facsimile of the dirty card that had been given to him on the battlefield of New Orleans. "Faval Bigore Poussin, Notary, Cockfights at Rodriguez's."

Then Jarvis seizes Convington and holds him up, for he is shivering as if he had the ague, and his lips twitch, and tears are in his eyes, as he gasps: "Do you believe—can it be possible—my darling?"

To this Kitson whispers: "Looks as if your darling would be as free as you or I. Looks as if this was the last day you would be her master. Looks as if she would flit away from you whenever she darned choose! Looks as if I get that extra three thousand in the Nita case," then cries: "Brace up!" for Convington has grown very pale, and is muttering to himself: "She's tired of the face that always says to her she is a slave."

But Jarvis whispers to him: "Tell the man to come up! Just give me a chance to slip round the corner and get out of the way, so Poussin won't see me. This affair is now in your hands. Pour brandy down ye—lots of it! Nerve yourself to fire yourself out of the purtiest fortune lawyer ever got for client."

So the attorney goes away, leaving Covington to fortify himself with brandy bathe his head with cold water, and give himself the manners of a villain, to draw a scoundrel's evidence out of him.

Then he sits and waits; suddenly his heart fails him; he fears Poussin has gone away. But a moment after, it is thumping harder than ever, for there is a knock upon the door, and to his muttered "Come in !" he sees, as the door opens, the old face with the cunning eyes, and the bent figure with the deprecating gestures, and hears in the low suave voice of Faval Bigore Poussin: "Monsieur Covington, I believe. I had the pleasure of receiving from you a tip upon the great four-mile race," and closing the door after him carefully, he sits down, Covington contriving to indicate a chair.

"Oh, you've come for another, have you ? May meeting in Kentucky, I reckon," says Bob puffing away at his cigar, though his fingers tremble.

"Not entirely. I—I have come on business."

"Business with me ? "

"Important business. I have been waiting for this time for over a year."

"What time ? "

"Ever since Prosper Tournay died. Monsieur Covington, you are a very lucky man; you have come by inheritance into the Tournay estate. You took possession of the property so quietly that I did not know of it; otherwise you should have had the pleasure of seeing me *before*. You have a very beautiful slave at the Tournay residence. I saw her this morning. She is your waitress, I believe; she was dusting the curtains in the window and she looked so timid, her eyes had even tears in them as she gazed on you, her master. I said: 'She has been guilty of some fault of menage; soon she will beg him to excuse her from the lash and he will kiss her tears away.' When I came back the blinds were drawn, the beautiful slave was having her tears kissed away,—eh, Monsieur Covington ? "

Here Bob, fighting to hold himself in the chair and not throw Poussin out of the window, and so destroy the affair at once, contrives to gasp: "Damned high-spirited ! "

And the notary goes on: "You looked so comfortable as the owner of it all, as you sat there smoking your fine cigar and reading the morning paper while your slave-girl did your bidding about the room, that I said: 'It is a shame to disturb a fine gentleman in so fine a property; therefore I will come—to him—not go to Monsieur Jarvis, who is the attorney for two beautiful slaves, who are *not* slaves.'"

"Not *slaves?*" screams Bob, in such a crazy tone that Poussin thinks it is the fear of awful loss, not the agitation of mighty joy and maddest hope!

"*Certainement!*" he purrs, "These young ladies are only slaves at my will."

"At *my* will, you mean!"

"No—pardon me—at *my* will. For Faval Bigore Poussin has a little evidence that can turn Mr. Covington out of the Tournay estate."

"You mean it?" whispers Bob, so tremulously that Poussin *knows* he's a villain.

So he goes on quite confidently: "Yes, Monsieur. Evidence I could sell to the young ladies you unjustly hold as your slaves, for untold money—evidence that their mother, Eulalie Camila, was not my slave to be sold—was never a slave—was never of a class or blood who can be slaves in law."

"*You mean she was white?*"

"As white as you or I! Of the purest Castillian blood!"

"Then why the devil don't you sell it to the girls?"

"Because I think Monsieur will pay me more money."

"Pooh!" says Bob, biting his cigar in two his jaws are shaking so, but forcing his brain to work. "You can't prove it!"

"I can prove it *to you!*"

"Then sell it to the girls!" he laughs, his nerves a-quivering so he can't keep still, and, springing up, goes staggering about, but finally, getting near Poussin, slaps him on the shoulder till he screams, and jeers: "Because you dare not!"

"I—I would prefer to sell the evidence to you, Monsieur!" snarls the notary, wincing.

"It's of no use to me!" sneers Bob, whose nerves are easier for their outbreak.

"But, Monsieur, if it is?"

"Very well, *prove* it to me!" And Covington falls into a chair and listens, the persperation standing in beads upon his forhead, he's so anxious.

"*Eh bien!*" says the little man. "Listen to my

story. In 1815 I was the agent of Lafitte's band.
After the amnesty proclamation, before Jean Lafitte
departed, never to be heard of again, he brought to me
three little children—two blacks, which, he said, 'you
sell, and distribute the money according to regulation
of the band,' and one white child, an infant girl, two
years of age, saying to me: 'I wish to make atonement
in this matter. This child is of high Spanish birth.
Her father, Don Hernandez de Rivera, was killed
when we captured the brig *Santo Espirito*, two months
ago. The mother sickened and died soon after she
saw her husband fall; our rough privateering ways
were too hard for her delicate soul and sensitive body.
Here are a few things from her father's body, and her
mother's neck, that will prove to the Spanish relatives
the identity of the child. Return her, either with or
without ransom.'

"Then I said: 'It shall be *with* ransom!' and sent
word to the Havana of the matter. But Don Hernandez de Rivera had no relatives in Cuba. The rest
of the family were in Spain, still torn up by the war of
Wellington. I knew they must be impoverished. I
said: 'Why demand a ransom *there*, when I can obtain
a greater price *here?*'—for the child promised to have
a beauty that would make men pay many piastres for
her—when she had become a woman.

"The child was brought up with the pickaninnies on
my place. In the state of servitude I placed her, education would have been against the law, except some music
and dancing—things that might heighten her value in
the eyes of an indulgent master—for she grew up beautiful as the sun in heaven, and very spirited. But at last
I conquered her, and she bent to my will as master.
Until, finally, Prosper Tournay, the poet-exquisite,
chanced to pass my way, and saw a wild flower growing on my plantation and wanted it, and I sold it to
him. And she cried out—for Tournay had a winning
way with women: 'I love him!' but pleaded for a
marriage. The marriage of a slave could not be legal.
But Prosper Tournay, to please his beautiful bondmaid, went through before me, as notary, a little ceremony that amounted to nothing were she a slave, but

to everything as she was not a slave ! For Carmelita Mira Estrella, daughter of Don Hernandez de Rivera, was called Eulalie Camila; for, of course, I changed the name."

"My God! If you prove this, Louise and Nita are free!" cries Covington, in such excitement that as he looks at him, Poussin smiles, thinking him a greater scoundrel, perhaps, even than himself.

"Yes; and the Tournay estates are also theirs!" he chuckles. "Do you think the evidence is valuable enough to pay——"

"Damned little for!" says Bob, for he sees the man has thoughts of making a demand for many thousands for his evidence.

"*Sacré!*" mutters Poussin: "You want it not?"

"Go, take it and sell it to the girls! Take it and sell it to the girls!"

"Monsieur will give nothing for it ?"

"I might, a little."

"Ten thousand dollars ? "

"Nonsense! How am I going to get ten thousand dollars for you ? I dare not give it to you in a check!"

"Oh, yes; of course. Aha! I see—Monsieur is a wise man."

"I will tell you what I will do!" says Bob. "I have three thousand dollars in the safe below. I will give it to you for the evidence—when you prove to me by your own affidavits and these trinkets that you speak of, and the entries in your ledger, and all collateral evidence, that it is of value to me—not before!"

"I came prepared to do that *now!*"

"Now! Here! Oh, my God!" And Bob is crying.

"Yes, it is hard to lose so much wealth. Monsieur must name a larger sum," laughs Poussin.

"Not a picayune!"

"I cannot speak for three thousand dollars!"

"Four thousand then!" And soon they agree to five thousand dollars, for Covington cannot haggle, and is thinking: "She said every breath of freedom I stole from her was centuries."

"When will you bring your papers ?" he asks hoarsely.

"I have them here. I came prepared. With five thousand dollars in my hands the evidence is yours to-night."

"Make affidavit to the facts you state! Sit there at that table!" gasps Bob, and takes an awful drink of brandy, his hand shaking the glass.

"The affidavit is already prepared. I had expected this," murmurs Poussin, and places before Bob a paper that seems blurred to him.

But forcing dazed eyes and reeling brain to their work, Covington sees that here is *certain proof*, and mutters, hoarsely: "Take oath to this before a notary!"

"No! I dare not before a notary!"

"Oho! Make oath before yourself! You're notary enough for me; I'll witness it. You must make this certain to me, before I buy."

"The money!"

"When you have sworn!"

"I'll do it now!"

Bob staggers downstairs to the hotel office where they think him drunk or crazy, but gets the money from the safe, and Poussin sits down to write his own acknowledgments with many chuckles, jeering: "This is foolishness! Into the flame it goes within the minute this man gets hand upon the evidence of beauty's freedom!"

But Covington flies in upon him, muttering, for his tongue seems heavy: "Here's your cash—now the affidavit!"

Finding it signed and attested, he places in trembling characters his name as witness to it, and taking this in his hand, and a little missal bearing the arms of the Rivera family and in it the true name of the mother of Eulalia Çamila, and the date of Mira's birth, and a locket taken from the dead mother's breast bearing the Rivera arms and crest, and two pages cut from the records of Poussin's ledger—in all with Poussin's affidavit—*evidence enough to free his love.*

Then he screams: "Out, scoundrel!"

But Poussin jeers: "O—ho—ho! Ha—ha—ha! We understand each other *thoroughly*. The slave is very beautiful; the estate is very valuable. Monsieur, *bon soir.*　Would you like a few tickets for Rodriguez's, or information about the Kentucky May events?" and, smiling in his face, bows and goes away, leaving Bob Covington with as great a lure as ever came to tempt man since earth rolled round.

He mutters, hoarsely: "She said when the cage is open, the bird will fly away.　I am tired of thy face, that always tells me I am a slave!"　He thinks of his financial ruin—of his mortgaged Blue Grass home.　He has but to place these papers in the lamp that burns even at his hand, and to-morrow morning be rich—to-morrow morning walk into the Tournay mansion and say: "Louise, behold thy master!" and the beautiful face is his, whether she will or no—his for all time. She must fawn upon him for her freedom—and for Nita's!

Then suddenly unto his eyes comes a picture of the sunshine he saw upon that face this very day, when his love thought there was a hope her dainty feet might tread the high places of mankind, that her young face might proudly meet the glance of all the world, and not droop, cringing with slave's humility; and he mutters: "No—by Heaven!　Though I *am* ruined —though my darling hates me *forever*—though I never see again her face on earth—*though her beauty is for another man!*—Bob Covington isn't built that way!"

———

CHAPTER XXIX.

"KEEP YOUR PROMISE!"

In a flash—as if he dared not wait—Bob buttons up the papers in his pocket.　Taking the missal and locket with him, and holding his hand tightly on his coat, for fear of loss, he goes out. slamming his door to stagger down the stairs.

In the street he runs, making for Martineau's house, and muttering, brokenly: " I have given her freedom— *all !*　She will be the Louise of old to others—*but not to me !*"

It is now midnight, but he thunders on the *avocat's* portals until they are opened by a sleepy servant. To him he cries: "Get your master up! I have news for him!" and in the private office waiting, gazes about and mutters: "Here she was first made a slave."

Three minutes after, Martineau, coming down in dressing-gown, looks affrightedly at him, and gasps: "In God's name, what is the matter?"

"Free! Free!" cries Bob. "FREE!"

"Free! Who? What?"

"Free! Louise *free!* Never was a slave! Here in this very room where she was put in chains, I take them off! *Free!*—a free mother bears a free child!— a white mother bears a white child—a wedded mother bears a legitimate child! *Free*, Martineau, FREE! LOUISE IS FREE!" And with the words he falls laughing and sobbing into the arms of the *avocat*, who is laughing and sobbing also, and they are like crazy men together.

Finally, Martineau, with lawyer's caution, falters: "Your—your evidence!"

"Ah! That was Jarvis's brilliant mind that gave to my darling her last chance in the world." And Covington puts the papers before the *avocat*, muttering: "Read them—examine them! Look at the collateral proofs!"

Then Martineau, reading the documents and inspecting carefully the missal and the locket and the registry within the prayer book, and Poussin's affidavit, holds them firmly in his hands, and says: "You are ejected from the Tournay estate!" next cries: "A noble action! But, *Grand Dieu!*—man—what a reward! Think what a noble wife she will make to you! Come with me!—your eyes must be the first to see hers burn in the light of freedom!"

"No," answers Bob, slowly, his face very pale, his lips compressed. Then he suddenly shocks the lawyer by gasping: "I—I shall never see her face again."

"Impossible!"

"I'm going away as soon as I have settled another affair," he mutters, brokenly. "Probably to-morrow. I owe you a good deal of money, Martineau, that in your generosity and the certainty of repayment you loaned me. I shall forward you a mortgage on my Kentucky farm for the amount; it is worth a hundred thousand dollars. I owe you twenty odd thousand dollars and three thousand more that you must pay to Jarvis for me. It is cheap—it bought—her freedom!"

"*Sacré!* What do you mean?"

"I mean—Louise told me to-night that I should never look upon her again unless I claimed her as her master; that were she free she would fly away from me—that she was tired of seeing a face that always said to her she was a slave. Ah, that was bitter, Martineau, BITTER!—when I was trying to give her—my darling—her last and only chance of being my equal—my companion—*my* wife in this fair land. Now go to her and tell her she is free."

To this Martineau says, determinedly: "Promise to meet me in this office in half an hour!"

"And if not?"

"Then I do not tell her! That you shall do yourself!"

"Go!"

Five minutes after, Martineau, rousing the servants, breaks into the Tournay house, runs along the hallway like a crazy man, and cries at the door of Louise's bedroom: "Come out! Come out, I say!"

She has not slept, and answers: "I cannot! I am imprisoned here!"

"Imprisoned?" And half opening the door, he says: "Nonsense!"

"I am confined by my word to Mr. Covington, my master, not to leave this room or communicate with anyone without his permit. Dear Monsieur Martineau, please go away."

But he repeats to her: "Come out!"

"Have I Mr. Covington's permission?"

"Of course! I come from him! Step out!"

"Mercy! What is it?" she screams. "*Mon Dieu!* Soulé!—Bob! Bob!" And hurriedly putting on dressing wrapper and her bare white feet in slippers, Louise flies into the parlor, gazes about and cries, affrightedly: "Bob!—he is not here!"

Then, Martineau hesitating, fearing the shock of sudden knowledge, she commences to sway and stagger
and give out, in piteous tones: "They're going to fight!
God has cursed me! To make my darling proclaim me
slave I have put upon him mortal danger! Bob came
to you to make his will—that's what brought you to
me!" And she wrings her hands and laughs in agony:
"They're going to fight for me, a slave-girl!"

"That would not be true!" whispers Martineau
"You are no slave-girl! Louise, you are *free!*"

"Free?—Ah, Bob has manumitted me!"

"You need no manumission! You never were a
slave—your mother never was a slave!"

"Not a SLAVE?" and she strides up to him.
Seizing from his hand the papers, and looking at them,
she cannot read, the words seem blurred, but he explains in whispered tones. Suddenly she begins to
understand, and it is as if the sunshine that has been
turned from her has come upon her fair face and she
sees the glorious opening of the world to youth and
beauty and to equal love.

Then from out her lips rings through the half-
opened casements, on the still, quiet air of night,
clear as angels' trumpet over Bethlehem:

"FREE!"

And a man outside, intently listening, mutters: "I
heard my darling's first cry of freedom! 'Twas like
the birth of a new child!" Then says, hoarsely, "By
Heaven, I'm happy anyway!"

Within the room, the girl, turning to the *avocat*,
whispers: "Where is he? He should have been the
first to hear my voice cry 'Free'!"

"He is going away, broken in heart, because you do
not love him."

"Not love HIM? Ha-ha-ha! Martineau!—not love
HIM?"

"Broken in fortune, that he has squandered to take
his chains off your wrists—to give you freedom—to
give you wealth!"

"Going away?" she gasps, as if she did not understand, then screams: "I remember now! Oh, God,
forgive me! I told him I was tired of his master's

face! Going away? *Mon Dieu!* Going away *un-happy?*" Then something flashes through her mind, her eyes become misty with passion, and a dreamy, far-away look is in them; she commands: "Bring him here!—to me! I will see if my Bob will go away UN-HAPPY;" next suddenly cries: "FREE!" and goes to gazing at the documents again, and sunshine flashes in her eyes and gladness ripples on her lips.

As he looks on, the lawyer starts. Louise has fallen on her knees; her white arms are raised to heaven. She is praying, but whether it is to God or to Bob Covington, Martineau cannot tell; their names are so mixed, and she is thanking both together.

He leaves the room, and, coming down the stairway into the courtyard, passes to the street; but at the very entrance of the house, stumbles in the gloom against a man, and, looking at him, says: "Thank God!—you are here!"

"Yes, I wanted to hear her voice cry 'Free'! Martineau—through these walls I heard it!"

"Come with me!" says the *avocat.* "She demands to see you. *Mon Dieu!* Don't hesitate! Come in—look at her face—it is a different one!"

Then Covington, following him into the parlor, even in his misery, even as he thinks he has lost her, is happier than when he had gained her. For he sees his love, her beautiful form draped in the clinging robes of night, holding in her hands the documents and muttering: "Free!" And though the tears are streaming from her blue eyes, her face is lighted by the sun of a new day.

Suddenly she looks at him, her lips twitch a little, and she falters: "Bob!" but does not rise.

To her he comes quite formally and murmurs: "Louise—I beg your pardon—Miss Tournay; my congratulations upon your release from cruel thraldom —my blessings on your new and happy life—my apologies for having treated, within two hours, a free-born maiden as my slave."

"Oh, you mean sending me to my room. Bob, that was just and right—whether I were slave or free. I'd obey you just as quickly now."

"Yes, mine will always be a master's face to you," he mutters sadly and turns toward the door.

But she, rising suddenly, takes a step toward him, murmuring, pleadingly: "You—you are going away?"

"Yes—to-morrow, if Soulé permits me."

Then her eyes blaze and she cries, piteously: "Would you make me the greatest monster of ingratitude since the earth began?" An awful reproach comes in her voice and eyes; she falters: "Ah! That's a brave revenge of a fine gentleman upon a free-born maid for the despairing words of a poor, tortured slave-girl"; next suddenly becomes haughty, and startles both Martineau and him by demanding, coldly: "Mr. Covington, are you a man of honor?"

"A man of honor?" stammers Bob, and throws the curls from off his brow as he mutters: "Don't you think I have done the square thing by you and little Nita?"

"No!"

"My God!"

"*Mon Dieu*, Louise!" cries Martineau. "This is monstrous! No man ever did so much for a woman!"

"For Nita—*yes!*" says the girl, airily. "For me—NOT YET! A man of honor keeps his word. Bob Covington, you made a promise in this very room that you would wed Louise, the slave-girl, in Christ Church, Canal Street, New Orleans, within the month."

"Louise!"

"That promise, I, Miss Tournay, the free-born maid, demand. There is now only one week left for you to make your word *good!* if you are a man of honor," and her fair, white hand is extended to him tremblingly, entreatingly, and the blue eyes gaze upon him as if he were not only her master, but her god.

The diamonds of her engagement ring flash in his eyes.

"You wish me—to keep my promise?" he says, slowly.

"For what did you make me free? To desert me and break my heart?"

"You would be happy as—as my wife?"

"I would be happy as your petted slave, Bob!"

He springs to her, and has her in his arms, and is muttering: "You forgive me for—for having been your master?"

"I will not forgive you, unless you *are* my master! The only value I place upon myself, that you have given to me, is to give myself back to you.—Oh, Bob! what are you doing?"

For he has gathered her to his heart, and she is laughing in his arms, and it is the *old* laugh—the laugh he has not heard for a month—the laugh of Louise Tournay, the freeborn maiden who will be his bride—in the sunshine of equal marriage before God and man.

From this scene Martineau has fled; it is too sacred for even his old and friendly eyes. He has been talking and explaining the matter to Pamela, who has by this time come out into the hall in schoolmistress negligée.

In the morning, however, a little pathetic note reaches him, reading:

Dear Monsieur Martineau:

Help me—save me from despair! In my joy last night, I forgot the awful thing I had done. Bob is going to meet Monsieur Soulé.

Of course he would face a thousand pistols rather than proclaim that I, his coming bride, had ever been his bond-maid or his chattel.

For God's sake, let me confer with you, that you may make the explanation to Soulé that my Bob never would.

Your distracted

Louise.

Five minutes after, the *avocat*, who knows in such an affair he must act quicky, is at the Tournay house. Here a beautiful but agonized creature comes to meet him, and faltering out the details of the catastrophe begs him for Heaven's sake to keep her from being bereft or thinking herself a murderess.

"I believe I can arrange the affair satisfactorily," says the *avocat*. I know Soulé well; he is a thorough gentleman and a man of honor."

"I am sure you can, dear Monsieur Martineau. I can't believe that I am to be unhappy *now*. We are to be married next Thursday week. Was it not a wonderful promise my Bob made to me? Did he not nobly fulfill it?" Then she smiles a little and says: "The only one in the house who is distressed is Nita. Her master gave her too many bonbons."

From this interview Martineau goes straight to Soulé, and exacting the most sacred promise of secrecy, makes such a representation to the Creole beau that just before the nuptials there comes to Louise an exquisite present bearing the card of Monsieur Hector Soubise Soulé, and on it is written: "My congratulations on wedding the noblest gentleman I have ever met."

But young Soulé is not present at the nuptials. The bright eyes of Louise, the slave-girl, shining even in the pathos of her captivity, have made his heart too sad. He has gone North, to try and forget the bride who will figure at one of the most exclusive and fashionable weddings that has ever taken place in the Crescent City.

For Bob, thinking it may add to his sweetheart's pride in herself, which he feels must have been humbled in the very dust in this month of her servitude, wishes to take his bride away from her native State with as much pomp of circumstance as possible.

To this purport, he has called in La Farge's aid, and suggesting to his friend his wishes in the matter, Henri has remarked: "Mademoiselle Louise should have a grand wedding here. The Tournay family is as old as any in Louisiana. My mother and sister, I will pledge, to do all in their power to place the daughter of Prosper Tournay in her proper station in New Orleans society."

And so he does. His mother and his sister calling upon Mademoiselle Tournay, the coming bride's table is soon covered with the cards of the elite of Creole society.

So it comes to pass, one bright May morning, to merry wedding chimes, with little Nita the maid of honor, and Mademoiselle René La Farge as bridesmaid, Louise, on Martineau's arm, walks up the aisle of Christ Church, New Orleans, a vision of white in tulle and satin and laces, upon her lovely brow the orange flowers that but a week ago had been forbidden by law to rest on her fair curls, to find Mr. Covington waiting for her at the chancel, his Creole friend acting as his best man.

The concourse is a large and select one; for to take part in any ceremony in which Madame Antoinette Marie La Farge is prominent, is social distinction.

This even impresses Mr. Kitson Jarvis, as he sits in a new and luxuriant black broadcloth suit, his enormous boots polished till they shine like fire, a big white posy in his buttonhole and a shirt front much too big for him, that was immaculate this morning, but is now stained by fallen drops from numerous cocktails, mint juleps and whisky straights; Kitson having celebrated this day himself. He mutters, *sotto voce :* " By snakes! Here are the Polks! Is not that old Monsieur Martigny and his wife and daughters ? Oh, Gehosh! This ere's a procession of the descendants of D'Iberville, Carondelet, Gayarré, Bienville, Ponce de Leon, La Salle, Cordova, and Friar Mark—if he had any. It is a meeting of the *old régime.*" Then he mutters: "Great Josh! And just to think—Whew!—if it hadn't been for your great brain, Kitson, what would that beautiful, exquisite lady-of-the-land, highfalutin, high-rigged bride have been right now?"

But Bob and Louise are coming down the aisle to the joyous strains of the wedding march, proclaiming happy nuptials.

Getting out before them, Kitson stands, one hand ready to doff his hat, and the other hand in his pocket, fingering a tiny portion of his thirty-odd-thousand-dollar fees.

Edging her way to him through the fashionable throng comes a woman of heavy jaw and determined mien, and whispers, jeeringly: " You're a great lawyer —your cases don't *stick !* "

" Oh—ah! Mrs. Combes—I remember you.   I'm thinking what you mean. You bet they don't stick when I get another big fee for knocking 'em sky high! Kitson Jarvis was the man that helped Bob Covington put the orange blossoms on that bride's head—But you'll excuse me; there's my little client Nita."

He steps to the carriage, from which the petite maid

of honor, in the prettiest of white dresses and white silk stockings and white slippers, looks out at him from over a big bouquet, as she sits beside Mrs. Joyce. To her he says: "How is Lawyer Jarvis's little client, this wedding morn?"

But Nita growls at him: "I hate you! You're the bad lawyer that keeps my cousin Bob from being my master any more. He doesn't give me bonbons now that he's not my boss."

"Gee-Whiz! The ingratitude of childhood!" chuckles Kitson, and turns away to catch a glimpse of an exquisite creature, all white satin and tulle and feathery lace, being assisted into another carriage by the tall Kentuckian.

"Great Crackey! here's the bride!" And he would step forward to salute the beautiful Louise, but suddenly there is a touch upon his arm and an old and weazened, dried up man, with cunning but astonished eyes, though dressed in a new suit of clothes, whispers in astounded voice: "*Diable!* I—I cannot understand, Monsieur Jarvis. *Nom de Dieu!* Monsieur Covington has married his—it is against the law."

"Ah, it would have been against the law," jeers Jarvis, "had Covington been what you are, and—damn it!—what perhaps I would have been."

A moment after, taking the arm of Martineau, the two walk off together, talking over the affair, with these curious words:

"*Adieu* the last of the Tournay skeleton," laughs the *avocat*.

"Ah," remarks Jarvis. "If I had not roused those old bones out of the closet you had them locked up in, and buried them twenty feet underground, it might have knocked those two turtle doves sky high. It must feel mighty curious to have a slave-girl for your *fiancée;* but that wouldn't be a marker to waking up some fine morning and finding the wife of your bosom was your *chattel personal*. Reckon I've been a blessing to both bride and groom."

"*Sapristi!* A good lawyer is like a good surgeon— a blessing when he operates successfully," murmurs Martineau.

"And I think I made a pretty good cutting up," replies Jarvis. "Thirty odd thousand U. S. gold dollars, and the thanks and blessings of both parties to the case!"

Some hours afterward, on the deck of the great steamer *Eclipse*, panting at the levee, her smokestacks throwing out great masses of vapor, her steam-valves throbbing, her enormous wheels ready to revolve, among its crowd of passengers, with all their varying interests, joys, sorrows, and distractions, stand Covington and the lady he delights to honor. La Farge and his other friends have shaken his hand and bidden him and his bride *bon voyage*, for Bob and Louise are going to their Blue Grass home.

The cry is "All ashore!" The gangplank is already taken up, when through the crowd upon the levee breaks Jarvis, with a yellow envelope in his hand, shouting: "Hi, Colonel, Hi!"

Two dozen distinguished individuals take off their hats and bow.

But Kitson shakes his head and cries: "I want *Colonel* Covington!"

"COLONEL?" yells Bob, "What the deuce do you mean?"

"Well, I've jist got to call you 'Colonel' now. The news has just come from Kentuck that you've been nominated for Congress."

But before he can say more, the great wheels revolve, and the vessel darts churning her way against the current of the mighty river towards the North.

And Louise, looking in her husband's face, her eyes flashing at the triumph of her adored, laughs: "Nominated for Congress, my Bob," then murmurs into his ear: "Now do you think there won't be a single man in your native town of Lexington to vote for you—because I am your bride?"

"It wouldn't trouble me much if they didn't," laughs the triumphant Benedict. "I'm happy enough without anything else but—" And he gazes on the exquisite creature—who is a marvel of brilliant beauty and tender love, in a perfectly fitting Paris-made traveling gown—so eagerly, so ardently that she retreats from him to a gorgeous stateroom that is decked with flowers.

But this is no harbor of refuge for her now. Blue Grass bridegrooms are not run away from so easily, and Bob is at the door with her.

"Do you want to come in also, Bob?" she says, blushing divinely.

"Great Pocahontas! Yes—rather!"

"Very well; if you demand, of course I must obey." Then she says, as her head falls upon his shoulder: "Bob, I have a secret for you. You're just as much my master now as when I was your—" His lips stop her words.

But she means it. For in those days strong-minded ladies were not so dominant as they are now, and the New Woman had not come to devastate the American rooftree and destroy the American fireside.

Finis.

APPENDIX.

The author desires to express his obligations to Colonel Sanders D. Bruce for information regarding the Interstate race on April 1, 1854, at the Metairie Jockey Club course, New Orleans.

THE FOLLOWING ARE A FEW OF THE LAWS OF LOUISIANA AT THE TIME OF THIS STORY (1854) THAT MAY GIVE SOME IDEA OF THE EXTRAORDINARY POSITION, PREDICAMENT, AND EMBARRASSMENT OF ITS HERO AND HEROINE.—ED.

FROM THE CIVIL CODE OF LOUISIANA OF 1825.

ARTICLE 2369. Every marriage contracted in this State superinduces of right, partnership or community of *acquets* or gains, if there be no stipulation to the contrary.

ART. 2371. This partnership or community consists of the profits of all the effects of which the husband has the administration and enjoyment, either of right or of fact, of the produce of the reciprocal industry and labor of both husband and wife, *and of the estates which they may acquire during the marriage,* either by donations made jointly to them, or *by purchase,* or in any other similar way, even although the purchase be only in the name of one of the two and not of both.

ART. 2379. Both the wife and her heirs or assigns have the privilege of being able to exonerate themselves from the debts contracted during the marriage by renouncing the partnership and community of gains.

FROM CIVIL CODE OF LOUISIANA OF 1853.

ART. 95. Free persons and slaves are incapable of contracting marriage together; the celebration of such marriages is forbidden, and the marriage is void; there is the same incapacity and the same nullity with respect to marriages contracted by free white persons with free people of color.

ART. 184. . . . An enfranchisement when made by a last will must be express and formal and shall not be implied by any other circumstances of the testament, such as a legacy.

ART. 184. (Stat. March 18, 1852.) Hereafter no slave or slaves shall be emancipated in this State except upon the express condition that they shall be sent out of the United States within twelve months after being emancipated.

ART. 187. The master who wishes to emancipate his slave must make a declaration of his intentions to a judge of the parish where he resides; the judge must order notice (specifying name, color, and age of slave or slaves, *Vide* Art. 185) to be published *during forty days*, by advertisement posted at the door of the court-house; and if, at the expiration of this delay, no opposition be made, he shall authorize the master to pass the act of emancipation.

Every person desiring to emancipate a slave who shall not have attained the age of thirty years shall present to the judge of the parish a petition; which petition shall be submitted by the said judge to a police jury, and if three-fourths of the members of the said jury, together with the parish judge, be of opinion that the motives are sufficient to allow the said emancipation, the petitioner shall be authorized to proceed to the formalities required by the civil code (posting of notice, etc.).

FROM REVISED STATUTES OF LOUISIANA, 1852.

SECTION 19. In order to keep slaves in good order and submission, no person whatever shall allow any slave whose care and conduct are entrusted to him, or her, and residing in New Orleans, to go out of said city; or any slave residing in the country to go out of the plantation to which said slave belongs, or where he is habitually employed, without a permission, signed by the owner or other person having charge of said slave, and every slave who shall be found beyond the limits of the said city, or beyond the limits of the plantation to which said slave belongs, or in which he habitually works, without a permission as above mentioned, or without a white person accompanying him, shall receive twenty lashes from *the person who will arrest* him and shall be sent back to his master who shall pay one dollar for his trouble to whoever shall bring back said slave.

.   .   .   .

SEC. 29. If any slave shall be found absent from the *house* or *dwelling*, or plantation where he lives, or usually works, without some white person accompanying, and shall refuse to submit to the examination of any freeholder, the said freeholder shall be permitted to seize and correct the said slave as aforesaid; and if the said slave should resist or attempt to make his escape, the said inhabitant is hereby *authorized to make use of arms*, but at all events avoiding the killing of said slave; but should the said slave assault and strike the said inhabitant *he is lawfully authorized to kill him.*